T0323147

Advance praise for *We Were Girls Once*

'Gorgeous and ambitious. Odafen writes women the way they should be written, that is to say, ecstatically. A lovely epic about female friendship and a country finding itself' Novuyo Rosa Tshuma, author of *House of Stone*

'Odafen writes with great insight and compassion about life, sisterhood, family, community and power. Each of her characters is so fully realised, their histories so richly drawn that they feel alive. This is a superbly written novel' Chika Unigwe, author of *The Middle Daughter*

'A gorgeous story of the redemptive power of friendship. With moving and immersive prose, Odafen invites us into the lives of three friends whose lives take remarkable turns, diverge and return to each other. Deftly, gracefully, she paints a vivid and unflinching portrait of Nigerian society of the past and present, its failures and triumphs ... I thoroughly felt this book' Francesca Ekwuyasi, author of *Butter Honey Pig Bread*

'*We Were Girls Once* is a beautiful, blazing book. The characters are complex and true, the setting vividly rendered, and the plot at once heartbreaking and mesmeric. This novel stands as proof that the political and the personal are always intertwined. Aiwanose Odafen is a master storyteller. I couldn't put the book down, and I couldn't stop thinking about it when I was done' Abby Geni, author of *The Lightkeepers*

WE WERE GIRLS ONCE

AIWANOSE ODAFEN

SCRIBNER

LONDON NEW YORK SYDNEY TORONTO NEW DELHI

First published in Great Britain by Scribner,
an imprint of Simon & Schuster UK Ltd, 2024

1 3 5 7 9 10 8 6 4 2

Simon & Schuster UK Ltd
1st Floor
222 Gray's Inn Road
London WC1X 8HB

Simon & Schuster: Celebrating 100 Years of Publishing in 2024

Simon & Schuster Australia, Sydney
Simon & Schuster India, New Delhi

www.simonandschuster.co.uk
www.simonandschuster.com.au
www.simonandschuster.co.in

A CIP catalogue record for this book
is available from the British Library

Hardback ISBN: 978-1-3985-0616-9
Trade Paperback ISBN: 978-1-3985-0617-6
eBook ISBN: 978-1-3985-0618-3
Audio ISBN: 978-1-3985-0620-6

By permission of Abner Stein, 'A Litany for Survival', The Black Unicorn
by Audre Lorde; W. W. Norton & Company © 1978, 1992 by Audre Lorde.

Typeset in Palatino by M Rules
Printed and Bound in the UK using 100% Renewable
Electricity at CPI Group (UK) Ltd

For my family

For those of us
who were imprinted with fear
like a faint line in the center of our foreheads
learning to be afraid with our mother's milk
for by this weapon
this illusion of some safety to be found
the heavy-footed hoped to silence us
For all of us
this instant and this triumph
We were never meant to survive.

A Litany for Survival
AUDRE LORDE

1

EGO

*The difference between a flower
and a weed is a judgment.*

UNKNOWN

1

Home

Sometimes it was one word, other times two. Stuttering at the corner of my brain, angling desperately to make themselves known. Whenever this happened, I was reminded of my father.

Here I was, thousands of miles away, in another country, on another continent, thirty-three years old, and still I could not break the hold he had over me, the power with which he pervaded my subconscious, controlling my actions, determining my thoughts.

In the early mornings, squashed between bodies as Londoners scuttled onto the Tube, pushing and shoving, I heard the condescending arrogance of his voice: *'Riff raff.'* At the office, when a colleague did or said something he would consider strange or colonial: *'White man's rubbish.'* But as always, he was loudest in my happiest moments – when I received a promotion or a complimentary email from a superior acknowledging my tireless efforts: *'You're a disgrace.'* I could never escape his words or the crushing feeling of inadequacy: the reminder that I would never be good enough.

On my 30th birthday, my mother had gotten me an enormous fruit cake decorated in icing with the words, *'Happy Birthday Ego Baby'*. My colleagues, assuming it was from a boyfriend, were afraid to cut into it, unwilling to offend. Speaking to my mother later, she cackled at their assumptions, then asked me, rather directly, if I had received anything from a romantic interest, until my stepfather shouted, 'Obianuju, leave her alone,' before taking the phone to wish me a happy birthday as well. My mother giggled in the background, a girlish sound that made me long for what they had.

Messages flooded my Facebook profile, strangers and friends – Zina posted three times and Eriife twice, because that was what best friends did – welcoming me to this great new age that solidified my spinsterhood. I went through the messages one after the other, liking and commenting, even the random *'HBD'*'s from people who couldn't be bothered to type in full. I kept it open as I worked, watching my notifications, waiting for his name to pop up. At midnight, wine drunk and forlorn, I stumbled onto his page to see he'd posted hours earlier – a newspaper article announcing a new business venture, a quote by the state governor embedded in it. As always, my grandmother – my mother's mother – was in the comments: *'Congratulations, my son.'* For minutes, my finger hovered over the block button, willing myself to end the torment, then I slammed my laptop shut, disgusted at my cowardice.

He'd been the one to add me on Facebook, a year after I moved to London, still struggling with the city's pace, the aloofness of its habitants. I'd stared at the invite on my phone, confirming that it was indeed my father, then left it unanswered for weeks, relishing the power to deny him something. Eventually, defeated by the uselessness of it, I clicked *'Accept'*.

As with everything else, my father used Facebook for his own aggrandisation: to announce a new government appointment, a new business venture, a new family. I became careful with my posts. Did he see them? Were they impressive enough? Did I give too much away? Were my words crafted appropriately?

Frustrated by my self-consciousness, I gave up on the platform altogether, long before privacy concerns began to surface in the news.

'What time is it?' Anna, a director at the law firm, asked, standing in front of my desk. The tightness of her bun made her blotchy face appear even sterner than usual.

I minimised the brief to counsel I was reviewing, then looked up, smiled politely and said, 'One o'clock.'

'Thank you,' she said, then walked away, her heels clicking on the tiles.

Beside me, Ceri giggled, and when Anna was far enough, she leaned in to whisper, 'Why does she keep doing that?'

'Doing what?' I asked, making a face, and we both burst into laughter.

'Might as well ask you for the date while she's at it, so you can go, "Year of our Lord Two Thousand and Fourteen",' Ceri added, and we laughed even harder.

There was a large clock on the wall, a watch on her wrist, a laptop on her desk, but Anna insisted on approaching me multiple times a day to ask for the time. When she wasn't asking the time, she said, 'What are you up to?' A seemingly innocuous question loaded with innuendo. Each time, I parroted off a list, creating more tasks as I spoke because I didn't want to appear idle.

'She wants you to know she's always there, watching,' Ceri

had explained to me once. 'Maybe she sees potential in you and doesn't want you to waste it,' she'd added with a wink.

I'd smiled and nodded, though I disagreed. It was no coincidence that I was the only person at the firm she did this to, and the only person that looked like me. Anna needed me to feel anxious, uncomfortable and out of place so that I would remove myself from where I wasn't wanted.

After five years at the firm, I knew I would never get used to the passive aggressiveness of the professional English setting. If there was one thing I missed about Nigeria, it was the blunt directness.

'Plans for the weekend?' Ceri asked, reminding me that it was a Friday. The days tended to merge into one another nowadays.

'Not sure yet, catch up on shows, then maybe a bit of work. You?' I replied in the semi-British accent I'd acquired at Oxford.

Ceri shrugged. 'Iain's birthday's in a couple of weeks so I have to find a way to sneak out the house and shop for some presents. Want to come?'

Ceri and I were not *friends* in the truest sense of the word – we shared no earth-shattering secrets – but we were as friendly as co-workers could be and, if I was honest with myself, she was the closest thing to a friend I had in the city.

'Sure, I'd love to,' I said, mentally cancelling my plans to watch television.

It was destiny that Ceri and I joined the firm on the same day, both young and eager, and over the years came to share binding memories: the time after our first dressing down by a junior partner, we hid in a bathroom stall, wiping away tears and assuring each other we were cut out for this brutal profession. I was at her garden-themed wedding to Iain, a bubbly Scottish man with a boisterous laugh; I'd silently screamed with her in the office kitchen as she showed off the engagement ring he'd hidden in a slice of cake. On St David's Day every year, she baked traditional Welsh cakes with cinnamon and dried raisins – a special box for me – and I said, *'Dydd Gŵyl Dewi Hapus'*. On Nigeria's Independence Day, I fried plantain, soft, sweet and slightly burnt, for us to share over lunch.

In the Uber home after work – I hated to use the Tube at night – I pondered what to eat while scrolling Twitter. I'd never bothered to try to get a driver's licence; the moment I landed in the UK, I'd concluded I would never get accustomed to driving on the wrong side of the road.

I was hungry. Staring down at the belly of my form-fitting suit, I considered the Lebanese restaurant not too far from my flat with its jovial owner and rich Mediterranean menu of mezzas, mashawi and platters. Sometimes his mother was around, and she went from table to table, asking diners if they were comfortable, assuring them they could ask for anything. She reminded me of my own mother with her maternal concern and persistent dishing out of unsolicited life advice.

I stopped off at the Chinese restaurant across the street instead, its owners a first-generation immigrant couple from Sichuan, punctilious in their politeness.

'What would you like, ma'am?' the wife asked as soon as I walked through the door, the red lanterns dancing above her. Her English was stilting and unsure, as though worried she might be required to speak beyond the words she'd committed to memory. When, in fact, this happened, she called on their son, a newly minted university student.

'How can I help you today?' he said with the estuary accent

of one who'd grown up in the UK, but when he turned to his mother, his rapid-fire Sichuanese Mandarin affirmed his connection to his parents' roots. I watched, enthralled, as her face transformed with understanding, and left, minutes later, food in hand, full of rapturous admiration for this family I barely knew. My country's colonial past ensured that I understood the language, yet daily life in London felt like putting on a shoe that didn't fit, that pinched at the edges in discomfort.

I walked home, eyes glued to my phone screen, accustomed to the path I'd trodden several times over. On Twitter, I moved through the carefully curated timeline that reflected my interests: news, sports, jokes, Nigeria. Every now and then, I branched out to others' timelines, going by an alias – @NaijaUKLawGirl – so my colleagues could never find me. Twitter came with its own madness but at least it was mostly devoid of the pretentiousness and boasting of other social media. I was no longer subjected to endless pictures of weddings and naming ceremonies and mindless epistles (though the latter would eventually rear its head in the form of *threads*). But most of all, the nonstop scrolling and constant barrage of needless information served as a distraction, relieving stress, and during late-night work hours, keeping my eyes open.

Occasionally, I volunteered legal advice, but mostly I tweeted about current events and Nigerian politics, desperate as I was to feel connected to life back home. *I'm Nigerian*, I proclaimed, even though I could no longer remember what harmattan felt like. I ignored news from the UK, swiping past without stopping. The country had become increasingly anti-immigrant: visa categories cancelled, new laws enacted, a hostile bill passed. The message was clear, reinforced via daily microaggressions that left me anxious.

My Twitter following had only just begun to grow when I took to sharing my experiences in the workplace:

My notifications were flooded with recollections of similar experiences.

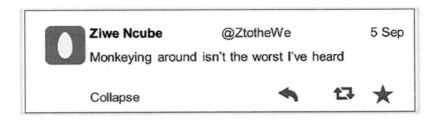

Sometimes I made up scenarios, seeking to confuse any colleagues who might stumble upon my tweets, but there was always someone who replied, *'That happened to me too!'*

*

I unlocked the door to my apartment and turned on the lights haltingly, listening for the *click* of the echo of the switches, acknowledging the emotion at the pith of my insides. Chilli oil and spices wafted from the takeaway and attacked my nostrils.

'Please make it spicy,' I'd said to the woman at the end of my order, reminding her I wasn't one of her paler customers.

'Spicy,' she'd repeated with a thumbs up and a familiar smile.

But now I was wondering where my appetite had gone. I felt it again, that gnawing feeling, malignant and rife: *loneliness.*

It wasn't the usual sort of loneliness, the type you grew accustomed to when living in a city like London, intimidated into inconsequentiality by overpopulation, the monumental structures and infinite bustle. It was a different kind; the kind that steadily worked a path through your consciousness, obliterating your peace and stability. It was devastating, humbling. I had no solution to it.

'You should get a boyfriend,' Zina had said the last time we'd spoken on the phone, her tone reprimanding like my mother's. We'd been discussing a new movie role of hers. 'You spend all your time working, before you know it, you'll be 40, then 50. Don't waste your best years o.'

'I'm not wasting my best years, Zina,' I'd said with a laugh.

'You're laughing? I'm serious. You've been there for almost ten years and I've never heard you mention a boyfriend, even a foreigner.'

'That's a lie!' I protested.

'Well, if you've mentioned anyone before, I can't remember, so it means you didn't date him for very long. You're tall, you're fine. Tell me, what's your excuse?'

I rolled my eyes. 'You're sounding like my mother.'

'*Oho!* So I'm not the only one that has noticed. Thank God. For Aunty Uju to say it, it means your case is critical.'

I laughed again, not the polite *haha* I used at the office, but an actual laugh that ricocheted off the walls, a Nigerian laugh.

'Get out! My case is not critical. Look who's talking! Are you married? Are we not the same age? Madam big-time actress. When is your next movie coming out? Make sure to mail me the DVD. When will Nigerian films come to Netflix *sef*?'

'Don't change the subject, at least I'm trying, I'm not like you please. Heaven helps those who help themselves,' she said. I could see her, stretched out on a sofa, shaking her head vigorously like she did when she disagreed with something that was said.

'Who said I'm not helping myself? I've just not found what I'm looking for.'

'What are you looking for? Do you even know?'

'Well, I know what I don't want.'

Dating in London was a dance, you were either a maestro or a novice, and I was a certified postulant, banging at the gates to be let in. I was ignorant of the basics: choosing where to hang out, creating the right *vibes*, dressing to be desired. In part, it was due to my Nigerianness. I was not like the born and bred Nigerian Brits, aware of social references and innuendos, and I refused to act like some other Nigerians, pretending they'd sung 'God Save the Queen' all their lives and never taken a plane from Lagos to Heathrow.

My phone rang as I bent in front of my refrigerator with the *dan dan mian* I no longer felt like eating.

'Nwakaego!' Eriife screamed from the other end.

The desolation dissipated for the time being.

'This woman, why are you screaming? You think we're still in university *ehn?*' I said, automatically slipping off the veneer I wore at work and donning *ehns, ahs and ohs* of Nigerian speak. 'Soye must not be at home for you to be shouting like this.'

'Ah. He is o. In fact, I'm tired of him,' she joked.

'How can you be tired of what others are praying for?'

We fell into easy conversation, even though it had been years since we were face to face. Her politician husband had received a promotion within his party and was getting ever closer to his dreams of one day becoming president. I burrowed into the warmth of my sofa, the *dan dan mian* forgotten by my side.

'I saw your boyfriend today o. In fact, that is why I called,' Eriife said after we'd spoken for a while.

I stiffened. 'He's not my boyfriend,' I retorted.

She hissed. 'Well, have you had another one since you abandoned him?'

'I'm sure he's a pastor now like his father,' I said, avoiding the question.

She pretended not to notice. 'No, he's into fintech now, and it looks like he's doing well. He came to the conference in a jeep.'

'That's nice,' I mumbled.

She laughed a knowing laugh. 'I know you won't ask, but he didn't have a ring on his finger. Maybe he's still waiting for you – you know you broke his heart, Nwakaego.'

'Why are you calling my full name? Call me Ego,' I deflected.

'You've been over there for too long. See how you're pro-nouncing your own name. *Ego*, like those British people. In fact, come home, come and marry him. How long are you planning to stay there?'

I rolled my eyes. 'See your mouth like *"come home"*. What will I do there? I have a job here, a life.'

'You can always practise your law; you can just renew your licence or whatever you people do. You'll be like an expatriate with your London experience, you can get a big position at one of these international firms.'

I chuckled. 'You think it's that easy? I read the news o. Nigeria is not that straightforward.'

'Yes, yes, I know. But things can only get better. You know elections are coming in a few months, Nigerians are angry, we're ready to change this government.' Eriife lowered her tone. I imagined her looking over her shoulder to make sure no one was listening. 'Don't say I told you, but my husband's party has a lot of plans, if everything goes well . . .' She let the promise hang.

'Madam president!' I hailed. 'I'm loyal to your government.'

She chuckled. 'When will you ever be serious? Anyways, you get my message. Come back. There's no place like home.'

The call ended an hour later with promises on my end to send the shoes she'd ordered online, and to consider her words seriously.

But in my sleep, there were no wistful images of home, nor of friends and family left behind, not even of *him*. There was only my father.

2

Witch!

'WITCH!'

That was what my father called my mother when he was angry, and he was angry often. His temper came like an unseasonable storm, triggered by the slightest disturbance, roiling and cataclysmic, destroying everything in its path.

'Witch!' The word reverberated off the pillars and through the walls of our home, surrounding us, imprisoning us in its echo. My mother ran, fruitlessly, from it.

'Ego, please take your siblings upstairs,' she would plead, her voice quivering as she glanced anxiously behind her, anticipating my father's presence. He was never far behind.

My father was handsome. As a young man, he'd been the one the women in church whispered about and fluttered their eyelashes at as they furiously swished their handfans against their faces after service. Years later, women would still stare and tilt their necks high to catch his unusually light brown eyes in spite of the gold band on his ring finger. My primary school class teacher always had some new insight about me she needed to share with him whenever he happened to pick me up from school. To my mother, whom she saw often, she only ever said a tight-lipped, 'Ego is doing well.'

When he wasn't my father, he was Chief Dr Chigozie Azubuike, the charismatic CEO of one of the country's largest trading companies. 'Leading from the Front: Transforming the Private Sector', as a business magazine whose cover he'd graced put it. He'd worn a designer suit for that feature, ordered directly from Milan. You could tell from the pictures that the photographer had been enamoured of him; everyone was enamoured of him – this extraordinary man who'd come from absolutely nothing to build a business that stretched the length and breadth of the country. At the soirées he held at our home, he charmed the nation's most powerful with his disarming smile and swaggering confidence. And then there was my mother, standing beside him, as she'd done from the very beginning, through it all.

But when the doors closed behind his guests, the caterers packed away their chafing dishes and the musicians and photographers turned off their expensive equipment, the clouds would gather and the storm would begin. Sometimes it was a shattered lamp or broken vase, other times, a fractured bone or swollen cheek; we were never left unscathed.

Each time, as my mother scrambled, pleaded and cowered to protect us, I would stare emptily at the black-and-white picture that hung in our living room, radiating charm and suave that matched Father's, the genesis of our predicament – a photo of the man my mother was in love with.

My mother Obianuju Azubuike née Nwaike was in love with a ghost: my great uncle Ikenna who'd disappeared during the Nigerian civil war, and it was for this reason she would end up with my father.

Her meeting my father was *fate*, or at least that was how my mother described it before her mouth no longer turned up in a smile when she spoke of their marriage. My father was a struggling reporter at a local newspaper, and she was a final year student at the University of Lagos. It was a Sunday in August 1978, eight years since the end of the civil war and eleven years since my mother last saw her uncle, Ikenna.

As a child, she'd planned to marry Ikenna, intricately plotting the details, calculating their ages and estimating the dates, until my grandmother had informed her that she could not marry her own uncle. But she could marry my father, and that was exactly what she did within a year of their meeting.

Fate. That was what connected them, the air alive with it that day. My mother's friends – my best friends' mothers, Aunty Ada and Aunty Chinelo – had forced her to attend church service by threatening to report her as a heathen to my grandmother, and there was no one my mother feared in this world more than my grandmother.

His voice captivated her, a mellifluous tenor that rang through the church auditorium, and rooted her to her seat as he belted out the lyrics to 'All Hail the Power of Jesus' Name', enthralling the entire audience. *Let angels prostrate fall,* but my mother had an entirely different subject of adulation in mind.

She never understood why my father chose her; of all the women there, he'd singled her out. Like a scene from a romantic movie, he'd asked to speak with her after a service, and as she followed him, dumbstruck, he'd simply said, 'Sister Uju would you be free on Tuesday after mid-week service? I'd like to take you out.'

Nat King Cole's 'Unforgettable' played on their first date, floating from the speakers of the restaurant across from the church, reminding my mother that that moment was indeed one she'd never forget. They bonded over their shared loss – he'd lost both parents to the war, and my mother, her precious uncle. My mother thought he was the most charming man – aside from Uncle Ikenna – she'd ever met, not that she'd met many before him. Whenever she spoke of this time, I tried to imagine my father as she described, to replace the image of the man I knew.

Four months later, under the shade of a frangipani tree at the city park, he asked my mother to marry him.

'No flowers, nothing! He just asked me to marry him. Can you imagine?' my mother always complained many years later. Perhaps it was her hesitation that would make him bear a grudge, but my mother wasn't ready. She was yet to graduate and she had dreams of travelling and breaking free, even if briefly, from her mother's constricting hold. And so she stared at my father in dazed silence as he lost his patience and asked in frustration, 'Obianuju, do you want to get married or not?'

My father zoomed off in his *tokunbo* Volkswagen after dropping my mother at home that evening, and my grandmother, hawkish as ever, immediately knew something was wrong. She pressed relentlessly until my mother confessed about the proposal, thus sealing her fate.

Whenever my mother spoke of Uncle Ikenna, she spoke of Nigeria's independence; her first memories of that illustrious time in 1960.

INDEPENDENCE: the rippling excitement, feverish anticipation and boundless – almost delusory – hope for the future of a country. Jubilant citizens paraded the streets, resplendent in their traditional garb, waving miniatures of the newly designed national flag as they shouted, 'God Bless Nigeria'.

'Biggest African State Nears Freedom', 'Hail Free Nigeria', the newspapers trumpeted in bold black ink. My mother was too young to read but she knew by the way her father held the pages that those indecipherable letters spoke of monumental events.

On October 1st 1960, they gathered around the black-and-white box television in their living room with plates of jollof rice and chicken and bottles of Coca-Cola like it was Christmas. Her father wore his Sunday best, complete with the red cap that denoted him a titled man in his village.

'Today is Independence Day . . . This is a wonderful day, and it is all the more wonderful because we have awaited it with increasing impatience,' the newly minted Prime Minister announced to the crowd and dignitaries – including Princess Alexandra of Kent, the Queen of England's representative – gathered for the Independence Day ceremony at Tafawa Balewa Square. *'And so, with the words "God Save Our Queen", I open a new chapter in the history of Nigeria, and of the Commonwealth, and indeed of the world.'*

Two years later, the zestful enthusiasm had waned, but not the hope, never the ardent hope. By 1962, it had become clear that an amalgamation of over 300 ethnic tribes and conflicting interests was never going to go smoothly, independence or not. A national census had already been cancelled, and a political crisis was brewing in the Southwest. But Nigeria was young, and its future was replete with limitless possibilities, and that was why Uncle Ikenna sent a letter to his elder sister – my grandmother – to inform her of his imminent return after years of study in England on a government scholarship.

My grandmother prepared for his return like it was the second coming of Christ – with utmost vigilance and cheerful readiness, even though the letter had arrived several months after it was written and its author never thought to mention a specific date. She kept it tucked in her bra as if the feel of the folded sheet against her skin assured her of the letter's existence, a promise soon to be fulfilled.

An insistent knock one afternoon alerted them to Uncle Ikenna's arrival. My grandmother's splitting scream closely followed, and my mother and her brothers ran out to see what the matter was. They found my grandmother engulfed in the arms of a strange man, weeping. When she finally collected herself, she introduced him to them as her brother, their uncle.

Uncle Ikenna's easy laugh and ineffable charm were unassuming, attracting without meaning to. My mother and her elder brothers fought like warring wives over him, each planning how to sabotage the other to ensure they got the most of his time. But my mother was the chosen one.

As the last child and only daughter, she was accustomed to being the exception, subject to a different set of rules, but never like this. Uncle Ikenna said her name – Obianuju – like she was royalty, as he handed her sweets and ribbons hidden in his pockets. He encouraged her to be unfettered, to speak her mind regardless of the moment. With him, perfection was never expected.

War came in July of 1967 in the way war usually came – with ominous foreshadowing amidst futile prayers. The independent union was not going well; there had already been several political crises across the country since '62, including a federal election crisis. And then in '66, a bloody coup d'état had thrown the country into further upheaval.

'FIGHTING BEGINS,' the Daily Times announced in bold

font on its front page, as if to say, 'it has finally happened'. But few had expected the Governor of the Eastern Region to announce the secession of the region from the republic. Before then, Uncle Ikenna and my grandfather argued in the living room about the state of the country.

'We must do something! We cannot continue to be persecuted in our own country,' Uncle Ikenna said. It was one of the last times my mother would hear his voice.

No daughter of my grandmother's was going to throw away a perfectly good proposal, and *definitely* not her only daughter.

Everyone knew the story because my grandmother never tired of telling it. She'd been married for many years with three sons, Kelechi, Ugochukwu and Ikechukwu. But she'd desperately wanted a daughter, someone she could bond with. And so my grandmother had prayed to both the God of her Christian faith and her ancestral deities, wearing amulets and reciting talismanic incantations, and as punishment for her infidelity to both, they'd sent her my mother.

'You should be grateful that you have someone like this. He reminds me so much of Ikenna. In fact, that was the first thing I thought the day I met him,' my grandmother said to my mother that night after my father drove off in '78, her eyes raw with emotion.

And when my mother said nothing, she barked, 'Listen to me! Tomorrow you will go and meet Chigozie and accept his offer. And you better pray he hasn't changed his mind or you won't have a home to come back to.'

My mother nodded in meek acquiescence, not for the sake of the fledgling love she felt for my father or the spectre of the man she saw reflected in him, but for the irrepressible yearning for her mother's approval.

At their white wedding, my father held my mother's hand in a deathly grip, like he was worried she would fly away. But she had no plans to escape. My grandmother's smile shone brightly at the front of the church, matching the lustre of the gold wrapper set and headtie she wore. In the pictures, she leaned heavily on my mother, pushing her deeper into my father's shoulders.

3

Love me jeje

My phone screen lit up, startling me from a daydream; wandering desultorily through time. Another Friday in September 2014. It wasn't yet midday and I was ready for the day to be done. I glanced at the screen:

Hey. Are we still meeting up today?

What restaurants do you like?

Zina had convinced me to join Tinder, a decision I'd already begun to regret.

'You cannot keep holding on to the past, Nwakaego,' she'd said.

She meant it in more ways than one.

'I'm not holding on to the past,' I said.

'Okay, if you say so.' She didn't sound convinced. 'You're in a country that's cold, don't you need someone to hold?'

We laughed. But she was right. I hadn't dated in a long time – a purposeful decision. Love was an emotion I no longer wanted; vulnerability a risk not worth taking. Yet, Zina was right.

At the office the next day, I googled: 'How to date in the 21st century.' The results were endless. I browsed through articles on *Cosmopolitan* floridly detailing why every woman needed a little black dress and what shades of lipstick went with every sort of dinner date; *Psychology Today* had a column on signs of doom in a relationship.

'I can't do this,' I told Zina vehemently. 'There is even *talking* stage? *Talking!* I talk enough at work. These people don't date like we do in Nigeria.'

'How do you know how we date in Nigeria? You've been there for so long. The dating market is rubbish everywhere,' she retorted.

'Hm. At least I know we take dating seriously – it is in preparation for marriage, not this thing they do here. I even saw "friends with benefits" on one page, what is that? And then I should join an app and be swiping? Normal people meet in person.'

Zina's screech of laughter rang through the phone. 'When did you start sounding like my mother, Ego? It's 2014! Everybody dates like that now.'

Tinder, the articles said, was a great way to meet people. For a week, I stared at the icon and willed my fingers to sign up. My first match was a white man named Jack, whose picture did not quite match the image I met in person, leading me to learn the meaning of the word 'catfish'.

'You're so exotic, so dark and beautiful, and your lips ...' he said on our first and last date, his eyes hungrily roving between my chest and my legs. *Exotic.* Would he have referred to an English woman that way?

My next swipe was a Nigerian British boy who assured

me he was a feminist and believed bills should always be split down the middle, to the smallest penny – he even kept a spreadsheet. I blocked him.

Then there was Liam, a mixed-race British boy with curly hair and a dashing smile. At dinner, he was gentlemanly – pulling out my seat and filling my glass – and had an easy-going air that lulled me into thinking that perhaps I'd been wrong after all. Until he texted the very next day asking to come over and spend the night.

'Can you imagine?' I ranted bitterly to Zina over the phone. 'After one date! What does he take me for? Is this how they do here?'

'Don't give up, Nwakaego,' Zina encouraged. 'I've heard some good stories about people who met their life partners on these apps. Or do you want to start attending Nigerian parties in London? You might meet someone there.'

No, I wasn't interested in attending parties. I forged on with Tinder and now had a date with John.

My phone beeped again. I breathed a sigh of relief as my mother's message came in:

Me and Matthew

I clicked on it, opening the messaging app to reveal a picture of her snuggling a furry Labrador. When she'd first moved to America, my mother had complained about the country's obsession with pets. 'They love their animals more than human beings. You see more outrage on the news when something terrible is done to a dog than to a person, especially a black person. Is that normal behaviour?' Months later, my step-father had gotten her Matthew and now she sent me pictures of him in sweaters and asked my advice on what treats to get.

Another message slid across the top of my screen from John:

Are you ignoring me? Let me know if you're coming or not so I don't waste my time.

I deleted the app – I needed to stop listening to Zina.

Zina was the reason I went home in May 1998.

'You no dey go your papa house? One would think you're homeless. A whole big man's daughter,' she said, cracking a groundnut shell with her slender fingers before throwing its contents into her mouth. Midterm exams for our second semester had just ended and while others packed up their belongings to return home for the break, we sat on old newspaper pages on the floor of our university hostel room eating boiled groundnuts in affable silence. Between sharp cracks of splitting shells, Zina loosened the worn braids she'd had in for half the semester; the once glistening lines were overrun with new growth and flecks of dirt and grease.

I hissed, looking up from the scattered shells in my fingers. 'You too, you no get papa house?'

Our eyes met and a loaded stare passed between us, saying that which didn't need to be said. The corners of Zina's lips turned up in a wry smile as she cracked another groundnut.

We were both on the run, desperately fleeing the turmoil of our parents' homes, finding comfort in each other's company and the shared understanding of never saying too much for fear of revealing the dysfunction, staying silent when others spoke fondly of their parents' love, wondering what it felt like, crushing the desire under our heels.

I broke the silence. 'You won't finish fast enough at the pace you're going. Eriife said she'll be here by three this afternoon. It's already 1.30pm.' I gestured with my chin at the unloosened braids held up in a rubber band.

With Eriife we were three: complete, as we were meant to be. Our lives had become entwined long before our births, at the back of a packed bus in the Southeastern parts of the country in the late 1940s. Our grandmothers had been unmarried girls then – about our age – on a one-way trip to Lagos to meet the husbands their parents had chosen for them. The twelve-hour trip on the dusty roads, surviving the near accidents, smell of passengers' unwashed bodies and crippling fear of the unknown had formed a bond so unbreakable it would last three generations. Our mothers had been brought up together, attending the same schools, sharing a hostel room at university – even before our births they had been determined to keep the tradition going.

Zina and I had come into the world months apart in 1981 and Eriife had joined us a little less than a year later. Aunty Ada – Zina's mother – always said it was a sign that we were to accompany each other in life, and every time she said this, my mother would nod in agreement and Aunty Chinelo would smile, a wide smile that brightened her face and made her cheeks puff up like a baby. At least that was how it had been until the tragedy of '97. Now our mothers rarely spoke of each other and Aunty Chinelo was gone.

Zina shrugged nonchalantly. 'Eriife is always late.'

I laughed. 'I'll tell her you said that.'

'I'll deny it,' Zina returned.

'She'll believe me, everybody knows you lie al— *aah!*' I shrieked as the shell Zina threw connected with my forehead.

I returned the favour with three shells of my own and soon we were squealing and hurling shells at each other, our familial troubles forgotten.

Minutes later, I was ransacking Zina's wardrobe for a spare comb to help loosen her braids.

'I'm serious. You don't have to *form* hard girl,' Zina said suddenly when I was on the third braid. 'You should go home. It might help you feel better.'

My first instinct was to pretend I had no idea what she was talking about, but Zina knew me too well. I sighed, 'I'm not sure.'

I missed my mother – the candid conversations we shared, the flavourful dishes only she knew how to prepare, her comforting hugs. But there was also the darkness, and for some reason, this time, I was afraid it would overwhelm me.

'I should organise some boys to beat up that fellow called Ademola or I should do it myself. God will punish him,' Zina muttered.

I giggled because I knew she was quite capable of doing just that. That was the difference between Zina and me – she didn't just talk, she acted; it was why we'd nicknamed her, 'Action Mama'. She'd been the one to lead the expedition to Aunty Chinelo's office during our lunch break in our second year of primary school. The three of us, just above table height, holding hands and crossing streets and busy expresses to get to the large office complex in Marina and upon our arrival, telling the gateman we were there to see our aunty and mother Chinelo because we were hungry and she had money.

Our mothers cried that day, more from relief that we'd not been killed or kidnapped than anything else, then they punished us, making us kneel in a line after we'd been fed plates of rice. I'd knelt the longest because our mothers were convinced I was the mastermind.

'Always coming up with bright ideas, this one. And always talking. *Cho cho cho*,' my mother said, sounding like her own mother. But I only talked, Zina acted.

'Maybe I shouldn't have turned him down,' I said to Zina's braids.

She huffed. 'It's a good thing you did, imagine dating such an idiot. And it still doesn't give him the right to do what he did.'

'October Rush,' she'd said to me a week into our first semester at the university. I'd been eager to immerse myself in the full experience. It was the relief of being away from home – from my father's stormy temper, my mother's ceaseless tears, my grandmother's interventionary visits, the black-and-white picture hanging eerily in our living room. And I revelled in it: the air devoid of the weight of fear and trepidation, the constant amiability. When people asked if I was related to *the* Chief Azubuike whenever I scribbled my name down for the endless activities, I laughed, a vague laugh that could never be mistaken for affirmation.

'October Rush,' Zina had repeated that first week when all had still been well. 'You've never heard of it?'

I shook my head.

'It's when first year students resume on campus, all the higher-level boys come looking for the girls because we're fresh blood. And very soon, all the finest girls are taken and all the senior boys have new girlfriends.'

'Well, it's been a week and no one has "rushed" at me yet,' I said.

'Like you would notice,' Zina muttered, turning away.

The very next day I met Ademola at the departmental orientation for new students.

'It is my honour to welcome you all to the Faculty of Law. My name is Ademola Adetayo and I am the Vice President of the Law Students' Society,' he announced to our class with a triumphant grin, the whiteness of his teeth augmented by his skin. He was dark, the kind of luminous dusk that stopped you in your tracks. He spoke with the inspired confidence of one who was accustomed to being listened to.

Halfway through his speech, I felt Zina's fingers pinch my side. 'He's looking at you!' she whispered.

'You're sure it's not you he's looking at?' I countered – Zina was the one they called *mami water* – and rolled my eyes, catching his. He winked.

'Ooohhh,' Zina squealed into my ear.

'SHHHH!' the girl beside us cautioned sharply, her hand moving swiftly across the pages of her notebook, jotting down his every word as if we would be tested on them.

Zina hissed. *'Efiko!'*

'Don't you know who he is?' Zina asked me once the session was over.

'You won't even congratulate me first?' I challenged. I'd just been elected as the class representative after a rather unusual nomination process.

'Always try,' my mother used to say, and so I'd put my hand up when Ademola had asked for volunteers for the role of class representative.

Zina laughed. 'You're already behaving high and mighty with me? If you now become president of the country *nko*? Anyway, do you know or do you not?'

'No. I do NOT.'

'That's why I'm here for you,' she returned. 'He's the son of a former diplomat and his family owns one of the largest law firms in the country. The rumour is that he's descended from a royal family. I mean his name literally means *"crown is added to my wealth"*. He's smart, tall, dark and handsome. He's hot cake! And he's winking at you!'

I stared at her, surprised by the amount of information she had on this stranger. 'We've been here for less than two weeks. How do you know all this, Zina?'

She shook her head. 'You should listen more to gossip, Ego. It might save you one day.' If only she'd known how prescient those words would turn out to be.

The following evening, I found a heart-shaped note stuck with tape to my door – *'Meet me at the cafeteria at 8pm'*. By 8pm, I was at the cafeteria wearing my most fitted dress, buoyed by Zina's encouragement despite my wariness.

Ademola's choice of place and time had been deliberate. The cafeteria was where everyone congregated after classes. The boys converged around the television at one end to catch up on the football matches, the couples whispered about their days to each other, and the hungry gathered around the counters screaming orders to the attendants. *Aunty give me big meat o. Not that one! Yes, yes. That one.* Ademola wanted people to see, to whisper as he ordered from the most expensive vendor, when he insisted I choose whatever I wanted with a possessive palm on my waist, and while he held out a chair for me to sit.

'You look beautiful,' he said when we were seated, staring at my dress.

'Thank you,' I said, pulling at its top in discomfort.

'You know I could make your time smoother here. All you need to do is trust me.'

The word went round – Ademola had a new girlfriend.

'They said he's your boyfriend o,' Zina informed me after class the next day even though I'd never had a boyfriend. I was still unconvinced.

'What are you waiting for? Are you playing hard to get?' Zina complained when over a month and a half had passed and I was still yet to agree to be Ademola's girlfriend. The tongues had become a wagging flame.

I wasn't playing hard to get – I didn't know how to – but there was an infinitesimal *something* that held me back. I could see fate playing the same tricks it had on my mother. Ademola's popularity, his charm, his commanding aura. The enticing smile that never seemed to fully reach his eyes, just like my father's. It was a fate I'd sworn never to repeat.

Maybe if I'd listened more to gossip, I would have realised how it appeared to everyone else – a first year student, a nobody, unyielding to the tireless efforts of a perfect boy who could get whoever he wanted.

Just before the Christmas break, Ademola ushered me to a corner table in the cafeteria.

'Ego, what do you want me to do? I don't understand.' He sounded frustrated, like he was at his wits' end. The top of his shirt was unbuttoned and the collar looked unironed; he was always impeccable. I stared at the collar, then at the empty plates of food – I'd offered to pay but he refused – and I wondered if I was the problem.

'I don't know,' I mumbled truthfully.

He grabbed my hand. 'Come spend Christmas with my family. We have a house in England, we can get to know each other better and you can meet my parents.'

My father also had a house in England.

I wondered what it was about me that convinced him I was the kind of girl to introduce to his family. Was it my height? My 'seriousness'? The novelty of my rejection?

We said goodbye with a clumsy hug. I wouldn't spend Christmas with his family. I'd made the decision without asking my parents. My mother would be uncomfortable and my father would see it as another opportunity for a business deal. Ademola's arms tightened around my waist as I pulled away and his face came down slowly, expectantly. Surely, I would not deny him something as simple as a kiss. I turned my head to the side and his lips connected with my cheek.

His eyes were hard when he raised his head. I saw my father in them.

The new year brought fresh rumours with it. Over the holidays, someone had taken it upon themselves to confirm my father's identity and I was accused of the greatest sin: pride. *Who does she think she is? Is her family better than his? His father can buy hers many times over.*

Then a new rumour formed, harsh and vindictive – I'd been assaulted in primary school. It was why I hated boys and wanted nothing to do with someone as good as a prince. And somewhere down the line, the story changed – I'd not turned down Ademola. He'd dumped me when he found out who I really was: bitter and damaged.

I felt a tear forming by the corner of my eye, blurring my vision of Zina's braid, and wiped at it hastily. Months later and the tongues still wagged.

'This place is dry. Let's listen to something,' Zina said, jumping up and taking the braid in my hands with her.

She returned with a device that served the dual purpose of

cassette player and radio. 'Let's check what they have playing on here,' she said turning the knob.

'Maybe we should listen to the news,' I suggested.

'By this time of the day? What are you expecting to hear? Another coup?'

I laughed, even though it was dangerous to do so. Our lifetimes had been a string of coup d'états, of waking up to the national anthem playing and a new face claiming control of the government, accusing the previous of corruption and then going on to do the same.

Keeping her ear to the speaker, Zina turned the knob, listening to the static until she landed on a station and turned up the volume. Then she twisted her waist as Seyi Sodimu and Shaffy Bello's voices blasted through, asking to be loved tenderly.

Love me jeje.

Zina had what people called half-caste hair, just like her mother. They had no idea what part of the family had produced such convenient hair; there was no known white ancestor lurking in their family tree. When water touched her hair, it did not shrink in the way mine did, coiling within itself, shielding its strands from moisture, nor did it dry as quickly, brittle and hard at the slightest breeze. In secondary school, the teachers let her wear her hair out, to share the beauty of her curls, while the rest of us were mandated to appear in neatly done cornrows. The hairdressers would spoil her hair anyway; they wouldn't know how to handle such fine hair.

By the time Eriife arrived, it was four o'clock and Zina's hair had been washed and blow dried, circling her face like a luxuriant mane, and we were clustered around the mini-television and VCR we'd combined our allowances to purchase, eating groundnuts.

'The doc!' I hailed as Eriife walked in.

'This place looks like a jungle,' Eriife commented as she made her way through the ruins of cracked shells and pulled off her lab coat.

'And you're late!' Zina accused, her eyes narrow.

Eriife laughed. It wasn't a sound we'd heard too often recently, and it tugged at my heart. 'I'm sorry, I was stuck at the lab. Unlike you, some of us don't have any semester break.' She turned to me. 'And Ego I'm not a doctor yet.'

'I'm preparing in advance.'

'Are you ready?' she asked Zina, rolling up her sleeves and sitting on the bunk. She'd learnt to do hair from her father's relative who owned a salon and was the only person Zina would allow to braid her hair.

'Ever ready!' Zina said, pulling out the packs of hair attachment, a pair of scissors, combs and a tub of hair cream from her wardrobe before settling between Eriife's spread legs.

'Ego, press play,' Zina instructed.

'What movie were you watching?' Eriife asked as she meticulously traced a line across Zina's head with a tooth comb.

'*Nneka the Pretty Serpent*,' I answered.

'Again?!'

'Zina won't let us watch anything else,' I complained, staring pointedly at Zina who deliberately ignored us, her eyes fixed on the screen.

'It's because they're both *mami water*,' I quipped and Zina's leg stretched out to kick me.

Eriife chuckled, her eyes not leaving the braid she was

deftly weaving. 'Are the both of you planning to use your break to only watch movies?'

'It's just me and you on this campus o. Ego is going home,' Zina responded. She did not bother to look at me – Nneka was calling out to the river spirit.

4

Any boy?

Chidiadi was the first to make me realise there was something wrong with my family.

'How many brothers and sisters do you have?' he asked in primary two, just before the rainy season came with heavy storms and chilly winds.

After our excursion to Marina to find Aunty Chinelo, Zina and Eriife had been placed in different classes; we needed to learn to make friends with others.

Chidiadi was much taller than me, the tallest boy in my class. It was recess and we were all gathered by the swings.

'Thu. I have thu sisters,' I replied through the space where my front teeth had been, thinking of my twin baby sisters who were still learning to talk. I glanced around the playground for Zina and Eriife.

'Any boy?' he asked, his thick brows coming together.

I shook my head no.

He drew a sharp breath, his eyes widening and his mouth taking on an 'O' shape. And when his friends looked with curious faces, he waved them over.

'Come and hear what she said. She has no brother, only two sisters!'

'I have two sisters too,' one of his friends said, smiling sheepishly and kicking his foot in the sand.

'But you're a boy. It's not the same,' he said.

'How is it not the same?' I asked.

'Every family should have a boy. That is what my daddy says.'

'Well, your daddy is a liar,' I retorted and stuck out my tongue.

'My daddy is not a liar!' he screamed before shoving me so hard I toppled into the sand, tasting dust in the space between my teeth.

I told my mother about Chidiadi in the afternoon, showing her the fawn-hued sand stains on my uniform and white socks. She listened patiently, then she slowly unbuttoned my dress and pulled off my socks, her face expressionless. When she was done, she dropped to her haunches, grabbed my shoulders and held my eyes.

'Ego, there are some people that believe that, but they're wrong. Very wrong. Don't listen to them. You will show them that you're better than them,' she said.

My mother had lost babies before my sisters, frail foetuses she never spoke of. My grandmother insisted that they'd been sons, the miscarriages an extension of her own eternal punishment for fusing what should never meet. She invited my mother for church prayer meetings and gathered prayer warriors in our home, screaming and shouting to cleanse the walls of evil spirits killing the unborn babies. When my sisters finally came in '85, she clucked her tongue in disappointment, patted my mother on the shoulders and said, 'God will give you more.' In defiance, my mother chose the names

Nkechinyere (whichever God gives) and *Nwamaka* (child is beautiful).

My father did not seem bothered at first – he had more important things to worry about then, like our almost abject poverty, until the elusive wealth he sought found its way to us and he was comfortable enough to insist we visit his village for the Christmas holidays, ready to remind those who'd looked down on him of the song 'Nobody Knows Tomorrow'.

It was after the new year service in '88. A woman in our village named Chinwe, whose husband Okpara owned a large supermarket in Enugu, had given birth to her second child and everyone was talking about it. It had been a mostly restful holiday spent eating roasted yam and *ofe akwu*, attending weddings and parties; even my father didn't scream as usual, too busy plopping his wealth on display.

'God is good! I'm so happy for her,' the women gossiped outside the church building.

'Congratulations!' men and women greeted Amaechi Okpara as he stepped out of the church.

'Okpara! Okpara!' the influential men's group cheered their friend, my father at their centre.

'My brother we hear congratulations are in order,' my father said and Okpara laughed from his belly like the big man he was.

'Congratulations, my brother. A son! You are now a man!' another man boomed, pumping Okpara's hand and grinning from ear to ear.

I watched my father's face change, the smug satisfaction disappearing from his eyes, replaced by a new realisation. He turned his head to stare meaningfully at my mother.

My mother cried more and ate less after that; she lost so much weight the hollows at the bottom of her neck looked like water-fetching bowls. At night she wept, heartwrenching sobs that shook her body where she knelt in front of the living-room couch in prayer. When the weather was hot, sweat ran down the back of her neck, and mosquitoes sang in the dark, but she seemed not to notice.

'God! Goooddd!' she begged each time, oblivious to my silent presence, her voice hoarse with anguish.

My grandmother invited a special prophet to bless our home. His oversized white gown dragged on the floors as he went from room to room spraying holy water and anointing oil and reciting incantations. My mother and grandmother followed behind him shouting 'Amen,' even though I was not sure they understood all he said.

When he was finished, he raised a battered wooden cross and smiled. 'It is done.'

Familiar black wrought-iron gates were waiting for me when I arrived home in May '98, high and forbidding and topped with electric wiring. A 'BEWARE OF DOGS' sign warned robbers away even though we lived in one of the most secure estates in the country, and there were no dogs because my mother was frightened of them then, and she had told my father he would have to find another house if he ever brought one home.

I pressed the bell and waited for our gateman, Usman.

'Ah Aunty! Long time! Welcome back!' he shouted through the peephole then quickly pulled back the bolt keeping the pedestrian gate locked. He reached for my duffel bag, and when I pulled it away, for the backpack on my shoulders.

'It's not heavy,' I insisted, removing his hands from my shoulders. I wondered if it was an innate reflex and that was all he knew how to do – serve.

I took in the expansive compound: freshly trimmed hedge-rows, the imposing three-floor edifice with its concrete pillars and wide white-painted windowsills, the alabaster winged angel fountain at the centre of the courtyard gushing crystal water, the open garage housing my father's numerous cars.

'Oga is not around?' I asked Usman, noticing an empty spot. My father owned several cars but he only ever trav-elled in his Jeep Grand Cherokee, with its customised plate *'Akajiugo'*.

The hand that holds the eagle – one of the names he'd assumed when he'd acquired the *ozo* title.

'He travel go village, some days now,' Usman confirmed. I nodded, relieved, and my steps quickened as I moved towards the front door.

My mother always kept a key hidden for me under one of the potted plants by the door, even though I almost never came home. Some days, she drove by my hostel and when I came down to see her, pulled me into a tight embrace, saying, 'I just wanted to see your face.' But even her coming was a reminder of what I was running from, and for the wariness I felt, guilt ate at my conscience.

Nothing had changed in my months away, yet something seemed different. I stared at the picture of Uncle Ikenna in its usual position and wondered if there had been any new word. Every couple of years, something arrived – a letter, a picture, a sighting claim – and my grandmother and mother would journey for days to seek answers to their decades of questions only to return with even more. Eager to keep my grandmother – his number one ally – in his good books, my father kept the ads running in the newspapers even though they'd all silently acquiesced that it was at most a futile effort.

'Mummy! I'm around,' I screamed and waited for my voice

to carry to her. Her response came, a tinkling laugh of joy so clear it sounded spectral.

'This one that you came to visit us today, I hope we're not owing your pocket money for the month. Or did you forget something at home?' she joked as she hurried down the staircase.

I laughed, feeling her joy. 'We finished our tests for the semester, we have a short holiday before classes start again. Where's everyone?'

'Your father travelled to the village and your sisters are with Mama for the weekend, you know she likes to spoil them,' she replied, pulling me quickly into an embrace. For the first time in weeks, I felt at peace.

'I missed your trouble,' she said into my hair before letting me go to grip my shoulders with a smile.

I laughed again, opening my mouth to respond. That was when I saw her eyes.

My mother touched her face. 'What? Why are you looking at me like that?'

'What did he do this time?'

I'd loved my father once – my tall handsome daddy with the voice that opened up the heavens and made angels *prostrate fall*. My first memories were of him swaggering into our small apartment at the end of the day, newspaper tucked in his armpit, a satisfied smile on his face as I ran into his arms screaming, *'Daddy Daddy'*.

With time, the memories grew darker: tears, blood, Mummy spending days at the hospital, the long holiday with Grandma and Grandpa. When we were asked to draw crayon pictures of our families in primary school, my drawing made my teacher ask my mother, 'Is everything okay at home?'

With age came understanding, and with understanding came the knowledge that my father was far from the paragon of perfection I thought him to be.

Yet the image of him with his newspaper under his arm remained in my mind, a cenotaph of better days. He'd been a simpler man then, an assistant editor at a local newspaper known as *The People's Voice*. He'd been determined to be just that when the military government took over on the very last day of '83, penning scorching critiques of the government's abuse of human rights and corruption scandals, refusing to be silenced until they came for him one afternoon. Even behind bars, he'd continued to protest.

In prison, my father was remade, scored of his humanity. I always blamed Nigeria for the man he became, whether it was because I had no one else to blame or that I wanted to believe that the nonpareil with the newspaper was who he was somewhere deep inside, I was not sure.

Our visits to the prison were drawn out and hollow, with him seated in silence, rotating jaundiced eyeballs here and there, staring but not seeing, as my mother spoke of false positives –the new provisions shop, how church members were organising weekly prayers on his behalf, her father's cousin that knew someone high up in the army – with forced cheer. And when I called, 'Daddy, Daddy,' he did not respond with a smile or his usual acclamation of 'My girl!' The only sound he let himself make were the munching noises as he stuffed his mouth with spoonfuls of the bowl of rice my mother always brought along, because if there was one thing he'd been running from all his life, it was hunger.

My father had been born into poverty – shameless poverty, he called it; the kind that couldn't be hidden. His mother's children had died in infancy, succumbing to illnesses, some said it was because she was cursed, others said my grandfather had spent too much time away from his people, trading in the middle belt of the country and the spirits no longer recognised his kin and couldn't offer protection. My father had been the one to remain, coincidentally, the very year the pipes were laid for clean water to come to their town, and his survival had inspired the ones after him to stay as well – even the spirits answered to clean water.

He might have overcome sickness, but he nearly did not survive hunger. His father was an uneducated trader who'd married late in life; he made up for the delay by marrying three wives, and what little they had was shared amongst all the children. They ate off the small farmland inherited from his father's father – a constant diet of cassava and yams. Eggs were split into the smallest quarters, a reward for the fastest fingers only, rice was for very special occasions, and bread was unheard of. They did not attend school until their hands could touch the other side of their ears because that was how age was measured then: in height and market weeks.

When others chose to pursue something useful like a trade or return to farming at the conclusion of secondary school, my father refused, insistent on his desire to study. Working as a labourer, he saved just enough to afford the West African Senior School Certificate Examination, the university entry form, and to support himself through four years of study, owning just four shirts and a single pair of sandals and eating a meal a day. He survived, as he'd done before.

5

Till death do us part

There it was again: the slight pinch at the corner of my brain whenever I struggled to recall something; this time, the details of the asset purchase agreement I was working on. I'd foregone the assistance of a trainee solicitor and taken the client call alone, and no matter how hard I tried, I couldn't make sense of shorthand in front of me. I groaned inwardly. Anna had already noted, with a triumphant smirk, that I'd been falling short of the pace I'd set for myself since joining the firm, becoming a solicitor long before even my British peers.

The scar at the side of my head itched, calling for my attention. I ignored it and tried again, focusing my energy on the thought, like the therapist had taught me. On days like this, it was a wonder that I'd managed to pass my exams. I heard my father's voice: *'Corporate law is not law.'* Once upon a time, I'd wanted to be a lawyer for entirely different reasons.

Sunlight glimmered through the glass walls, providing a shimmering view of the City of London. Pushing away from my desk, I shuffled to my feet, taking a moment to balance on my heels, and headed for the lunch room, deciding coffee was what I needed to wake my mind up even though it had never worked for me as it did for others.

Ceri was waiting by the coffee maker; an excuse to chat with Rayan, the handsome British Pakistani senior solicitor who'd joined the firm a year before us.

'He's cute, isn't he?' she'd said to me once.

'We should ask Iain,' I'd returned pointedly.

'Come on, I'm allowed to have a crush!'

I waited at the other end of the room, refusing to be drawn into conversation. Words had feet, travelling faster than their owner.

The lunch room was for talk: questioning why Miley Cyrus had ridden a hot dog on her comeback tour, banter about Manchester United's performance a year after Sir Alex Ferguson's retirement and futile wails '*Noooo*' when George Clooney and Amal Alamuddin obtained a marriage licence.

It was bizarre to me the level of possessiveness exhibited over celebrities, the derangement and rabidness of fans' social media comments, more so if the celebrity was British: '*There's something about her.*' '*He should have chosen an English rose.*' '*She's trapped him.*' I was convinced it was some form of national madness.

In the early days, the lunch room had provided fodder for my Twitter account, attracting a band of loyal followers:

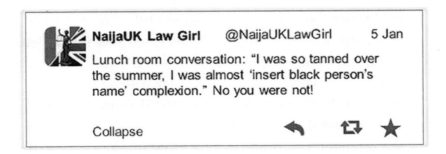

NaijaUK Law Girl @NaijaUKLawGirl 5 Jan

Lunch room conversation: "I was so tanned over the summer, I was almost 'insert black person's name' complexion." No you were not!

Collapse

NaijaUK Law Girl   @NaijaUKLawGirl   3 Feb

Overheard in the lunch room: "I don't get all the fuss about golliwogs, they're pretty enough dolls, and let's be honest, some people do look like them."

Collapse

 NaijaUK Law Girl   @NaijaUKLawGirl   6 May

Overheard at work: "Our government is making the right choice, so many immigrants are ruining the country." *stares in immigrant*

Collapse

'What do you think, Ego?'

I blinked. Ceri was staring at me with curious eyes.

'Think about what?'

'The referendum.'

'What referendum?'

Rayan chuckled. 'She's asking about the Scottish independence referendum. The results were announced last week. They voted to remain, 55 to 45 per cent.'

'Oh.' I was aware of the referendum and its result.

'Rayan thinks it was the right decision and that it was wrong to *"upset the order of things"*,' Ceri said. 'What do you think?'

'Yes, everyone benefits from the Union remaining together,' Rayan added.

For a moment, I stared at Rayan, astonished he'd been the

one to parrot such a phrase – *upset the order of things*. To aspire above a given station was anti-British, rooted in the nation's very structure. But from an immigrant?

'Or you don't have an opinion?' he offered.

I always had an opinion. 'The people should have what they want, either way,' I said cautiously.

'Is that it?' Ceri demanded; she knew what I was really like.

I cleared my throat uncomfortably. 'Yes, there is a conversation to be had about the benefits or otherwise of remaining in the Union,' I said eventually. Rayan smiled. 'But your home country is independent is it not?' I continued. 'That wouldn't have happened if people hadn't been willing to *"upset the order of things"*, as you put it.'

Rayan bristled visibly. 'I'm British.'

'Yes, but you're not only British, are you?' I challenged.

Sensing the rising tension, Ceri glanced harriedly between the both of us. 'Rayan thinks the monarchy holds everything together.' She gave a wobbly smile. 'God save the Queen, innit?'

On my Twitter page that night, I wrote:

NaijaUK Law Girl   @NaijaUKLawGirl   22 Sep
I'll never understand why the British are against ambition. What is wrong in aspiring for more? Enemy of progress spirit.

Collapse

The retweets came, the favourites accumulated, someone replied:

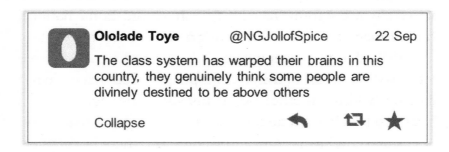

The frustration in the words hinted at more but there was only so much 140 characters could take.

Frustration had spurred me in '98.

If you don't do something about it, I will. The words I uttered that spurred my mother to challenge my father when I returned home that May, words I would come to deeply regret; it was the only way to guarantee she would stand up for herself.

But before I spoke those words, I ate the sweet spicy jollof rice my mother made, savoury steam rising from the pile of grains on my plate.

'Don't choke yourself o,' she said, laughing as I wolfed down the meal.

In the kitchen, she reminisced about her own time as a student, her face aglow with the memories. 'In fact, Adaugo and Chinelo—' she said, in the midst of conversation, then froze, realising her error.

She blamed herself for Aunty Chinelo's death, for not doing something to prevent it, even though it had little to do with any inaction on her part. Childbirth took many. But Aunty Ada blamed my mother for some reason neither of them would share, and so she blamed herself.

But it was more than Aunty Chinelo's death this time. I felt it in the way her frame trembled, in the trepidation I'd sensed the moment I walked through the door. I led my mother out of the kitchen, keeping my arm around her. When we were settled in one of the gold-threaded settees in our living room, I held my mother's eyes and asked her again, 'What happened? What did he do?'

Divorce was a cardinal sin; to deliberately seek to put asunder what He had joined together was to fault God himself. Marriage is till death do us part.

When the rumour first broke in July '96 that one of the church's women leaders, Sister Bolatito, was to divorce her husband, the adults were left stunned. They gathered at Aunty Ada's to discuss it.

'It's not possible,' Aunty Chinelo insisted, folding her arms.

'She wouldn't be the first or the last,' Aunty Ada countered.

'But she's a church leader,' Aunty Chinelo whispered as though imagining the fact itself made her co-guilty of the sin.

'It's probably a lie. She and her husband wore matching *aso-ebi* to church four Sundays ago,' my mother said.

Aunty Ada stared at her. 'Obianuju please be serious!'

'Will her family allow it?' Aunty Chinelo asked, looking between them for an answer.

'She has her own money. It shouldn't be much of a problem for her,' my mother answered, sounding to me like she wished she could switch positions with Sister Bolatito. Sister Bolatito was from an influential family and had inherited several properties upon her father's death; he'd left a will behind.

'But what about the church? She's a leader, she's even a member of the Marriage Council,' Aunty Chinelo insisted.

'Do you think people will insist that they remove her from her positions?'

'Why? Did she kill anyone?' Aunty Ada said.

'Don't worry. Nothing will happen,' my mother concluded.

'Even when our parents are going the wrong way, we must encourage them to live godly lives,' our Sunday school teacher said the very next Sunday, staring pointedly at Sister Bolatito's daughter.

By August, the pastor had begun to receive conveniently anonymous messages and warnings of the church descending into the ways of the world, rewarding the fallen with leadership positions.

The climax came, befittingly, at a women's general meeting; one that would end in a brawl. A group – seeking revenge for personal grievances – demanded Sister Bolatito's immediate removal from her position. My mother returned home that day with a torn blouse, missing braids and lipstick smears. For years, the image would be imprinted in my subconscious; the ruin of my mother's blouse, waving like miniature flags, a warning of what happened when women sought to leave their marriages.

The child looked just like him, my mother said, a tiny replica.

I stared at her, my mouth slightly open, my brain suspended by shock; at no point had it occurred to me that my father would go that far.

A son. My father had a son by a woman that was not my mother. And her people had come to demand that he marry her traditionally.

'Divorce him,' I said, and even I couldn't believe the words that had come out of my mouth.

'Divorce him,' I repeated, shrugging off the instinctive

guilt. 'We can talk to Mama Bidemi's son, he's a lawyer, he can hel—'

My mother raised a palm, closed her eyes and shook her head rapidly. 'Stop. Stop it.'

I held her gaze, unflinching. 'If you don't do something about it, I will.'

We were the reason my mother had stayed: I knew it, she knew it, we all knew it. 'Think about your children,' was how my grandmother chastised her. It wasn't only that my father held the financial reins – he could afford to send us to the best schools, to feed and clothe us – but also what would happen when he passed. 'Protect what belongs to your children.'

At my grandfather's funeral in '95, my mother had wept loudly, rolling herself in the dirt, muddying the ankara material she wore with his best picture printed on it. But at the meetings afterwards to discuss what little property he'd held that survived the war, she'd not bothered to participate.

'Everything will go to your uncles,' she'd explained when I asked. To my teenage mind, it had seemed unfair, heinous even, but she'd seemed unbothered, happy to let her brothers have it all – or perhaps I'd mistaken resignation for indifference.

'Who are you planning to leave all this wealth you're accumulating to?' Elder Ijeagha, a distant relative, asked my father not too long after the funeral, gesturing at our ostentatious living room with his nose, his most prominent feature, which he couldn't keep out of other people's business. My mother was away and I was glad she couldn't overhear their conversation. 'You better find a son.'

My father said nothing.

*

If you don't do something about it, I will. I threw down the gauntlet knowing my mother would have no option but to take it up.

The horn of my father's Jeep made a distinct sound, a blaring that announced itself and the size of the vehicle that carried it. Given to extravagance, he acquired a new vehicle every year, sometimes he sold off a vehicle or two to create a balance, but annually, we memorised the sonance of a new horn. When the beep came, demanding at the gate, we hurried to alter ourselves; turning off the television, changing clothes, hiding in our rooms.

This time, when the blaring came, days later than expected, I felt excitement rather than trepidation. My skin prickled with anticipation, like a soldier eagerly awaiting war.

My father had a ritual: he returned from travel, he took a long shower, he ate, then he took a nap. Only after all this did the rest of his day begin, and that was usually when my mother approached him to discuss anything of importance.

I slept off watching the clock, waiting for the moment to arrive. In my sleep, an earthquake shook our sphere, seismic tremors running through the walls and foundation of our home leaving visceral cracks in the blocks until they gave way, collapsing in heaps of concrete, twisted metal and dust.

Voices pulled me from fitful sleep.

'We took an oath before God and man. You should be ashamed of yourself!' Her voice shook, and I wondered once again what had happened to the girl my mother's brothers often described.

'Your mother was fire o,' Uncle Ugochukwu always said, chuckling at the fond memories.

It was why I told my mother repeatedly that I would never

get married. 'I don't see the point,' I explained. I didn't want to say I feared I would become like her one day.

'What did you say?' my father asked, his tone portentous. I jumped out of my bed and ran out, aware of what was coming next.

Stop, please, I wanted to say to my mother, the same words she'd said to me earlier. But she'd found her voice and she was not going to back down. 'I said you should be ashamed of yourself! How old is she? Nineteen? Twenty? That girl is young enough to be your daughte—'

The first blow was so vicious I staggered and stumbled on the staircase, clutching at the rails for balance, even though I wasn't its recipient. I heard my mother scream, then the sounds of a scuffle.

He was bent over my mother's body, landing blow after blow, not caring what part of her they connected with, screaming in her bloodied face; deranged. When he was like this, my mother always begged me to hide, to protect myself and my sisters from his feral rage but, this time, I wasn't going to cower.

I rushed at him from behind, no strategy or plan, just an end goal. He was no small man, but the force and suddenness of my attack was just enough to knock him off balance, giving my mother room to escape.

'Leave her alone!' I screamed at my father, and for a moment, he just stared at me, seemingly unable to believe his eyes. It was the first time I'd ever raised my voice at him. Our relationship was one of tacit tolerated co-existence: he funded my school, he made sure I had a roof over my head and enough to eat. He was my father and I was to respect him as such, to never interfere in any other aspect of his life, most especially, his relationship with my mother.

My mother stumbled to her feet, but instead of running, she pulled at my arm. 'Nwakaego, please go upstairs,' she begged, tearful.

I pulled my arm from her grasp and faced my father. 'Have you not done enough? You got another woman pregnant. You should be begging her not to leave.'

My mother burst into tears and moved to put herself between us. 'Think of your school. Please go upstairs.'

My father, who'd been quiet all along, sneered at my mother. 'Why are you begging her? See for yourself the kind of mother you are, just look at what you raised. And you're wondering why I found another woman?'

'You're shameless!' I screamed.

I would think of this moment in the future: the fire and humiliation in my father's eyes as he rushed at me – I watched the back of my mother's head connect with the wall as he threw her aside – and did something he'd never done before. The first blow was painless, enveloped by surprise, the sting of the second had barely settled before I felt the third.

When oblivion finally came, I welcomed it, thinking about how my mother had had to endure for too long.

6

Nwakaego

Nwakaego. Child is greater than wealth. When my parents chose my name, they'd had nothing, but they had me. I was a reflection of them: their faith, hope and every desire.

I was rarely referred to by my full name. Instead, I was *Ego.* Wealth. I was their wealth long before fortune came, turning its wheel and changing their lives. I loved my name and the meaning it carried, and I wore it proudly as an emblem. When strangers asked, I never introduced myself as *Ego.* Instead, I said, 'My name is Nwakaego, but you can call me Ego.'

My mother only ever called me by my full name on three distinct occasions: joy, anger and urgency. When she would stand at the bottom of the staircase of my father's mansion, trying to catch my attention, she would scream *'Nwakaego'* and I would come running down. Whenever a teacher accused me of bad behaviour, my mother would pull me aside, anger and disappointment etched in her face, and say, 'Nwakaego, what happened?' In the face of my father's rage, her voice would come again, urgent and pleading, 'Nwakaego, go upstairs with your sisters.'

I grew accustomed to it, that resonant call that demanded my attention and sought to remind me of who I was. I was wealth, my mother's treasure. But that day, even my mother speaking my name could not wrestle me awake.

Nwakaego. Nwakaego. Please wake up, a *bat kol* prayed, overarching and omnipresent like the voice of God within this dimensionless universe, but I remained in a loop of unending oblivion. Then the darkness disappeared, replaced by memories long suppressed. There was my father, a newspaper tucked under his arm, and me, screaming as I ran towards him, arms stretched. My father again, running to pick me up after a fall. My father, driving off in a strange van as I stood beside my mother weeping. My father returning home with the blank eyes of a stranger. So it continued, through the years until memories were overtaken by nightmares in this formless world.

Nwakaego, the voice called over and over, but I could not answer.

Living under a dictator was like living in a hamlet at the bottom of a mountain with a large boulder at its peak, a boulder with a shaky foundation. Some days, smaller stones crumbled down, hitting your roof and that of your neighbours, tingling the aluminium but causing no real harm. Other days, larger stones slipped through, causing injuries to some but not all. But you all lived in the perpetual fear of that inevitable day when the boulder itself would descend, crushing your very existence into dust. It was how we lived in a military regime and in my father's house.

There were many before it, but my first memory of a coup d'état was in August '85, not long after I turned four. My parents sat, anxious, by a small radio in the early hours of the morning as the national anthem came on, followed by the cultured voice of a trained military officer. My father had returned from prison at this point and the cracks in his person had begun to show, but they were united in their hatred of the military government.

The speech was too complex for four-year-old me to follow but I read the meaning from my parents' sighs and nervous glances. If they felt a modicum of relief that the man who had jailed my father was no longer in charge, it did not show. I would view those same expressions again, in the penultimate month of '93, but by then they'd grown wary, anaesthetised even to the incompressible turbulence. There'd been a brief moment of hope during the '93 elections when my mother had hummed the catchy campaign jingles with glee and debated about the candidates with her friends, brimming with excitement at the prospects of a civilian government. On election day, she'd returned late in the evening with a large ink stain on her thumb she flaunted with pride – she'd voted. But it did not take long for the country to descend into the convoluted military maze we could not seem to escape – the cancellation of election results, demolition of democratic systems, crackdown on dissent, the inevitable collapse of the economy and the widespread impoverishment that followed. We were in a lateral world, there was no up or down, only sideways.

'This country is finished,' Aunty Ada told my mother.

'Don't be so pessimistic,' my mother chided.

'Pessimistic? Obianuju, open your eyes and look around you. Where are we headed?'

The end of a dictatorship was sparked by the beginning of another, or in rare circumstance, a grudging acquiescence to international pressure and the democratic will of the people. The coups, however, were not always successful, and when this happened, we were subjected to a gory display of nationalism in the form of radio retellings of bodies bound to wooden stakes decimated by firing squads: a clear warning of the consequences of treason.

Fear. My father always said that only a truly powerful regime was able to install itself in the mind of its people. Fear was the way to control the masses; entrench fear and they would never defy you – they would pray to their gods, begging and pleading for intervention, but never revolt.

By '94, I'd learnt that fear all too well: to avoid my father's presence, to speak only when spoken to, to listen for the timbre of his voice and the weight of his footsteps, to see him when he wasn't there.

There was an audacious, almost daring manner in which this new government went about its brutality. Its omnipresence was alive in the most intimate corridors of our lives, even our classrooms. When we deigned to discuss politics, we said to each other in hushed tones, 'Do you want them to come and carry you?' By *them*, we meant the special forces that had taken to disappearing dissidents, so much so that it became a running joke – *Do you want them to come and carry you?* – because we feared that we or someone we loved would be the next victims of this cannibalistic government, never to be seen or heard from again.

Proverbs 11:10. It was a scripture we memorised in Sunday school, saying the words over and over again. *When the righteous prosper, the city rejoices, when the wicked perish, there are shouts of joy.* Our teachers told us it was why we were to live righteously; there was no worse conclusion to life than to have your demise cheered by the city as bowed-headed family members followed behind in a procession of shared shame.

It was this manner of jubilation that permeated my new world: screams of joy, strings of festive music. In my universe, I was in an ancient, fortified city, surrounded by a cheering mob as a body wrapped in simple linen passed in a lonely procession in our midst. A troupe played from an exalted position – lyres and trumpets and flutes. I turned to ask the identity of the dead that caused such celebration but the crowd had disappeared. But the music – I could still hear the music and cheers. The strings had begun to sound modern – electric – and the trumpets were joined by saxophones. A baritone voice led the festivities and asked others to join, and I moved towards it. As I did so, the world around me disintegrated. I was blinded by sudden light.

Kool and the Gang's 'Celebration' blasted from a speaker as I opened my eyes, the encouragement to party distracting from the unfamiliarity of the faded yellow walls and the dull ache coursing its way through my skull.

'It's a celebration!' someone shouted.

The head of state was dead.

Nurses gossip – it was how I knew a mother had slapped a paediatrician with the bottom of her shoe, leaving a sole-shaped imprint at the side of his face; the hospital had descended into pandemonium as everyone tried to appease both parties. It was also how I learnt I'd lain unconscious, my mother by my side, the voice I'd heard, for over a week. Their chatter was how I found out that my mother had cried into the telephone at the hospital front desk, her face battered and swollen, as she'd begged my father for the money needed to perform the surgery that saved my life. He'd said no.

'Maybe he's not the real father,' one of the nurses said.

There was a special kind of disappointment that came with

expecting little from someone and still being let down by their actions. I'd hoped, assumed, thought that at the depth of his being, my father loved me, and at the very least, wanted me alive. But the evidence to the contrary sat on the surgeon's desk in the form of the keys to my mother's Mercedes Benz sedan. On her knees, she'd handed over her car keys – a gift from my father – pleading for my life. Why they accepted, I wasn't sure; I wouldn't have been the first patient left to die because I didn't have the means to pay for my treatment. We read similar stories in the newspapers or heard about them through someone that knew someone that it had happened to all the time. Perhaps it was the frantic desperation in my mother's eyes or the elegance of her clothes or the fact that she'd driven to a government clinic in a car like that. How could such a person not afford to pay for a life?

'Extradural haematoma is not something patients recover from overnight,' the doctor told my mother, his voice low in an ineffectual attempt to avoid waking me. I'd been conscious for over a week but the doctors insisted on keeping me in the hospital for observation.

'We've run all the tests,' the doctor continued, then looked down at my file in his hands. 'And she seems to be recovering well, but we'll have to wait and see. To put it simply, losing blood from the brain means there's a deficit. Luckily, she's regained most of her abilities – it could have been much worse – but she will still need to undergo cognitive therapy for three to six months, depending on how she responds and how fast she recovers.'

My mother nodded, her hands folded in front of her in abject humility. 'But will she be fine? Will she be able to go back to school?' Her voice cracked; I'd never heard her sound so afraid, not even when my father was raging.

'Not immediately. She'll need some time to recover, maybe a few months. Considering the side of her brain affected, she might have some issues with short-term memory loss or small lapses. I'll put you in touch with the therapist we usually recommend before she's discharged.'

'Thank you doctor, thank you so much,' my mother effused as he turned to leave.

He stopped at the door to pull something from the front pocket of his lab coat. 'I was asked to give this to you, your payment has been received by the accounts department,' he said, handing my mother her car keys. And I felt hope bloom in my chest that my father wanted me to live after all.

Two weeks after my return to consciousness, the doctors signed the papers discharging me. I left with a note to a therapist and a bag of medication, and found my sisters seated at the back of my mother's car. The direction we headed was not my father's house.

My mother turned on the radio. When Mariah Carey's 'Always Be My Baby' came on, we sang along, crooning the lyrics in disjointed voices like our lives hadn't just been turned upside down. I bent my neck to the side, to feel the breeze and sun beating against my shorn head and the cranial scar that contoured it – a confirmation of life.

7

Almost British

It was impossible to ignore because the entire country was alight with it in the *ember* months of 2014 – especially Twitter.

 Britain No 1 Citizen   @DavidJo52598764   4 Oct

Ebola at our borders, our schools, NHS and public services under strain and we keep letting these good for nothings into our country

Collapse

 No to Referendum   @EUCitizen   12 Oct

Flagshaggers won't talk about anything else when there are far more pressing issues in this country than a referendum on leaving the European Union!

Collapse

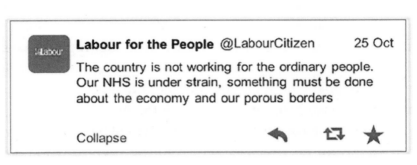

Election season was upon us, and despite my best efforts to avoid the discourse, it trailed me like a sinister shadow of gloom with immigration at its centre.

The news cycle was set up to thwart anyone who sought the solace of avoidance. Fleet Street headlines were read on the news, talking points repeated and debated on morning and evening shows and included in stand-up routines, until they seeped into everyday consciousness. It was a phenomenon that had to be experienced to be understood and I often marvelled at the effectiveness of this machinery in moulding society.

Politics in Great Britain, I'd learned, was split, just like my hands, into left and right; each side spouting differing ideologies on how they believed the country should be run. It was extraordinary when they were united on any given issue, as was the case when the Labour Party announced it would implement immigration curbs if elected in the upcoming elections.

In 2010, the Conservatives had been voted in on the back of a promise to significantly lower the number of immigrants to the country to 'tens of thousands', a promise they'd failed to keep, but one the populace demanded.

A lesson in the art of the boogie man: bombard the airwaves with enough insidious stories and carefully worded headlines about a group of people and they become no longer human but the cause of every societal issue: higher taxes, rising cost of living, a collapsing system. For good measure, employ people who look just like them to sit on panels and insist there is nothing insidious about it all.

'I read this great column by Hannah Switch the other day,' Leo – short for Leonidas – a senior solicitor who'd worked at the firm longer than me, said in the lunch room one balmy morning as a group of us waited for the coffee machine. 'It's on the new housing tax on council flats and homes above a certain grade and the income it brings to the government. Too many people have leeched off the government for far too long and are costing us more money than they bring to the country.' He had an upper-class accent that indicated Eton and then Oxbridge as an nth generation attendee – someone who had no idea what it was to live in a council flat.

Bile crawled up my throat and I swallowed it down, training my eyes on the patterns on my mug. Leo often featured unknowingly on my Twitter account:

NaijaUK Law Girl   @NaijaUKLawGirl   9 Jun

What does it mean when your colleague looks you square in the eye as he talks about immigrants leeching off resources in the break room?

Collapse

 NaijaUK Law Girl   @NaijaUKLawGirl   7 Jul

"No need to get uppity about it," a colleague to me this morning over a minor disagreement on a client file. Does England have a factory where it produces these posh boys? How are they all the same?

Collapse

Rayan nodded slowly. 'Ah Hannah Switch ... she also has some astute columns on the immigration crisis and the potential danger it poses to our systems and culture, and the need to create a hostile environment for *illegal* immigrants.' I wondered if he emphasised the word 'illegal' to underscore the difference between them and him.

The next day I would tweet:

 NaijaUK Law Girl   @NaijaUKLawGirl   29 Sep

The Good Immigrant Myth: The belief that only certain types of immigrants deserve to be treated with humanity

Collapse

It would spark a debate.

 Ziwe Ncube   @ZtotheWe   29 Sep

Some immigrants play into this and consider themselves superior to others, the difference is circumstance and opportunities!

Collapse

 Bayo Adesanya   @BigBayo   29 Sep

The superiority complex won't shield them from the immigrant experience, they should carry on. Idiots.

Collapse

 Semo and Garri   @OyinkanB   29 Sep

Whether we like it or not, some are better than others, let's stop pretending abeg

Collapse

 Jamaican Gal   @CaseyWhite   29 Sep

Be careful or they'll say you're in support of illegal immigrants. Home Office come knocking on your door.

Collapse

'The situation on the Mediterranean is preposterous,' Leo continued. And I thought with disgruntled admiration that he said *preposterous* in a manner only a posh English man could, a blonde curl at his temple vibrating. His ice-blue eyes fixed on Rayan's face, awaiting his endorsement.

'Absolutely,' Rayan responded in an almost exaggerated tone. 'Hannah's a fantastic writer and doing a good job keeping us informed in these times.'

Efulefu was what my mother would call someone like Rayan: a man who'd lost his way from his roots.

'Do you have something to say, Ego?' a posh voice asked.

I glanced up, realising in a panic that I'd hissed loudly. Every eye in the lunch room was trained on me.

'Hannah is married to that MP, isn't she? She isn't as unbiased as you might think,' Ceri interjected. I appreciated her boldness and support, though she had less to lose than I did.

Leo did not glance in her direction. His eyes held a glint of malice that suggested he'd been waiting for this moment, and I worried that he'd come across my Twitter.

'Yes, Ego?'

Ceri shook her head at me frantically but I'd never been one to take good advice; there was only one man I feared and we shared a name.

I straightened my back and held Leo's gaze. 'The policies are inhumane,' I said simply.

He laughed, mockingly. 'Inhumane? You think it's humane for immigrants to come over here and deny hardworking British citizens resources their taxes pay for?'

'People just don't leave everything and everyone they know behind and brave such conditions without reason, you know that, right?' My voice shook as I struggled to get my rage under control; it was possible to bottle anger without knowing it.

'I take it you're speaking from experience,' Leo said, a sneer on his lips.

I bit the inner corner of my lip, refusing to take the bait.

He waved a dismissive hand. 'It isn't our fault their countries are corrupt,' he said drily.

'He thinks he's one of them,' Ceri said to me later with a sad tut.

'Who?'

'Rayan,' she clarified. 'He thinks he's not working class anymore because he rubs shoulders with Leo. He'll learn the hard way.'

Where I'd viewed the conversation through the lens of race, she'd only seen class.

'Who does he think he is?' Eriife fumed when I recounted the exchange to her over the phone. 'Are you not almost British? You pay your taxes. By next year you will get your papers.'

I chuckled at that – *almost British* – like it was a status to grow into. Would I become like Rayan when my new passport came in the mail?

'You see this is why I said you should come back home. You not only deal with nonsense from clients but this as well? Why will you stay in a country that treats you like a visitor?'

She sent me articles after that, headline after headline saying I was unwanted. Addicted to suffering, I clicked on them and picked my way through the comments – anonymity meant people were the worst versions of themselves.

Go back to your country, they screamed, and each time, I came away feeling exactly as Eriife had described: a visitor.

*

Back in '98, Sister Bolatito's boys' quarters smelled like bleach, and the soap-marked smudges on the windows indicated that they'd been cleaned in a hurry ahead of our arrival. But it was the best we had.

On the way there, my mother had stopped by a NITEL call centre to call her mother to let her know we were not coming home. She returned to the car with red eyes and a running nose, indications that the call hadn't gone well, but she did not say anything, and we knew better than to ask. Instead, my sisters made fun of my low-cut hair as my mother drove in edged silence; when we stopped at a red traffic light, we bought plantain chips from a hawker with change my mother kept in her glove compartment, filling the car with noises of tearing sachets and crunching.

Sister Bolatito stood in front of her gate to welcome us, and as we approached, she screamed for her gateman, an elderly man with a limp.

'Welcome, welcome,' she said, sounding out of breath, opening our car doors like we were august visitors.

To me, she gave special attention, assisting me from the car and looking me up and down, staring at the scar on my head.

'How are you feeling, my daughter?' she asked. Before I could respond, she was at the boot of the car, helping my mother pull out the belongings we'd brought along.

The boys' quarters was a bungalow at the back of her compound, sitting behind the main duplex where she lived. It was in England I learned that boys' quarters were a colonial relic; where the servants stayed while their masters lived comfortably in the main house. But in Nigeria, they were the norm, extra rooms for the help and where extended family members stayed when they visited.

We scrubbed the place in her absence, starting with the

smudged windows. And when we were done, we unpacked our belongings in the living room and two boxy bedrooms.

'The two of you can take the larger bedroom. Ego and I will share the other room,' my mother said, and the twins squealed like we were on holiday. As they rushed to their room, we could hear them arguing over which side of the bed belonged to the other.

'Teenagers,' I grumbled, like I wasn't one myself, and my mother smiled tentatively, the first smile I'd seen from her in a while.

Sister Bolatito's house was nothing like my father's. There were no marble sculptures gushing out crystal water, no gardeners pruning away at foliage at the crack of dawn, and no steward to prepare continental dishes at her whim. But she had a buxom woman, Mama Yejide, who took care of the running of the household. In the mornings, Mama Yejide knocked on our door to inform us that breakfast was ready and told us when the washman was coming so we could bring our dirty clothes out for laundry.

My mother expressed excessive gratitude for these gestures. She'd always been a polite person, but she seemed to wear a new skin. I recognised it – it was the same one of perpetual servitude my father's workers wore – I'd just never thought I would see it on my mother.

Money commanded respect, sometimes for oneself, and my mother didn't have any. The night we arrived at Sister Bolatito's place, she assembled us in the living room of the boys' quarters to inform us of her obvious decision.

'I feel it's important for you to know what's going on,' she started, then cleared her throat. She pulled at the sleeve of her blouse, looking unsure and we stared at her in pensive silence.

It wasn't the first time we'd assembled like this, but that was over ten years ago and then she'd lied, told us we were going to spend time with our grandparents. But even back then, I'd known the truth.

'I've left your father,' my mother said finally and my sisters gasped. 'We're not going back,' she announced with finality.

'What about school?' Nwamaka whined. I turned to stare at her nose. It was how I told them apart: Nwamaka was the one with the slight crook at the edge of her nose that mirrored my father's, the only blemish in his features. As children, Nkechinyere had been the one to mirror my father's temperament but at some turning point between child and teenagehood, they'd switched personalities.

'You can keep going to school. I'll take you myself every morning,' my mother said.

'Are we going to live here forever?'

My mother blinked rapidly, like she was trying to calm herself. 'No, we won't live here forever. We'll find a solution, I promise.'

'Did we leave because of Ego?' Nkechi asked, pointing at the scar at the side of my head. It was her turn for us to stare at her.

My mother had always done her best to shield them from the reality of my father, even when he made it almost impossible. As the first child, I'd been the one to bear the responsibility of knowledge.

'It doesn't matter. I'm fine,' I quickly interjected.

My mother stared at her hands. 'I'm sorry,' she whispered.

The weeks afterwards restored some sense of normalcy as we developed a routine – my mother went out every morning to drop my sisters at school, then she returned to take me to therapy. In the car, we said little to each other, listening to music instead.

Therapy was uncomfortable, like pinching at a scabbed wound continuously. My therapist, a small woman swamped by her lab coat, encouraged me in exercises and drills to recover my neurocognitive skills. Cognitive remediation therapy, it was called. Each day, we listened to recordings in American accents that instructed me to press buzzers or indicate when I heard certain letters or words, perform maths equations and embroider letters to create language.

At the end of the sessions, she said, 'Well done, Ego. You're doing very well,' pronouncing *Ego* in a Lagos accent, then scribbling feverishly in notepads before handing out assignments and exercises to practise at home. As time passed, I grew bored and listless, fatigued by the routines and encouragements to journal, but I did not tell my mother because I knew the sessions were costing more than she could afford.

While I was at therapy, my mother sold her belongings to amass funds for us to start our new lives – the ornate jewellery, bejewelled wrappers and custom shoes. My father had money but my mother did not, it was a baffling phenomenon to explain to an outsider so I never bothered. Yes, it was possible to be married to such a wealthy man and have nothing of your own. My father hardly, if ever, handed my mother raw, hard cash but he'd ensured she lived and looked the part of the wife of the man he was. It allowed others to make assumptions of their own, painting spurious pictures of our lives that differed bluntly from the reality.

When she wasn't looking for a buyer for her assets, my mother went job hunting. On those days, she returned with scarlet eyes and slumped shoulders and I knew it hadn't gone well.

At night, she slept uneasily, rolling this way and that, and I wondered if even in sleep, she couldn't get away from my father.

Zina visited often; it was the least she could do after encouraging me to go home that day.

'*Molo!*' she shouted as I opened the door the first time and she saw my almost bald head.

'Fool,' I said, slapping the door in her face, and her laughter echoed through the heavy wood.

She was the first person to know where we were, my mother having informed her of our location before even her own siblings; she hoped the companionship would improve my disposition and my dissatisfaction with the fact that I couldn't yet go back to school. But if anything, her visits made me long more for what I couldn't yet have.

The three of us had filled our JAMB university admission forms together. Zina had carefully penned 'Theatre Arts' as her choice for her course of study, Eriife, 'Medicine', while I scribbled 'Law'. We all chose the University of Lagos, determined to continue our mothers' legacies. But two weeks later, Zina purchased another JAMB form, and in the course of study box, she wrote 'Law', defeated by her father's will.

Our fathers were alike and yet so different: they'd both been born into nothing and by the sheer force of their wills made their fortunes. But whereas my father mostly ignored mine and my sisters' existence, Zina's father's will extended to every area of his children's lives. And so, when he'd insisted that his first daughter would only take up a profession he considered reputable, neither of us had been surprised, just disappointed.

'Can't your mother talk to him?' Eriife asked Zina as a tear blotched the paper.

'There's no point,' she said.

I knew the feeling.

Eriife visited only when she didn't have classes, which wasn't often. 'I'm a medical student, not like you jokers,' she told us, and we laughed, accustomed to the jabs. But on one of those afternoons when Eriife wasn't there, Zina confided that she'd been spotted around campus with an unusual older student. 'Don't ask her, when she's ready she'll tell us what she wants us to know,' Zina said.

In my absence, the world had moved on: classes continued, tests were given, Ademola had a new girlfriend (and he'd received hearty congratulations that he'd escaped my bad luck), exams were looming, the sky was still blue and rain still fell, drowning walkways and reminding the beach to push back. I wondered if this was how the dead felt, watching the earth stretch to cover the hole created by their former existence.

'Do you know who he is now?' I asked Zina, another day. We sat with bowls of popcorn watching a movie on the small television my mother had purchased to keep us entertained.

'She's still not said anything but I did some digging, trust me,' Zina said.

I laughed. 'Of course, I trust you, Madam FBI. What did you find?'

'He's a former student leader, during the NADECO days, when they tried to pressure the head of state to hand over power to Abiola, but got too involved in national politics and had to leave school for a while because the military men were looking for him.'

I wrinkled my nose. 'Do you think that's why she didn't tell us about it? Is he still on the run?'

Zina gave me a look. 'The head of state is dead, you know that.'

I did.

Glancing at my face and guessing my thoughts, she reached out a hand to tap mine comfortingly, 'Don't worry, she'll talk to us when she's ready.'.

'Isn't he too old for her? Is that legal?'

She chuckled. 'This is Nigeria.'

'I don't like him,' I grumbled, and she laughed.

'You don't even know him.'

My mother sold her car to make up the money needed to rent an apartment. By then, Zina already had a boyfriend of her own: a man so tall the top of his head hit the roof of his Peugeot as he dropped her off at our gate. I didn't like him either.

Sister Bolatito had marked our departure with a grand lunch in her living room. We were the only ones to attend; the church ladies no longer socialised with her and I could tell she would miss my mother's companionship – the animated remarks as they watched home videos, commenting on the characters like they were real people: 'Don't do that, stupid girl. Oh God, she's going to die!'

'Ladies and ladies,' Sister Bolatito said at the lunch, causing us to burst into laughter. Then she gave her speech, thanking us for our stay. My mother gave a speech as well, a less confident one, but a speech nonetheless. At the door of our new apartment, just before she left us, Sister Bolatito pushed a thickened envelope between my mother's fingers, telling her to take care, and my mother wept, loud broken sobs, as they hugged.

At first, my mother did not tell anyone where we'd moved, and we lived in tentative peace. Then she told my grandmother and days later, my father was at our door with an entourage, all wearing the charcoal uniform of the police force, clicking handcuffs around my mother's wrists and driving off.

Sister Bolatito stayed with us the nights our mother was away; she'd been charged with kidnapping and I wondered how you could take your children to the same school every day – a school their father had never visited – and still be accused of kidnapping. It was one of the reasons I wanted to become a lawyer. Our laws seemed to me mere suggestions, tools of manipulation of the powerful and not edicts to protect the everyday man.

Days later, my mother was returned to us – a warning to return to the status quo or be punished. And I wondered how much further my father would go. Nasir, my father's business partner, always said he was not to be credited for their remarkable success: 'Chigozie is inevitable.' I pondered on those words as my mother walked through our door, smelling of dirt and stale urine. Inevitable.

'You don't like anyone,' Zina countered when I voiced my thoughts about her boyfriend.

'He's not good enough for you,' I said. There was something much too ordinary about him for my liking and he carried it like it was an accomplishment, not wanting to be better, and Zina was anything but that. He would want her to be ordinary one day and she wouldn't be able to be.

It was why they called her *mami water*, the creature whose beauty seduced men to their deaths; she'd inherited her mother's stunning features and her father's yellow skin tone. Even that wasn't what made Zina different, there was a fire in her eyes, a recklessness and willingness to tread the borders of caution that left people curious.

'It's a waste of time anyways, might as well have fun,' she said. We exchanged a look.

'Have you met him yet?' I asked, referring to the man she was to marry the moment she turned eighteen.

'Not yet, but soon.' She looked away, and I could feel the helplessness rolling off her.

'I don't understand your father. Why is he doing this? Who even does this in this day and age?' I said, voicing our shared frustration.

Zina shrugged, feigning nonchalance. 'It's a family tradition. It doesn't matter,' she said. 'It's not like talking about it will change anything.'

'And your mother? What is she saying?'

She shrugged again as a corner of her mouth turned up. 'Well, let's just hope he's young and not some old man.'

8

Patriotism

Patriotism in London in 2014 meant attending boozy parties where the latest Nigerian releases were blasted from out-sized speakers and posting a green-white-green flag with the caption *'Naija for life'* on the first day of October. On Independence Day that year, I tweeted:

NaijaUK Law Girl   @NaijaUKLawGirl   1 Oct
God bless my home country even as I hustle to make it in this new one. Anyone throwing a bash? send my invite o

Collapse

Someone replied:

Jamaican Gal   @CaseyWhite   1 Oct

Sending independence greetings sister like you did for us. Tek a break from Twitter and come turn up in South London

Collapse

It was the beauty of the London scene – the blend of cultures and, for many, a shared history of colonisation and migration. At the Notting Hill Carnival, flags were waved and worn as clothing, music – from the townships of Jamaica to the streets of Lagos – blasted on speakers as we swallowed Trinidadian roti and Guyanese pepperpot. On Twitter, we fought faux diaspora wars for supremacy and threw accusations of appropriation and influence, but in reality, and in truth, we were one – pledging allegiance to a country that had become our home.

Patriotism, to my great uncle in the '60s, had meant running off to join a new army to fight for the country he dreamt of and debated about daily with my grandfather. To my mother, in February of 1999, patriotism meant voting in the upcoming presidential election, the first since the '93 military coup. I was to turn 18 that year – not before the elections, but still – and I shared my mother's excitement. When the campaign jingles came on the television, I called for her to come watch. I visited home more often now.

The ghost of Uncle Ikenna's allegiance came calling a few weeks before voting day – someone finally had conclusive information on his whereabouts during the war following years of stony silence. My mother packed her bags in a barely suppressed frenzy, having applied for leave at her new job as a clerk at a government parastatal. By then I'd long resumed classes, immersing myself in the usual routines.

I had returned to school four months after the incident to find I'd lost my class representative position; the class had voted in my absence, not for a temporary but a permanent replacement. The doctors said I'd done well to recover so quickly but it felt anything but well to return to classes and struggle to recall names, places, dates, to fall into an occasional stammer when called upon to speak, to spend extra hours poring over notes, pleading with the letters to stick. Lecturers were willing to make concessions but only so much, and by the middle of the semester, I was sure I was bound to fail.

'I swear I'm doing my best,' I tearfully admitted to Zina when a test result came back. I'd been brilliant all my life, and having my nimble brain so viciously snatched from me, I had no idea who I was anymore.

'It will get better as you heal,' the therapist told me. 'Keep doing your exercises.'

My father began to wage a different kind of war when my mother did not return to him even after her stint in a police cell. The gossip magazine covers were melodramatic with jagged lines running through glossy pictures of my parents, the stories salacious and outrightly defamatory. I read the details from the faces of others, the remorseful manner in which they rushed to tuck the pages in their bags and pockets when I was near, as though in possession of an illegal substance.

'Have you read this?' Zina asked, slapping one of the magazines on my bed one evening.

'No, I haven't,' I replied calmly, continuing to iron the dress in front of me.

'Why?' she asked. I could hear the incredulity in her voice.

'Because I don't want to know. What's the point?'

She threw up her hands, her consternation apparent. 'You could at least try to know why everyone keeps talking every time you pass by.'

'They've been talking about me for almost a year now.'

Zina sighed as she balanced on my bed, just beside the smoking iron.

'Don't burn yourself o, *biko*,' I shouted, snatching the iron and placing it on the other end of the bed.

'I've read it, do you want me to tell you what's in there? It's really bad.'

'No.' It couldn't be worse than any of the usual slander men adopted when women left them: accusations of infidelity and poor parenting.

Zina rolled her eyes. 'What are you even ironing for God's sake? It's Friday evening.'

'I know.'

'And? Where are you going?'

'To the party,' I said with a triumphant smile and Zina stared, stunned.

Someone popular was throwing a party; I wasn't sure who, but the fliers had been lying around the porter's desk as I'd passed, the red letters asking to be picked up. And as I stared at the gratuitous promises of fun and good music, I decided I was going to attend. Perhaps doing something out of character would help me find myself again.

Ceri was throwing Iain a birthday party, their first as a married couple.

'I hope it's not one of those parties you people have in this country that's just alcohol and chatting,' I joked as she handed me the invite. Going to my first party as a student in England, I'd been flummoxed to find people standing and drinking as house music played in the background. I'd thought in horror: *No food? Not even fried meat or puff puff?*

I wore my most comfortable slacks and a fitted turtleneck sweater I thought flattered my figure. They lived in a redbrick house in a quiet neighbourhood just outside London with a sizeable garden – a home for a couple hoping to have a family someday, unlike my cold urban flat.

The aroma of cooking wafted through the air as Ceri led me down the hall, walls decorated with family pictures, towards the noise of the garden.

'Where's the birthday boy?' I asked, infusing as much cheer as I could into my voice.

'Forget the birthday boy,' Ceri said. 'There's someone I want you to meet. I just know the two of you will hit it off.'

I immediately knew that this person, whoever they were, was black. Not because she'd offered to introduce us, but in the certainty she felt that we would get along.

It was similar to the way my classmates in grad school had asked if I knew their friends from Ghana or Burkina Faso and I'd had to explain that two francophone countries separated Nigeria and Ghana and that we did not even share the same lingua franca as Burkina Faso.

P-Square's voices crooned the melody to 'Chop My Money' from a speaker somewhere and I glanced at Ceri in surprise.

'It's so good, isn't it?' she said. 'It's afrobeats, I thought you'd like it so I included it in the playlist.'

My throat clogged with gratitude at the thoughtfulness of the action.

'Ego, I'd like you to meet Rodney,' Ceri announced when we were standing in front of a man so well proportioned, I was convinced he'd been designed and not birthed.

'Ego. Nice to meet you,' I said, extending my arm as my skin prickled with a sensation I hadn't felt in ages. Shyness.

'Be nice, he's a good guy,' Ceri whispered theatrically before scurrying away.

'I take it you're from Nigeria?' Rodney said when she was gone, holding my eyes with confidence. Could he sense the attraction?

'I take it you're not,' I joked in return.

He smiled and I was tempted to swoon.

'How did you know I was Nigerian?' I asked, curious.

'I grew up in South London with lots of Nigerians and so I can tell when I meet one. Unfortunately, parts of the borough have now been gentrified, it's losing its flavour.' He said *losing its flavour* in a tone so tinged with poignant regret that I knew I liked him at once.

Ceri wasn't always right understanding the complexities of my identity, but she was right about Rodney. He was British, a third-generation descendant of grandparents who'd moved from Jamaica with the Windrush generation. He told me that although his grandparents were no longer alive, he worried about the new immigration act that had taken out protection from forced deportation for that generation. I told him the government said other protections existed. Neither of us thought the government could be trusted.

'Their generation helped rebuild this country after the Second World War, dedicated their lives and this is how they're repaid. You're never considered truly British as long as you're not white,' Rodney said.

'Do you feel more Jamaican than British?' I asked him.

He wasn't sure, England was the only home he'd known, born and bred. But in England, he felt Jamaican, in Jamaica, he felt too British.

Music played on – an intersection of British pop and rock interspersed with the occasional afrobeats song. Games were *'roaring'* and competitive and everyone cheered as Iain cut into his cake. Banky W's 'Yes/No' played when Rodney asked for my number, ardently beseeching a lady to be his lover, and I gave it without hesitation even though I was unsure what my answer was.

In 1998, Nigerian songs did not dominate our airwaves, not because we were unpatriotic per se, but because there weren't as many options, and we still suffered from a Hollywood-induced obsession with everything American, not knowing that one day, it would be cool to be Nigerian.

Zina and I arrived at the party together in almost matching outfits: barely above the knee tube dresses – hers blue, mine red – that would have had our mothers screaming. I pulled at the hem of my dress as we walked in, feeling self-conscious, and Zina slapped at my wrist.

'Return of the Mack' was winding down, 'Doo Wop' just kicking off, bodies contorted into shapes on the dance floor, drawing closer and closer. A hand waved from the other end of the room at Zina – it was much too dark to make out the face – and she waved back, recognition lighting her own face.

'Move around, mingle, I'll be right back,' she said as she hurried away.

It was like losing your mother in the middle of a busy marketplace, searching for anything or anyone familiar that could direct you to safety. I missed Eriife, she'd always been my companion whenever Zina went off.

Spotting a bar in a corner of the room, I moved quickly towards it. A man who looked much older than everyone else was mixing and pouring drinks, smirking and winking at the drunk girls waving empty glasses, asking for refills. Just beside the bar, where the lights from the disco ball lights barely flickered, was a small cove of chairs, and I settled into one of them, pulling at my dress and muttering how I'd made a mistake in coming.

I did not notice the lone figure leaning against the wall until it moved, then I jumped, startled. He was tall – I could tell that even from my seated position – much taller than I was, and wide, and I worried I was in danger until he smiled, a calming smile.

'Why not grab a drink?' he asked, gesturing towards the bar. His voice took me by surprise. I wasn't sure exactly what I'd expected, but I knew I would never forget it.

'No, thank you. I'm fine,' I said, trying to make out his face, then I looked away, conscious of the fact that he was watching me watch him.

'You look like you shouldn't be here,' he said after several minutes of silence.

I did not respond.

Daddy Showkey's 'Diana' came on then, and every corner of the room screamed with the lyrics. The DJ was good, making me grateful for the noise that prevented this strange person from talking to me; I could still feel his eyes roving over my face with interest.

'So why are you here?' he asked, persistent, when the song ended and a foreign one replaced it.

I turned to look at him. His eyes were shiny, not the usual white. 'Because I want to be.'

He smiled, showing equally white teeth. 'Then you should enjoy it.'

'Who said I'm not enjoying it?'

'You don't look like you are.'

I cocked my head to the side and stared up at him. 'Are you enjoying the party? You're in a corner all by yourself monitoring what others are doing.'

He laughed, a deep one that came from his chest. 'Fine, I concede,' he said, moving from the wall to stand beside me; I shifted uncomfortably. Placing his glass on an empty seat beside me, he extended his hand. 'Care to dance? Maybe we can both be of use to each other.'

I stared at his extended hand, suddenly emboldened, drunk on adventure. I grabbed it and allowed him to pull me in the direction of the dance floor.

The music was too loud, the floor packed with sweating bodies but neither of us seemed to notice. I moved because he moved and he moved because I did. How long we were there for, I wasn't sure. Each song seemed to wind the web that drew us closer, our eyes never leaving each other.

The rhythm slowed as it drew closer to midnight and the dance floor emptied as bodies began to cling to one another, and he placed a cautionary palm on my hip, his brow raised, asking if I was okay with it. I nodded and his other hand moved to cover the opposite side of my waist. Of their own accord, my arms rose to circle his neck. And he smiled a smile of encouragement, like he could tell I was out of my comfort zone. A force beyond our control seemed determined to pull us closer, and by the time Joe's 'The Love Scene' came on, we were plastered to each other, our lips inches apart. I'd never been kissed before but I knew I would enjoy kissing him.

The DJ changed the music then, a hammer shattering the glass of the moment, and the dance floor began to fill quickly.

Zina emerged from the crowd, screaming my name. He pulled away as she rushed towards me.

'I think your friend is looking for you. Hope you've enjoyed yourself,' he said in that voice.

Questions floated through my addled mind. What was his name? Would I remember if he told me? Was he a student? What department? Would I see him again? But I could not force myself to mouth any as he turned away and moved through the crowd.

'I've been looking for you everywhere,' Zina said the moment she was by my side. 'Who was that?!'

I blinked. 'I'm not sure.'

Haunted – that was what I was. For months afterwards, I looked out for him everywhere, listened for his voice: at the cafeteria, in class, at the school chapel. But it seemed I'd conjured him that day, a fantasy of my own making.

'How is it possible for someone to just disappear like that?' I asked Zina. And I thought to myself that I'd finally experienced a fraction of what it was like to live like my mother, stranded in time, longing for answers and closure.

When she returned from her journey seeking answers to Uncle Ikenna's disappearance, I only asked one question, 'Did you get an answer?'

She nodded mechanically, the tears spilling uncontrollably down her face, her shoulders shuddering and I put my arms around her.

On election day, my mother did not go out to vote. She lay in bed, a photo album in her lap, her eyes aflame. And I wondered if her patriotism had been because of Uncle Ikenna all along.

I liked Aunty Sally because she didn't pretend to be Christian; she was incapable of pretence, speaking her mind at every turn. She said more people needed to be told they were stupid so they could be aware of that congenital defect in their persons. 'Imagine going about not knowing how much your stupidity affects others?'

Aunty Sally was a woman comfortable in her success, appearing only in well-tailored clothes, having fought her way to the top of a bank, not an easy feat. Perhaps that was what inspired such confidence, the knowledge that she could take on the best. Her introduction into our lives brought a spark that had been missing, a fire that needed to be lighted, motivating my mother to do what she'd been unable to thus far.

'Obianuju, you should get a divorce. I'm serious,' she told my mother in our new living room with the fading paint and popcorn ceiling.

'We went to university together,' my mother had told us with a nervous smile as she introduced us to Aunty Sally for the first time. 'We ran into each other at the market some days ago.'

We greeted her 'good afternoon' in unison as we'd been raised to do and Aunty Sally let out a guffaw. 'You don't have to be so polite, this isn't the *Sound of Music.*' Then she pointed at me and turned to my mother. 'She looks just like you. My God! It's like a time machine.' And I felt it, that suffocating sensation that came when I was reminded of the similarities between us.

There was a Rolls-Royce parked outside my hostel, its grill badge glinting in the sun, the week my mother finally filed for divorce from my father, assisted by a lawyer Aunty Sally hired. I was aware of what the licence plate read even before it honked in my direction: Azubuike.

A tinted glass window at the back seat rolled down and my grandmother shouted my name – *Nwakaego.* I walked towards the car calmly, unwilling to create a scene by refusing to acknowledge them.

The leather of the seats smelled fresh, like they had just been pulled from plastic and I thought of my mother as she counted the change in her bag to make sure there was enough money for bread the next morning.

My sisters had become vocal in their dissatisfaction with our new lifestyle, complaining at every turn.

'Why can't we go back?' Nwamaka said. 'You and Mummy can stay here.' We were the ones with an issue with my father.

'I miss Daddy,' Nkechinyere said. She did not miss him – there was nothing to miss – but the life we had lived with him.

'And mosquitos are always biting me, just look at my legs. I was voted best legs in my class before,' her twin added.

'Will the both of you please shut up!' I shouted.

Nwamaka opened her mouth to respond but froze as she looked behind me, and I turned to see my mother standing by the door, silent. I thought she looked smaller than her usual height, shrunken in herself.

'My daughter,' my grandmother said, her smile patronising as she shifted to make space for me in the back seat. My father stared at me in loaded silence, like a fighter evaluating his competitor.

'Good afternoon,' I said to no one in particular.

'Good afternoon, my daughter. How are you? How is school?' my grandmother said.

'Fine,' I said, waiting.

My grandmother stared at my father expectantly, as though they had a conversation planned, and he cleared his throat.

'Erm, I'm sorry for what happened. It was never my intention to cause harm.'

I had never heard my father apologise, and for a moment I stared at him, mesmerised.

'*Ehen*, your father has apologised,' my grandmother said, placing a placating hand on my thigh. 'He is very sorry. He has told me so several times himself. Please talk to your mother, encourage her to forgive him. You know she listens to you.'

I smiled, saccharine, nodded and said, 'Okay,' then opened the door to leave. I could feel their eyes boring into the back of my head.

'Wait,' my grandmother said as I was about to close the door. 'Take,' she said, stretching a stuffed envelope in my direction. I collected the envelope with a thank you, because I thought it would be stupid not to, and I gave it to my mother, telling her it was from Aunty Sally. I did not pass on their message.

The next time the Rolls-Royce was parked in front of my hostel, my mother's lawyer had made demands of my father, moving ahead with the case.

'You were married to him for how many years. You cannot leave with nothing. I won't allow it,' Aunty Sally said to my mother.

'Did you not talk to your mother? Why is she acting like this?' my grandmother demanded in the car.

'No, I didn't,' I said evenly.

'What kind of child are you? Your father has apologised. He said he is sorry. What more do you want?'

I laughed an empty laugh.

'What is funny?' my father asked.

'The fact that both of you can come here so shamelessly after so many months and expect me to convince my mother to return to that hell is what is funny.' I turned to my father.

'I almost died, do you know that? I still have the scar on my head, I still struggle to remember people's names. But I should help you? You! As far as I'm concerned, the both of you can go straight to hell. I'd spit on your graves.'

A vein throbbed in my father's head when I was done, and I knew if given another chance, I would be dead.

9

Democracy

'What is going on in your country, Ego?' my mother asked me over Skype in the middle of November 2014. Matthew lay docilely beside her on the sofa and my stepfather was out getting bagels.

'Bagels? For breakfast?' I was alarmed. Bagels were not what we considered breakfast back home. I marvelled at how America had changed my mother, and wondered why Britain hadn't done the same for me, or perhaps it had, and I'd chosen, obstinately, not to acknowledge it.

'It is not my country,' I retorted with unintended force.

My mother's brows creased together with concern. 'What is the problem, Nwakaego? Is everything okay?'

Nwakaego. She expected me to open up, in the same way she sent me new pictures of Nwamaka, stolen from blogs and clipped from society magazines Nkechinyere sent over, and spoke of her longings for reconciliation, mourning over a daughter who was still very much alive.

I dragged a hand across my forehead. 'I'm sorry, I shouldn't have spoken to you like that,' I said, feeling remorseful.

'Is everything okay? Talk to me.' She studied my face, her eyes squinting with concern.

'I'm fine, I promise, just a little stressed from work,' I offered.

'Do you want to take a break and come spend time with me here?'

'No.'

I could tell my answer hurt her. In her eyes I saw a haunting fear that she would lose me in the manner in which she'd lost my sister.

'Why this sudden clamour to leave the EU?' she asked me, returning the conversation to safer grounds. 'What happened to the age of globalisation? Anyone with a basic sense of economics knows it's a bad idea.' She'd studied Economics in school.

I sighed. On the television panels, the ones where they pretended to have a balanced debate, they spouted admonitions of sovereignty and the rights to determination: *Britain should be making decisions for Britain!*

Take back Britain was the mantra. *From whom?* was what I wanted to ask.

I told my mother.

'But immigrants are not to blame for the state of the economy.'

'You're right, I know you're right, but many don't,' I said.

She shook her head.

'I guess that's the good thing about democracy,' I said. 'They'll vote on it eventually and decide for themselves.'

'You said "they",' she observed. 'Won't you vote?'

I shrugged, unsure.

'But is it really democracy if they're lying to the people?'

'What is democracy?'

On Twitter, I asked:

NaijaUK Law Girl   @NaijaUKLawGirl   14 Nov
Do you consider the UK your country and do you feel any interest in having a say in its affairs?

Collapse

But I already had my answer.

At the revival of democracy in Nigeria in May 1999, we were informed that the presidential villa had been exorcised like it was a perfectly normal phenomenon to have a presidential villa exorcised of the demons of a dead military dictator. Preparations were feverish, and miniature flags waved on the streets again, evanescent hope in Nigeria restored. This was indeed a new beginning, our first people-chosen leader in 15 years, our departure from being an international pariah to the nation we were meant to be, and yet, the excitement was cautious as we waited with bated breath for reality.

Before the elections, Eriife had invited me and Zina to a rally on campus organised by her boyfriend's party. At the rally, she stood on a wooden stage and espoused the virtues of democracy and our right to vote.

'We've lost her, haven't we?' Zina said quietly, watching Eriife. And I understood what she meant. Eriife had always been outspoken, sharp-tongued even, but the woman in front of us was far removed from the girl we knew. Eriife of the past did not use words like 'compatriot' nor did she contort herself to please an audience.

'Are you not a compatriot?' I joked. But Zina looked on like one mourning a lost relative.

We did not wait to meet Eriife's boyfriend after the rally.

On Democracy Day, my mother cooked rice, just like her mother had cooked on the first Independence Day, and we formed a circle around our television to witness this transition into a new era. Uniformed men swinging booted feet in unison like marionettes, martial music – a retrospection of less pleasant times – ringing in the arena, aeroplanes huffing national-coloured smoke: green, white, green. My mother clapped like she was seated with the six thousand spectators packed in Abuja's Eagle Square and needed to be heard above the din, her smile bright with sheer joy; this was what her generation had been promised.

A knock came as the swearing-in ceremony began and I ran to open the door, leaving my mother to bask in her state of wondrous rapture, because I hoped, or rather, willed it to be Zina.

'What do you think?' Zina had asked, pushing the picture in my face, not giving me an opportunity to look elsewhere.

'He's young,' I said, in genuine relief. He looked to be mid-20s, his haircut a recent style.

'At least you didn't say, "I don't like him", like you always do,' she joked, mocking me.

'Have you met him yet?'

She shook her head no. 'He and his family are coming to see my father this month to formally begin the process.' Her tone was carefully flippant.

'Are you ready?' I asked, not sure what else to say. It seemed like the sort of question you asked your friend who was on the verge of marriage.

'Chuka wants to make a counter proposal to my father. He

thinks he can change his mind,' she said and giggled like she thought it cute.

I hissed. 'That fellow? Does he even have the money to pay your bride price? Or he plans to sell his Peugeot? Can that old thing even buy a bag of rice?'

Zina laughed and I joined her, then we laughed even harder, her palm rising to slap my shoulder, and I was certain we'd both gone mad.

We told each other everything. Yet Zina only left a note on my bunk the day she disappeared; only a week after she'd shown me the picture: *Ego baby. I'm not ready to marry anyone biko. I'm going away for a while. I can't tell you where but just know I'm okay. Chuka is with me. Don't be annoyed ehn. It's for your own good. I still love you plenty.*

I told my mother because I had no one else to confide in, because I was scared that something would happen to my friend and I would be the unwitting accomplice who remained silent when her voice was needed, and because I wanted her to be prepared for the possibility of Zina's father coming after us. Who else would know Zina's whereabouts if not me?

'Nwakaego,' my mother said, using the tone that told me she was serious. 'Are you sure you don't know where she is? Who is this Chuka? Do you know where he lives?'

'No. I don't know anything,' I said and sobbed into my hands, feeling useless.

My mother rubbed my back in soothing circles. 'Don't worry, everything will be okay.'

'Obianuju,' Uncle Kelechi, my mother's eldest brother shouted as I opened the door.

'Kelechi at least enter the house before you start shouting, this thing is heavy,' Uncle Ikechukwu grumbled behind him, his hands full with a bag of rice.

It had been months since either of them had bothered to look for us.

'What would Papa say? He must be rolling in his grave,' Uncle Kelechi had said to my mother the last time I saw him.

'I'm not going back,' my mother said.

'Why not think of your children? This isn't life,' Uncle Ikenna added, circling a palm in the air at our sparse living room. My mother looked contrite then.

Now, my mother wiped her hands nervously on her skirt as she stood.

'This your democracy day celebration is serious,' Uncle Kelechi said, grinning, charming. 'Where is my own plate of rice?'

My mother burst into tears. She cried too often now.

The Academic Staff Union of Universities (ASUU) welcomed the new government with a strike. Our lecturers instructed us to go home to wait it out, the union wasn't going to budge this time, they'd given past governments too many opportunities to meet their commitments.

'Are we not human beings? Will our families not eat?' a lecturer complained aloud to his colleague in the hallway.

The days were languid, blending into one another until they became a single infinite and meaningless existence. Eriife was consumed by her new boyfriend and, automatically, by his first love – politics.

'Nigeria has so much potential,' she said to me one day. 'Don't you want to see a better country?' She rarely spoke about becoming a doctor anymore. And I began to wonder if this person had always existed or had been created by this man and her ardent affection for him.

'Nice to meet you,' he'd said the first time I met him, gripping my hand tightly and holding my eyes through the thick lenses of his glasses, and I thought to myself that he had probably learned it from one of those books on power and getting others to do your bidding. Eriife bounced beside him, nervous, eager for him to be liked. But my opinion had been formed even before I set my eyes on him, for the sole reason that he'd taken her from us.

'He's tolerable. I can see why she likes him, but I still don't. He should date his agemates,' I told Zina over the phone. The phone number had been taped to our hostel room door days after Democracy Day with the words, *Ego baby, call me. Friday, 5pm.*

'Are you mad?' I'd screamed into the landline at the NITEL call centre and the attendant perked up in her seat, suddenly interested in my conversation.

Zina's cackle rang across the line. 'Nwakaego, never change.'

'It's not funny. How could you do this without telling me. I've been so worried. I'll kill that Chuka if I ever see him, just warn him never to cross my path.'

'I wanted to make sure that if the police arrested and tortured you, you wouldn't have anything to tell them,' she said.

I sighed; she was joking but she wasn't.

'I'm psychic, I left at the perfect time,' she boasted after the strike was announced.

I hissed. 'When are you coming back?'

Zina did not answer.

A thanksgiving service was how my mother wanted to celebrate my father finally agreeing to sign the divorce papers but she did not want to return to the church we had attended with him, the one where they had met. But still, she wanted a thanksgiving service because that was what you did when you received a major victory: you thanked God.

The church was a few streets from ours, and because buses did not move around as frequently on Sundays, we legged the distance, my sisters complaining nonstop.

A bungalow in the middle of a plot of undeveloped land that reminded me of our village parish in the East met us with a billboard that announced God's presence was indeed there. There was singing, clapping, dancing and a choir performance. When testimonies were called for, my mother joined the band of people gathered by the side of the altar, and I stood to clap encouragingly when she was handed the microphone.

She did not use the word 'divorce'; instead, she said God had delivered her from certain death. The congregation stood to applaud.

Newcomers were encouraged to wait behind after the service, and my sisters and I were separated from our mother, sectioned off to join the *youths*. A girl about my age distributed fliers, reciting a well-rehearsed monologue about the church and its programmes for young people willing to serve God. Then she announced she was stepping aside for one of the leaders – the head pastor's son – to take over.

It was one of those moments where the world rotated on its axis to a standstill. A bright light had come on in the room and in my universe: months of fantasies and questions answered. Fate did indeed exist.

Perhaps it was because Rodney did not live in London that I felt comfortable flirting with him.

Work had taken him temporarily to Bristol the week after we met and, on the phone, and in text messages, he described the beauty of the city and its superb culture – he was keen on experiencing culture everywhere he went and I found it an admirable quality.

He sent flowers from his favourite florists with notes that accentuated his love for poetry. And yet, I remained unsure.

Then one day, he informed me he was coming to London to visit and I called Zina in panic.

'He's fine and he has sense? My dear, that combination is rare these days, even over here,' she said. 'Give him a chance.'

'Dorobucci' banged out from a speaker somewhere behind her; on her Blackberry Messenger, the one only her closest friends had, her name was *DoroZina*.

'I don't know,' I said, torn by my own hesitation. 'Something just feels missing.'

'Nwakaego, when will you let go of this boy?'

I'd known it was him before he opened his mouth to speak, releasing the voice that had haunted me since the night of the party. Our eyes connected, and for a moment, he froze. The room suddenly felt hot and airless, and my skin prickled with awareness.

I blinked first, realising we were being watched, and stared down at my hands, my mind whirring. I heard him clear his throat to continue speaking, welcoming newcomers to his father's church.

We were handed cards when the session was over to fill in our names and addresses. People milled around the youth leaders when they were done, asking questions and making conversation.

I marched towards him, wielding my card like a weapon.

'I'm done,' I said, pushing it in his face. He did not look at me as he collected the card and tucked it in with the several others in his hand. I did not move along.

'So, this is who you really are? A pastor's kid,' I said, challenging him.

It was then I knew it was possible to see a blush on brown skin.

In London, I did not attend church because it reminded me too much of him, of our time together and how dazzling the world had seemed then, sparkling rays of light dropping from the sky, clothing everything in colour.

He hated his name – Daniel Chukwuemeka Igwe. 'Who chooses the two most common names possible for their child? Every pastor's child I know is either David or Daniel and every Igbo man is Emeka or Arinze. Even my surname is common,' he complained often, and each time, it made me laugh, at how superficial it was, how human. He rolled his eyes when others complimented his looks or his voice, and when I told him he was handsome, he scowled like I'd uttered an insult, but this one thing, this was his Achilles heel.

For him, church was an obligation and he could not understand why I chose to attend voluntarily. My mother rarely attended church after that Sunday but I became a constant, joining the youth ministry even though I'd never participated at our previous place of worship.

'I enjoy it,' I said every time, and his raised brow said he didn't believe me.

Until one day, he leaned in and said, 'Enjoy it? Or enjoy me?'

A smug smirk lined his lips as a visible shiver ran through me.

As a child, I'd memorised scriptures, committing them

to heart, believing the words. I wanted to be good, sinless, perfect before God; an impossible task.

'God can turn the heart of the most wicked man,' our Sunday school teacher had preached, citing Pharaoh in the Bible. And it made me pray for my father, that God would make him a different man, keeping a diary of my prayers and a catalogue of changes I sighted in his behaviour. But then he would descend once more into the man I'd come to recognise and I would lose my faith, cursing God and swearing not to believe. Later, I would return, counting my sins and pleading for forgiveness, unable to stop believing because faithlessness left me bereft of the protection of hope.

It was why I returned to church that listless strike season, because it all seemed to be falling apart and I was in need of reassurance that my life was indeed controlled by a being who had my best interests at heart.

I prayed for Zina, I prayed that she would be safe, that her father would change his mind about her marriage, then I prayed for my father, that he wouldn't change his. Then I prayed for my mother; my prayers for her were haphazard as I was unsure of what to say, scared to leave anything out, exposing her to danger.

When the pastor made altar calls, I was tempted to rush towards him, to renew my faith, launder it, because then, maybe, just maybe life could finally resume.

But Emeka saw church differently, having viewed behind the curtains the cogs turning the wheels of the machine, and it had left him stolidly unimpressed.

'Is this why you didn't tell me who you were? Why you ran away?' I poked that Sunday, refusing to move after handing in my card.

Finally, with a sigh, he rolled his eyes towards me. 'I did not run away!' He seemed affronted by the very suggestion.

'Then what was that?'

He shrugged, a slight raise of his shoulders.

'Well, I don't believe you,' I said, shifting my feet, unsure of what to say next.

He leaned in and lowered his tone, making sure no one else could hear. 'What's your name? I should at least know the name of the girl I nearly kissed.'

I blushed, flushing with sudden heat; he would always know how to do that – make me blush.

10

Pastor Kamsi

The version of our story Emeka always told was that I'd refused to let him go after that church service, but the reality had been a natural gravitation, an instinctive connection of adjoining puzzle pieces.

'Nwakaego, but you can call me Ego,' I'd said to Emeka that first day and he smiled like he'd expected that to be my name.

'Who is he?' Nkechi asked on our way home, her eyes alert. We were in the backseat of a bus we'd been lucky to come across on our trek home.

'Where did you meet him?' her twin added.

'I don't know,' I mumbled, hoping my mother wouldn't notice.

'Who?' my mother asked, turning her head.

'No one,' I blurted, and she smiled that motherly smile of knowledge, but didn't poke any further.

The following Sunday, Emeka and I sat in a corner where the ushers had stacked the used chairs at the end of service, to talk.

'For the record, I didn't run away. I just want to make that clear,' he told me.

'Are you sure? The way you disappeared, I thought you were a ghost,' I said.

He laughed. Then we talked and talked – he hadn't meant to dance that day, but he'd seen me seated, looking lost and out of place and he'd been compelled to ask me to dance.

'So, you ask every girl you see sitting alone to dance?'

'I did not say that. You love putting words in people's mouths, do you know that?'

We were both students at the same university, I would discover, but he was in the Computer Science department.

'So, if my mother hadn't come here to share her testimony, what would have happened?' I asked, hoping I didn't sound too eager.

'We would have met eventually, I'm sure of it,' he said, his eyes settled with certainty. And I believed it, because he did.

With Emeka came expectations – of character and behaviour.

'My father was not always a pastor, you know,' Emeka said to me much later. We'd known each other for a few weeks at this point, and I could now read his facial expressions – the way his brow arched when he was unimpressed, how they flattened when he was annoyed. This expression was new, and I filed it in my mind to put a label to it later.

'Really? How come?'

He slouched further down in his seat. The seats beside the stack of chairs at the back of church had become our spot.

'When I was five, he was a banker, then he quit his job to start a marble importation business. The business was doing very well, at least we lived well enough. Then one day he said he'd received a calling from God. He went to a mountain to pray for forty days and forty nights. When he returned, he was haggard and thin. He visited a pastor friend that he considers his mentor, spent a few days there, and next thing you know, our lives had to change.'

It was hard to imagine Emeka's father – with his hulky towering frame, platyrrhine nose and hard jawline, the man who stood on the pulpit every Sunday to command the congregation – being so easily influenced.

'That must have been hard,' I said, knowing what it was to have life upended by a singular event.

'You have no idea!' He chuckled and adjusted in his seat, bringing his eyes to my level. 'So, are you finally going to tell me about yourself?

'You make me feel short,' I said, deflecting, pushing at his shoulder.

He rolled his eyes. 'Please madam, you are short.'

'I'm taller than most guys.' It was true. I was even taller than my mother, whom many considered tall.

'Well, you're short to me,' he said and patted the top of my head like an uncle.

'You should play basketball.'

'Nwakaego, stop dodging the question.'

It was the way he called my name, with such authority, the way he held my eyes, daring me to lie.

'I've told you about myself,' I said. 'What else is there to know?'

'You know what I mean.' He took my hand and rolled a finger over the surface. 'Don't think I haven't noticed that you won't say anything about your family. It's all very top level with you. I want to know *you*.' I would always think of those words whenever I thought of him – *I want to know you* – and how no one had ever said that to me before.

I couldn't seem to hold back after that. He knew the questions to ask, astute and probing without ever seeming intrusive.

He'd heard of my father, read about him in passing in a magazine, but never thought he'd be seated at the back of a church with his eldest daughter; he wanted to know how that had come to be. And I told him, rubbing at the scar cushioned between my braids.

When I was done, I waited for him to withdraw, to run and never look back. Instead, it seemed to remove the final barrier between us, and he shared even more: his struggles with his own father, the knee injury that had prevented him from playing basketball, his plans to become a programmer. Perhaps it was because he was a pastor's child that he did not run away; he'd seen and heard the worst of society and nothing shook him anymore.

He reached out and stilled the fingers moving restlessly against my scalp. 'You do that a lot.'

'Oh, I didn't realise,' I said, immediately self-conscious. I tried to move my fingers but his hand had covered them.

We stared at each other in silence, and I thought we were going to kiss. Then he smiled, his teeth white and large. 'Stop looking at me like that, we're in church.'

It rained the day he met my mother. He arrived at our door soaked through, and I was afraid my mother wouldn't like him. He'd been the one to suggest meeting her so we could spend time together outside of church activities. I'd been reluctant but he'd insisted.

'So, this is the reason you're going to church every day of the week?' my mother said, her smile teasing.

She laughed and Emeka joined her, and they laughed together like they shared a secret about me.

'I like him,' my mother said after he left. She'd invited him for Sunday rice that weekend. 'He's calm and mature for his age.'

I grinned, relieved.

'So that thing you said about never marrying, I hope you've told him,' she teased.

'Mummy please, we're just friends.'

'Okay o.'

Emeka visited on weekdays after that, and we spent hours playing chess, even though I lost to him all the time, and talking about books we'd read and the films we liked to see. We argued often over what films to watch.

'You're a snob,' I told him.

He puffed air from his lips. 'Because I don't like Nigerian movies? Please. They're too dramatic and are always trying to teach a lesson that shouldn't be taught.'

'Not all of them. There are some really good ones, you know. Films are meant to be a reflection of society; I think they reflect our society fairly well. Our people believe in witchcraft and blood covenants, and men still throw their wives out of their homes.'

'Well, our society isn't ideal,' he conceded.

I loved sports and he didn't, unable to keep track of the names and scoring techniques – except basketball, he loved basketball – but he tolerated the screaming football matches and tension-filled tennis rallies for me. We kissed for the first time the day Serena Williams won her first Grand Slam, in a studio room at the back of the church; it was a room people rarely used but I'd wanted to watch the match and he'd collected the keys so we could use the television kept there. The ball from Hingis' racquet went long and I jumped on him, screaming with unbridled joy, and he fell back, taken by surprise. Then in a moment of heady excitement, I kissed him, losing myself in the moment as his arms tightened around my waist.

'We can't waste all our days indoors because the government

has decided to be stupid,' he announced the next day, dragging me along to Apapa Amusement Park.

'We're too old for these things,' I complained.

'No one's ever too old for enjoyment,' he said.

At the counter, he paid for tickets and sugared popcorn. On the rollercoaster, I clung to him as I screamed into the wind, thinking what a relief it was to have my own person.

Then there was Pastor Kamsi. Pastor Kamsi with the voice of authority, who brought down fire and brimstone when he prayed, whose *tongues* could shift the atmosphere. Pastor Kamsi the youth president. He'd earned his position dedicating most of his adolescent life to the church, and now that he was an adult, it was only right to appoint someone who could relate to the experiences of youthfulness and lusting for the things of the world.

'Bloody stiff-necked hypocrite,' Emeka mouthed beside me during a youth meeting and I covered my face with my palms to hide my mirth.

'I hear you're new here,' Pastor Kamsi said to me the first time we interacted, refusing to let my hand go. It was after a midweek service and attendees milled around him, vying for his attention but he'd called to me and Emeka as we walked by.

Pastor Kamsi lived for the veneration: the sister who had felt the spirit move like a current of worms through her body when he prayed, the mother whose son had turned his life around thanks to his teachings.

At the prayer conferences he organised, he took centre stage, speaking in tongues and laying hands, convincing sinners to turn to God. Following the services, he was inundated with requests for guidance and prayers.

The church sisters discussed his unwedded status with vested interest. 'He's so in the spirit! Whoever marries him will be so lucky. God will always be with them.' And I wondered if God was only ever with Pastor Kamsi.

On the Saturday he stopped me and Emeka on our way out of the hall. Holding my hand longer than necessary, he made small talk about the service and the atmosphere of the Holy Spirit, waiting to be gifted the adulation he was accustomed to. Then he asked, 'Sister Ego, do you know God's purpose for your life?'

I looked at Emeka, taken aback by the question. He shrugged.

'I'm not sure,' I said.

'Well, that is terrible. You should want to know, or you'll end up living a meaningless life. Perhaps you need some counselling and prayers.'

'Thank you,' I said with a stifled smile, pulling my hand from his.

He wilted at my rejection. I could tell from his expression that he thought I had a bad spirit.

'What was that about?' I asked Emeka as we walked away.

He smirked. 'You're probably the first person to reject such an offer. He doesn't usually make them you know.'

It had never occurred to me how busy the life of a pastor and their family was until I met Emeka: the Tuesday midweek services, Wednesday leadership meetings, Thursday deliverance services, Friday prayer meetings and Saturday evangelism walks. And Emeka attended them all.

'You don't have to be here all the time, you know,' he told me.

'Then I'd never see you.' He smiled. 'You know, sometimes I wonder if you really believe in what you're doing, it seems like you're going through the motions, like a civil servant,' I said.

He paused to give my words some thought. 'It's not that I don't believe per se. I mean, I believe in Jesus and what he taught but I've seen behind all of this. Kamsi can shout on that pulpit all he wants but he can only rise to a certain level within this ministry, do you know why? The general overseer at the very top is Yoruba and Kamsi is not. Yes, tribe matters even though we're supposed to be one body in Christ. My father sacrificed everything for the church, and how do they pay him back? They owe his salary every other month while some pastors live large at the headquarters. So, forgive me if I'm not impressed.'

He always referred to Pastor Kamsi as Kamsi and I knew this indifference to authority was his own act of rebellion.

'What would make you stop believing?' I asked.

'I don't know.'

He'd never thought of not believing, and I realised that, like me, he feared falling into that abyss bereft of hope.

Just before the turn of the century, ASUU and the government reached a compromise, and my mother was in love again. She would never admit it, but it was clear in the way her eyes twinkled when his name came up and how she ran around the living room on the days he visited, propping up the weathered sofa pillows.

A strange man with deeply chiselled cheekbones and curly hair had visited one day when my mother was out; he left a note, saying she would know who it was from. She'd wept as she read it, holding the note to her chest and we'd stared in awkward silence, perplexed.

'I'm so sorry, I realise I didn't introduce myself the last time

I was here. I'm Akintunde Ajayi but you can call me Akin,' he said the next time he visited, and I stared at him wondering where I'd heard the name before.

'Uncle Akin,' my mother said, bouncing between her feet. I was reminded of Eriife and her politician boyfriend.

'Akin. Isn't that the name of the man Aunty Ada was always quarrelling with Mummy about?' Nwamaka said later.

'Not quarrelling really, more like cautioning, that she should stay away, she's married blah blah blah,' Nkechinyere corrected.

'Hmm,' her twin grunted.

'They were friends many years ago, before she even met Daddy and he was always sending her letters,' Nkechi continued, refusing to allow my mother's name to be besmirched.

'Well, if Daddy finds out, he's definitely not signing the divorce papers.'

There was foreshadowing in Nwamaka's words. It had been months since my father had informed my mother's lawyer he would sign her request for a divorce and yet he'd done nothing, blaming his dawdling on the Nigerian judicial system.

'The world might end before he signs,' I joked.

The frenzy of Y2K had taken over the airwaves, warning of the year computers – whose programs allowed for only two-digit years – would melt down and the world would collapse in an apocalypse. In '97, we'd heard stories of a religious cult that had committed mass ritual suicide in preparation and I'd wondered what level of fanaticism would cause people to follow someone so dedicatedly. I would soon see it in the way people revered Pastor Kamsi.

I called Zina to inform her classes were to resume soon, but instead of her voice, I heard Chuka's. After months at an impasse, Zina's father had changed his mind – he would wait till she graduated to arrange her marriage.

'She left this morning,' Chuka said. He sounded neither happy nor relieved, and it struck me that he'd hoped to tie her to him with desperation.

A month before the close of the century, the civilian populace of Odi village in Bayelsa state was wiped out, every building torched to the ground by the Nigerian military as ordered by its Commander-in-Chief, the country's president. Their crime? An 'ambush' attack on policemen by a gang on its outskirts. My mother commented that the demons of tyrannical dictatorship still roamed the presidential villa despite the exorcism.

11

Valentine's Day

There was an obsession with purity, a single-faceted almost ghoulish obsession. In the home videos we watched, there were two classes of women: the pristine sect, wearing ankle-length clothing and forgetting to do their hair, and the unholies, who had boyfriends, went to parties and wore fitted clothes. The first always ended up with lives full of love, laughter and godly children, and the latter would bask in their indulgence for a while before it all fell apart.

In the hostels, between classes and over languorous weekends, girls congregated in their underwear and nightgowns discussing important subjects like who was dating who, who was pregnant and who was most likely to get married.

'Did you see the Range Rover that came to pick up Amoke yesterday?' Chioma asked during one such week-end. The chosen location: Zina's bedside. Eriife was there, her first visit in a long while, and I was relaxing on my bed, chewing on a Goody Goody caramel bar and staring up at the rotating ceiling fan, wondering how the weather could be so hot.

I knew Amoke, the prettiest girl in the Microbiology department.

'The windows were tinted, you know,' Chioma continued.

Chioma was what we called a hustler – she could tell the price of a handbag by looking at it and knew how much it cost to import weaves from China. If there was money to be made, Chioma was at the forefront, selling shoes, bags, soaps, creams, earrings, unwilling to be left out. Most of the time, we admired her.

'I saw it o. She's so lucky,' someone said. I was too fatigued to look. The voice sounded like Hajara, our class represent-ative. Hajara who was consumed by the subject of marriage and 'settling down,' Hajara who said *God please* when she heard another student had gotten engaged.

'I like how she's kept herself, doesn't associate with all these small schoolboys and now she's with a big fish. I hear the guy is almost forty,' Chioma said.

'FORTY?' I didn't have to guess who it was this time; I could identify Zina's voice anywhere.

'Yes? Is there anything wrong with that? Amoke is mature for her age. He's rich and has his own business, plus he's ready to settle down as soon as she's done with school. *Dey* there, allow all these small boys to play you instead of finding mature men ready to marry,' Chioma said.

'I can imagine their conversations,' Hajara said, her voice dreamy. 'So mature, what their home would look like, prayers for their future children, things like that. Not all this non-sense small talk.'

'Thank you, my sister,' Chioma concurred.

Eriife disagreed. 'She's just nineteen? Max, twenty? That's just somehow please.'

I was surprised to hear her speak that way, considering her own boyfriend's age.

'I heard he sent a big box on her birthday filled with Chanel handbags, perfume, et cetera,' Chioma continued, ignoring her. 'Would you believe she has her own car in his compound? And his workers already call her madam!'

'*Hay* God! Please do my own,' Hajara said, and I turned my head in time to see her jump up and clutch her bosom in excited supplication.

Zina hissed. 'You're always jumping, Hajara. Do your own what? What exactly is it you're always wanting God to do?' Zina shook her head, as if in pity. 'The both of you are thieves. Would you say all this if Amoke's boyfriend didn't have money?'

I chuckled to myself, until their heads turned in my direction and I realised I'd done so out loud, reminding them of my presence.

At church, Pastor Kamsi had insisted Emeka and I start attending special services when he'd found out about our relationship. It wasn't like we'd gone out of our way to hide it; I'd been attending the church for going on two years, but someone had finally asked Emeka directly instead of whispering behind our backs. Now, every weekend I sat in on a *Sisters' Vigil* – a gathering on chastity, a religious study of the art of seduction as depicted by Samson and Delilah.

'God, we return all the glory untampered to you,' Sister Charity, the women's youth leader, said at the beginning of each session. I always wondered where she'd learned such a phrase and how she did not find it funny that it was possible to tamper with such glory.

'As a woman you must know your place in society,' she said during these services. 'Many of us have forgotten our place in society. Every night, I cry to myself, asking, are these our future wives and mothers? Goddddd!'

After the services, I would demonstrate to Emeka, bending over with an imaginary microphone, my voice cracking with practised anguish, 'Are these our future wives and mothers? Goooddddd,' and he would laugh till tears ran down the sides of his face.

'There's grace in femininity,' Sister Charity taught. 'Many of you want to become men by your conduct, it is the new age thing. In the body of Christ, there are different organs and each organ has its function. Imagine if the neck suddenly decided it wanted to be the head? As a woman you must know your place.'

'Is this what they're teaching you in your classes?' I asked Emeka after several weeks of the same thing. 'Because I'm not sure I can continue listening to this every weekend.'

'No, it's not, I'm sorry,' Emeka said, turning my palm over in his studiously. I'd come to accept he wasn't talkative.

'No? What do they teach you then?' I demanded, affronted.

He traced a flexion crease. 'Just other things, you know, like godly men in the Bible,' he said and leaned closer, 'and avoiding temptation from jezebels.'

'I've never tried to seduce you!'

He raised a brow, reminding me of our first kiss; he'd mastered the art of communicating with his body parts – a raised brow, a sly smirk, a subtle swipe of his fingers.

'Well!' I blustered. 'I was excited, that's all.'

He laughed, throwing his head back, and for a second I forgot my annoyance. 'For the record, I don't mind being seduced by you,' he murmured. 'You know we only agreed to this so they wouldn't invite our parents for a chat. How do you feel about my father asking your mother why her daughter is trying to corrupt his son?'

'It's none of their business. We haven't even done anything.'

It was a silent agreement between us that we weren't ready, and so we kissed, exploring with our hands, but nothing else.

Emeka sighed, no longer joking. 'You're right. You don't have to go. I can talk to Kamsi if anything comes up, but God knows that fellow is stubborn.'

I decided to attend one more service, to satisfy my conscience that I'd indeed tried my hardest. That afternoon, we prayed. Sister Charity stood at the pulpit pronouncing prayer points and waiting for the congregation to repeat them after her, before dissolving into a deluge of rapid-fire tongues.

'Sisters, slap your thighs and say after me – my laps shall not be the graveyard for any man, I shall not be a Delilah!'

I did not attend the sessions after that; Pastor Kamsi decided that the only appropriate measure was for me to be placed under his direct supervision.

Valentine's Day '01 was when I looked in the mirror and decided I liked the face I saw reflected in it, the year I decided I was beautiful.

'You're so beautiful,' Emeka said often, but I dismissed it as the words of a young man with eyes coloured by bias.

I did not like my face. Whether this was because it reminded me of my mother's face, or the fact that it was too ordinary to be called pretty, or the way it crooked at the side when I smiled, showing the least attractive of my teeth, I wasn't sure. But then again, I did not like myself very much. I was not 'cute' or 'portable' as the boys said, the kind of girl that made them want to offer protection, be nicer, kinder, instead they joked I was one of them.

But around Emeka, I wore shiny block heels with pointy fronts, and it wasn't because he was taller. He did not make me dislike my height, nor the fact that I wasn't a useful sort of tall: skinny and stretching upwards like a band, worthy of walking a runway or athletic with shapely arms.

Valentine's Day the year before that, the one just before Sisqó's 'Thong Song' was released, radiating through every student radio, making the girls desire thighs and butts thick enough to move, Emeka and I were at a crossroads. We'd survived several tests by then: the test of patience when he'd taught me to drive, his screeching matching the car brakes as I desperately tried to pull to a stop; the test of fundamentally disagreeing on animals, he liked dogs but I could not stand any living creature that wasn't human. But there was no way over this.

'He's not officially asked me to be his girlfriend,' I had complained to Zina in our hostel room the week before.

She had no interest whatsoever in Valentine's Day, having recently separated from Chuka. 'He wasn't good enough for me,' she'd said simply with a shrug and I wondered what had made her finally realise that.

Zina had created her own dance floor in the middle of our room, arching her back and gyrating.

Eriife looked up from her position reading on Zina's bed, chewing on *kuli-kuli*, her face lined by mild bemusement. 'What have the both of you been doing since?' she said to me.

'I don't know,' I mumbled, suddenly frightened.

Kr-kr-kr-kr, Eriife chewed, waiting for me to answer; *kuli-kuli* was a noisy snack. Zina paused her dancing, the music blasting around us.

'Can you stop that? How can I think when you're both making all that noise,' I snapped.

'*Ewo,* so I shouldn't eat again because you're in distress? You're not even happy I'm visiting? Please please,' Eriife replied, her chewing getting even louder.

Zina wiped at a sweat drop at the corner of her forehead. 'I don't even know why you're stressing yourself, that boy literally carries you on his head like a basket. Send someone to call him now and he'll appear. You don't need any official status to confirm what's going on.'

But I did; I needed an assurance that it wasn't a figment of my imagination.

Zina shook her head. 'You worry too much. That boy likes you a lot.'

On Valentine's Day, the hostel buzzed with anticipation. By eight in the morning, the usual suspects had already begun receiving gifts, cakes and cards. At noon, wild screams shook the hostel walls as four double-layered cakes arrived, hoisted by hefty delivery men, one with a proposal in the form of a fondant ring and the icing letters *Will You Marry Me?* Zina and I stopped by the lucky recipient's room, one of the many pilgrims present to confirm the stories with our own eyes.

'Congratulations o. Have you told him yes?' Zina said, perusing the cakes at length.

The girl stared at Zina like she was simpleminded. 'He's just one of my toasters, we're not even dating.'

'Maybe he should have proposed with a real ring and not icing so she can take him seriously,' Zina murmured on our way out of the room.

Zina was yet to broadcast her unattached status so it wasn't too much of a surprise that for the first time, no one came knocking at our door announcing that she had a visitor waiting. I had no expectations myself; Emeka had never asked me to be his girlfriend.

Roses arrived by three, so red that they looked like they'd been carefully painted, then a box of chocolates and finally, a cake in the shape of a heart.

'Whoever this boy is must really like you o. Real roses are expensive,' I told Zina, convinced they were for her. But a note accompanied the cake, one that read: *I love you so much Ego – E.*

Love. We'd never used that word before. Were we truly in love? What was it to be in love? Was love the intensity of warmth I felt around him? The awareness of completeness? Like life would be okay no matter what?

'So, you didn't get me anything?' Emeka asked me later that evening, in the alcove of a restaurant on campus, the walls decorated in red balloons, Westlife's 'Swear It Again' playing in the background.

'I didn't expect anything. You never asked me to be your girlfriend,' I confessed.

He stared at me. 'I have to ask? I thought it was obvious.'

Then he asked.

'Sometimes I feel like you have no expectations of me,' he said later that night as we walked back to the university dormitory.

'Is that good?'

'No.'

Valentine's Day the following year, the year I accepted I was beautiful, I bought him a pair of Air Jordan sneakers and he got me a collection of books – Zadie Smith's *White Teeth* and Anne Rice's The Vampire Chronicles series – I'd wanted for a while. At dusk, we walked by the shores of Bar Beach, our feet soaking in the sand, listening to a cassette of my favourite songs he'd compiled on his Walkman.

On our way home, we passed a woman selling roasted corn by the roadside who looked about my mother's age. Emeka wanted to buy corn.

'Is she your girlfriend?' she asked him. He nodded with a timid glance in my direction. 'She's so beautiful. Such a lovely smile, *nwa mama*. Take care of her o.'

In my bed that night, I stared at my face in the mirror, and for the first time, I liked it.

12

Mentor

'The country has to work for everyone,' I said to Rayan in the lunch room as November 2014 drew to a close. Speaking up the first time had unshackled my tongue. Perhaps I'd stopped caring about what I said because I'd fully accepted my status as a 'visitor', ready to leave when the time was right.

America burned with uprising – on the streets and in the media. British news shows, anchors and commentators discussed the issues as purely an American problem.

'We should be grateful these things don't happen in the UK,' Rayan said after the riots broke out in America in reaction to the grand jury's decision not to indict the officer who'd shot Michael Brown.

'What things?' I asked.

'Race issues,' he said with such contemptuous disdain I was tempted to burst into laughter.

'You think there are no race issues in the UK?'

'There's barely any racism in the UK.'

'You're joking?'

He wasn't.

'Of course, there are occasional issues,' he obliged, 'but here we treat people according to their behaviour and not their skin colour. And of course, there's the issue of class. But you have to admit that we've progressed beyond Dickensian England and towards a more equitable society.'

'I don't know,' I said, giving it some thought. 'I think it's impossible for the country to move on from the issue of class or race when its very structure is set up to reward that – the very hierarchy of the British system is titular and then you look at the influx of migrants from former colonies and how that has influenced their treatment. Racism is well and alive here whether we like to admit it or not.'

'I disagree. Focusing on race or blaming it for all the issues in society is why many don't progress and it creates unnecessary tension and conflict. Look at London, it's such a multicultural city. Look at the both of us and where we are.'

Not for the first time, I thought how British he was in his desire to avoid ruffling feathers, and how easily he'd been convinced not to be on his own side.

'Looking at America,' Rayan continued, 'it's clear to me that all racial conversations serve to do is ignite and, quite literally, burn society to the ground. Imagine if people blamed the events on that young man's response to the police – he could have simply not run.'

'People have been shot even when they did that,' I responded calmly, watching his face for anything that would suggest a change of heart. He blinked and I realised he was not the type to question his beliefs deeply. They were like cards hidden at the back of his pocket – produced when questioned but never deeply perused.

'Well,' he said slowly. 'Our police have never gone about shooting people and that's why we're not America.'

Of course, that was also false, but I was too exhausted to burst his carefully constructed bubble. Instead, I tweeted:

NaijaUK Law Girl   @NaijaUKLawGirl   25 Nov

At least Americans are having some sort of reckoning about race, in the UK we just pretend and gaslight ourselves into oblivion. Keep calm and carry on innit?

Collapse

For the first time, the replies spun out of my control. People raged at me to move back home or go face the butt of a gun in America. I tweeted again:

NaijaUK Law Girl   @NaijaUKLawGirl   25 Nov

Golly, Brits really really do not want to talk about racism in this country

Collapse

Amy Jones   @AmyJones67   25 Nov

@NaijaUKLawGirl I've followed you for a while and I'm disappointed, you really think the UK is as racist as America? Why not move there then and find out?

Collapse

Jamaican Gal   @CaseyWhite   25 Nov

@AmyJones67 @NaijaUKLawGirl Please! The
British are the founding fathers of racism. We live
in this country, we know what we're talking about

Collapse

Ziwe Ncube   @ZtotheWe   25 Nov

@AmyJones67 @NaijaUKLawGirl This country
would lose it's mind if a black person married into
the royal family

Collapse

Amy Jones   @AmyJones67   25 Nov

@ZtotheWe @NaijaUKLawGirl Well only Harry's
left and he likes blondes so guess we'll never find
out!

Collapse

When a rally was organised, I considered taking time off
work to join.

'It's a waste of time,' Rayan said. I'd developed a soft spot
for him despite our differing opinions – we were both trying
to make the best of life in a country that could never be ours.

Leonidas walked by then. 'You should spend more time with
Rayan,' he said to me. 'He would make a great mentor for you.'

It reminded me of Emeka and the conversation we'd had at my mother's new flat not long after Akin came into our lives.

'*Mentorship*, according to the Oxford English Dictionary, can be defined as "the guidance provided by a mentor, especially an experienced person in a company or educational institution". AND a *mentor* is an "experienced and trusted adviser",' I read out to Emeka.

'That's the British definition,' he said, amused. He found it bizarre, hysterical even, that I'd taken a bus to Lagos Island and scoured bookshops until I'd purchased bulky hardback copies of the Oxford English and Merriam Webster dictionaries to prove my point, but he understood my frustration.

ASUU were on strike again, and our days were once again supine and purposeless. Emeka was meant to have graduated from university that year, but the strikes meant an extra nine months at the very least. But frustrating as this latest strike was, the origin of my frustration was Pastor Kamsi.

Without classes to provide plausible exoneration, church had returned to the frenetic schedule of the previous strike, Pastor Kamsi insistent that without these activities the youth would be led astray. And for my refusal to attend the weekly *Sisters' Vigil* sessions, he'd adopted me for forceful mentorship. He insisted the youth appear in church daily, and that I accompany him for his meetings and man the front desk at his office.

'I'm sorry,' Emeka had apologised after Pastor Kamsi announced the new rules at a youth meeting. 'Honestly, I would have left all this, but who will pay my school fees if my father kicks me out?'

I laughed; I understood what it meant to be beholden to someone.

'You know my father used to say that if you spend every

day in church, you'll never get to do anything in the world you're supposed to shine in,' I said, taking Emeka's hand as we left the church premises. Later, he would tell me it was the first time I'd ever spoken of my father with a smile.

The sermons were seditious, the doctrines bordering on heresy. Our true hope and desire as Christians was to live lives of wealth and dominion, and the quality of our lives was determined by our faith, and by our giving. Ten per cent was the portion of our income to be donated, and as students, our pocket monies were not exempted, even though we hadn't worked for them.

We were to believe enough that we wouldn't seek secular solutions, like hospitals, for our ailments but instead depend solely on our faith, even unto death. If we were sick, it was because we didn't believe enough, didn't give enough to God – why else would He allow evil to befall us? Our greatest adversities in life could be solved if only we gave more. God had become transactional, an automated teller machine.

His words would flash in my head whenever I struggled with my memory, and I would wonder if the accident had happened because I hadn't done enough. I would withdraw into myself, and Emeka would spend the rest of the day asking, 'What's wrong?'

Then there were demons, winged bloodsucking creatures that hung in the shadows, summoned by sin and evil, by relatives who despised your progress and desired your downfall, by witches and wizards disguised as friends.

Outside the church auditorium, plastic tables covered in white cloth were lined with spiritual handkerchiefs, anointed bottles of water and olive oil that could grant protection.

The people flocked to Pastor Kamsi, and our mentorship meetings grew into full services. At the altar, they laid their problems before God remade as a man, crushing their glasses under their feet, throwing away their medication, donating their very last kobo.

They lined the corridors of his office, seeking personalised sessions and special prayer meetings. They pleaded with me to write their names down when he was fully booked for the day. 'I will wait,' they insisted. It fascinated me that they were mostly young women, my age or slightly older. Were we raised to be more judgemental of ourselves? To feel inadequate and unsure, continuously seeking external assurance?

A new pattern developed. It would take me a while to notice. Pastor Kamsi was never to be challenged; his word was truth and life. *Touch not my anointed and do my prophet no harm.* Those who dared to question were scorned, immediately silenced. He'd successfully created his own shrine within the youth ministry.

'It's a cult!' I told Emeka.

'You don't think that's a bit extreme? I mean I don't like him very much – but a cult?' Emeka asked.

I went dictionary hunting the following weekend. And now we were in my mother's new flat, which she shared with Akin whenever he was in the country. My father was still to grant their divorce. But my mother carried on with her life, refusing to despair. She'd signed up for a part-time master's degree at the University of Lagos and made new friends, inviting them over for lunch and loud philosophical discussions in our living room. Aunty Sally said it was the happiest she'd seen her.

'They swallow everything he says hook, line and sinker,' I said to Emeka. 'What sort of madness is this? Have you noticed that other young men in church cut their hair like him?'

Emeka blinked, surprised. 'Well, I haven't noti—'

'You should start paying attention,' I interjected, incensed. 'He's a man! Flesh and blood. I've been sent to buy paracetamol when he has headaches but people can't wear glasses? My God, even Zina thinks he's weird.'

Zina had attended a service out of curiosity and never returned. 'If you want to see me, come to my house *abeg*,' she'd said afterwards.

Emeka sighed, acquiescing. 'I understand what you mean. Unfortunately, my father likes him. He has a way of getting young people to listen, plus he's bringing in a lot of money for the youth ministry. There isn't much we can do unless he commits a crime or something.'

Pastor Kamsi's influence seemed only to multiply. His promotion to regional youth president came as a surprise to no one, except maybe me. And when ASUU called off the strike, inviting us back into our classrooms, Pastor Kamsi moved his sessions to weekends and weekday nights. By the middle of the semester, he'd published a list of *inappropriates* covering every facet of life – hairstyles, clothing, songs – he considered unacceptable within his ministry and disciples.

The Lagos armoury explosion happened at the beginning of the year of Emeka's eventual graduation, a four-year course that had become five, delayed by the decayed system.

The year before, in 2001, we'd watched, beaming with jingoistic patriotism, as one of our own was crowned Miss World, her hair slicked up, weave-on twisted into a tower atop her head, gleaming drop earrings dangling from her ears.

'I didn't like her response to the question. I don't think it was the best,' Emeka said as Agbani Darego was called, Priyanka Chopra in glistening blue and silver as she transferred the crown to her successor's head. My mother took it all in, waving a flag a similar green as the victor's dress, the one she'd bought for democracy day.

'You're not patriotic,' I said to Emeka, my tone accusatory.

He folded his arms against his chest. 'What does it mean to be patriotic? Does that include telling lies?'

I rolled my eyes. 'Nobody is saying you should tell lies, but you're being overly critical. Were you expecting a dissertation? She's the first indigenous African and Nigerian to win the Miss World pageant, you should be happy.'

'I'm happy, proud even, but I'll still say the truth,' Emeka said. 'If she knows what is good for her, I hope she gets away from this place as soon as possible.'

I slapped him hard on the arm. 'You don't love your country. It's not like America or any other place is lined with gold.'

'Loving my country means being able to tell the truth about it. As it is, Nigeria cannot do what other countries can for her. It's all about opportunities. Do you know the kind of money she can make abroad? Isn't it better for her to do that and come back here to help others? How many people eat three square meals here?'

'There are poor people over there too, every system has its problems, especially for black people. I'd rather be a first-class citizen in my country than a second-class citizen over there.'

Emeka chuckled. 'My dear, this "first-class" citizen, how "first-class" an experience is it?'

My mother briefly disentangled herself from her euphoria to shock us by saying, 'He's right.'

Obianuju Azubuike née Nwaike, who hummed the national anthems – *anthems* because she sang the pre-1978 version as well – when she was bored, who joined the interminable queues to register to vote every election season there wasn't a dictator overseeing us, who still said 'Nigeria will be great', agreed with Emeka.

'He's right,' she repeated.

'Why?' Emeka and I said at the same time.

'Emeka already said: opportunities. See how well Akin is doing over there. Also, they have working systems and laws that protect even the most vulnerable citizens, especially women.' I heard what she didn't say: were we citizens of a different country, she would have been free of my father by now.

'Akin has a PhD, it's unfair to compare him with the average immigrant. You have to remember that Nigeria is a relatively new country compared to others,' I replied.

'It's very easy to say all this when you're not suffering. Nigeria comes for everyone eventually . . .' Emeka said, leaving me with an eerie sensation of foreboding that would stay with me for days.

Like comets, a series of successive events came, determined to change my conviction. Bola Ige's death came first, shot dead in his residence in Ibadan as we prepared for our semester exams.

'A Senior Advocate of Nigeria. Minister of Justice and Attorney General of the Federal Republic of Nigeria,' I said to Emeka as I paced the room aggressively. It was a day to Christmas and instead of singing carols and revelling, I was in a windowless room at the back of the church.

'Ego, please try to calm down,' Emeka said.

'You cannot understand what this means,' I retorted.

'You're not a law student,' Zina added before Emeka could defend himself.

'I'm sure they'll find the killers,' Emeka assured us.

'They know who killed him,' Zina said with assured

finality. Years later, she would say to me, 'If the death of such a man can go unpunished, who are we?'

On the afternoon of the armoury explosion, Emeka's parents' bungalow breathed brandy, warm, smooth and spicy as his mother baked. Food was her language, cooking how she expressed her love – from the bags of rice stewed into jollof for motherless children, cakes gifted to the children's church, coolers of fried meat carried along on condolence visits. She was the type of woman born for nurturing, her buxom undulating arms created for giving love through fervent embraces.

Mrs Agnes Igwe had worn a fancy church hat complete with feathers and flowers the first Sunday afternoon Emeka sweated, a nervous sweat that beaded around his forehead and rolled down the side of his face, because his mother had requested I stop by their house so she could meet the 'tall girl' he was always with. She would always call me his 'friend', never adding the 'girl' as a prefix; a purposeful obliviousness.

'Do you speak Igbo, my dear?' she asked.

'Not very well,' I replied, anxious that this was reason enough for her to consider me unsuitable.

'Why?' she asked.

'My father did not like my mother speaking Igbo to us, he thought it would affect our English pronunciation,' I answered truthfully.

'Hmm,' she grunted, with neither disapproval nor approbation.

She kept the brandy hidden in a top corner of her kitchen cabinet because it was a dereliction of the church's policy to avoid drink. She was wary of visiting members seeing it proudly displayed, but she needed brandy to bake her fruit cakes.

The afternoon of the explosion, the kitchen tap was leaking, the pipes rusty, and Mrs Agnes had barely taken off her Sunday clothes before returning to the kitchen as she did every week, refusing every offer of help.

'Emeka, please remind your father about this tap,' she shouted.

'Yes, ma,' Emeka shouted back, before mumbling about how his father never remembered anything. He always returned from church late in the evening, barely uttering a word as he ate his cold dinner, wrung of his tolerance for people by hours attending to the problems of others.

'Seventy percent of all the funds raised go to the headquarters, most of the rest goes to church activities and whatever is left, church members use up with all their problems. My mother pays for almost everything at home,' Emeka had told me once. He'd seen the questions my lips were too polite to ask, aware of the imperfection of my own parents' situation: why his father only possessed one suit, why his younger sister had been sent home for not paying her school fees, why he never changed his clothes. But you could never tell by the way Mrs Agnes sang in the kitchen, glorious choruses declaring the wondrous works of God.

'They really love God,' Emeka said. I believed him.

The floors shuddered and the walls convulsed. Mrs Agnes turned off her gas oven and screamed for us to all run out. 'Earthquake! Earthquake!'

'Oh God. My cake will collapse,' she complained when we were all safely outside. 'I was supposed to give it to Sister Jumoke. Her husband just lost his job and her son's birthday is tomorrow. When did this country start experiencing earthquakes?'

The ground vibrated under our feet one last time, then there was a heavy silence. Before long, others gathered on the street to noisily question what had happened. On the news that night, we would learn that there had been an accidental detonation of explosives at a poorly maintained military base that had been marked for decommissioning the previous year. For the hundreds killed, thousands injured and left homeless, and the many that would go unaccounted for, it was yet another symptom of the home they'd not chosen, a sleight of hand dealt by the lottery of birth.

'Lives are so dispensable here,' Emeka remarked a week later at the funeral of a church member who'd lived close to the military base, his eyes frozen on the low-cost wooden coffin.

After the service, Mrs Agnes pulled a cooler from the boot of her car and shared packs of rice with the attendants. Pastor Igwe stayed at the front of the auditorium with the widow, and when the crowd had dispersed, I saw him fold an envelope into her hand – money he did not have.

At Emeka's graduation, his father insisted that only Nigerian songs be played, nodding his head vigorously to Majek Fashek's 'Send Down the Rain'. And I wondered if he was where Emeka's disdain for patriotism had originated.

13

Whispers

I had a demon in me. A demon of disobedience who inhibited me from acceding to authority and advice, and Pastor Kamsi was determined that I be exorcised of it. Of course, it had nothing to do with the whispers floating around about my taking up with those he'd condemned.

Names had been attached to Pastor Kamsi in the past: Akachi in the choir whose mezzo soprano was said to rival the angels, Veronica the children's church teacher with a penchant for hugging babies, and the new attendee who'd just joined the youth ministry.

For the while that their names were affixed to his, these women breezed in and out of Pastor Kamsi's office, consorts of the monarch, barely acknowledging my pedestrian presence.

Parishioners acquiesced to their elevated status. 'Greet Pastor Kamsi when you see him,' they said.

And the women blushed and swished their hands as though swatting at flies and said, 'Me *ke*? No o.'

He was mentoring them, he insisted, but their coquettish smiles and flighty laughter hinted at more. Then the tide would turn and the once favoured consorts would suddenly be cast out. Parishioners would turn their backs, shutting them out of circles and conversations of which they'd once been the centre.

Stories circulated in the space these women had once occupied, disparate yet connected in theme: disobedience, a disquieting lack of spirituality, arrogance, abortive efforts at seduction. No one was sure of the origin of these tales, but they always came from someone who knew someone who was close to Pastor Kamsi, and this someone would never lie about such things because they loved God.

It was a sight to watch these women fold into themselves, sitting in a quiet corner of the church auditorium, no longer leading songs or calling for prayer, having lost their zeal for Kamsi's God. I was reminded of Ademola and the girlfriends he'd dated after his attempt with me. For the duration of the dalliances, they burned brightly, spearheading conversations and debates on law, unofficial first ladies of our department. The lights always went out once it was over, and they were left covered in the dust of defeat that coated their tongues and prevented them from speaking as eagerly as before. A curated version of the truth always followed. Once, all we'd heard was that the girl had added nothing to him, and it had seemed like a sensible enough reason to end things.

'You don't think it's strange?' I asked Emeka.

'I don't think *what* is strange?'

'The way all these stories pop up whenever Pastor Kamsi falls out with people.'

Emeka raised a brow that asked what direction I was headed.

'I try not to listen to church gossip. I hear enough from my parents at home – imagine what I'd hear about myself.'

'I don't listen to gossip,' I protested, 'but whenever I ask after someone Pastor Kamsi was close to or *mentoring*, I hear all sorts of terrible things. Where else would these stories come from?'

Emeka shrugged. 'I have no idea. I try not to pay too much attention to Kamsi. I see him as a sort of necessary evil at this point, nothing either of us says will change anything.'

'Evil should never be necessary,' I said.

I stood to take the microphone at the next youth meeting. Emeka glanced up at me with surprised eyes. I never spoke at these meetings.

'I've noticed a disturbing pattern that has developed, and I think it is necessary to speak up,' I announced into the mic. 'We must not always agree with one another or with everything our leaders say or do. We are not sheep, and this is not a cult, there is no reason why one of us should be ostracised or pushed aside because of unsubstantiated rumours or fallouts. We cannot progre—'

The microphone was cut off.

'Thank you, Sister Ego,' Pastor Kamsi said into his. 'That isn't the subject of today's gathering. Please let us endeavour to stick to the purpose of this gathering.'

Later, he called me aside. His tone laden with concern, he said, 'You're rebellious. It is demonic. I was hoping working closely with me would break this spirit but nothing has changed. I'll keep praying for you because I see something in you that you cannot see in yourself.'

It was when the rumours formed a halo around a young face that Pastor Kamsi announced to the congregation that he was 'courting'. *Courting,* the old-fashioned term denoting seriousness, a declaration of his plans to marry.

A woman surfaced from nowhere, pumiced of all personality and charm, a tabula rasa for his use. On Sundays, they wore clothes sewn to match, colours and patterns blending and beginning together. She walked five paces behind, carrying his bags and bible, she did not speak except when called upon, and when she did speak, it was in deference to what he had said already – the ideal spouse.

'She's like his secretary,' Zina interjected as I described them.

Eriife laughed. 'Isn't Ego his part-time secretary or whatever already?'

'I honestly don't know why you still go there,' Zina said.

The halo of gossip had revolved around an orphaned teenager from a troubled home whose grown-up sisters had brought her to Pastor Kamsi for counselling and guidance. Something had happened, something bad enough that her sisters had pulled out of the church and threatened to involve the police, something so terrible the church council of elders had pulled Pastor Kamsi aside and issued an ultimatum on his marital status. I'd known the girl, seen her cherub-like face as she wandered into the waiting room asking to see Pastor Kamsi, watched her appearance and clothing transform over time, like the others before her.

'My father won't say anything, my mother won't either,' Emeka said when I pressed him for answers.

'Are you sure it's not . . .' I said.

'What you're suggesting is sinister,' Emeka said. 'Don't think too much about it or your mind will travel too far.'

Unlike before, there were no salacious vapours to whet the appetite, only silence that soon morphed into paramnesia. Was she really a teenager? Had anything even happened? What was her name again?

I was sent to purchase suya for Pastor Kamsi and his

soon-to-be wife, my final errand for the weekend; I barely had time to study as it was. Waiting for the meat drenched in *yaji* to cook, I watched sparks fly from the hot coal under the grill, the only source of light around us. My mind wandered, focusing on the teenager's face I seemed unable to forget.

When I returned, they were waiting, plates of rice in front of them. I opened the paper bags and oily newspaper and stood in a corner, lingering in case of further instruction before going home.

Cynthia – for that was her name – selected the largest pieces from the bags and placed them on Pastor Kamsi's plate, her fingers moving mechanically.

'Are you mad? Make sure you clean the stain,' Pastor Kamsi shouted suddenly. An oil stain was spreading through his trouser leg. Cynthia desperately wiped at it.

Her eyes turned in my direction, nervous and ashamed, reminding him of my presence.

'What are you still doing here?' he demanded. 'Get out!'

The whispers died away after that and soon no one spoke of the cherub-faced girl, only of Pastor Kamsi and his soon-to-be wife.

During the six-month-long strike of 2003, the campus photography studio shut down; Mr Silas, the personable proprietor of Studio Da Best, was leaving the country. Students were his market and the incessant strikes meant the hostels were often empty and no one had anything to celebrate. When we heard the news, a group of us assembled, refusing to allow this to happen in the same year as our graduation; we handed out fliers by roadsides and promised to stop by with our families and friends.

Studio Da Best was where we held time as a frozen object

in our hands: birthdays and special events marked with poses and balloons and cakes; the last day of exams, our faces transforming every year, losing the dewiness of youth. Mr Silas, now middle-aged, had opened its doors on his return many years prior from the United States.

'They chased me away with their racism. Such bullshit. I'd rather be a pauper here *mehn*.' He said the 'mehn' like he said 'bullshit', in a twisted American accent, to denote his foreignness, his choice of return that placed him in a slightly higher echelon, because they were not words average Nigerians used.

Emeka had begun his compulsory year of national youth service and I convinced him to stop by for a snap in his khaki uniform; his posting to a primary school meant he had less time on his hands. I returned to Zina who had a new boy-friend whose name I didn't always recall. Eriife was still in school – back then, the College of Medicine didn't always go on strike when others did.

In the evenings, Zina and I watched TV soaps, voraciously tailing the characters' lives, caught up in their romances and betrayals.

'I should probably get pregnant,' Zina said flippantly one such evening.

I turned to stare at her. 'Pardon?'

She looked at me then laughed. 'You should see your face. Oh my God.'

'Repeat what you just said.'

'I'm joking.'

'You sounded serious.'

She sighed. 'Well only partly. We'll soon graduate, when-ever these people finally decide to call off their strike. I've begged and begged my father. He's still insisting I get married; he might delay it till we're done with law school, but only just.'

'You think getting pregnant for what's his name would help? You'd be making your father's point for him.'

Zina sat up straight, her smile gone. 'You're so judgemental, do you know that? You've never even given him a chance. You're lucky your father barely pays attention to you. Do you know what it feels like to have mine breathing down my neck every day?'

We didn't speak for days after that.

'Nothing,' I told my mother when she asked what was wrong.

But Zina refused to let things calcify between us as they had with our mothers. Barely a week later she was at our door with a bowl of the spicy rice I liked – we called it Mallam Rice after the smiling Hausa man who sold it – and Craig David's latest album wrapped in film.

It would never occur to me to tell her that the reason her words had struck so hard was my awareness that my father wasn't ignoring my existence; he just hadn't found a use for me yet.

Elections that year were violent, but then again, they always were: riots, killings, sudden disappearances were the norm, rather than the exception. My mother insisted on going out to vote, even when Akin advised against it. Her chosen candidates for president and governorship did not win, and for weeks afterwards she lamented how the masses never voted for the best people to take the country forward.

Eriife's boyfriend's party secured a second term for the Lagos state governorship and a state dinner was held to celebrate. Eriife obtained an invite for us – cursive letters underneath the state coat of arms, embossed in gold on hard cream cardboard paper, delivered in an embellished white envelope.

My mother considered it an affront: 'Is this her way of rubbing it in that they won? A party of thieves.'

I chuckled. 'Mummy, I doubt she knows who your preferred candidate was.'

'Hmm,' my mother grunted. 'Her boyfriend better become president one day the way she's running around, carrying him on her head.'

The state dinner fell on my mother's birthday and Akin informed us that he was throwing her a surprise party, not that she could have attended the dinner anyway – my father was usually front and centre at such events.

Akin took my mother shopping to get her out of the house so we could hang the balloons and lights in her absence. We chattered while we worked, pinching pieces of beef and chicken from the feast the caterer had brought over.

'Stop chewing and keep hanging. We don't have much time left,' Emeka instructed from his position atop a ladder, like an overseer on a farm.

'Yes, sir,' Nkechi responded with a mock salute.

'These service people have taught you how to be bossy ehn,' I said. '*Oya* come and help me blow this balloon. I have meat in my mouth.'

The shoes were how I discovered that Nwamaka had been in communication with my father: brand new Steve Madden slinky platform mules hidden at the back of her closet, where I was searching for a duster. It all fell into place: how my father had known our new address, why police had come to harass my mother in Akin's absence, and why my father had accused my mother of adultery in court.

Picking up a mule, I called for Nwamaka.

She came running, her smile wide and unaware. 'Yes? Did you find it?'

I raised the shoe and watched her smile disappear.

'Since when has this been going on?' I asked.

It was the ultimate betrayal. Our mother had sold every valuable she owned to afford my sisters' fees, taking on side jobs and investment schemes, vehemently rejecting Akin's offer to help. 'They are my children, I can do this,' I'd heard her insist, the only time I'd ever heard them argue. Their love was one in sync, making up for time lost. But that day my mother had insisted, and Akin had given in, even though he'd argued – quite reasonably – that he earned in foreign currency. He held a position as a professor at a university in the United States, having migrated not long after my parents married.

'Yes? I'm listening. And don't even bother lying,' I said to my sister.

'It–it's not as bad as you th–think.'

'How bad do you think I think it is? How are you any different from Judas Iscariot?'

'You've already concluded without giving me a chance to explain! He came to my school, okay? He said he would make things easier for us and that he's sorry, he wants to be a good father. He's willing to do better if Mummy gives him a chance.'

'And you believed him? After all this time?'

'Are you not tired?!' she demanded. 'Of living like this? Have you forgotten how it was before? How we lived? The kind of things we had? Mummy wouldn't even collect money from Uncle Akin, and Aunty Sally has to go behind her back to do anything for us. I'm tired of feeling like a pauper, of watching my classmates throw things that my father can afford in my face. He said he's sorry, what more do you want? He even asked me to bring you next time I'm coming to see him.'

'God forbid!'

'He's still our father whether we like it or not.'

I raised the braids by the side of my head and pointed at the scar etched in skin. 'Maybe you've forgotten but I cannot forget. I don't have that luxury.'

We pretended all was well when my mother returned, beaming as she unwrapped the brand-new Nokia 2100 Akin had purchased as an additional surprise.

'Isn't it too much?' she said, laughing as she encircled her arms around him.

Nwamaka's eyes held mine, saying our father could afford even more.

Aunty Sally coordinated the cake-cutting countdown and Sister Bolatito led the closing prayers.

Zina had a gift for my mother too. 'Happy birthday, ma,' she said as she handed a wrapped package to my mother.

'You knew about this too?! Thank you, my daughter. Come, come and take a picture with me. I must remember this day,' my mother said, dragging her to go find Mr Silas who we'd booked for the event.

Months later, our mothers would barely glance at each other at our graduation.

14

America

Things with Rodney ended before they'd even started, and I thought to myself afterwards that there'd been nothing to end.

'Nwakaego, what are you doing?' Zina said with a deep drawn-out sigh, not really expecting an answer.

'He just wasn't for me,' I told her.

Rodney had returned from Bristol in early December avidly expectant. We'd been talking for over a month and things had been progressing smoothly. He was, I felt, the universe's attempt at making a mockery of my excuses for remaining encumbered by the past – I'd wanted perfection and it had sent it my way and yet I was dissatisfied.

'Why?' he asked me when I finally found the voice to say no, his eyes the image of a lost puppy.

I thought of what to say and settled on the truth, with the dawning realisation that I would never find better. I could tell by the way his eyes crinkled at the corners and clouded over that he could never understand. He was kindness and beauty, a chance at newness and I'd turned him down.

After I ended things with Rodney, my mother called. I was lying in the dark even though it was day outside, the heavy blackout curtains doing their work.

'Nwakaego, come and spend Christmas with me and Akin in America,' my mother said. I'd spent every Christmas in London the same way: watching *Home Alone* in bed with microwaved food, wondering if anyone would notice if I died alone in my apartment.

'I'm fine here,' I said.

'You're not fine, I'm your mother and I know you're not fine,' she said. 'Will you wait until I die to finally come and visit me here?'

'Don't talk like that!'

She laughed. 'Talk like what? Do you think I'll live forever?'

I typed up a leave request that night. Akin insisted on paying for my flights and my mother begged me to let him.

'He wants to feel like a father figure to you, he sees you and your sisters as his children.'

Boston airport brought Lagos to mind – bustling crowds, constant motion, restless anticipation, everyone on a journey somewhere.

Akin stood at the arrivals terminal with a sign that read my name like there was a chance I would walk by him.

'Nwakaego!' he called, waving his card high and I rushed into an embrace that filled me with a warm sensation of safety.

'Your mother is in the car,' he said to me, taking my lone box. 'Is that all?' he asked, looking behind me like he expected a trolley filled with baggage to appear.

'I have a backpack too,' I said with a laugh, pointing at the bag at my back.

My mother was pacing anxiously by the side of a silver Ford Edge in the parking lot when we arrived.

'She's here!' Akin announced when we were close enough. My mother did the running this time, pulling me into her arms and squeezing me so tight that my stepfather was forced to say, endearingly, 'Smallie, she's coming home with us.'

'I used to think London was cold,' I said as we drove down the snow-covered roads and high-rise buildings to Cambridge, Marvin Gaye's 'Let's Get It On' playing on the car's stereo, 'but Massachusetts is COLD. I can feel the chill in my bones.'

'At least you came here from London,' my mother quipped. 'Imagine how I felt arriving from hot hot Lagos. I thought I was going to die.'

Akin laughed. 'You should have seen her that first winter, always shivering. Our heating bill was through the roof.'

'Ahn-ahn, it wasn't that bad.' My mother slapped a palm blithely on his shoulder, and he shot her a look of such ardent devotion that I turned away, feeling like an intruder.

He'd been her first true love before she'd even known it, the one who'd endured through the years despite distance and marriage to my father and even though she never said it, I knew she wished she'd married him instead.

America was shimmering in colour: sparkling Christmas lights in the likeness of reindeers and sleighs, giant decorated trees covered in glowing orbs.

'You people really take Christmas seriously here o,' I commented as we passed a deer-drawn sleigh composed entirely of lights.

'But you people decorate London for Christmas too – I've seen the pictures,' my mother said.

'Not like this o,' I said. Or maybe I didn't go out enough during Christmas to remember.

'Christmas is a big tradition here, bigger than Thanksgiving I think,' my mother admitted. 'Even those that don't believe do something. And they've managed to export the obsession to the rest of the world.'

'The entire thing is capitalist anyways,' Akin said glibly. 'A way to get the masses to open their purses.'

'Oh God, you're about to go into lecturer mode again,' my mother groaned.

'America is very capitalist,' I said.

'Don't encourage him!'

'But it's true,' Akin said with a cheeky grin. 'How else would what is meant to be a Christian celebration of the birth of a Hebrew messiah turn into all sorts of merchandise shilling. Corporates are pulling in millions of dollars annually from this.'

'England is capitalist too,' my mother said somewhat defensively, and I wondered when America had begun to mean so much to her. Did she wave flags on their Independence Day too? 'Most western countries are.'

'Well at least we have the NHS,' I teased. 'We're not telling our people to die if they cannot afford healthcare.'

We did not speak of Nigeria or the state of *its* healthcare system.

Akin laughed. 'She has a point.'

'I thought you said it wasn't your country,' my mother grumbled.

Their home was how ours might have been in the absence of my father's ever-present iron fist. There was no garish furniture, no gaudy chandeliers dripping from the ceilings; it was a home that embraced instead of intimidated.

'Please treat this as your home,' Akin said to me after he'd lifted my box up the stairs; my mother was downstairs in the kitchen, anxiously banging pots and pans together.

The sincerity of his words was evident, but left unsaid was his true desire – to take the place of my father. I questioned how much he wanted to wipe my mother's memories of her years with my father.

Despite Akin's insistence that Christmas traditions were capitalist conjectures to fleece the populace, he took us shopping the following day, laughing at my mother's excitement as she grabbed a giant turkey and purchased more lights that could cover the circumference of their home. He climbed ladders and cut through paper ornaments, sharing in my mother's joy as the lights came on, his eyes not on the decorations but her face. He would do anything for her, I realised with a dull ache in my chest.

In America, my mother listened to classical music, the symphonies floating through the walls. She'd only just concluded her PhD programme at the Massachusetts Institute of Technology where Akin taught and had taken up a postgraduate position on the department faculty. Occupying a prominent position on their living room wall was a framed photo of my mother in her graduation gown, cheesing at the camera. She'd refused to let us come for her graduation – 'Don't waste your money. Do you know how old I am?' – but from the way her smile lit up the frame, the prominence of the print of her name at the bottom – Obianuju Nwaike, her father's name – I knew it meant more than I could know. Life was beginning for her at last.

'American media is too focused on America,' I observed one day as I watched the evening news with Akin. 'You would think the rest of the world doesn't exist.'

A fledgling bond had begun to form between us. Akin

possessed a genuine curiosity, an eagerness to learn, but it was the sensitivity with which he seemed to move through life that was most endearing. He was an encyclopaedia of experience and knowledge and yet he was in no way boastful or arrogant, and I found myself willing to talk, to share my thoughts.

'American racism is more overt than British racism,' he'd said to me during a conversation about my Twitter; he did not understand Twitter, but he understood race as a foreigner. 'And the British are less willing to discuss it because class disparities take prominence over everything else there.'

'Yes,' I concurred. 'Class issues are ingrained. But they would die before they admit something is racist.' I mimicked a British accent. *'It's rude, not racist.* It's also part of the stiff-upper-lip culture of not talking about your problems. Personally, I think it's how the establishment has been able to keep the masses from revolting. If you don't speak about your problems, how do you get angry enough to protest?'

'Now,' he said, 'It's American exceptionalism at play. America is in love with America, it's high on its own Kool-Aid. I moved here before the internet became a thing, and let me tell you, it was so hard to find news about any other country. I felt like the country was suffocating me. I wrote letters back home to assure myself that another world existed.'

I thought to myself that it was why he'd never developed an American accent, despite having lived there since the '80s – a refusal to be subsumed by America.

'You know we had a running joke in class during my postgraduate programme,' I said, 'that anyone speaking about a country outside of America should put up a map and flag so the Americans could know where they're talking about.'

Akin laughed long and loud until I wondered if he only found the joke funny because I'd told it.

It was at a large store that our bond was truly solidified. We were getting groceries when I went searching and came face to face with a wall of guns. In a fit of panic, I bolted down the aisle and through the nearest exit I could find. Later, I would think of it as an embarrassing overreaction.

Bent forward, on the verge of hyperventilating, a hand soothingly rubbed my back until I'd gathered myself. I looked up to find Akin, his face a mask of concern. It was more care than my father had ever shown me.

A store attendant passed by. 'Is everything alright?'

Akin looked to me for a response. I nodded slowly.

'Is she your daughter?'

'Yes,' I said with assurance.

Akin lamented the big corporates that held the country in its grasp. 'There's no reason for guns to be sold in a grocery store. Year after year we lament school shootings and we let it continue in the name of freedom? Freedom birthed in fear!'

It brought a change in our relationship, a gradual eradication of its limitations.

My mother wanted to go shopping, just me and her.

'You don't spend any time with me,' she said. 'You're always talking to Akin.'

'You should be happy I love him as much as you do,' I teased.

Understanding her need for time alone with me, Akin dropped us off at the mall with stern instructions to call him when we were done.

'Ahn-ahn, you're talking like we'll get lost. I know Boston o,' she said.

We moved between clothing stores, pop music playing from the speakers, lanky salespeople observing our movements.

'You should buy that,' I said to my mother when she tried on a cocktail dress that hugged her hips and accentuated her cleavage.

'You don't think I'm too old for something like this?'

'Nobody is ever too old to look fine. You don't even look your age.'

'You should try on something. Maybe somebody will see how fine you are in America and keep you here,' she joked.

I smiled. 'I don't want anybody to keep me here. I'm not ready to write exams to become a lawyer in America too.'

She faced the mirror, rubbing her hands against the dress. 'Akin told me what happened the other day,' she said suddenly. 'Why didn't you tell me about it?' I sensed in her tone a creeping angst that I'd begun to keep things from her.

'It was nothing,' I assured her. 'I've just never seen guns in a store before.'

'It's not nothing. You should tell me; I want to know.'

I nodded.

She turned away from the mirror to look at me. 'I've never understood the gun laws here. They say it's to protect against bad people but isn't it easier to make sure nobody has guns at all? But that's America for you, they do everything upside down. Even their measurement system is different.'

I laughed. 'I know. Who else uses Fahrenheit in the name of God?'

'During the riots, I was so worried. There are deep racial tensions and grievances unaddressed in this country. What if it breaks out into a full-on war?'

'I guess they compensate for that with heavy investment in law enforcement,' I said.

She decided against getting the dress, so we went into another store, shuffling through the racks. An auburn-haired teenager brushed roughly against my shoulder, not bothering to apologise.

'Some of them don't have manners here. They don't teach them respect,' my mother said with annoyance. 'You should hear the things they say to me on campus. When the Ebola pandemic started this year, someone asked me the last time I visited home, as if that would determine how closely they could approach me. Can you imagine the rubbish?'

'It was the same in England, even some of my colleagues started acting funny, educated people o.'

There was a minor queue at the register so we waited for our turn. My mother spoke cheerily about the new church she had joined in the city and the diversity of its congregation.

Then she said, staring at me, 'You've lost weight.'

'Thank you.'

'I mean it in the Nigerian way.' Then in Igbo she added, 'You're not eating well.'

A voice spat suddenly from behind us, 'You're in America, you know.' We turned to find a big-boned woman with inky hair tied in a tight knot at the top of her head. 'You should try to speak English.'

In the past, I would have brushed it off, but something had changed in the past months. 'You're very stupid! Was English the language your ancestors met in America?'

My mother pulled uneasily at my shoulder. 'Nwakaego, leave it. Let's go,' she whispered. 'They carry guns in this country o.' In Nigeria, she would not have let it go.

We took an Uber home because my mother was too distressed to call Akin and wait for his Ford to arrive. Our driver, Hailey, was a chatty brunette woman with delicate model-like features. 'Have some sweets,' she said, offering us a bowl.

Our journey was laden with silence and my mother stared out the window in thought, until I asked her, 'Do you miss Nigeria?'

'If our country worked well, would we even move here?' she said, not answering my question, falling silent again. More than anything, her pride had been hurt.

'Here we are,' Hailey announced, parking in front of the terraced house. As my mother rigidly made her way out of the car, our driver looked in the rearview mirror and said, 'Your braids are so pretty,' even though they had layers of undergrowth budding underneath. And in Hailey, I saw another kind of white woman; one who bore the guilt of people like the woman in the store and sought to make amends.

Close to Christmas, Kwaku came for dinner with his white wife and two sons.

'He's one of the other Africans on the college faculty,' Akin explained before they arrived. 'You know we Africans have to stick together.'

Kwaku's accent reminded me of Mrs Mensah, my Ghanaian English teacher in secondary school whose accent was the object of jokes amongst my classmates. '*Werser*,' Zina mimicked once. 'They over-emphasise their vowels – is that how to speak English?'

'It's still better than our local accent,' Eriife had said.

'My good man!' Kwaku said at the door, pulling Akin into a half embrace and thumping him on the back. Behind him,

two biracial men towered over a tiny woman with honey-
blonde hair and an oval face. Kwaku made the introductions:
'My wife, Sophia and our boys, Yao and Kofi. Yao, our last
born just finished high school but Kofi is a lawyer in New
York, he's visiting for the holidays.'

I stretched my hand out and was abruptly pulled into
an embrace.

'I'm a hugger,' Sophia said.

Over dinner, the conversations were focused on the midterm election results. 'They show a deep dissatisfaction with
the current state of things,' Kwaku said.

'Dissatisfaction at what exactly?' Akin responded, passing a plate of jollof rice. 'Yes, there are issues, but we cannot
pretend that there's no racial factor at the bottom of all this.
A particular sect of this country is affronted by the fact that
a black man was elected – not once but twice.'

Kwaku shoved a spoonful of rice in his mouth and said
to my mother, 'Ah madam, your jollof rice is good, almost as
good as ours back home. But Ghanaian jollof will always be
the best eh.'

She laughed at the banter. She'd recovered from the
encounter at the clothing store and it made me question
how often it had happened. 'Our jollof rice is better than
yours jare.'

To Akin, Kwaku said, 'The issue with us black people is
that we don't want anyone to criticise Obama. Next thing,
we mention racism. We're too protective of him; he is not
faultless, you know.'

'I'm not saying he's faultless, but the issues are not at the
core of the problem. It's going to be worse at the general
elections,' Akin said. 'Something has shifted racially in this
country, especially in the last couple of months with the riots.'

'Yes, but let's also look at the last few months,' Kwaku said. 'The response to the riots? Benghazi? IRS scandal? Ebola? And then he threatened to take away their guns? You know how much they love their guns here. Then the Citizens Pathway Program, that's enough to start crying about borders being unsafe and letting criminals into the country.'

Akin shook his head in disappointment. 'Ah Kwaku, don't tell me you're one of those who move here then vote against the very policies that helped you.'

'Of course not! I'm not a sell-out, brother.' Kwaku appeared affronted by the mere thought. 'I even gave my children Ghanaian names; I'm not trying to be one of *them*.' The emphasis on 'them' was clear.

Akin nodded, acquiescing. 'But you also agree that Obama has been unfairly criticised.'

Kwaku chuckled. 'The major problem is that Obama is not the liberal hero people want him to be. He's too right-wing for the left and too left-wing for the right. It's like he saw what everyone wanted him to be and decided to stick firmly to the middle, pursuing bipartisanship that does not exist.'

I yawned unconsciously, a reflexive response to the drawn-out conversation.

'See?' Akin said with a smile. 'We're boring our visitor from Britain.'

'Why don't you tell us about the UK, Ego?' Sophia said softly, startling me. It was the first time she had spoken.

'Yes,' Kwaku concurred. 'How are the politics there?'

Their eldest son Kofi's eyes were immediately alert behind his spectacles and I had the distinct feeling that he was paying close attention.

I chuckled nervously. 'Well, it's pretty much the same in terms of the right-wing creating boogie men to scare people into thinking how they want. I think the main difference is the absence of the particular brand of evangelical religious fanaticism that is American. The crusades of the late '70s and '80s were successful at spreading it to Africa and certain other parts of the world but not Europe.'

Later, when they were gone, my mother said to me, 'I think Kofi likes you.'

On Boxing Day, we were up early to watch the English Premier League. Football had always played a part in my relationship with my mother; we'd followed the World Cup together and lamented Nigeria's defeat in the knockout stages.

'Do we call this an offshoot of colonialism or what?' Akin mocked. 'Waking up on Boxing Day to watch another country's league football.'

'Call it whatever you want,' my mother retorted with her tongue out as Manchester United versus Newcastle United lit up the screen.

'Okay o, I'll prepare breakfast,' Akin said and planted a kiss on her cheek.

'He's a good man,' I told my mother when he was out of earshot.

She smiled, but it was a sad smile. 'Are you ready to tell me what is bothering you?'

I recoiled. 'Why must something be bothering me?'

'Can you tell me why you've been going about like you have the world on your shoulders? Or why you won't give Kofi a second glance? He's come to visit three times and you never look interested in what he has to say. And you won't tell me what happened to that Jamaican boy that liked you in London.'

It was impossible to hide anything from her. 'You've

started talking like Americans; they always want to talk about how they feel,' I said.

'What is it?' she pressed. 'Is it Emeka?

That was when I burst into tears.

15

White light

All Emeka spoke about in 2004 was how the internet was going to change the world. It was a wave, he said, so propulsive and unremitting that the universe would have no other option but to capitulate.

'The internet is the next big thing, I'm telling you,' he said to me for the umpteenth time, gripping the steering wheel as we drove towards the Lagos law school campus. We were on our way back from a cyber cafe where he'd taken us to set up email addresses.

'I don't see why I need an email address,' I complained as he pulled me into the shrouded room with CPUs humming in unison. 'Who will I email? No one else has one.'

A small bespectacled man tore out time tickets with login details as Emeka handed him the cash needed for an hour for the both of us.

'Where did you learn how to type so fast?' I asked. We'd learned to use typewriters in secondary school, but those keys differed in style and weight.

'I come here often,' he confessed. 'I'm a computer science graduate, you know.'

Eventually, I settled on 'egolove81@yahoo.com'. Years later, I would have to open a more professional sounding email address, but at that moment, it didn't matter. Emeka sent me an email to mark it, my only personal email for a long while:

Hi, it's me.
   Yours always,
   E.

I teased him about how serious sounding his email address was: danielemekaigwe@yahoo.com. He was more foresighted than I would ever be.

He had completed his year of compulsory national service, and despite all his efforts, still hadn't secured a job.

'Can you imagine, they wanted me to type letters every day on their new desktop computer. Do they even know what a computer scientist is?' he'd blustered after his last interview. There were two things I'd always known about Emeka: he never panicked and he never lost his temper. But watching him blow hot that day, I wondered if that was what Nigeria did, took you apart until you were left a varmint just trying to survive.

We stopped to buy fuel for the car his father had loaned him.

'There aren't enough tech jobs in the market – the kind of jobs I want,' he said, as he pulled in front of a pump and turned to speak with the attendant.

'Maybe you should take that typist job first so you can have something to do. You have to eat,' I said as we pulled out of the filling station.

'I don't want to eat. I want to code, to build, to change the world!'

I laughed. 'You don't want to eat *ke*? It's only those that eat that can build anything.'

He smiled. 'You're laughing? You know this will be you soon, right? Looking for a job like every other graduate in this godforsaken country.'

Emeka was right. Zina and I often talked about what we would do when law school was over. We were more than halfway through and we worried for our future. Law firms were notorious for paying graduates barely enough to survive, and you needed to have certain connections to get your foot through the door. Every now and then, Zina still fantasised about becoming an actress. 'It's possible, you know!' she said.

'I think what I need to do is to leave this country. See the type of companies being built in America,' Emeka said. He spoke about America often and with longing now.

'Why not build something here?' I said. 'You can be a pioneer. The market is still young and ripe. If we all leave, what will happen to the country?'

'Madam Patriotism please, you've started again. You don't even vote. I can believe your mother at least.'

I frowned. 'That's unfair. I turned eighteen after the elections in '99 and last year's were violent.'

'I'm just teasing.' Emeka sighed. 'Anyways, it's like Bola Ige's friend said at his funeral: "Nigeria is worth living for but I'm not so sure that it's worth dying for."'

'I'm pregnant,' Zina announced a month later in our hostel room. A newspaper was spread in front of us and we'd spent the last hour studying it for any topic that might come up in class discussions; our lecturers insisted on analysing the latest cases and judgements.

Once, during one of these evenings, we stumbled on an article about my father. There was speculation that he was under investigation for corruption by the Financial Crimes Commission for the government contracts he'd been awarded over the years.

'I'm sure he'll be fine,' Emeka assured me, when I pulled the torn-out page from my handbag to show him. 'He's bloody Chief Azubuike!'

Though Emeka did not say it, I could tell that he was surprised I would still worry about my father.

'Zina, I'm not in the mood for your jokes this evening *abeg*,' I said, turning a page, nervous that I would come across my father in bold colourful print.

'I'm serious.'

'I don't understand. Pregnant how? Are you sure?'

'I've not taken a test yet, but I'm late by a week, and I can feel it.'

'Is it . . . what's his name again?'

'Bayo? Yes.' As if it wasn't bad enough that she was pregnant, she'd chosen to get pregnant by a Yoruba boy. Her father would kill her.

'Why?'

'I told you. I don't want to get married yet. I'll tell my parents I'm pregnant and they'll leave me alone.'

'You don't want to get married so you chose to get pregnant instead? Do you realise how stupid that sounds? Can you take care of a child in this economy? Does Bayo even have a job?'

Zina bounced off the bed and threw the newspaper to the floor. 'You're so arrogant, you think you know it all. So tell me, wise one, what should I do instead? You think you're better because you spend all your free time with Emeka and at that church that is more like a cult. You think his parents will let their precious only son marry a girl from a broken home with a father in the newspapers? You better wake up!'

During my first year of postgraduate studies in the UK, I snuck into a workshop at the Department of Psychiatry. At the back of the hall, I listened to the speaker – a white man with salt-and-pepper hair – discuss how humans react to trauma: some people might display characteristics associated with post-traumatic stress disorder, many more would exhibit resilience or effects that fall outside diagnostic criteria. Panic and anxiety were normal; fragmented and incomplete memories were not uncommon. I took notes feverishly, underlining words and phrases in red pen, in a bid to understand what had taken place that day. What had really happened and why did the memories slip from my brain like cloth through my fingers? How could such a life-shattering event feel so remote yet so present?

It was meant to be a simple errand. We were done with law school exams and in that hapless space of waiting for our final results and the graduation list to be published, to see who hadn't wasted their parents' money. Zina and I were barely on speaking terms even though we shared the same living quarters. In the mornings, we tensed to keep our bodies from brushing as we passed each other.

Pastor Kamsi had organised a conference at the other end of the city and needed someone to carry supplies from the church. It was a rainy day, the clouds dusty grey. Emeka had another job interview and couldn't help. Instead, he paid for a taxi to take me to the hotel where Pastor Kamsi was lodged, with a promise to pick me up once his interview was over.

At the hotel reception, I was told I was expected and handed a key. I was meant to wait when I was done. In the elevator, I hummed along to the music. In the room, I arranged the supplies – brochures, handkerchiefs and bottles of oil – in a corner and sat on the bed to wait.

Fingers like tentacles up my thighs awakened me. There was whirring in my ears, there were grunts like an animal on its way to slaughter, there was pain, then there was white light.

My mother held my hand as we waited. It reminded me of the time we'd waited outside my principal's office in my third year of secondary school because I'd punched a boy in the face for referring to another girl as a prostitute. *Ashewo.*

'Nwakaego, what happened? You're not the violent type,' my mother had said to me then.

This time, she sat in silence, gripping my hand too tightly. I stared at the faded walls of the building thinking about how my father would never be caught dead in such a place; marble-floored private hospitals were more his thing. I felt a sudden wetness on my hand and turned to study my mother's face. Anger and irritation surged in me. What would crying solve? Why was she crying when I couldn't?

I'd searched for the Nokia 2100 in my handbag when I was sure he was gone. My mother had handed it down to me after Akin had upgraded her to a 6600.

'Mummy, please I need your help,' I said, and she was there within an hour.

In the car to the hospital, I heard his voice again, 'I'm sure you've done it before with that boyfriend of yours. Did he make it as enjoyable as I did?'

We hadn't because I'd wanted it to be special, and Emeka had understood. *Special.* That word felt so flimsy now.

'You better not tell anyone, if you know what's good for you,' he'd said as he redid his belt buckle. He chuckled, like I'd said something funny. 'Anyway, you can try, they'll never believe you.'

Perhaps it said something about me that I'd continued to spend time with him despite the stories that had floated about for years, even though a niggling had persisted at the back of my mind. Was it pride? Arrogance? Did I think I was special? That he wouldn't – couldn't – touch me?

'Next person,' the nurse called as my phone rang. Emeka's name flashed across the screen. A phone had been his first major purchase at the end of his youth service, bought with savings from his monthly government *allawee*. He'd held it up triumphantly, and I'd wanted to rub the top of his head like a proud parent.

'Nexxxttt!' the nurse screamed. My mother pulled me to my feet.

In the room, she explained what had happened to the nurse in hushed tones, and I wondered if she felt the shame I felt. My bag vibrated and I pulled my phone out to see ten missed calls, all from Emeka.

'*Ndo*, sorry my dear,' the nurse said to me, pulling out her kit. 'We have to run some tests and take some samples, then we'll give you drugs to prevent anything. Just lie down there,' she said pointing at a gurney in the corner.

A message flashed on the screen as I stretched out on the hospital bed. I would read it later: '*Where are you?*'

'Are you sure?' the officer at the police station asked the following day, smacking chewing gum as he eyed me suspiciously.

'What sort of question is that?' my mother demanded.

'Madam na so these small small girls dey do. Instead of them to say that they were with their boyfriends, they'll say it's rape when they're caught,' he said.

The station smelled like urine, and stale moisture that had transformed into mould climbed the walls.

'I'm sure,' I said to stop my mother from railing at the only help we had.

'How old are you?' another officer asked. He looked more sombre than his counterpart.

'Twenty-three,' I answered.

'Ahn-ahn! Big girl like you?' the smacking gum officer exclaimed.

'Madam, you'll have to file a report,' the sombre officer said, pulling out a long dusty notebook from under the desk.

My mother called Aunty Sally who made calls to the absent Divisional Police Officer (DPO) in charge of the station. We paid to fuel the police vehicle that followed us to the church premises.

It wasn't how I'd imagined our parents finally meeting. I still hadn't spoken to Emeka. He'd called and called and sent text messages until I'd allowed the handset's battery to run out, watching the neon-coloured display blink until it went dark.

'Are you okay? Is something wrong? Please talk to me.' I could feel the panic in his words; Emeka who never panicked, but I had no idea how to say what needed to be said.

He came to our house, knocking insistently until my mother was forced to politely explain that I did not want to see him. But now his parents knew and soon, he would know too.

'We don't take our brethren to court,' Emeka's father said. He'd been the one to post bail for Pastor Kamsi. We were in his office at church, and I realised it was my first time there.

It was just how I'd imagined: on the walls, a picture of the general overseer at the headquarters hanging beside portraits of the president and an artist's depiction of Jesus Christ, a mahogany bookcase stacked with spiritual guidance books and various versions of the Bible, a chestnut desk cluttered with letters and pamphlets.

Beside her husband, Emeka's mother watched me like I wasn't the same person who'd insisted on slicing onions and tomatoes for rice just the previous week.

Pastor Igwe stood up to pull a Bible from a stack in the bookcase. 'First Corinthians six verse one. New International Version,' he read out when he was seated.

'If any of you has a dispute with another, do you dare to take it before the ungodly for judgement instead of before the Lord's people?'

'Look,' my mother said. 'I know the Bible like everyone else in this room. What has happened is a crime and I am not letting it go until justice is served. If this is why you've called us here, you're wasting your time.'

'The pastor involved says you're lying, and it's your word against his,' Mrs Agnes said.

'It's not just her word against his, we have the DNA sample from that day at the hospital,' my mother said.

Mrs Agnes looked at her husband. 'DNA? Do we use that in this country?' Then to my mother, 'It still doesn't prove anything, the intercourse could have been consensual.' I realised she couldn't say the word 'sex' aloud, it was too lurid for her.

Pastor Igwe sighed. 'Madam, are you married to the man you're living with? Where is her father? Why are you not here with him?'

My mother huffed, insulted. 'What does that have to do with what we're discussing?'

'I'm trying to understand what circumstances at home would have caused her to come up with such a tale against a man of God. I can personally vouch for Kamsi as a man of God. We know she's had issues with him in the past and has pushed against any form of mentoring and guidance.'

Mrs Agnes gripped my hand just before we walked out of the office. 'Nwakaego, tell me the truth as a mother, why would you do this? Why not just tell the truth?'

They were convinced the devil had chosen me to try to ruin Pastor Kamsi.

I dropped a note in the prayers and testimonies basket before we walked out the church building:

Pastor Kamsi raped me.

16

Big guns

They wouldn't stop fussing: my mother with her minute-by-minute checkups; Aunty Sally and her bottomless gift baskets and packages; Sister Bolatito's drawn-out visits with coolers of rice and chicken; even Zina and Eriife's sudden affinity for spending hours in doing nothing but chatting aimlessly. Eriife whose life had previously revolved around her boyfriend; Zina whose thickened middle connoted problems of her own. I didn't understand it. I wasn't sick, I wasn't dying. I was still the same person, the same Nwakaego – wasn't I?

Anger had settled over me like a fresh crust. Why had any of this happened? What had I done wrong to be deserving of this? In the mornings, I scrubbed at myself thoroughly, scalding and bruising in the process, willing this new membrane away, this ever-present feeling of disgust and irritation. Some days, it boiled like bile at the bottom of my belly, then rose up in my chest and I entertained thoughts of driving to Pastor Kamsi's house and creating a circle around it with kerosene, lighting a match and locking both of us in, of watching the flames consume our bodies. Other days, I woke up leaden, trudging between my bed and the bathroom and nowhere else. Those days, I existed in a state of nothingness.

The therapist encouraged me to talk about my feelings, said that speaking would help me feel better. But who was she to say so? In our sessions, I watched her head bob from side to side in animation, eyed the tuft of hair that had escaped the sleek relaxed bun at the top of her head, thinking of how much money she was costing my mother. 'She's shielding her mind,' she told my mother. It wouldn't work until I cooperated. It angered me how much she felt she knew about me, a woman who until a few weeks ago had no idea I existed, that she could suddenly speak about me to my own mother like an expert.

The church headquarters had called in the big guns: the Chief Superintendent of Police, the Assistant Commissioner of Police; people whose ranking surpassed that of an ordinary Divisional Police Officer. Aunty Sally made calls, but no one was willing to risk weathered alliances over such a flimsy matter, a promiscuous lying child.

'Your case cannot be proven in court,' the regional pastoral head told my mother. 'It's best for yourself and your daughter that you leave all this now. She's still young, there's no need to ruin her life over this.' *Ruin her life.* I would have laughed if it wasn't so funny.

My mother called my father. She'd held out over the years, refusing to budge in even her most vulnerable moments: when we had no money for basic amenities and sat in pitch darkness without power supply; when she'd spent all she had on our school fees and had no money for food. In those moments, she'd prayed instead, clasped her hands together, looked to the ceiling and waited for a miracle. And each time, whether by the force of her faith or the intervention of the Almighty, a breakthrough had come, a timely remediation that was nothing short of miraculous.

But this time, she called my father. Akin had been the one to encourage her to do so; I was his daughter, he knew people, he would be able to do something. And so, my mother dialled a number she'd sworn to never call again.

Much like Pastor Kamsi in earlier years, my father had remained outwardly single; a disconsolate bachelor abandoned by his unstable wife who had taken their children; his son's mother was too unrefined. It did not stop the stories of his new much younger girlfriends from reaching our ears.

Usman was still at the gate when we arrived. '*Hay* madam! Na you be this? Welcome o.' He poked his head outside the gate as if searching for something, then he looked myself and my mother up and down. Realising we hadn't returned with any baggage, his smile waned.

'Is your oga around?' my mother asked.

He was around; he'd told us he would be.

'Yes, ma,' Usman said.

The compound was the same: the blooming ixoras, open garage and majestic columns. The steward opened the door; that had changed, replaced by a bulletproof structure.

My father was sat behind the mahogany desk that had always been at the centre of his study, but now there were even more bronze plaques lining the walls and corners. He was still handsome, the only indication of ageing the grey strands in his hair and new lines under his eyes. He asked to speak with me alone. He demanded this slowly, with the brass of one aware of the power he wielded.

'Nwakaego,' he said when we were alone, leaning forward in his seat. I started; it was a while since I'd heard him call my name. He laughed. 'So, you're finally here. After asking you to come and see me for years, I sent your sister – you even collected my money, remember? – and now you've come to me of your free will.' He threw up his hands. 'It's okay, I understand. I can't say I didn't deserve any of it, I only hoped you'd give me the respect deserving of a father.'

He relaxed in his cushioned chair. 'Anyway, that's not why you're here. Your mother says you need my help.'

'Yes,' I said, ashamed.

He swept his hand forward. 'Go ahead, tell me what happened so I can know exactly how I can help.'

'Hmmm,' my father said when I was done speaking. 'These are the kind of *riff raffs* I tried to protect you and your sisters from when we were still a family. Would any of this have happened if your mother hadn't refused to listen to reason? All because of a child, a child whose mother I'm not even married to. He's upstairs by the way in case you're wondering, I hired a nanny and special tutor for him. I take care of all my children, make sure they get the best as long as they're under my roof. Unlike your mother who has given herself to prostituting for that lecturer that goes and comes as he likes, I'm still honouring my vows. Did you see any other woman here when you walked in?'

'No,' I said meekly, clenching my fists in my lap.

'Regardless of all that had happened, you're still my child, and so of course I'll help.' He paused. 'On a simple condition.'

I waited for him to speak. It was like making a deal with the devil, you never knew what he would ask of you.

He nodded, taking my silence for acceptance. 'Once I take on this case, two things might happen: one it might go away quietly; two, if they resist and people get wind of it – this is the more likely reality– it will get wider coverage in the newspapers. I'm already dealing with some issues, you might have already seen some of it in the papers, I'm not in the mood to deal with any more noise, and I'm sure you don't want the world to know what has happened to you. I have a solution that can work for the both of us. You remember Chief Badmus? He used to be a regular at my parties back in the days.'

'Yes, I remember.'

'Good. Well, he now sits on the board of the Financial Crimes Commission. He has a troublesome son he's looking to marry off, you know, make him into a responsible young man with a family. I've told him I have a brilliant daughter who's practically done with law school and he's very open to the idea of a union between our families. We can tidy up the wedding within the next three months. He will ensure that this case with the commission gets snuffed out, and even if your case eventually gets to the public, you'd be a respectable married woman by then, no one would dare speak ill of you, to your face at least.' He was exultant in his brilliance, his ability to always come up with a solution.

I said nothing, stunned by the proposition.

He continued. 'If you're worried about this son of his, I've done some background checks of my own and there's nothing about him that can't be handled, and if it gets too bad, their family is wealthy enough to get you a separate home.'

'You're asking to sell me?' I mouthed finally.

He frowned, the vein in his head started to tick. 'What nonsense are you talking about? I'm providing a solution for the both of us and that's the best you can say?'

I lurched to my feet.

'Nwakaego, think of what you're about to do. You're my daughter, I know you're not stupid. You have to be realistic.'

I moved towards the door and turned the handle.

'I know you're not stupid, and so I'll give you till the end of next week to make up your mind. If I don't hear from you then, consider yourself dead to me.'

In my room, I listened to the CDs Emeka had burned before it had all come crumbling down. I still refused to see him or pick up his calls. He blamed himself, I knew, though I wasn't sure to what extent, until the first email arrived, lodged at the top of the screen on my visit to a cybercafe.

> I'm so sorry, I should have been there that day. It's all my fault. I shouldn't have let you work with him. Please forgive me.

But it wasn't his fault.

> Remember all the promises we made to each other, the future we planned together. Don't you still see it? Was our love only a passing thing for you? Did you love with the fear of losing?

I did love with fear, but with the fear of transformation, that he would one day become a man I didn't recognise, just like my father.

The third email was brief:

> Nwakaego, I still love you. Please talk to me.

Was I supposed to be grateful?

> Are you afraid of what I think about you? Nothing has changed for me. I still see you the same. I'm so sorry.

But everything had changed, irrevocably so. I would never be the same person again. The last email had come with an MP3 attachment: Lighthouse Family's 'High'.

Emeka delivered an invitation to his mother's birthday party. My mother spoke with him at the door.

'I think you should speak with him,' she said to me when he was gone. 'You both deserve closure. He's not his parents.' She handed me the card. 'You don't have to go, but maybe it's an apology on their part. Maybe they're going to do the right thing now.'

Gospel music tinkled as I arrived. I'd come late, deciding at the last minute to make an appearance. Emeka's sister answered the door. She smiled up at me.

'Emeka went out to buy drinks, many more people came. He'll be back soon.'

I hid behind the crowd as 'Jesus' was spelled out and the knife sliced through the icing. Just as the music picked up again, a familiar figure stood and clinked on a glass with a spoon.

'Attention everyone,' Pastor Kamsi announced. The gathering went silent. 'I have the special permission of the celebrant to do what I'm about to do.'

The room murmured. Emeka's mother's eyes met mine.

Pastor Kamsi pulled Cynthia forward and dropped to a knee. Ecstatic screams engulfed the room, as Cynthia, joyous tears streaming down her face, nodded and accepted the ring he slid unto her finger.

Emeka's mother continued to hold my eyes as understanding dawned on me: this was why I'd been invited, to witness this engagement, to put an end to my demonic ways, to see Kamsi thrive regardless. Was Emeka aware? Had he brought the card to me knowing what would happen? I couldn't breathe.

My phone rang as I rushed towards the door. A strange number. I hesitated, thinking it was Emeka. 'Hello, is this Nwakaego Azubuike?' a woman asked.

'Yes, this is she.'

'Your attention is needed at our hospital. An unconscious patient – Zinachukwu Okafor – put your name down as her guardian.'

It was all white: white walls, white sheets, white overalls and white nurse caps. I imagined I'd taken a detour and somehow ended up on the other side. That would have been a lot better than reality.

They needed blood. Zina was low on blood and the hospital's blood bank was down on O-negative. I flinched as the needle pricked my arm. We'd joked about this before, in secondary school after the biology teacher announced we were going to be studying blood types. For the class experiment, we pricked our fingers with lancets and placed our blood on glass slides to be studied under microscopes. 'A, B, O,' our teacher announced before he added the anti-Rh serums. We were the only two in class that belonged to the O-negative blood group. 'The universal blood donor type,' our teacher informed the classroom. 'This blood type offers the lowest risk to other blood types and can be donated to others. However, should they need blood transfusion themselves, they can only receive from other O-negative types.'

'Ah thank God, I have one close by. Hope you hear that Ego,' Zina said laughing. 'If I'm ever in an accident, you're the only one that can save me o.'

'Instead of you to pray that we're not in the accident together,' I retorted, joining in her laughter.

Now here I was, watching my blood gradually fill bag after bag held by a nurse who did not smile. She handed me a small packet of juice when she was done. 'Take that and sit still for at least fifteen minutes. I'll bring your friend's belongings to you,' she said. Then she was gone.

'She walked in here bleeding profusely,' the doctor had explained in his office after I rushed into the emergency ward, screaming for help. He pulled a small white bottle from his lab coat pocket and held it to me.

'What's this?' I asked.

'It seems your friend took illegal abortion pills. Somehow she was able to find her way here when she started bleeding. If she'd come in any later, she'd be dead.'

His words frightened me, how close I'd come to hearing different news.

'As you know,' the doctor continued, 'abortion is illegal in this country, and I should be reporting this to the authorities. However, I think what is paramount now is ensuring she's fine. I'd advise you though to encourage her to report wher-ever she got these pills to NAFDAC before they manage to kill others that aren't as lucky.'

I called my mother because I couldn't stop crying, because I felt like a little child suddenly lost in a bustling station, people running helter skelter, without a parent to hold their hand.

Zina opened her eyes as I waited, weeping into the spot-less bedsheet.

'Good to know you would have cried at my funeral,' she croaked over my head.

I jerked up and wiped at my face, relief washing over me. 'Are you mad?!'

A wan smile crossed her face. 'You said babies were expensive.'

'You should call her mother. I would want to know if you were in such a situation,' my mother said to me later while Zina slept.

I found Zina's phone in her bag and called Aunty Ada. 'Zinachukwu, where are you this child?' she railed across the line.

'Aunty Ada, it's me, Nwakaego,' I said.

And with that natural mother's instinct, she immediately knew something was wrong. 'What happened?' she breathed.

My mother met Aunty Ada at the hospital entrance, engulfing her in an embrace, assuring her Zina was fine. Aunty Ada cried and cried, then she nodded, encouraged, as my mother spoke to her.

Death had separated them, near death brought them back together.

17

Commonwealth

A form with an unfamiliar globe emblem was on my bed the month Nwamaka told us she was leaving. *Commonwealth Scholarships*. In future, I would think of that day with the ancillary mirth of my classmate Njoki's favourite statement: '"Commonwealth" – what is so common about the wealth? Should be called Association of Former Colonies.'

'I overheard a few people at the office talking about it so I asked some questions then stopped at the cyber cafe to check for the form online. I think you should apply,' my mother explained, pushing the pages towards me.

The results had been pasted on the notice board at the campus. It all seemed too mundane: months of sleepless nights, exacting dress-coded classes and unsparing lecturers, all for our names to be printed on these flimsy papers pinned to the corkboard, pins that would loosen with time, sheets that would get wet when rains fell.

'Is my name there? Can you see it?' Zina shouted, jumping up from beside me. The boards were crowded, students shoving their way to the front so they could trace their numbers and those of their friends with their fingertips, followed by shouts of joy or heads bowed in disappointment. 'If you've seen your result, move now, let others check theirs. Please!' someone shouted.

'Yes, move!' Zina supported, still stretching her neck. 'Ego, you're tall. Move forward and check for both of us. I can't see anything,' she said to me.

It both amazed and disconcerted me how resilient she was. One day she was in a hospital bed, pale and seemingly at death's door, and now she was bouncing up and down like it had all been a moment of shared hallucination. Aunty Ada had fought with her husband after Zina went home, a bitter and rancorous fight that had made Zina speculate that her parents might end their long-standing marriage.

But in the end, Uncle Uzondu caved and Zina's engagement was called off.

'I can't believe it. I don't even know what to do with myself now that I can do anything I want,' Zina effused.

Our names were listed in the second-class upper division, and I felt an auspicious elation that my life would not end up a total waste like my father had predicted. I could hear Emeka saying with a pert smile and an arched brow, 'Not bad for a girl that claims to have lost her brain.'

He was yet to email me since the party, and I wondered if his sister had told him I was there. If it was guilt that kept him from reaching out or if it had all been a ploy. But Emeka wasn't like that.

My mother continued, 'It's a very good opportunity,' she said. 'I think it would be good for you to go somewhere different for a while. Uncle Ikenna . . .' She paused like she always did whenever she spoke of him. 'Uncle Ikenna really enjoyed the time he spent studying in the UK; he always spoke of it very fondly. Of course, a lot must have changed since then, but the quality of education is still very high, and you'll have access to a much better system over there.'

I considered my mother's words and the possibility of leaving, then I pictured my life if I stayed, without the connections to lobby for the right jobs, without protection from the realities and wickedness of the country. The next day I went to the cyber cafe to look at schools, then I printed all the forms and instructions one after the other, determined not to leave anything out. At home, I filled them in painstakingly, first with pencil, then in pen once I was sure of the words.

In a packed hall, I took the IELTS test, bristling at having to take an exam to prove my knowledge of the only language I'd ever spoken.

'Come and apply with me,' I encouraged Zina.

'Please please please. School never tire you? I'm leaving law for you people, I'm going into acting,' she said. And I concluded that there was something about near death that had unshackled her, left her inimitably fearless.

The morning Nwamaka left, my mother sat on the edge of my bed as the sun came up, forming an orange globe through the reflection of my bedroom window. She looked nervous as she said, 'There's something I've been meaning to tell you.'

I waited, expecting the worst. She dug in the pocket of her dressing gown and pulled out a black box.

'Akin asked me to marry him before he left,' she said, handing it to me. Akin had been gone for weeks, had she hidden the box in her gown all this time? 'I wasn't sure of how and when to share, but I thought you should know.'

On her face, I read what she did not say: that she hoped for my support and approval, that she needed someone to say she was doing life right. And not for the first time, I felt like the parent in our relationship.

I opened the box and stared at the platinum band, the simple stone that sparkled where it hit the light. 'It's a beautiful ring. What did you say?'

A corner of her lips turned up. 'I said yes.'

'You're still married.'

She stared at her hands. 'I know. He said he'll wait till whenever your father gives the divorce.'

Just as he'd promised, my father had sent a letter stating explicitly that he now considered me dead to him. We'd filed a case against Pastor Kamsi but the courts were on strike due to nonpayment of allowances and Barrister Ogbu, Aunty Sally's lawyer, who was also handling my mother's divorce case, wasn't hopeful about the outcome. 'I'll be honest with you. Rape cases barely go anywhere in this country. In fact, since this country gained independence, we've had less than 50 convictions. And I'm told the church has hired a Senior Advocate of Nigeria to take on the case. It will be tough. But if you want to go ahead . . .'

'I like Akin,' I said to my mother. 'He makes you happy.'

That evening, Nwamaka's boxes were arranged by the door. She was a university student now, and like her twin, a few years from finishing if the strikes would allow.

'He's promised to pay for all my fees and everything else going forward so you don't have to worry about any of that,' she said to my mother. 'He'll also sign the divorce papers as soon as the courts open since your mind is already made up.'

Nkechinyere grabbed at a box and began to pull it towards their room. 'You can't do this. I thought we talked about it?'

Nwamaka wrestled the handle from her twin. 'We might

be twins but we're not joined at the hip. I'll live my life how I want it.'

My mother wept when she was gone, sobs so strangled, I called Akin to calm her.

'I failed, I failed as a mother,' she said over and over.

The acceptance tasted like sawdust in our mouths. My mother was yet to recover from Nwamaka's departure, and I could not muster any excitement at the prospect of leaving her behind.

'*Congratulations Nwakaego,*' it said.

'I'm not going,' I told her.

'I will not allow you to waste such an opportunity,' she said.

And so, I submitted the acceptance letter to the government office in charge of the scholarship applications to be included in my file, convinced I wouldn't even be invited for an interview.

The lead interviewer stared at my name and profile long and hard, then she asked questions I thought too simple for such a prestigious scholarship, and I wondered if she'd recognised my surname, if she knew my father somehow and would use it as leverage one day to seek a favour from him. But the other interviewer seemed just as impressed. 'It was good to meet you Nwakaego, expect to hear from us soon,' he said.

We read the marriage announcement in the newspapers as we waited for the results, routinely scanning the pages of the dailies for a publication of the list.

Wedding bells are ringing in the households of Chief Dr Chigozie Azubuike and Chief Olanipekun Badmus as their children Nwamaka Azubuike and Olufela Badmus prepare to tie the knot. The much-anticipated event is expected to take place later this year and will be graced by the crème de la crème of society.

A thick envelope was delivered to our doorstep later that week – I'd gotten the scholarship. Akin drove me to the passport office to get my picture and biometrics taken. I applied for a visa, fearful that I'd be rejected, but the sandy-haired interviewer informed me I could come pick up my passport in three weeks.

Aunty Sally organised a send-off party; Aunty Ada and Sister Bolatito insisted on handling the cooking.

My mother's brothers presented me with a well-padded envelope. 'You're only the second person from our family to go to *obodo oyinbo* to study, we're very proud of you. Represent us well, you hear?' Uncle Kelechi said on their behalf, pushing it between my fingers.

At the airport, my mother cried, until Nkechi told her, 'You'll see her again; she's not dying.'

Before I walked towards the check-in point, my mother shoved an envelope in my handbag.

'I have an allowance,' I protested, realising it was more than she could afford.

She shook her head and zipped the bag closed. 'I'm your mother. It's what I'm supposed to do.'

At Oxford, we cycled: to class, to the store, to the city centre, to the weekly open marketplace.

'The city's mascot should be a cycling monkey,' Njoki said even though she refused to buy a bicycle. 'A car will blow its horn and I will panic and fall down. God forbid.'

We were the only black Africans in our class. On the very first day of the programme, the Dean had boasted about how

Africans made up five percent of the set, an increase from two percent the previous year, but a majority of the *Africans* had turned out to be white South Africans who rarely, if ever, associated with the darker of our collective. Most times, we could barely tell them apart from the other foreigners, until they opened their mouths to speak.

'We're nothing but mere statistics, but at least we can benefit from it,' Njoki joked at the African Society cookout, and everyone laughed.

At Oxford, tradition was upheld in its most historic form – the sub fusc at exams, the physical submission of printed assignments at the exams school, weekly debates at the Union, college dinners in vaulted halls with pictures of dead benefactors hanging. The ancient city was the school and the school was the city, or so we were told.

In my first days there, I did not have friends, and I blamed this on the fact that I hated drinking, the acrid aftertaste and burning sensation as the alcohol passed from mouth to gut. If there was anything graduate students loved to do, it was drink; restaurant hopping, weekend pub crawls, house parties, there seemed to be a constant flow of alcohol. In the beginning, I tagged along, desperate to make the most of my experience, then as the day waned into darkness and spirits heightened in bloodstreams, I discovered that I was the only one without the added sheen of humour alcohol provided, and as others guffawed at the stale jokes, I gaped at them, lonely in my mirthlessness.

There was also the problem of funds. For many students, Oxford was simply another stamp in the book, not a fragile lifeline to survival. Having parents that descended from old money, had links to Asian royalty and sat on the boards of multinationals meant there was always an exciting city to visit, a new restaurant that had just opened down the street, some competition with another school that required a trip. Their lives were free of the creases of scholarships, the limitations of allowances. I envied them their superior passports that did not require visas to move between borders, the ease with which they could travel through life.

An Indian classmate called Aarav asked why my English was so good. I stared at him for a long minute, feeling my accumulating frustration mount even higher. An American had already asked how I'd flown to England and if we had access to the internet back home; a professor had looked around the class for someone to answer his question, he'd stopped at my raised hand and my name tag, stared at the letters for mere seconds – what was so hard about pronouncing Ego? – and called on a girl named Jessica instead.

'You're Indian, right?' I asked.

'Yes?' He seemed confused by the line of my questioning.

'Then you should know we were colonised by the same country, and so of course I speak English. Don't they teach that in secondary schools in your country? At the very least, I know India gained its independence in 1947.'

People avoided me after that. I imagined Aarav going round whispering, 'You wouldn't believe what she said,' and so kept to myself, hiding in my college room.

Njoki sought me out after a lecture. 'So you're the one that put that Aarav in his place. It's great to officially meet you,' she said.

I looked around, unsure of who she was speaking to.

Njoki continued, 'I can understand the whites, even the snooty white South Africans with their Afrikaans accent, but how can Asians join them to look down on us? Are we not suffering racism together?'

She laughed, and I thought her laughter brash; it reminded me of Zina. Later she would tell me, 'I've been gauging you from afar. For a while, I thought you were one of those fake Africans that like to lounge in the sun during summer like they're looking for a tan and talk about how warm it is.'

Through Njoki, I discovered the African Society and the constant battle between the Nigerians and black South Africans for supremacy, the Congolese students and their winding flexible waists, the monthly cookouts where the Ghanaians insisted on cooking jollof rice with basmati rice. Once, a Namibian tried to invite a white South African student in the African Studies department to the cookout.

'Please bring out your phone,' Chukwuka, the society president said to him when he informed us. 'It's not too late, uninvite her before she gets here. Blacks only!'

In our gatherings, we had unrestricted freedom to discuss the culture shock we'd experienced without the veneer of politeness.

'I must say I admire how they've managed to maintain so many old structures; some of these buildings are almost a thousand years old,' Sylvester, the Namibian, said.

'Yes, they preserved theirs while going everywhere to destroy others', Njoki retorted.

Time passed quickly as the chilly autumn turned into sunless dreary winter that hurriedly transitioned into murky spring and sweltering summer.

Njoki complained about how ill equipped the buildings were for the change in weather. 'Heaters everywhere, and not a single air conditioner in the rooms. I have to open my window and invite insects in because I'm sweating.'

Soon we were conducting research for our final thesis and

spending hours in supervisors' offices, and even more time in the career counsellor's office seeking help with our job searches. I admired the utility of the careers office, the actual support it provided, unlike the one during my undergraduate years where the officer had reviewed curriculum vitaes with an ennui that said she'd only taken the role to avoid unemployment herself.

On the day we wore sub fusc for the last time, Njoki pulled at her neck ties and said wistfully, 'You know, I'll miss this thing.'

At the ceremony, my mother clapped the loudest when my name was called, Akin's ring blinking on her finger. Afterwards, people commented on what a handsome couple my 'parents' were.

18

Breathless

The year 2015 opened with a flourish: new client jobs, net-working dinners and talks of possible promotion. But the trip to America had snuffed the wind out of life and a new inextinguishable longing settled in its place, driving my pace at work.

It was ineffable, even to me, exactly what I longed for. I'd done well for myself – for an immigrant at least – with a job in the Square Mile (*and* in the Magic Circle of law firms), an annual six-figure salary and an apartment situated in Canary Wharf. It was more than many could hope for. And yet my days were shadowed by gnawing discontent.

Sensing the disequilibrium in my soul, Eriife sent articles florid with stories of young professionals and artists who'd moved back home and found purpose and success. 'This could be you,' each message said, and yet I didn't want it to be me, at least not yet, I told her. But afterwards, I searched their names on social media and snuffed around their Instagram pages, imagining myself in their place, picturing life in a city where the sun did not just shine, it burned.

Zina thought otherwise. 'Don't mind Eriife and her pol-itician tongue. This country is hard; have you forgotten so soon? No amount of money can protect you from the non-sense, one day you'll be sick and you'll wish you were in a country with decent healthcare.'

I shopped often, spending money I'd once hoarded and scrimped to send home to my mother before she'd informed me she was moving to America with Akin.

'Nkechi has a job now and has moved to her own flat. Who will spend all this money you're sending? Please keep some for yourself,' she'd said then. And still I'd felt an annoy-ance that rankled at her decision, a possessiveness over her person. She was my mother before she was Akin's wife; their wedding was a simple affair at the marriage registry at Ikoyi. Now we'd formed a new bond exchanging stories of racist aggressions we faced.

'You should have heard the way she called out the bill! Is it because of my accent? Does being African automatically make us poor?' she said. And I wanted to remind her that not too long ago, we were that: poor.

I no longer glanced at the shop attendants that tailed my movement with wry amusement. It had first happened at Oxford, in my very first week, on the day I'd stopped by a shop for a thicker sweater. I'd spent a few minutes browsing, working the currency conversions in my head, when I'd noticed a blonde shadow. I'd read about it on online forums and immigrant chat rooms – *prepare to be followed around any shop you visit,* they said – and I'd scoffed. To experience it so ineluctably was jarring. I'd marched up to the attendant and pulled out one of the shiny 50 pound notes my mother had tucked in my bag at the airport and said, 'Where is your counter? I'd like to pay for this sweater,' and taken satisfaction in watching her face turn beet red. With time, I'd begun to view them with tolerant amusement.

Now they no longer amused me. I thought of Njoki who used to say, 'Those working-class teenagers steal more than any of us, but how would they notice when they're too busy following us around like policemen and looking at our notes under lights like they work at the Bank of England? Who would come to their country if ours were working properly? Such cold people, you greet them and they answer with their nose.' I thought of calling her – it had been a while since we'd spoken – to hear her speak of colonial theory and laugh at her jokes. But I worried she would no longer be interested in such conversations, too far removed from the problems of blackness in a foreign land.

Braids were the reason Njoki had returned to her country. 'Listen, you're already at a disadvantage with your accent and immigration status. You have to try to get in first, then once you're comfortable, you can do whatever hairstyle you like,' I advised her, but she refused to take out her braids in favour of a weave-on for job interviews. 'Why should I pretend to be someone else? You think I've not noticed how you've started twisting your tongue for these people?' she protested.

'It's not being someone else; it's being smart. I'm still me. I'll always be Nigerian inside,' I said.

'Well, I want to be Kenyan outside,' Njoki said.

The interviews had all returned the same result: polite rejection. 'Even their rejections are very British,' she joked. Still, I sensed a plaintive sadness at their refusal to hire her, an Oxford graduate.

She bought a plane ticket to Nairobi the day my job offer came; a small role to build experience so I could apply for a trainee solicitor position.

'Why not come stay with me? We can get a small apartment and you'll look for a job while I work, and when you get a job, you can pay me your half of the rent,' I proposed.

'Nah, I think the ancestors are calling me back to the fatherland. I'll be better off there anyways,' she said. 'This place was already driving me mad.'

We kept in touch via Facebook and intermittent phone calls but our friendship had begun to feel like a distant waning thing. In her last uploaded picture, she was laughing with a dark-skinned man, a man she hadn't told me about.

The outfits were ill-suited for the coming weather I knew, the tops sleeveless and loose fitting, the dresses cropped and lightweight cotton. Still, I shopped, saying to myself that I was taking advantage of the discounts, and not the yearning that knocked insistently. The worst of winter was imminent and yet I shopped for the sun.

Like the Hydra with its multiple heads, other forms of loneliness emerged with a central character at their fore: Emeka. He came to me in dreams, dreams so poignant and lucid that when I eventually opened my eyes, they left me feeling adrift, unsure of reality.

In the middle of the erratic winter that opened the new year, a radio station played Shayne Ward's 'Breathless' and the Uber driver turned the volume up. *'Now that's it for Throwback Thursday, shout out to Shayne Ward. Hope you lovers out there enjoyed it,'* the radio host sounded out as the final strings of the song died and I realised I'd stopped typing as the song played.

In my apartment that night, I allowed myself to think of him, the most I'd obliged myself in a long time. Opening Facebook, I searched for his profile, scrolling past multiple

Daniels and Chukwuemeka Igwes – he'd been right, his name was indeed common – until I stumbled on a thumbnail that resembled the person I knew. *One mutual friend,* the subtext underneath said. I clicked on it and Zina's name popped up.

I scouted the picture folder for signs of a wife or girlfriend and found only pictures of him smiling in the sun on holiday, at tech conferences and with t-shirted colleagues all wearing the logo of his startup. He'd grown a beard and it added a ruggedness to his looks I liked. I wondered if he'd ever visited the UK and thought of calling Zina to ask for her password so I could view pictures only available to friends, then I imagined her reaction and thought better of it.

I'd never told Zina but I'd dated in my first year in London. A proper working-class English boy named George that Njoki – who I'd never told about Emeka – had described as 'so pale!' when I sent her his pictures.

'He likes West Indian cuisine, and reggae music and afro pop,' I'd said in his defence.

We'd met at a work conference, and for weeks, flirted off and on, until I agreed to go on a date. He kissed me that evening in the car, his tongue darting about my mouth with purpose, and I enjoyed it, inviting him upstairs to my apartment. There, we continued, our hands rushing up our clothing until he reached for the edge of my underwear and my body turned solid.

We never spoke after that, and every now and then, I thought of calling him to offer an explanation. But how did you say, *'I was raped'*?

Change was coming; Eriife was sure of it.

'Ego, the people are tired. They're ready for real change, and we will bring it,' she said.

In English politics, the left was the 'progressive' side, the side that wanted a more socialistic approach to governance, feeding programmes and general healthcare, and the right favoured the capitalistic approach, staunch proponents of trickle-down economics and retention of systems and 'values' as they were. Each side considered themselves *right*, and every social issue and figure was politicised along these lines. In the digital sphere, it was an interminable battle to see who could one-up the other, who could be in creation of the most raucous cacophony; there was no nuance, no complexity. There was only right and wrong, and the other side was always definitely wrong.

Back home, our problems were more elemental – there was the kleptomaniacal ruling class, and there were the people. And it reflected in our daily language, in considerations of duty to self and country. It wasn't about capitalism or socialism; it was about those who greedily pocketed the nation's coffers, who implemented policies to ensure monopolistic advantage for their cronies and utilised institutions to pursue political grievances, who exhibited a blatant disregard for the rule of law.

And so, when people tried to initiate conversations along the translated Western political lines, I found it absurd. There was no 'service'; resignations were an anomaly. There was *us*, and there was *them*. And there were those willing to sacrifice their mothers to join *them*. Over time, especially as the parliamentary election results were announced in favour of the conservative party, I'd come to wonder if it was the same in England as it was in Nigeria, albeit in a less obvious form.

But Eriife assured me that it wasn't like previous times. Rising insecurity in northern states and numerous accounts of corruption amidst rampant and abject poverty had unsettled the people, made them hungry for different. Campaigns were in full swing and camps of the two main political parties formed hard lines. Then the parties declared their candidates.

'I thought you said people wanted change?' I asked Eriife. 'How can your party declare a former military dictator as a candidate, the same man that put my father behind bars in the '80s?'

'It's been thirty years, Ego. Are you going to hold that grudge for so long? He's a refined democrat now. This is politics, we had to go with someone that can canvass support for us in certain parts of the country. Read our manifesto; we're for the people. Hope you're seriously thinking about my proposal, come home. We're winning this,' she said. She forwarded a link to me when the call ended. A multinational was seeking a Chief Legal Officer. Her message said:

> Send me your CV, I promised them that I have the right candidate for the role. See how much they're willing to pay you. In dollars! As an expatriate, they'll cover your living expenses, and the cost of living is lower here and you won't be paying all the multiple taxes over there. You better not ignore me.

I sent my resume to satisfy the agitation inside.

I ran into Emeka's aunt on Kensington High Street, shopping bags brimming with clothes and shoes caught tightly between her fingers. I'd met her once, on a Sunday afternoon in Emeka's parents' living room, and I thought then, as I did now, that she did not look like a pastor's sister. Her skirts rode up her legs, brushing the top of thigh-high boots, and multiple gold pieces were arranged in a tower along her neck. Her makeup was heavy handed, her lipstick a red that was intended to shock.

'She's a proper rebel that one,' Emeka had said then.

'Nwakaego,' she called from behind as we passed each other. I hadn't heard my name pronounced properly in England in years. I turned.

'*Ehen!* I thought it was you. Longest time! It's me, Emeka's Aunty Ngozi.'

We chatted briefly. She was in London on holiday with her newest husband; she had the glow of a newlywed. Before she left, she pulled a card from her bag and jotted down two phone numbers.

'That's my hotel. I'm leaving on Sunday, but you can stop by any time before then. The first number is mine, I'm roaming so you should be able to reach me. The second is Emeka's, that boy has refused to marry or date for years now, please call him. I don't know why you broke up, but Emeka is a man now, he's more mature, I'm sure you can work it out.'

They never told her.

At home, I logged into my old email address and dug beyond the newsletters and alumni emails for the last email I'd received before I left Nigeria, one I hadn't opened since the first time I read it:

Dear Nwakaego,

Your mother told me that you're leaving Nigeria soon. Please don't be annoyed with her. I've been pestering her for a while now; I even stopped by her office and waited till she was closing for the day. You're so lucky to have her, she's wonderful.

I know what my mother did. I've been silent all this

while because I know what she did and I had no idea how to fix this without sounding like I'm making excuses. So instead, I decided to write to say how sorry I am.

I'm so sorry, Ego. I should have known that something wasn't right when she asked me to invite you to her party. I was so eager, so hopeful for her to believe you, to believe me that you wouldn't lie that I excitedly brought the card to your door. Please believe me when I say I had no idea he would be there that day, I would never do that to you, ever.

I'm sorry I wasn't there that day, I'm sorry I couldn't protect you better. I should have believed you when you said there was something wrong about him, I shouldn't have let you keep working with him, I should have fought harder against the church establishment, I should have done something.

I want you to know how happy and proud I am of you that you got this scholarship. Not bad for a girl that claims she lost her brain. I've always believed you were a star, that was all I saw when I saw you – a star much too bright for this place.

I don't think I have any right to say this, but I love you. The words seem so useless because I should have done better. I'm not asking you to forgive me, I understand why you can't. Instead, I'll hold out hope that in another life, in another time, we will meet again and then I'll be able to show you just how much you mean to me.

Yours always,

E.

I'd lived in the UK long enough to qualify for a citizenship application.

'You better not return to this country as a Nigerian,' Zina warned me. And so I applied for British citizenship, compiling the documents needed to be considered. As I pressed the submit button on the portal, I immediately questioned my decision to do so. I couldn't say I loved the United Kingdom; wasn't one supposed to love the country whose citizenship one sought? It had given me a new lease on life, but I felt no earnest devotion when I saw the flag or when the anthem was played. Perhaps I did not love Nigeria either; I hadn't chosen to be born there. It was a strange place to be in; one of emotional statelessness.

The offer for the Chief Legal Officer role came, and when I turned it down, they raised the pay offer; Eriife had informed them I was on the verge of a different citizenship.

I handed in my resignation the week the new Nigerian government was sworn in. Eriife posted pictures in our group chat at Eagle Square wearing the party's chosen colours and waving the flag.

'*I belong to everybody and I belong to nobody*,' the former dictator announced in a lauded speech.

'See, I told you he was reformed,' Eriife wrote.

'Mtchew,' Zina wrote.

'Oh my God, why? Did you get another job?' Ceri asked, her voice high with panic, when I informed her of my decision.

I thought about how to explain my decision in a way that she would understand. Eventually, I settled on, 'I'm going home.' Then we both cried into our coffee. On my final day at work, Anna smiled, happy to be rid of my discomfiting presence and Rayan said, 'You're making a mistake. Where else would you find the opportunities you have in this country?'

Ceri organised a send-off; a party at her house where

afrobeats boomed endlessly from the speakers until I was forced to approach the DJ – a cheeky Welsh lad – to congratulate him on a job well done.

Rodney stood in a corner, his eyes studiously tracking my every movement like I was a specimen he wished to understand. He said, 'You could always change your mind.' I knew he was referring to more than my decision to move back home.

I shopped, consciously this time, for Nkechi, Zina and Aunty Ada, Eriife and her family, for Nwamaka and her two children. My sister now lived the life my mother once did, appearing in magazines for parties and events only the rich attended. I'd found out about her children from a Nigerian blog.

I attended church the weekend after my British passport came in the post; I never wanted it to be said that I'd never attended church while I was there. Leaving Nigeria had made me less religious; Njoki said it was because back home, we relied on God for things other more responsible governments provided for their citizens. Instead, I hungered for a different kind of God – a companion and a friend.

The night before my flight to Lagos, I sat in a corner of the Sichuanese restaurant waiting to order *dan dan mian*. 'Very spicy,' the owner said with a blinding smile and a thumbs up before I could. Then I watched her move to the next table – a white couple – and call for her son to translate after several attempts to take down their order.

At the door, she said, 'See you soon!' And I wanted to say, 'Not soon – I'm leaving. I'm going home.' But I did not know how.

In my room, I opened the only item I was yet to pack – my

laptop – and clicked on the tab I'd left open since I'd first opened it; a source of inspiration as I taped boxes to be shipped and folded blouses into veritable squares. Then I clicked *Reply*.

2

ZINA

Friendship is a sheltering tree

SAMUEL TAYLOR COLERIDGE

19

Country

Nwakaego loved to use run-on sentences where a simple word would do; a true lawyer that one. That morning, the sky still a drab overcast of grey, my phone vibrated on the nightstand by my bedside. I rolled over to pick it up. A WhatsApp message: *'I'm coming home.'*

I was jolted fully awake. Ignoring the rhythmic snores beside me, I pushed my way out of bed and walked over to the veranda, then I dialled the international number underneath her name.

Three years had passed since we'd last seen each other at the Heathrow terminal. Ego's years abroad had barely changed her, although there was a sophistication and confidence that now clung to her like the high-end clothes she wore. Later, I would realise it was success.

Over pricey coffee and dainty pastries – her treat – we'd caught up; there were things that couldn't be said over the phone.

'Remember that guy that lived in the flat beside your mother's? The one that had a new girl over every day? Well, he got a government appointment and now owns a flat in Ikoyi,' I told her.

'Is that so?' she responded, eyes wide as she wiped sugar from her lips with a napkin. Years back, she would have used her tongue.

The glass walls of her flat offered an uninterrupted view of the city. And yet she clicked the curtains closed as we arrived, dragging my bags towards a room where she said with a sardonic smile, 'I got a two-bedroom in case anyone came to visit, but they never come.'

'Ego, this is really nice, you've done so well for yourself,' I remarked, looking round at the expansive space and elegant furniture, aware that I sounded almost in awe. Did I appear local and unrefined?

She shrugged dismissively. 'They say those of us abroad wash dead bodies to survive. Well, mine is paying off.'

Later, she said, 'Some of our people here act like we didn't all arrive by the same plane; they think they are better than others.'

'Well, some came by boat,' I joked.

'Don't joke. That's an actual crisis,' Ego reprimanded. The old Ego would have laughed; if there was anything we Nigerians did, it was laugh at the most morbid of situations. How else would we survive? But this new Ego was more socially sensitive, more aware of appropriateness and correctness.

I thought her well settled in her new life. In the beginning, she'd spent her money on phone cards, expressing her awe at every new discovery: *'Would you believe I have access to free proper health care over here? And I'm not even a citizen o; the lecturer told us to call him Adam, how can I call someone older than my father by his name?'*

But she'd lost that sheen of excitement and naivety.

'You're one of them now, a proper Britico,' I'd told her that day.

'Hello?' Ego answered.

'You're serious,' I said, my voice gruff. It wasn't a question. The simplicity of her words held only one meaning – she would have carefully pondered over the decision for months. Ego wasn't like me; she didn't just jump into the deep end.

'You're just waking up? Zinachukwu, your mates are already searching for their daily bread.'

I hissed. 'I was on set till 3am this morning, this woman. Or you've forgotten not all of us work a nine to five? And don't change the subject.'

'Oh,' she said.

'Yes, *oh*. Who sends that sort of message first thing in the morning like this? *"I'm coming home."* Are you Jesus Christ?'

She laughed. 'I've forgotten how cranky you are in the morning. I didn't know what else to say and how else to say it and I wanted you to know.'

I sighed. 'Why?' I asked, stating the real cause of my frustration.

'Why? I can't stay here forever, it's not my country.'

'My dear as long as you live there, it's your country. Did we ask to be born here? Did we even create this country? Some people came and merged us together and created borders between tribes and called us a country and now we have a passport. My friend from Lagos has relatives in Cotonou across the border. You've been there long enough to apply for citizenship, that should be your primary focus now; when is your red passport is arriving? Not *"I'm coming home"*. To do what? When?'

'I have a job,' she said. 'It's a senior legal position at a multinational – chief legal officer actually – I just accepted their offer. I don't have to start until September, so in a few months.'

'You purposely didn't tell me you were applying. I would have told you to not bother. I smell Eriife's handiwork all over this. I've told you to stop listening to her politician speak. This place is a fucking hell hole.'

'I know it isn't all roses. You know me, I wouldn't make such a decision lightly.'

I knew her – it was why I knew I couldn't change her mind. 'Is it because of *him?*'

'Who?' she said, feigning ignorance.

'You know who I'm talking about. *Him.* Are you coming back for him? Ego, you should never make life-changing decisions for a man, you of all people should know that.'

She sighed. 'It's not because of him. I miss home. I'm lonely here. You say this is my country but it doesn't feel like it. I don't even feel welcome here. I miss the food, the music, the people. I miss how much concern we show for one another. Here, everyone minds their business. I could die in my apartment tomorrow and no one would know for days. I can't continue to live like this. You were the one who said I shouldn't throw the best years of my life away.'

I felt tears gather in my eyes and leaned over the railings. 'Ego, please. Have you forgotten what this place is like? You've forgotten what they did to you?'

Puffing smoke from my lips, I observed the clouds disperse into contours of bright blue, an array of pastels splintering through. My mood was indisputably grey after the call. From the veranda, I could see the shanty towns that sat on wooden stilts on the Lagoon that bordered the Island. I'd spent my last Christmas there, distributing packs of food and drinks, watching half-naked bony children man boats with sticks, jarred by the reality of such dire poverty adjacent to the most immense Nigerian wealth.

I considered opening a bottle of wine. *It's too early*, I thought. The gateman staggered out of his room then, a plastic bowl in hand, and pulled at the gate latch. A few minutes later, he returned with a full plate of steaming beans. I was reminded of our most recent estate association meeting.

'Our main agenda today is discussing a worrying phenomenon that has come to our attention,' the council chairman said. 'Whereas this area of Lagos used to be for people like us who can afford to create our own haven within this city, recently, we've noticed a rising number of shanties and structures, selling one thing or the other on our streets, and miscreants lurking. How long before these people invite criminals into our homes?'

Unconsciously, I laughed.

'Yes, Miss Zina, do you have something you'd like to share with us?' the chairman said.

I straightened. They wanted me to say something, so I did. 'You live in the poverty capital of the world and you don't expect to see poor people? Do you stand on your verandas? Listen, I'm not saying this isn't an issue that should be discussed, but let's be honest here, how much do you pay your gatemen and live-in workers? Where do you think they purchase the food they eat? Or the minor items they need without disappearing long enough for you to notice or discomfort you somehow? Let's be serious.'

Behind me, I heard a ruffle of sheets and feet pattering. Then the hum of an electric kettle boiling. Minutes later, Halil walked onto the veranda, clutching two mugs. He extended one in my direction and planted a peck on my cheek as he murmured good morning.

'What's wrong?' he asked. 'You don't smoke so early in the morning except when you're – how do they say it – upset.'

I wanted to tell him he hadn't known me long enough to make such a claim, but it felt unfair to transfer my aggression, so instead I said, 'My friend Ego, the one in the UK, she's coming back.'

He frowned, and I thought the ruffled curls at his forehead gave him a boyish look. 'Isn't that good news?'

'She's not visiting, she's moving.'

I was yet to tell Ego about him, this Turkish man with boyish curls I'd met at a cafe on a day off. Filming for a picture had just concluded and I'd strolled into a posh café – the kind with expatriate customers and white owners that switched up menus daily, somewhere I wouldn't be mistaken for a character I'd played. I felt, rather than saw, a pair of eyes attach themselves to me as I sat at a table. Their owner: a man pale enough that I knew he was foreign but tanned enough that I knew he wasn't the usual *white*. In Nigeria, there were different types of white people: the Americans and Northwestern Europeans, usually employees of oil companies and large multinationals, and the others. 'Those ones are stingy, they won't give you anything, because they don't have that much themselves,' my friend Tari – short for Ayebatari – always said. Eventually the man approached my table and politely asked to take the seat opposite. His eyes were an unusual shade of green.

He ran a furniture company – Halil Furnitures and Fittings – having come to Nigeria to seek his fortune after years of trying to make it as an architect in Turkey. A friend who owned a business in Nigeria had mentioned the opportunity and he'd taken a leap. Now, he serviced contracts for government institutions and homes; everyone knew Turkish furniture was good. Or was it his accent and olive skin? Regardless, he sat a step higher up the social ladder than most Nigerians.

'You seem to like tea. You should come to my place, I have a whole *err* collection of Turkish tea you should try out,' Halil said to me that first day.

In his apartment that mirrored a capsule from another country, he ran his hands down my arms as the water boiled, murmuring against my neck in splintered English. Then I said no and removed his arms. And for a moment, it seemed he'd never considered the possibility of my saying no, or perhaps no other woman had said no to him before.

We drank the tea in awkward silence that was sporadically broken by Halil's attempts at conversation – stories of his grandmother who made Turkish sweets, his siblings and the mountains back home.

At the door, he apologised and asked me to come again.

Zino called as I sat in traffic at the Lekki toll gate. At different points in the road, tar had already started to disintegrate but we continued to pay the toll, for what exactly, I wasn't sure. I handed a note – the most battered I could find – to the attendant and moved forward to join the rest of the traffic.

At the junction that faced the grand Oriental Hotel, a beat-up Toyota swerved into my lane, barely missing my bumper, and I rolled down my glass to give him a piece of my mind.

'Madam, look where you're going now!' he shouted. His windows were already down, the AC of his car probably in need of a mechanic.

'You're a fool. Go and learn how to drive!'

'*Waka*. All these women wey no sabi drive, who buy you this motor sef?'

My phone rang then. 'If you want to die, go and die in your house, don't endanger others,' I screamed as I clicked on the screen of my dashboard. My eyes connected with an image of myself on a billboard ahead and I quickly wound up my glass.

Zino was laughing.

'What's funny?' I growled.

He laughed even harder.

'If you called to laugh, I'm not in the mood.'

'You're lucky we don't have proper paparazzi in this country. You would have ended up on some pages today.'

I hissed. 'Paparazzi *ko*. Who has fuel to chase anybody about in this economy? Anyways, we still have those blogs.' The traffic light at the next junction stopped us.

'Yes, but someone has to record or take a picture to send to them, and to be honest we just don't care as much as they do over there. Our mentality is: yes, you're a celebrity, and so?'

'Maybe when we finally have 24/7 electricity,' I quipped.

He laughed.

'I know you didn't call me to philosophise about our paparazzi culture. So what's up? Talk to me,' I said.

'I got wind of a new project coming up in a few months. It seems like the sort of thing you'd be interested in; different storyline and everything. I like what I see so far and I'm thinking of putting money down, maybe get the director to shoot some scenes in the Western Cape. Where are you headed now? Come to mine, let's discuss.'

My ears perked up. 'I have a meeting with a director but I'll come over once I'm done.'

'Hmm,' Zino grunted. 'Be careful, many of these people are not straightforward.'

It was my turn to laugh. 'Zino abeg come and be going. You're talking to me, remember? I'm not exactly a new flower in this business.'

'Zinachukwu, the ying to my yang,' Zino greeted me at his doorstep, pulling me into an embrace. He always said it was no coincidence that I was Zina and he was Zino; destined to accompany each other from birth, even though he was ten years my senior.

'Erezino, my love,' I responded, tightening my arms; Zino gave the best hugs.

Zino's house was a masterclass in interior decoration, an analogy for unbridled sensuality: the dark walls, velvets and hanging lights, the abstract paintings and sculptures. But everything about Zino was sensual: his body sculpted and lean, his manicured hands branded by a gold signet ring, his clothes tailored to a crisp fit, pedicured feet covered in Italian leather.

'He's gay,' another actress whispered to me during a production. A blog had carried the gossip but blogs carried gossip about everyone; there were rumours about me floating around that I never bothered to acknowledge.

But I could see why many would assume Zino was gay. In our decade of friendship, I'd never known him to have a girlfriend or discuss an attraction to anyone.

'So is it true?' the actress asked me.

'Is what true?' I responded.

'Is he, you know . . . ?' she demonstrated with her eyes. 'I know you're his friend.'

'I don't know,' I said truthfully. She raised a brow, indicating her disbelief. 'I don't think it's any of our business, to be honest,' I added.

In 2014, after the Same Sex Marriage (Prohibition) Act was passed, we'd discussed the legislation over a bottle of Antinori Tignanello.

'It's the poor who will bear the consequences,' he'd said. 'The poor are subject to the rules; the rich do as they want, in silence of course.' He clucked his tongue. 'Quite unfortunate.'

'Ego is moving back here,' I told Zino when we were done discussing the potential project, a film focused on something outside the usual themes.

'You're unhappy about it.' He wasn't asking. 'Did she say why?'

'The usual: she misses home. But I know Eriife convinced her that this new government will change everything. She already has a job. She applied without telling me, can you believe that? Eriife's husband and the director of the company are friends, I've seen pictures of them online.'

'Did you watch the speech on democracy day?' Zino asked.

'No, why would I?'

It was the cause of our first major disagreement: he wanted to vote and I didn't. We'd participated in several protests together, lifting placards and screaming for the country we wanted, but in February that year, I refused to vote.

'Protests are a part of being Nigerian, the ballot is the ultimate protest,' Zino said.

'I don't like the current system – we both know that. It isn't ideal. But I will not be voting for a man that jailed my friend's father and turned him into a monster.'

'I'm not voting for him either. I was a teenager when he was head of state, my memory functions perfectly,' Zino countered.

'So you're voting to keep the status quo?'

'It's better than not voting. You vote for or against what you want or don't want. I'm disappointed in you.'

I'm disappointed in you. I blocked his number for a week.

The whole country had been taken up in the frenzy. *Change!* On Facebook, people documented epistles for and against the sitting party and its momentum-bearing opposition. Family members issued blocks and insults, old newspaper clippings and conspiracy theories drifted about. Hashtags trended. Elections are not won on social media, the incumbents responded. Detailed manifestos, promises upon promises. Change was coming.

'We're going to regret this,' Zino said as the results were announced.

20

Wild

Acting came easy when you'd spent the better part of your life playing a character. I was always going to be wild; Sister Teresa at my father's local diocese said I needed to be monitored or I would go astray. That had been the first sign of the incompatibility between my parents: doctrine. My father was a staunch Catholic, the sort who mouthed Latin phrases like *'Deo Ggratias'* and *'Anima Christi'* and my mother was a screaming, waving, jumping Pentecostal. In the early days, they reached a compromise: they would rotate attendance between each parish until the other one was convinced to abandon theirs to serve God the only right way he could be served.

Until Sister Teresa uttered that word about me. *Wild.* An animal to be caged. At seven, my breasts came, round pointy things jutting out of my blouse and my father agonised about my waning childhood, that I would mature too quickly, attracting men like scavenging animals to prey, and lose my flickering innocence. He measured my skirts with his eye, adept at calculating their length above and below the knee, turned off music with the slightest corrupting lexicon and locked the doors in his absence.

It was only appropriate that I inherited my father's fair skin and my mother's features – looking like neither of them and both of them at the same time. My father might have been the reincarnate of a Prussian sentry but it was in the shadow of my mother's person that I matured.

Adaugo Okafor née Omimi. The paragon of perfection. Adaugo with the flawless chestnut skin, sculpted oval-shaped face and teeth like coconut meat. Neither too tall nor too short; the perfect height for a woman. Adaugo who did as she was told without question or pause. Adaugo who had graduated at a ripe age with a good degree and returned home with an enterprising husband.

'Your mother never gave me any trouble, so please don't kill her for me,' my grandmother often said. And when my mother complained about our trouble, she murmured, 'You must have gotten it from your father's side.' But it was in the mirror that our likeness and disparities were most apparent, as my mother slid her fingers into hair that was just like hers – hair that made others question our heritage. Twisting the black thick strands into cornrows, she would stare at our faces side by side, and her eyes would ask how her offspring could be so unlike her.

My period arrived at nine, gushing like it could no longer bear to hold itself back, thickening my hips and widening my buttocks, staining my best skirts. My father mourned as if bereaved, then bundled me over to an all-girls Catholic boarding secondary school.

At St Mary's Girls, we put on a daily performance, for ourselves and for the benefit of others, the chapel our amphitheatre, 'Salve Regina' our chorus. At mass, we stood, we knelt, we stood again, the shawls on our heads inert, the hymnals in our fingers dogeared. For the Eucharist, we bowed our heads in contrived penitence and received the sacrament in acknowledgement of confessions we'd never given. Then we said *'Amen'* and became ourselves again.

We purported to believe the stories of Madam Koi Koi, the spectral woman who walked the halls of the hotels at night in clacking heels; we testified to have set eyes on her fiery red heels and the image of her other ghostly counterpart: the headless girl who made her own braids. We'd even heard the cries of the bush baby that positioned itself by the clothes hanging line at the edge of the undeveloped bush paths, but we'd grabbed our checkered house dresses and Sunday whites off the line and run in the opposite direction.

We played a sullen disinterest, revulsion even, for the opposite gender even though we were fascinated by sex: its meaning and the act. We stole biology textbooks from the senior girls and studied the drawings, then we read lascivious romance novels for the seriatim. In my third year, when I'd given up tearful scenes during visiting days, pleading with my father to withdraw me from St Mary's, a scandal broke and made its way to our parents: two soon-to-be-expelled students were caught in a bathroom doing God knows what. My father pulled me out at the end of the term before I could be tainted by their immorality – an unceremonial end to an act.

Troubled. That was how Pastor Matthew described me to my mother the Saturday afternoon I was found kissing a boy at the back of the church auditorium, his fingers deep in my bra. The devil had a strong hold of my life, the kind that goeth only by prayer and fasting. In the midst of the mothers the following Sunday, their tongues wagging in rapid fervent prayer, I knelt for deliverance and waited for God to move, to send a new spirit and change me.

Kanyinulia needed money again.

'Sisterly!' she shouted over the phone.

I rolled my eyes even though I was aware she couldn't see me. 'Nulia, you only call me "sisterly" when you need something.'

Her wardrobe was lined with the newest designer releases. On Instagram, she'd posted a picture of herself a week earlier, seated on the bonnet of a brand-new car with the caption: *'Work hard, God will do the rest. Glory be. #tearrubber #mercedez-benz.'* And yet she needed money.

My sister had inherited our mother's penchant for shopping. It was how my father had appeased her: a bag, a new pair of shoes, gold that glittered against her skin. And he would be absolved of all his wrong. He was ill-tempered, erratic even, not violent, not angry. Once, he'd smashed the blender my mother had purchased, accusing her of teaching her children to be lazy. For hours, she'd picked at the glass pieces with bleeding fingers, refusing our assistance. The next day he'd come home with cardboard boxes bearing the labels of her favourite brands, and she'd pulled at the seals with her taped fingers like a child on Christmas morning.

'Ahn-ahn, I can't greet my sister again?' Nulia joked.

'I'm not your only sister,' I reminded her.

Our parents had had us in quick succession – Zinachukwu, Urenna, Apunanwu, Jachinma, Sofuchi, Kanyinulia – until they'd landed on the treasure they sought: a son. Ifeadigo – *the light has come.*

'Well, you're my best sister,' she replied, her voice a lilting song.

I laughed. 'You sound just like Jamie,' I said, referring to her three-year-old son. Nulia. A baby that had a baby. 'I'm still not your only sister. Jachinma even has a supermarket. Allow me to have peace please.'

'Please now. You know you're the only one that understands me. Apunanwu doesn't even pick my calls, and she's earning in dollars, that stingy girl.'

It wasn't just Nulia's calls, Apunanwu no longer answered anyone's calls since she and her family moved to Canada. My mother said her children would grow up to be borderless, with no knowledge of self and home; they would pronounce their names like white people did.

Urenna, Jachinma and Sofuchi had formed a clique of wives who behaved like wives, posting pictures of their children's school parties and sports days with captions like, *'Congrats to my lovely daughter on completing Year 4'*, the others dropping heart and smile emojis underneath with their comments: *'It is the Lord's doing.'*

Then there was Nulia and me. My defiance had only served to strengthen my father's resolve. Initially, he'd acquiesced to my mother's tearful request after my return from the hospital that he allow us live our lives without the guillotine of an early arranged marriage over our heads. But just months later, he announced that he'd accepted a suitor for Urenna, then Jachimma, then Sofuchi and Nulia, citing me as a cautionary tale. The others had accepted their fate without contest. They were their mother's daughters; pliant, eager to prove they were unlike me, the disappointing first child. But Nulia showed up at my door when her turn came. 'Zina, please,' she pleaded, like I was her only hope, and for a while at least, I was.

With the aid of a police officer, they dragged her out of my home a week later, kicking and screaming and begging. 'You will not ruin her life like you ruined yours,' my mother said, her finger pointed at my face. I did not attend the wedding.

'Zina, please now. I promise, I'll spend better this time. I'll be more judicious,' Nulia begged.

'So you even know the word "judicious"?' I cackled. 'I saw your new car o. Or you think you're the only one that likes good things?'

'Zinaaaaaa. Pleeeeaaaasseeee.'

'Okay, what about your job? Where is your husband?' Her husband worked at a local bank as a marketing officer, slowly moving up the ranks. A steady hardworking Catholic man who provided for his family, grateful to have such a beautiful wife; the sort of man my father had chosen for all his children. Nulia treated him with stolid indifference, and I often wondered if she would have liked him more if she'd chosen him for herself.

'Why are you asking about him?' she asked.

'Is he not your husband?' I retorted.

'That's not why I called you. It's just a quick loan. I promise I'll pay it back.'

I hissed. 'You still haven't paid me back for the last time and you've bought a new car. Maybe next time I'll see a new house on your page.'

There were no pictures of her husband on her social media. Occasionally, she posted pictures of her son, but only on special days, like his birthday or the new year.

'Zina, please now.'

'What do you even need the money for?'

'I need to sort out some things, just a few gaps here and there. Please now Zina.'

'I'll think about it,' I responded.

I scrolled through her Instagram again after the call. There were several pictures of me, and of us together, glossy pictures at red carpet events, at promos and premieres, each caption clamorously vaunting. They said: see my sister the actress, don't we look alike, aren't we one? In them, I sensed a dissatisfaction at the simplicity of her life, an eagerness to live vicariously through mine.

As children, she'd been just as vocal declaring who she looked up to: '*I'm just like Sister Zina.*' I opened my bank app and entered a figure that was twice the amount she'd requested for transfer. It was the least I could do for having the life she'd wanted, for not doing enough to ensure she'd been able to live it.

It had begun as an escape, an ambition to be someone else, anyone but myself. But actors need co-stars, and so I'd recruited my sisters.

'Why am I always the daughter? I want to be the friend,' Nulia had complained.

'Because you're the youngest,' I explained.

'At least you're not the husband or boyfriend,' Jachinma quipped, rolling her eyes.

'You're the tallest, you took Daddy's height,' I said, defending my casting decision.

We always drank Coke, either real (stolen from the fridge when our mother wasn't looking) or imaginary bottles; we gulped Coke because that was what they did in the American movies. We said '*Oh my God*' to express shock and '*shit*' – pronounced 'shirt' – when we spilled our drinks; the drinks always spilled, it was how the Americans did it. Until my mother told us they drank water in America too, and that she would punish any child she caught calling the Lord's name in vain.

From romcoms, we drew inspiration for our acting – the swooning, the music, the chance meetings and endings that sparkled. It was possible to exist in a world with effervescent magic.

'You're a natural,' the casting director said at the very first audition I attended. My parents had given me an ultimatum: find a job or get out of the house. My presence was too strong a reminder of a failure on their part. But the text I received weeks later indicated an interest in hiring me for anything other than the role I'd wanted.

'Isn't every industry like that? Men will take advantage once they hold any power over you. Plus you're very pretty, you should be used to it by now,' Eriife said when I told her what had happened.

But still, I refused to give up. Ego was at Oxford by then, but called often, asking how it was going. 'Very fine. Everything is going well, I read another script, another role came up,' I told her, my voice so shrill and full of false cheer, that it seemed to be another role I was playing. If she suspected any dishonesty on my part, she pretended not to notice.

'You're wasting your life,' my mother said, standing in the doorway of my room like a ghost in the early hours of the morning.

'Did I do something?' I asked. I'd only just woken up.

'"*Did I do something*"?' she mimicked. 'Every day you go out and return jobless. If you'd only listened to your father, you'd be married to a responsible man, you would have stability. But look at you, loafing about like a waste of space.'

I said nothing as her words pierced through. I'd learned that speaking only encouraged her to say more.

'You even have a law degree. Your father could have gotten you a job with a decent law firm after your marriage if you'd listened to him. Now what are you going to do? You really think you can be an actress just because you're fine? Are you the finest person to ever be born? Me, your mother, am I not beautiful? I was even more beautiful at your age. Did you ever see me abandon my responsibility to chase ridiculous ambitions? Who do you think you are?'

Beauty was a double-sided curse. It announced your presence, generated an unwanted buzz and desire within others that you had no control over; it created assumptions about your person, it meant you were hated for a face you didn't create, even by your own mother.

'The East is where everything is happening. Why not go there?' someone advised after another failed audition; a time before Lagos became a filmmaking hub.

At the back of the bus to Onitsha, I counted the only money I had, feeling hopeful. Ego had called the week I'd purchased the tickets. 'I had some extra this month so I sent you something. Go to Western Union with your ID card o, make sure you don't forget it,' she said. But I knew there was no extra money, she was sent a fixed sum every month as part of her scholarship arrangement.

'I don't need it,' I protested. 'How can you be sending me money from your scholarship allowance? Things are so expensive over there. Chioma said when she visited London with the savings from her business, she could barely buy anything because she kept converting to naira in her head.'

'Akin sent me something for my birthday, you know he earns in dollars,' she said.

'You're lying, your birthday isn't until next month,' I retorted.

'He sent it early.'

'Nwakaego, I don't need money!'

'That one is your business. I've sent it already, go and pick it up from Western Union.' She knew. She'd pretended not to know, but she did. I wondered if that was why I hadn't gotten any roles, if my acting was so poor that even my friend knew I was struggling.

The man at the Western Union counter stared at my ID card for a while, whether he was looking at my name or the caricature portrait, I wasn't sure. But eventually, he counted the naira equivalent to £500, shoved it in an envelope and handed it over.

21

Boundaries

We shot the final scenes of the movie in South Africa: a retelling of an old Nollywood movie about a group of con artists who stumble on illicit loot; a story of poverty and its desperations. Zino was eager to make it a memorable one, and having come on as an executive producer, he put forward the funds necessary to do so.

'I've been in the business long enough to spot a good project,' he said to me. 'We need to push the boundaries, tell more stories. Our people are incredibly talented, they just need the backing of entrepreneurs and the government out of their way.'

Zino's irrefutable passion for all things Nigerian irked and confounded me. The blue American passport kept secure in a safe box in his room and the bottomless funds in accounts across multiple banks meant he could leave, turn his back and never have to deal with the inanity, and yet not only did he stay, but he remained committed to creating an element of transformation one way or another. He was as unconvinced as I was convinced that the country was irredeemable. At the airport, they checked his passport quickly, respectfully, while I was subjected to inquisitorial questioning.

'If all of us left, who would stay to fix things for the millions who can't afford to go?' he often said. I concluded he had a penchant for fixing things, the same way he'd pulled me back from the edge at the start of our friendship.

In Onitsha, I'd slept in boarding houses with peeling walls, rats that scurried at night, scavenging for their next meal, munching on the skin of human feet when they couldn't find it. The bathrooms had no running water and so we depended on the filmy water that rose in the well at the back of the compound; we killed the earthworms that slithered up the drain with salt and shouted for whoever was behind the broken door to finish quickly so others could bathe.

'Do you know anybody here? Who sent you?' one of the casting directors asked at the first location I tried. His eyes moved up and down my frame, settling meaningfully on my hips.

'She's a fine girl *sha*,' his counterpart commented. To me, he asked, 'What's your name again?', shuffling through the papers in front of him. 'You're okay, still new, but let's see.'

For my first role, I was paid twenty thousand naira, barely enough to cover rent for a decent room. I spent the money on food and new shoes; the soles of every pair I owned had been eaten in by the tar of the streets I'd trudged. The next role paid just ten thousand naira more, and the next. A director recommended me to another director, and I played a role that lasted more than ten minutes on screen; I was paid eighty thousand naira.

It was how I lived for a year, role to role, side job to side job, avoiding the ingratiating leers and surreptitious taps, the spoken and unspoken requests and suggestions, unwilling to return to my parents, defeated and at their mercy. Until one day, at the edge of the River Niger, I met Zino, and it was only then that my life truly changed.

In the Witteberg mountains of the Western Cape, we taped the adrenaline-packed car chase scenes, and exchanged fire between warring gangs.

'This is what I'm talking about!' the director said from behind the screen. Zino sat beside the director, cross-legged and expressionless, half of his face covered by oversized dark glasses. He was always hands-on with his projects.

We took a trip to Mossel Bay for the skydiving scenes.

'Ready?' the instructor asked as the door opened, filling the plane with a rush of cold wind.

I smiled. 'It's what I do.'

His brows creased in confusion.

'Live on the edge,' I clarified.

On our final night in South Africa, a team dinner was held in the hotel restaurant to celebrate the success of the shoot. I stayed in my room to video call Ego. She'd booked her flight, some of the boxes she'd shipped ahead had already arrived at my house. I'd given up on convincing her not to come back, and now our conversations focused on concrete plans for her return.

Her tweets gave no indication of the life-changing decision she'd made:

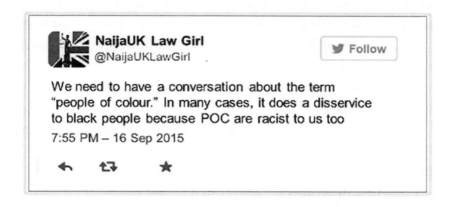

NaijaUK Law Girl
@NaijaUKLawGirl

Follow

We need to have a conversation about the term "people of colour." In many cases, it does a disservice to black people because POC are racist to us too

7:55 PM – 16 Sep 2015

I wondered if someone had said or done something racist to her. Through her, I'd come to understand what it was like to discover what it meant to be black. In Nigeria, our prejudices were tribal, amplified by decades of colonial-forced cohabitation.

There was a knock at my door: Zino, wearing a fashionable belted two-piece and holding a bottle of champagne in one hand, two flutes in the other.

'I was told you didn't join the party,' he said as I let him in. 'So I came to make sure you weren't moping about.'

Locking the door behind him, I said, 'I had a call with Ego.'

'Oh, I see. That's lovely. When does she arrive?' He settled in an armchair.

'In two weeks,' I replied, plopping on the bed and staring up at the ceiling.

He chuckled. 'You act like she's signed a death warrant. We both live there, you know.'

I huffed. 'Well, I can't speak for you, because like I've told you several times, you're strange.' He guffawed. 'But I only live there because of my acting career. I can't imagine going to London – where the glass ceiling is almost titanium by the way – or Los Angeles to hustle for roles with my accent, passport and African-sounding surname. Even Nigerian Americans are still trying to get roles without being accused of taking roles from African Americans. You think if I'd been born elsewhere or had a different career, I'd be in that country with you? Please.'

'Well, shouldn't you be celebrating this illustrious career that has kept you tied to your beloved country?' He waved the flutes and bottle of Dom Pérignon.

I laughed. 'I wouldn't call it illustrious.'

It wasn't *illustrious* – as yet – but it was surreal, even after so many years. To be cast as a lead in a movie that made it to the screen of a cinema, to travel to locations for shoots, to have my face printed on billboards.

'The goal is to be too good to be rejected, to be more than a pretty face,' Zino had told me back then as he'd drilled me through hours of practice and training. I did not object because I was hungry and desperate – the perfect recipe for docile compliance – and I still thought he wasn't human. It had been too fortuitous, the sort of intervention my mother would label as divine.

We were the same, you see, he'd explained to me. His father had rejected him for refusing to participate in the family business, for not outwardly representing the sort of men their family groomed. He'd survived on a sizeable inheritance left to him by his grandparents, an inheritance he'd managed to multiply. But even the mention of an inheritance seemed too alien to assure me we were anything alike – my grandfather had perished in the rampage of the civil war, and my grandmother had followed him years later in a small, thatched hut in our village.

Erezino was a name he'd chosen for himself, to detach

himself from the legacy of the father he'd been named after, a name on his passport he never showed me.

'You brought the expensive one,' I chimed as Zino uncorked the champagne bottle.

'Nothing of mine is ever cheap.'

'Touché.'

I watched as he filled the flute, tiny bubbles forming against the glass surface. 'Thank you,' I said as we clinked flutes. 'What are your plans after this?' I asked after taking a sip.

'Some new proposal I got the other day. The script looks decent but the powers that be already have their choice for lead actress fixed.'

'Hmm,' I said, swallowing a gulp this time. 'Do I know her?'

'I don't, but she's light skinned, has a London accent and a decent following on social media, and that seems to be enough for the team. The things people care about these days.'

I giggled, suddenly feeling light. 'I'm fair skinned too.'

He held my gaze. 'You can act,' he retorted in a deadpan tone. 'Seriously, I don't understand what's happening. We have local talent that can be polished, but we'd rather give an amateur with the right accent and connection the role. It's preposterous.'

'"Preposterous",' I repeated, swallowing more champagne. 'You sound like Ego. I only use that kind of word in written speech.'

'You just love to pretend you aren't as smart as you are.'

I turned to the side and picked up my phone. The champagne had already begun to take effect, turning my mood. 'We should listen to something, this conversation is getting too serious,' I said, scrolling through my playlists.

He raised his flute. 'Go ahead.'

I settled on Westlife.

Zino groaned. 'Not this again.' He'd always complained about my attachment to boybands, but as always, he let me have my way. 'Can't Lose What You Never Had' came on as we continued to chat.

'You know,' I said as the chorus played. 'Ego and I used to listen to this album so much when it came out. But this song was always my favourite. It's a love song but that's not what I hear when I listen to it.'

'We focus too much on romance as a society anyway.'

I nodded. 'I can't lose what I never had so I might as well take a chance.'

He knew my story. On the night we met, he'd poured red wine into crystal glasses and shoved one between my jittery fingers. Then he'd clinked our glasses and said, 'Here's to being rejects, the ones our parents would rather not have.'

In a different society, it would be considered strange – obscene even – to travel back and forth through a monument to the man responsible for the death of your grandfather, a man whose very memory was a grisly reminder that your tribe had lost the civil war. I thought of this as I prepared to head to the Murtala Muhammed Airport to pick up Ego.

'*Have you seen the new cabinet list? What utter bullshit,*' Zino texted me as I drove towards Eriife's clinic so we could go to the airport together. Ego's flight was due to land in an hour. The traffic light changed before I could respond.

Eriife was standing outside the glass double doors in a tailored navy trouser suit despite the blazing heat as I pulled up. It had only been a few years since she'd opened the clinic with her husband – their pictures splashed across the newspapers as they cut the ribbons – and it had already gained a reputation for its great quality of care, a rarity in a country like ours. There was a time when I would have looked forward to this trip together to the airport, before our connection had become only a dreary elegy to the bond our mothers had shared.

Eriife had wanted me to campaign for their party's candidate for presidency – now the newly sworn-in president, a man I despised – to wear t-shirts and appear in TV interviews, to espouse words I held no belief in, to become the person she now was.

'Can't you do this for your friend?' she'd said when I turned her down, her eyes burning with the sting of betrayal. We were in the sprawling duplex she shared with her husband and hadn't seen each other in months even though we both lived in Lagos. When she'd called, asking if I had time to come over, I'd thought it was to rekindle the connection we once had, the days of laughing on hostel bunks. I'd been mistaken.

'You know me better than that,' I said that day. But did she?

She'd been the first to know about my boyfriend after my parents had pulled me from St Mary's, the first to meet Chuka, because she saw men in the same way Ego did, through the lens of her father. I was the one who still bore the secret of the day after Aunty Chinelo's death, the day Eriife had said, her voice laden with guilt she did not understand, 'I hate my father, he's the reason she's gone.'

Eriife's separation from us had begun in the smallest of ways: missed hangouts had turned into birthday parties and major milestones, until we'd grown accustomed to her absence. Now, I was the semi-famous face she called on for political campaigns.

I stopped the car long enough for Eriife to get in then pulled away from the driveway, noticing her chauffeur-driven Land

Rover SUV following closely behind. I wondered why she'd asked to go together instead of just meeting at the airport.

We travelled in unbroken silence, until I said awkwardly, 'Ego says you got her the job.'

'Oh. Did she?' Perhaps she was surprised that she'd cropped up in our conversations at all. She shrugged. 'It was nothing. They needed someone, I only made the connection.' She looked out the window, her lips tight together.

We did not speak for the rest of the journey.

Ego looked different and yet the same, pushing a trolley piled high with luggage, wearing a chic jumpsuit and large sunglasses. She was no longer the broken young woman that had left the country, desperate to escape.

'Well, hello there,' I said, Eriife standing stiffly by my side like a stranger. People milled past, dragging luggage and sending stares my way.

I'd been anxious that Ego's return would be the end to the utopia of our friendship, that it would reveal our bond had been a version of our previous selves we'd clung to, that we would be so changed by the years apart we would no longer connect. A short visit and phone calls were different from living day to day.

We hugged, clutching one another for several seconds, our perfumes mingling, our weaves blending.

Ego pulled back first and raised her sunglasses to dab at her eyes, I kept mine in place. Then she hugged Eriife. 'We should probably not be doing this here,' she said and laughed. I took the trolley from her hands and pushed it towards the car park.

'Ahn-ahn, you have a Range? What else haven't you told me?' Ego said as we stopped by my car and I clicked the doors unlocked. She turned to Eriife, 'Did you know she had a Range?' Eriife shrugged.

'It's not that big a deal,' I said, loading her boxes into the rear.

'Not that big a deal? Since when?' she said, then stared at me. 'You've changed, you're calmer.'

'Me?' I cackled.

In the car, behind the tinted shade, she unzipped the front of her jumpsuit to just below her breasts, then she reached behind to pull at her bra hooks.

'What are you doing?' I asked.

'You don't know that part of the reason I was crying was because my bra was too tight?'

I laughed. 'Why didn't you take it off on the plane? You're a mad woman.' She hadn't changed. I turned on the engine.

'Jesus!' she screamed several minutes later, as I manoeuvred between lanes. 'You drive like a mad person. You've not changed o.'

'We're all mad in Lagos.'

Eriife remained quiet in the back of the car.

For a while, Ego stared out of the tinted window at the broken tarred roads, hawkers and beggars hanging by the windows, street sellers, their wares spilling off the pavements, the ramshackle yellow buses and their passengers jumping on and off, the passers-by constantly screaming, cursing and sweating. I wondered if she was reconsidering her decision in the glare of the reality of Lagos.

I opened the compartment by the passenger side and pulled out a CD, waving it in her face. 'I bought something to commemorate your return,' I announced, pulling off the film.

She pulled away from the glass and shook her head. 'Who

buys CDs in this day and age?' She stared at the cover and Craig David's face. 'Oh my God! *Born To Do It!* I haven't listened to this in forever.'

I grinned as she pushed the CD into the player and the intro guitar notes tinkled through. 'We were so obsessed with him, my mother wanted to break our player.'

She sighed. 'What a time, life was so different.' She turned to look at the rear seat. 'Eriife, why are you so quiet? You were talking my ear off on the phone, and now that I'm here, you're quiet?'

Eriife laughed a stilted laugh. 'I'm just tired. It's been a long day at the clinic.'

Ego's eyes slimmed in a squint, perceptive as ever. 'Or are the both of you fighting?'

Forced laughter from Eriife and me followed.

'You're not serious,' Eriife said.

'Remember Jide that used to DJ all the school parties?' I said, changing the subject. 'His father got him a job in a ministry, and now he's an assistant director in Abuja.'

Ego let the issue go with a stare that said she would address it later. 'You don't mean it? Remember how he used to help us transfer songs to our phones? Your flip Motorola with the "Good Girls" ringtone? Every time I hear that song, I remember your phone and your night calls.'

We smiled, settling into the cushioned embrace of the past.

'That was when you were still serious about being a lawyer,' I said to Ego.

'Yes o, every time, justice this, justice that,' Eriife chipped in all of a sudden.

Ego rolled her eyes. 'Ahn-ahn, I'm still a lawyer now, it's just a different version of law. Man must chop.' She glanced at Eriife. 'And look who's talking? You did not let us hear word about medicine but your clinic is now a side hustle, madam politician.'

We laughed again, Eriife joining in this time, and for a while, we were girls again, alive in a time before life separated us.

Ego shook her head. 'You wouldn't believe the escalator stopped working as soon as I got on it. What can we ever get right in this country? And the officers kept asking for money. I had to adjust my accent immediately so they'd know my British passport is just for show. I accidentally packed my Nigerian passport in one of the boxes I sent over.'

I grinned. 'What accent were you using before? The nasal one you use to talk to your colleagues in the UK?'

During her first year in Britain, she'd called me, fuming with barely contained anger: *Can you believe my classmate said he can't understand me when I speak? That I pronounce words in a weird way. This, from an Australian. An Australian! He's mad. I'm not changing my accent for anybody.'*

A beggar knocked on the window by my side as we waited for a traffic warden to pass us. I pulled a bank note from my handbag and rolled down the glass to hand it to him.

'You didn't give anything to the last one that knocked,' Ego observed.

'He's a child,' I said simply. We both understood the significance of those words.

At home, the security men lugged Ego's suitcases up the staircase; we'd dropped Eriife off at her clinic with glib promises to meet up later.

Ego had commented on how the streets had changed as we transitioned from the mainland to Lagos Island and then my estate. 'The disparity in this country is so jarring.'

She flapped the skin of her jumpsuit as she settled into a

sofa. 'The weather is so sweltering. Has it always been this humid or has it gotten worse?'

I giggled. '*Oyinbo*. I can't wait for you to meet Zino,' I said, picking up an AC remote, 'the both of you can be speaking English together.'

The AC bristled, then it grumbled to a stop. The lights flicked off. The power was gone.

I laughed even harder. 'Welcome home.'

My mother arrived as I arranged the platters delivered by the caterer on the dining table. Ego had just taken a bath, the generator was running, and the air conditioners in the living room gushed frigid air.

'You should think of getting a solar generator and inverter installed,' Ego said to me. 'You know everyone is going green, we can try to save the planet.'

I huffed. 'Nwakaego, please! Like Africa is contributing anything significant to the global warming numbers. We have more pressing problems.'

'We still have to do our part.'

My mother walked in without looking at me even though I held the door open for her. 'Obianuju informed me that my daughter is around,' she announced, marching across the threshold.

'Good afternoon, Aunty Ada,' Ego said, rushing to-wards her.

The last time we'd set eyes on each other, her eyes had burned with fire as she gripped my chin between her fingers. 'I hear you now smoke,' she spat out. 'Is this the sort of life you want to live? Did I fail as a mother?'

I'd wrenched my face from her palm.

Her face, so like mine, twisted with revulsion. 'God is

punishing you, do you know that? That's why you're not married. That's why you don't have any children. You killed!'

This time she pulled Ego into a bosomy embrace. 'Nwakaego, my daughter. You're looking fairer! So fine! Is that what the weather over there does to you?'

'Ah yes, Aunty, the sun doesn't shine at all.'

22

Murderer

In my diary that day, I'd penned: *I don't think I can go through with this.* Journaling had come naturally to me from the time my father purchased a sequin-backed notebook covered in glitter on my seventh birthday. A miniature padlock sealed my secrets in.

He loved to write, despite his limited education, and he was determined that we have a different sort of life from the one he'd had, working his parents' farm after his father's death in the war, selling grounded cassava and millet in the village marketplace. The missionary school in an adjoining village had been a godsend, where he learned and acquired an affinity for literary education, and even that euphoria was short-lived. It was in his fourth year that his mother passed away, taken by a sudden illness they were too impoverished to treat, her children distributed amongst relatives. An uncle that traded leather imported from China claimed my father.

Hard work, wit and an endless determination for perfection saved him, he always said. In truth, it had been *igba boi*, the years-old apprenticeship system of servitude that had saved our tribe from impoverishment in the years following the civil war. And after a decade of serfhood, working at his uncle's behest for little or no pay, learning the trade, he was rewarded with enough capital to start his own. Now, he trained others from the village, just as his uncle had done for him. He did not have the tremendous wealth that Ego's father had acquired, but enough to do his part.

The money laid the foundation; his quest for knowledge built the scaffolding. In his library, he collected cases of books and tapes on the art of business, research into trades and their shortfalls. His ability to critique was second to none, to pull apart a perfect-sounding idea, until he was left with the rubble of its initiative, to determine a fault ahead of others. It was the same critical eye he turned on his children; it was the eye he'd used selecting my mother.

His expectations were laid out early enough that there was no cause to say: '*I didn't know.*' Perfection was the requirement, regiment the tool, conduct the yardstick. Perfection was not obtained by hope but by will, a will to prove he was better than where he came from.

In his eagerness to determine, my father unknowingly gave me freedom – my journal was the one place he could not reach, where his hands could not lord over. My initial journal entries were simple: recollections of the day, of words spoken and unspoken. Soon, they transcended to thoughts and feelings, a recount of flaws and admission of mistakes. Years later, I would re-read them with new eyes, realising the girl I'd been – striving and failing to ever acquire his approval.

Bayo claimed to be different. When he said he wasn't like my father, I should have known that he would be the one to turn my life upside down. It was the same with all of them: I was a prize to be won, a target to be acquired, a shining new trinket to be displayed on the arm. But with Bayo, there was a golden goodness about him; he was the sort of man that wouldn't cause hurt knowingly.

He'd been too shy to approach me and so he'd sent a note from the back of the class. And I'd tucked it in the corner of my bag, forgotten along with the others, until a bespectacled gangly young man walked up to me weeks later with a nervous smile and introduced himself.

'He's a sort of shiny brown,' I told Ego in our shared room. She never remembered my male admirers' names and I was eager for her to remember this one.

'Hmm,' she grunted, a brow raised. She never took me seriously. 'You're too fickle,' she told me once. And I knew she'd learned the word in literature class in secondary school; when our teacher had described Romeo in *Romeo and Juliet*, he'd used the word 'fickle'. But I wasn't like Romeo, switching affections between Rosaline and Juliet in a matter of acts; I was just aware of my reality. Until then, dating had been a sport, a distraction as I awaited the inevitable.

Bayo laughed easily, artless joy expressed at the simple things, untroubled by life's gloom, like a child you constantly wanted to keep happy because their happiness was so pure it brought you joy. I craved to be as unburdened as he was. To have parents like his, hardworking stable-jobbed, spectacled, smiling parents that told you to do whatever, to be whoever, because they would support you regardless. To be able to say 'I love you' so easily, because you'd only known love.

On his bed, between sheets with cartoon drawings that smelled like baby powder, we made love for the first time; his first and mine. Chuka had begged to be the one to take my virginity, on his knees in a flat his father had rented for him for school. He'd begged with tears in his eyes, telling me how much he loved me and how much he was willing to do for me, but it only made me wonder how many others he'd pressured and guilted into sex the same way, women who had given their consent unwillingly.

A pregnancy wasn't something I'd planned, even though I made it appear that way to Ego. Perhaps that was what the Sunday school teacher at my mother's church had meant by life and death in the power of the tongue – to joke about an event, and have it transcribed to reality.

It had been once, one time when we'd had sex without a condom. We were laughing, joking like we always did, then we were pulling at each other's clothes, and by the time we realised it, we'd gone too far.

'We'll be fine,' Bayo said, his smile reassuring, believing. And I thought that he wouldn't make a bad father.

On the same bed, I handed him the paper bag with the six pregnancy tests I'd taken.

'What's this?' he asked with the jaunty smile of a child unwrapping birthday presents.

I waited for him to open the bag.

'You look so serious,' he said, laughing as he poured out the contents.

Then his smile disappeared. He picked the sticks one after the other, and stared at the double lines that declared me pregnant.

'Are you sure these aren't faulty? You should get a proper test at the hospital,' he said, his voice carrying the excessive optimism of a child seeking to escape punishment. I pulled out the printed hospital test from my bag and handed it to him.

'It's not that bad,' I said finally, when he remained mute

after several minutes, his head in his hands. It was a role I'd never played with him: blind optimism. 'Now, I don't have to get married to someone else anymore. Remember we planned to talk to my dad once we're done with law school? Now, we can just tell them we're going to get married. Your parents are always supportive, my mum and your mum can help out with the baby while we work and try to stabilise ourselves.' It rushed out quickly, like I was grasping at a rope slipping from my fingers.

I left the room when his head remained in his hands, smoothing the bedsheet with my hands, wanting to leave the perfection of his life as I'd met it.

His text came two days later:

Hi Zina, I'm so sorry it's taken so long to say anything. I did not realise it then, but I'm not ready for such a serious commitment as raising a child, or marriage even, and that's why I've been grappling with the reality ever since. I also realise that at the end of the day, it's your body and your decision, and I'll support you regardless.

Even the message sounded so innocent, like a wide-eyed infant waking up to the reality of the world.

Girls had abortions every day, we just pretended they didn't happen, like it wasn't illegal, like there weren't back-end doctors and herbalists with solutions to such a minor problem.

I called Chioma. She knew everyone and everything there was to know. 'Ahh, Zina I thought you were sharper than this. How can you let one of these small boys mess up a shining star like you ehn? A whole fine girl?' I wondered if she expected a response to her question, if it was only the 'ugly' girls that made mistakes. 'I'll make some calls. Expect to hear from me soon.' A final cluck of her tongue and she was gone.

Days later, she squeezed a white pill bottle in my palm at the back of a restaurant. 'Don't tell anyone I gave you o. I'll deny it, I swear.'

I thought of calling Ego to talk, but knew I couldn't, in the face of her own struggles, mine seemed inconsequential. And so, I wrote in my diary, to myself, to the child I wasn't brave enough to have. Then I swallowed the capsules.

I heard my parents' voices through the walls when I returned from the hospital, mostly my mother's.

'Uzondu, is it until she kills herself? I told you when you started this that you shouldn't force them to marry so early. Must you always have your way?'

I did not hear my father's response.

I laid in bed and pretended to be asleep afterwards when my mother came into the room. 'I know you're not sleeping. Open your eyes,' she said.

I opened them, one after the other.

Her arms were crossed across her chest. 'I hope you're happy with yourself. Can you see what you've done? Me and your father and arguing over this. What kind of child are you?'

When I was five, I broke a plaque that had been gifted to my father as I wiped it. The splintered pieces had scattered across the floor of the sitting room. Alerted by the sound, my parents had rushed into the room seconds later as I hurriedly tried to gather the pieces, then my father said, 'Look what your daughter has done.' An argument erupted almost immediately, my mother questioning why I was labelled her daughter. Afterwards, she'd pulled me by the ear, holding a broom in her other hand and said, 'See what you've done. Are you trying to scatter our home?'

It was the same tone she used now: 'You're not only trying to kill yourself; you're trying to destroy your family.'

It would take a week, but the cramps would eventually dissipate, aided by the capsules the doctor had handed out at the clinic, with the warning, 'She's very lucky, had she come in even an hour later, she might be dead by now.' My mother had nodded with tears in her eyes, and for the first time, I thought she didn't see me as a burden.

An uncharacteristic silence shadowed me about the house. Suddenly the dining room was empty when it was time to eat; my plate, covered and isolated at the middle of the glass table; the living rooms deserted of siblings fighting over the television remote control. In the kitchen, we occasionally bumped into one another, by the refrigerator or by the sink, and before our eyes could meet, they bowed their heads and hurried away. It dawned on me that they'd been instructed to avoid the impurity of my person.

The novelty of my near-death wore off eventually and my mother paid a different kind of visit to my room, with a Bible tucked underneath her armpit, the lilac-embroidered volume my grandmother had given her on her wedding day.

She was settled at the edge of my bed when I came out of the bathroom, wrapped in a towel. 'Good morning,' she said, moving the Bible to her hands.

I stared at her, droplets of water falling off my skin and pooling in a small puddle at my feet along with my stomach. Finally, I murmured, 'Good morning, ma.'

She nodded, accepting my greeting then said, 'Get dressed quickly, I need to talk to you.'

I rushed through the routines and pulled on a house gown,

then I sat, tentatively, by her side. She flipped through the pages of her Bible in silence until she settled on the page that interested her. She placed her thumb on a scripture and asked me to read it aloud.

'Thou,' I started.

'Read the scripture,' she instructed.

'Exodus 20:13. Thou shall not kill,' I read out loud, realising what this was about.

'Do you know why I've asked you to read this?' she asked.

I said nothing.

'Do you?'

'Yes, ma,' I mumbled.

'I don't think you do. Or you wouldn't be so unremorseful.'

I stared at my clean hands. 'Do you realise what it is you've done? In your foolishness and selfishness, you've taken away a precious life, a child that deserved to live. Your hands are covered in blood!'

In the hospital, I'd overheard the nurses gossiping about me, the girl who'd killed her own child and nearly killed herself in the process. I tried to picture a baby, my mind conjuring a hazy blur – or babies, I'd never tried to find out. In my hospital gown, I drifted to the maternity ward and stared through the glass at the small helpless creatures, name tags attached to scrawny arms, nurses carrying bundles moving in and out of the room.

A nurse stopped by my side and asked, 'Madam, are you a new mother? Would you like to see your baby?'

I opened my mouth to answer but the words stayed frozen on my tongue. I'd been a mother less than a week before and just like that, I wasn't. I turned and walked away.

Now, as my mother launched into her diatribe, I saw a baby, a plump colicky infant that would have been the perfect fusion of Bayo and me, a child not too light and not too dark, a child with pudgy arms and legs, that would have one day grown into a toddler, a teenager and an adult.

My mother was still speaking. 'I've done my best to raise you right, but still you've chosen to make all the wrong decisions.' She paused. 'Are you even listening to me?' she demanded.

Her palm cracked hard against the side of my face before I could respond; I felt each one of her fingers imprinted on my cheek. 'Don't you realise what I'm telling you? You've killed! You're a murderer!'

23

Flowers and floodings

Rain thundered down when the naira fell, clobbering the pavements, filling the soakaways and blocking sewages, a homage to what had until then been a steadily burgeoning economy.

'Keep all your money in dollars o. Don't say I didn't warn you,' Tari shouted over the phone. She was on the set of a movie but promised to be back in time for our monthly gathering.

The streets flooded, the water rising above ankle and then knee length. On social media, residents posted videos of canoes on the roads, sloughing floodings from their cars and furniture floating about in discoloured water. And our gateman caught fish, a flatheaded whiskered thing squiggling about in a bucket. 'Aunty I catch fish! I catch fish!' he screamed, holding the bucket up to my face so I could take a look.

I smiled, amused by his childlike excitement, wondering which fish farm had lost its pond. 'Where you catch am?' I asked.

'For the other street, the water plenty for that side. Aunty I wan make pepper soup, make I bring some for you?'

I laughed as I recounted the events to Ego, describing the squirming catfish in the bucket and his offer of pepper soup. We were in the living room of my house, watching soaps on TV; she was living with me while work on her new apartment was still underway.

Ego gave a strained smile, then said, 'After all these years, how can the supposed capital of enterprise in the continent look like this every time rain falls?'

I could feel the smile disappearing from my face. She'd been back for a little over six months and the ecstasy had slowly worn off; all that seemed to be growing in its place was a caustic disillusionment at the state of the country. She couldn't say I didn't warn her.

At first, she'd continued to tweet about British problems until I'd asked her if she feared her followers finding out she'd moved back home. 'Do you think they'll look down on you?'

After that, she began to tweet about Nigeria: excitement at the things she'd missed, the changes borne over time until frustration found its way in, and her followers began to ask if she still lived in the UK.

NaijaUK Law Girl
@NaijaUKLawGirl

🐦 Follow

What can be done about the state of Nigeria? We cannot continue like this!

5:30 PM – 3 Apr 2016

NaijaUK Law Girl
@NaijaUKLawGirl

🐦 Follow

Yes, our leaders are terrible but so much of our current issues can be traced to our colonial history. I wake up everyday cursing Lord Lugard

2:53 PM – 12 Apr 2016

Ego looked at me. 'But it's true! What's the point of paying taxes? Can we even blame this on global warming? Tomorrow, we'll call ourselves the Giant of Africa.'

My smile returned. 'You're always talking about global warming and making the earth safe again but tomorrow you'll complain when I call you *Britico* or *Janded*. Anyways, we can't blame this solely on global warming. The government keeps giving licences to all these real estate developers to push the ocean back and build houses and luxury apartments – you're going to be living in one soon – and our garbage system is an absolute waste.'

She sniffed, ruffled. 'I'm still the same – global warming is just important.'

I giggled slowly at first, then it turned hysterical. 'Just look at your face! Are you sure you're still Nigerian?'

Her eyes widened. 'Serious? Me?'

I shook her shoulders playfully. 'You've forgotten that the first rule of being Nigerian is to laugh at the state of Nigeria ehn? You have to enjoy the little things, the catfish and pepper soup incidents or you'll run mad in this place. What were you expecting? I told you this is how it was. Or do you want to go back? Your passport is still red, you know.'

She exhaled and pushed herself deeper into the settee. 'No, I don't, I was running mad over there. I just expected things to improve, how can we still be dealing with the same problems from ten, fifteen years ago?'

'Isn't almost every country like that? Dealing with the same issues from ten, twenty years ago?' I couldn't believe I'd said that.

'True, most governments are inefficient.'

'It's just that our system in particular is set up to fail. I mean how much has really changed since we inherited it from our colonial masters? Many of our laws go as far back as before independence or before we became a republic. Let's start there.'

When the rains subsided, Ego and I visited Aunty Chinelo. Eriife was busy – with what, I wasn't sure. The bouquets occupied the back seat: blush pink camellias and fragrant lilies. Nwakaego had found a list online that said camellias symbolised love and devotion and lilies were for purity and beauty; she'd chosen the camellias and I'd wanted the lilies and so we found a florist who could deliver both.

'My fellow yellow' was what she'd called me, because we'd both been *yellow pawpaws*, me and Aunty Chinelo, but her *yellow* had a red undertone that coloured her cheeks when she laughed too much, which she did often, and one time, I overhead her telling my mother that a white man must have snuck into her ancestral line along the way. Then she'd laughed and laughed, in a way my mother would have called unladylike if I did it.

Almost twenty years had passed since her death, but the

memory remained unblurred in my mind, like a tape on unrelenting repeat: my mother running out of the house in a blouse and wrapper and the first shoes she could find; my mother returning, her wrapper limping at her waist, her hair scrambled and untidy. 'Chinelo! My Chinelo!' she'd screamed, and I knew the worst had happened.

'Did you remember to carry the broom and rags?' Ego asked as we buckled into our seats.

'Yes, I did. We have everything. You worry too much,' I said, starting the car and pulling out of the gate. Edikan, the gateman on duty, waved excitedly as we passed.

'I promised my mother I'll call her when we get there. Nkechi said she'll see us there. She has a meeting at work.'

'What about Nwamaka, her twin? Have you spoken with her yet?' I asked, turning a corner.

Ego shifted in her seat and stared out of the glass, as though searching for something. Was her sister passing by? 'We've spoken,' she said finally. 'If you call that speaking,' she added.

'What happened?'

'I got her address from Nkechi and went to visit her. She lives in one of those mansions in Ikoyi now.'

'That's nice.'

'I don't think she's happy. Her eyes look just like my mother's used to. Something or several things are not right but she wouldn't talk to me. I know it's been many years but we're still sisters.'

'Does she talk to Nkechi at least?' The twins were so identical and yet so unalike, and I'd always wondered how it was to see your face mirrored in another but not your person. Was that how my mother felt whenever she looked at me?

Ego sighed. 'She stopped speaking to all of us when she got

married, and it was only last year she reached out to Nkechi. And even she doesn't know what's going on. I feel like it's all my fault. Maybe I should have married him instead, you know. I was older and tougher; I could have handled it.'

My brows furrowed. 'Nwakaego, please don't speak like that. Blaming yourself is not going to change anything. Give her time.'

She wiped at a corner of her eye. 'But may—'

'No buts. Take a tissue from my bag,' I ordered. 'Have you heard anything about your place yet?' I asked, changing the subject.

She cleared her throat, as she dabbed tissue against her face. 'They're still making final touches to the apartment.'

'Still? After how many months? Didn't they know you were coming? They should give you the contractor's number so I can call them and show them small madness. In this Lagos, you have to make sure people know they don't have the monopoly of madness, you can't be using British gentleness for them.'

Ego laughed, and I was relieved to hear the sound. 'To be fair, the company has offered a luxury furnished apartment in the meantime but I told them I'm okay where I am.'

I slapped my steering wheel, deliberately dramatic. '*Hay*, this woman! So you want to be eating my free food. Are you not a thief like this?'

Ego laughed even harder and I smiled. 'But jokes aside, you're lucky that your office is handling this house matter for you. You even have a driver that comes to pick you up every day.'

'How so?'

'Ah! I didn't tell you what I suffered house hunting in this Lagos when I first moved back from Onitsha? One landlord said he doesn't rent to single women, another said how is he sure I'm not into *ashewo* business, that he doesn't trust women that are into acting. The real estate agent that was taking me around was telling me that I should try to understand, that my car is too big, that even he had had his sister's car towed so she could walk around a little and meet a man? Can you imagine the nonsense?'

Ego's guffaw rang through the car's interior. I didn't add that eventually, I'd given in and taken the agent's car around until we'd finally found a place I could rent.

The headstone was clean when we arrived, devoid of dirt and moss and the weeds sprouting around it had been cut and cleared. My mother had visited; she was the only one who never dropped flowers.

Ego video-called her mother and I stood aside awkwardly as she turned the camera to the gravestone so Aunty Uju could see its condition; we'd wiped it again and arranged the flowers. Lilies, pure and beautiful, like Aunty Chinelo, too good for this world.

I heard the sound of sniffling and I moved away to pull out a cigarette from my bag. I watched Ego talk to her mother from behind my sunglasses, remembering how I'd wished my mother loved me like Aunty Uju loved her daughter.

Ego eyed the cigarette between my lips when the call ended, considering whether to make a comment. The first time I pulled a cigarette from my bag, she'd screamed in comical horror, 'You smoke now?' And since then, she'd been given to launch into regular lectures on the habit. 'You can die early. Do you know that?' she warned once. I'd shrugged and noted the surprise in her eyes that death was hardly enough to scare me.

I tried to form an O with the smoke from the cigarette, just like I'd learned to do on set, to provoke a reaction out of Ego this time, but it came out mushed. Her eyes were bloodshot; emotionally exhausted.

'Nkechi texted to say she can't make it. She'll come on her own,' Ego said, ignoring my cigarette.

I put my arm around her shoulder; in heels, I was nearly her height. 'Let's go,' I said. Then I put out the cigarette and crushed it under my heel.

'Did something happen between you and Eriife while I was away?' Ego asked suddenly in the car on the drive home.
I waited till we arrived at a crowded junction, the cars squashed as close as possible together in unmoving traffic, then I turned to look at her. 'No, nothing happened. Why?'

'She said the same thing, but the both of you are lying.'

I folded my arms across my chest. 'Why do you think we're lying?'

'You don't talk to or about each other. You think I haven't noticed? You act like the other doesn't exist. When I went to visit her and her family, you suddenly had a meeting with your friend Zin—'

'I actually had a meeting with Zino,' I interjected.

She hissed. 'That's not the point. She wouldn't even come to your house to visit when I suggested it and she's never called your phone in my presence.'

'What if she calls it in your absence?' I joked. Ego was in no mood to joke. I sighed. 'You're overthinking this. People grow up and grow apart. We're different people with different lives. We don't have much in common and we don't have to be friends just because our mothers were friends.'

'Is that all? Are you sure?'

The car in front of me moved and I turned my attention back to the roads, escaping giving an answer.

I dragged Ego along to our monthly gathering because I did not want her moping at home by herself.

'Remember not to take anything too seriously, these women are all actresses, they're different,' I told Ego as we neared Tari's house – it was her turn to host. 'And most importantly, don't judge. I've told them I'm bringing my friend who's just returned to the country. It's why they've allowed you to come, they're curious about you.'

'I haven't just got back.'

'As far as most people here are concerned, you've just got back. You were there for over ten years. You're a proper IJGB,' I said.

'Ahn-ahn!' Ego exclaimed as we drove through the gilded gates of Tari's home. A uniformed policeman saluted as we passed. 'Is this your friend royalty or what?'

I laughed, moving towards the car park. 'No, she's married to a former footballer.' Tari's husband had played for a club in a first-division league in Europe until an unfortunate injury had ended his career, and then he'd returned home with his millions to live like a king at the official age of thirty but his wife was thirty-five and we all knew he was older than she was.

'Why do footballers like actresses and beauty queens so much?' Ego said as we walked the distance to the house, her eyes grazing over the sports cars and motorcycles. Luxury wasn't something that shocked her; she'd known it for a decent part of her life.

'Shhh, someone will hear you.'

Stewards greeted us at the door and in the corridor leading

to the living room, brandishing trays of small chops, puff puff, stick meat, peppered snails, samosas and plantain balls. Tari loved to put on a show, in her outlandish yet amiable war with Cassandra for primacy.

Cassandra was married to a retired British vice chairman at an oil company, a man old enough to be her father. He had a family in the UK, a daughter and a son young enough to be Cassandra's siblings. Cassandra lived an independent life; her husband did not breathe down her neck or question where she went or who she met with. She shuffled her time between London, New York and Lagos, and she was already in the process of applying for British citizenship. Often, the other women deferred to her with a grudging respect that she'd managed to climb her way to a pinnacle.

'Ah you're here, my darling,' Tari said, rising from a gold-plated armchair in a thigh-length sequinned dress that shimmered against the chandelier lights.

'I've never seen such garish furniture. My God!' Ego whispered beside me.

'Is anyone else here?' I asked just before we exchanged air kisses.

'No, you know they're always late,' Tari responded, rolling her eyes. Then turning shining eyes to Ego, 'Is this the friend from Britain? It's so lovely to meet you, darling,' she said and traded air kisses before I could respond.

I was ignored while we waited for the others, Tari's full attention taken by Ego as she hounded her with questions about the UK and the places she'd been to. 'I love going to Harrods. That's where I get all my clothes, nowhere else – except the Italian designers of course,' I heard her say. I smiled, amused by Tari's effort at foreignness, the extra 'r' that adjoined her high-pitched tone, the unnatural way she laughed. I wouldn't tease her in front of Ego.

Cassandra arrived next, her high-priced weave brushing the top of her bottom. 'I had to go for brunch with my husband and his friends,' she explained. Zahrah rushed in behind her, spurting apologies in her American accent, and as always, Marve was the last to join us. 'I'm so sorry guys, I was at a seminar,' she said, pushing her designer handbag into a corner by her side, like she expected it to be snatched from her. Her name was Marvelous, assigned to her by her very religious mother, but she'd shortened it to Marve, because Marvelous was simply not cool enough.

Our friendships were ropy, but we were connected by our shared profession; we knew and had worked with each other at some point in the past, and most importantly, we were friends with Tari. And Tari had been the one to suggest we meet once a month to 'catch up'. 'We all need friends in this business.'

'What seminar is that?' Zahrah asked, picking up a stick of meat and turning it to the side before taking a bite.

'It's an exclusive ring masterclass for only those that can afford to pay. It was wonderful, you should have seen the big big women that attended, all of them single and searching,' Marve said.

I shook my head and bit into a samosa. 'Ring masterclass? Why would you waste money on such nonsense?'

'I'm the only one that's not seriously attached in this room and you're asking why? I already have a calendar date I've marked. I must have my own ring by then,' Marve responded.

'Zina isn't seriously attached,' Zahrah pointed out, waving her hand with the diamond engagement ring in my direction. Her family was well-connected with vast farmland up north and ties within the government. She'd spent most of her teenage years in America and only returned on her father's insistence. Now she was set to marry a childhood sweetheart from an equally well-connected family.

'How come the rich only always marry each other?' Tari had commented behind Zahrah's back, her voice coated in malice. She'd married her own husband by sheer luck. He'd told his mother he had no interest in dating any of the foreign women in his club's country; he'd wanted a home-grown woman instead, and she'd gone over to Tari's father's house to request his well-behaved daughter on her son's behalf.

'You marry the people you know, Tari. They grow up together, lunch together, school together. Who else do you expect them to marry?' I'd replied.

'Zina isn't serious please,' Marve said now, swiping her hand dismissively.

Tari screamed with laughter, the other women joined, including Ego, that traitor. 'Zina, can you see your life outside? Everybody knows you're not serious.' Tari's accent was Nigerian again.

'Please please please. Don't start,' I said, raising a palm.

Tari wrinkled her nose in my direction before saying to Marve, 'I could introduce you to my husband's friends. Many of them are footballers.'

Marve sat up straighter.

'Don't listen to her,' Cassandra interjected. 'These footballers and sports people are never faithful partners. My husband's friends are settled, and they don't have the time and energy for such nonsense.'

Tari rolled her eyes, and just as she was ready to respond, a small Filipina woman shuffled into the room, Tari's weeping daughter attached to her hip. 'What happened?' Tari demanded as she jumped to her feet and followed the woman out of the room, her battle with Cassandra abandoned.

Ego studied Tari and her nanny as they left the room and I knew she would comment on this when we were alone, the reason Tari had thought it necessary to fly in a nanny when there were many Nigerians who could handle the position just as well. 'It's not like they speak French. And she could have hired our Cameroonian neighbours for that. What is with the Nigerian obsession with pale skin?' she would say.

In Tari's absence, I introduced Ego to the others. And they chirped at her in excited and ardent curiosity. Marve in particular didn't understand why Ego was single, and Cassandra could scarcely believe that Nwakaego had spent ten years in the land of the white man and returned without one.

24

Murky waters

The murky waters came to me at night again, as they'd done since the day my mother first called me a murderer. Rising from their centre was a face that haunted, plump and rosy. It had my eyes and nose; its lips were not mine but its father's, and from it, gurgled water that steadily darkened: copper then sepia, mahogany then crimson. I was at the edge again, unable to take the plunge to save it. And like previous times, an invisible hand prodded me from behind until I was suspended in the air then pulled underneath the bleeding waves of my own making.

In Onitsha, I'd been convinced the hand and fingers were my mother's, jeering at my lofty ambitions and failures. Then, the dreams had left me shaken and convinced I was cursed. Why else was I living in a boarded room with sporadic electricity supply and well water for over a year, unable to make any tangible progress?

'Is everything okay with you?' Binyelum, the girl who lived in the next room, asked one day. We were queued outside the bathroom with our buckets full of well water, waiting for its current occupant to vacate the cubicle.

I turned to blink at her. 'Why would you ask that?'

She leaned in and lowered her voice so the others behind us wouldn't hear. 'I heard you screaming in the night. And it did not sound like the other type of scream, if you know what I mean.' She winked at me. 'It wasn't the first time too. Is everything okay? Are you having bad dreams?'

'I'm fine,' I said and tried to turn away.

'You know the devil likes to pursue fine girls like you,' Binyelum persisted, leaning even closer. 'My pastor specialises in prayers for women like you. Very powerful prayers, and you'll stop having these dreams.

I could see my mother laughing as I knelt the following Wednesday in front of Binyelum's pastor. Zina who'd run away from the church, who'd dodged attending mass with her father and labelled her own mother a fanatic, kneeling for prayers of her own will. 'You demon, let her go!' Saliva flew from his mouth to my face, but I was desperate for the shower, anything that would redeem my soul.

The dreams continued unabated, sharpening in vividity. I avoided sleep altogether, running from them, and the skin underneath my eyes began to darken. Then I started to forget my lines and directors no longer had recommendations to offer, and even the minor roles that had become a means of sustenance began to wither away.

My mother called one night as I lay awake in the dark, calculating just how much I had left to spend. I pressed the green telephone answer button, convinced it was an error on her part.

'Zinachukwu,' she said as soon as I accepted the call. No, it wasn't an error.

'Good evening, ma,' I answered.

'How are you?' she asked.

Hope bubbled in my belly at the concern in her voice. 'I'm fine,' I said. 'How is everyone?'

'We're fine, we thank God. Your sister Urenna is getting married soon and I'm calling to let you know.'

'Oh,' I murmured, feeling the hope fizzle out.

'"*Oh*",' she mimicked, before unleashing: 'Is that all you have to say? I said your younger sister is getting married and you say "oh". Won't you talk about coming home to see your sister? Leave all these reckless fantasies and settle down to build a decent home?'

The beeping from the call ending sounded in my ear before I could say anything.

I drank catfish pepper soup the very next night, the spices burning a path down my throat and clearing my sinuses. I paid the restaurant owner with a quarter of what was left of my money. I handed over the remaining fraction to a taxi driver and asked him to take me to the River Niger Bridge.

The bridge hadn't been rehabilitated in decades, but it was the connection between the east and the rest of the country, and as always vehicles milled through: trucks carrying goods to be sold, oil tankers delivering petroleum products, long buses transporting those seeking their fortune elsewhere. We waited in the car as evening turned to dusk. I asked the taxi driver to play his favourite CD, and the highlife tunes of Ebenezer Obey burst through the player and we sang along; my father loved Ebenezer as well.

At three in the morning, when the traffic had thinned, besides the occasional vehicle and travellers' bus, I stepped out of the taxi and waved the driver and his questions away. The railings were rusty, and moss grew at the bottom of the stone. I stared at the river below, how vast, majestic and murky the waves looked in the night light. Would they find my body? It was probably better if they didn't. It was how I deserved to be remembered: the *mami water* that suddenly vanished, never to be heard from again.

I gripped the railing and lifted a leg to the other side, bracing myself against it to lift the other. I did not see nor hear the feet running in my direction until an obstinate arm grabbed mine and pulled me from the ledge.

The bed was drenched in sweat when I opened my eyes, sweat so copious it saturated the sheets, and soaked through the mattress. I picked up my phone to look at the time: 4am. I pulled my nightstand drawer open and scattered my fingers through its contents for the pill bottle Tari had given me almost a year ago when I'd casually mentioned that I almost never got any sleep.

'Bad dreams,' I'd said flippantly.

'They'll help calm you down so you can sleep. How do you think I survive the stress of all this?' she said, folding my fingers around the bottle after the others had left.

'I don't want to abuse drugs,' I said and pushed the bottle towards her. Her face fell and I realised I'd hurt her feelings. 'I don't mean you abuse drugs,' I quickly added, in an attempt to rectify my error.

'They're just sleeping pills. You can read the prescription at the back. I struggle with sleep too and they help me.'

'Were they prescribed by a doctor?'

She looked away and I knew the answer. 'Thank you,' I said, taking the bottle from her.

Now, I turned the cap open and slipped two capsules between my lips the way Tari had described – bite, break, swallow – and slowly faded into dreamless slumber.

Roses, scarlet and perfumed, decorated my living room

when I finally sauntered down the stairs in the morning; they could only have been from one person.

'Good morning, our queen. Look at the time you're waking up. You're lucky it's a weekend,' Ego said as I ambled down the stairs.

'Good morning to you too. I see Emeka has finally gotten my address,' I retorted, pointedly staring at the roses as I settled into a seat across the dining table.

The slices of bread in her fingers suddenly became very interesting. 'What do you mean? They could be for you.'

My laughter was a shrill echo. 'Nwakaego please. Who would send me flowers? Or you think I don't know that lover boy's signature? Aren't those the same type of roses he always sent to our campus room? Now he can afford to send you plenty and my whole house is smelling like a garden.'

'What do you mean who would send you flowers? What happened to your handsome Turkish guy, Halil? He was here just last week. I liked him.' It was the fact that everyone seemed to like him that disconcerted me. Liking came with expectations – of settling and permanence.

'We had a quarrel. He's Muslim, I'm Christian,' I said blithely.

Ego's eyes formed slits. 'Since when did you become religious, Zina? You both drink wine, a lot of it, and I've seen him sleep over a couple of times. Last I checked, these things are unacceptable in both your religions.'

'We had a random conversation about church and suddenly he went into this rant about how my religion is false, and then tried to kiss me afterwards. Anyways, it doesn't matter.'

She giggled. 'You're so temperamental. You're just like my mother's brother Ikechukwu. Would you believe me and Nkechi had to go and beg him yesterday to return to his own home? He said his wife insulted him, and that she only did it because she was the one who built the house with her business funds.'

I was unamused. 'Ego, don't try to change the subject. Why is Emeka sending roses to my house?'

We stared at each other in tense silence until she decided to tell the truth. 'I sent him an email before I returned to Nigeria. We've been in touch since I got back to the country. I know what you're going to say, but he's not the reason I came back. We both needed some form of closure, you know.' Her eyes took on a faraway look. 'We met up at a restaurant to talk and . . . at first we weren't sure what to say to each but then he asked me how I'd been, took my hands and said he'd missed me . . . you should have seen his eyes. He's just . . .'

'Hmm,' I grunted.

I expected to feel anger, frustration even at her decision to connect with him again, but the only emotion I could conjure was admiration for her ability to be so fixated on one person for so many years.

'Nothing's happened. We're just friends,' she blurted out. 'We hang out at restaurants, go watch movies together, things like that.'

'Friends don't send these many roses to each other.'

She squeezed her eyes shut. 'Fine. We kissed a few days ago.'

'*Ay!*' I screamed. 'Nwakaego Azubuike. Now you're telling the truth! So these are the extracurricular activities you've been engaging in after work? No wonder you're always late.'

Tears gathered abruptly in her eyes and my amusement vanished. 'Zina, I don't know what to do,' she wailed.

Breakfast was cold by the time Ego stopped crying, and by then, we'd moved to the living room and I'd lost my appetite.

'It's not your fault, I want you to always remember that. It was never your fault,' I said, my arm around her shoulder. 'And I understand that it's not his either.' I had no issues with Emeka, I just wanted Ego to forget, to move on from the horror of that period.

'He's still the same; he hasn't changed,' she said with a small smile.

I thought of asking about his parents, but I glanced at her face and thought I'd allow her dream, if only for a little while.

The Cosmopolitan was buzzing as I arrived from a meeting with a financier, servers scurried about with platters above their head, an aroma of fried food and alcohol lingering behind them.

'Do you need me to accompany you?' Zino had asked over the phone before the meeting.

'Zino, I'm going to be thirty-five soon,' I said to him. 'I should start going for things like this by myself. They said they wanted to meet me directly, not even my agent.'

'Be careful,' he had said.

Now Zino murmured as I took the seat beside him. 'How did it go?'

'Long story,' I groaned, feeling my frustration at the day's events kick in.

I'd arrived at the investor's office suited and eager to impress, until he'd arrived alone, and I instinctively knew what the meeting was about, just as I'd known the first time a director had slipped a note in my direction.

'What would you like to drink? We've all placed our orders,' Dapo shouted, his voice overshadowing mine. The others at the table nodded. The group of us were friends not because we were *friends* but because we all knew each other, and in Lagos, that was as good as friendship.

'A mojito is fine,' I said, reeling off the first cocktail that came to mind. Dapo raised a hand to call a waiter.

'Mojito? Please, that thing tastes like rum and toothpaste here, never order a mojito in Lagos,' Simi said, batting her lashes in disgust. She had moved back to Nigeria from Texas over five years ago but still complained with the superiority of one who'd only just returned, and I'd come to accept that being a returnee was the only personality she possessed.

'You're right. That thing tastes awful,' Zutere concurred beside her, even though he'd spent all his life in Lagos and his consulting firm salary meant he could only afford to travel once a year.

'A daiquiri then?' I acquiesced, feeling tired.

'Syrup and sugar,' Simi chimed in dismissal.

Zino's hand covered mine, telling me to ignore Simi; he could tell I wasn't in the mood.

My phone buzzed, a text from Ego: *I can't make it today, have a date with Emeka. Have fun!'*

'I prefer your actress friends to those guys,' Ego had said to me the first time she'd met them. 'Minus Zino, of course. It's impossible to dislike Zino,' she quickly added. 'When is he coming to visit? He makes the best conversations.'

'Why do you prefer them?' I asked.

'They might be aspirational and maybe a little provincial but at least they're well aware of who and what they are. These other guys are living in another universe. Imagine Zutere saying he doesn't go to mainland Lagos. Don't human beings live there? I left British classism to come and meet its younger brother in Lagos.'

'I take it it didn't go well,' Zino remarked, staring at me studiously.

Dapo screamed before I could respond; he had only one

volume. Zino squeezed my hand; we would talk later. 'My hand has been up for how many minutes! Why is customer service so bad in this country?' Dapo said.

'Oh my God, tell me about it,' Simi said. 'At the dress shop yesterday I literally had to scream. They act like they're doing you a favour.'

A waiter appeared then with a menu and Dapo asked for a strawberry daiquiri. I flipped the menu open even though I'd already placed my order. New prices were taped over where the old ones had been. 'The prices have changed?' I asked, my tone incredulous.

'I know, right?' Dera had been quiet until now. She ran a boutique PR agency and did not pretend to have any airs.

'This country is going to the dogs,' Zino said flippantly. 'The government is borrowing us to the ground, fuel price has doubled within two years, inflation is on the rise. How is the average citizen expected to survive? What will the poor eat?'

'The country isn't that poor,' Zutere said. 'There's a lot of opportunity for growth and the economy will pick up again. It's just a matter of time. I mean look at the sort of high-class jobs coming to the city. We have to stop being pessimistic and be innovative instead.' He was a certain kind of Nigerian – the kind who saw the rest of the country through the eyes of Lagos.

'It's very easy for you to say the country isn't poor because you're sitting in Lagos. Lagos isn't Nigeria. We cannot innovate our way out of poor governance,' I countered.

'We just need to let go of capitalism,' Simi said. 'Capitalism is the root of all our problems. I mean it's not just in Nigeria; there are disparities in the US – it's what everyone talks about on social media.' She loved to Americanise conversations.

'Our system isn't a capitalist one either,' Zino said, sounding like he'd had enough of Simi's nonsense. 'If our country was even close to a capitalist country, there would actually be a free market across the board and the central bank wouldn't be wasting funds manipulating the country's currency. And to be quite sincere, most of the online discourse around capitalism and communism sounds like something out of the '70s before the end of the Cold War, not a lick of modern economics knowledge between either side.'

There was a stiff silence after that, a tension that crackled as Simi sulked at her phone screen and no one seemed sure of what to say. It was a shift in dynamics; Simi always led the conversations, the others tagging along, and Zino looked on in bored tolerance. I was the wildcard, choosing when and how to participate.

'We should try not to be too drawn into this extreme Western division of left and right,' Ego had said at our last gathering, then she giggled. 'That reminds me, when I was at Oxford, a lecturer in one of these courses about humans asked us to mention strong leaders, so I thought since we're in the UK, I might as well mention Margaret Thatcher. You know in Nigeria, everyone refers to the Iron Lady when we want to describe someone as tough, but I had no idea about her policies or anything like that because it's not the sort of thing we talk about. Oh my God! The class went silent and her face turned really red, and she went, "Oh, well Margaret is a bit like marmalade". I was so confused. It was later that my friend Njoki made me realise my error – I'd mentioned Margaret Thatcher to a lecturer from Liverpool! I was so sure I was going to fail the course after that.'

Ego had narrated the story because she'd found the events funny and I saw that she expected them to share the humour, because they were Nigerian and they were supposed to understand, but they'd stared at her in snide condescension. 'People died, that's not something to laugh about,' Simi said on their behalf, her self-righteousness polished and shining.

Well, except Zino, he'd laughed and laughed until Ego and I nervously joined in.

'We're venturing into film production and have several projects in the works and are interested in bringing in a few actresses on a sort of layered deal to star in our movies and represent some of the brands under our umbrella,' the investor had said in his office. 'I'm Charles, by the way.' And I'd nodded in enthusiasm and listened to his plans for the projects, until his hand crept up my knee then continued its journey up my skirt, nearing my crotch.

'You'll come around in time,' he said when I lurched to my feet to leave.

25

Forgiveness

Forgiveness came easily because I'd learnt it from my father; he caused offence often and expected to be forgiven just as frequently. He wasn't a bad man, just flawed. At his core, he loved. It was a love that pervaded and instilled its will, but it was love all the same. Love that wanted the best for its recipient.

Halil stood outside my front door, a bouquet of tulips blocking his face from view. 'You're not taking my calls,' he stuttered through the petals. I let him in.

'Will you listen to me now?' he asked when the flowers were displayed in a vase on my dining table, adding a radiance to the living room. The lines underneath his eyes said he hadn't slept properly in a while, and I thought he looked like a sad little boy.

I folded my arms and nodded for him to continue. 'I'm so sorry, Zina,' he said, then grabbed at my arms until they came free and pulled me to him; that was the problem with being just below average height, everyone assumed they could fling you about. 'I didn't mean any of it, I know I was wrong. We don't even care about things like that.' He kissed my neck, creating a trail to my ear and I felt my resolve weaken.

'It won't happen again?' I said.

'I swear on my life it won't,' he averred. We kissed and I thought his tongue tasted like *lokum*.

I stared at the flowers after he was gone, running my fingers over their delicate surface, careful not to disturb them. He wanted to meet up for lunch later in the day, spend the evening tasting the assortment of teas that had just arrived at his place. Guilt had coursed through me as I gazed at him; he was good and yet I seemed unable to give myself fully to him.

'I think you purposely go for men you think nothing serious can happen with and if, by some random accident, it starts to get serious, you run,' Ego had observed just the previous week. I'd taken the comment personally and she'd come to my room that night to offer an apology.

I'd always been the one with the problem. In the beginning, they pursued – a hot ardent chase – enchanted by the novelty of it. Then I gave in, and I became too much: too intense, too expressive, too determined to make things happen. And every time this happened, I wondered if I'd lost my appeal, that shine of newness. 'Men love the chase, you have to keep them chasing regardless of status, that is the trick,' Tari always said. But I did not know how to be any other way, my life was a spectrum of extremes. And now? Now, I'd learned not to care.

How long before Halil was just like the rest of them? Malvin who said he found me rather strange, Deziri who thought I didn't have the right personality for a wife, Jachike who only kept white friends (in Lagos!) and assumed I shared his light-skinned aspirations to be considered Caucasian, Tade who loved video calls until I'd begun to reciprocate and he claimed that I was too forward.

Then there was Bayo. He'd come to see me at the hospital – by then it was too late. 'I don't want to see him,' I told Ego, regretting the words as soon as I said them, but Ego delivered the message.

His letter, arriving at my house a week later, only just managed to escape my mother's eye:

Dear Zina,

I don't know how else to reach you and you won't take my calls. I'm so sorry. I realised my mistake when it was too late, when it dawned on me just how close I'd come to losing you. I was selfish and immature in my response. I should have been a source of support and provided assurance. Of course, I wanted a baby with you. You're smart, funny and beautiful. I was afraid of what my parents would think. It's so stupid to think about it now, but that's the truth. I've always made them proud, and I worried they would be disappointed in me. I was wrong, I was so wrong. I've never felt what I feel with you with anyone else. Please give me another chance to make this right, to fix this.

I never responded.

'I leave to check out my place for a few hours and you have a boyfriend again,' Ego joked as we lugged empty moving boxes to her room.

I rolled my eyes. 'Ego, please don't start.'

'Start? I'm happy for you, at least you'll stop spending your weekends watching soap operas.'

'How's the apartment? Is it ready now?'

'Yes, it's quite nice actually. It's well furnished too. I

literally just have to carry my luggage and boxes there and I'm good to go.'

I huffed, unimpressed. 'It took them over a year; it's the least they could do.'

'You know I saw some of my neighbours in the parking lot and for a second I thought I was back in England – they're all white. Apparently only expatriates live there, and the rent is about forty thousand dollars per annum. Thank God, the office is paying. How can they be collecting rent in foreign currency in Lagos?'

It was something she would tweet about, I knew, but for now, her focus – online at least – had shifted to foreign politics and had been firmly placed there for several months, meandering from rants about Brexit to comments on the US election cycle, even though she insisted over and over that she detested politics.

Her reaction to the Brexit votes had made me question whether she loved England far more than she let on, but for America she held a special affinity.

'Americans have a way of making everything a performance,' she told me. 'Even the way they debate their politics on TV, it's all so Hollywood.'

On the morning of the election results, she came into my room before the sun could find its way out, her face hewed with sorrow. Her phone displayed the electoral map of America, unusually red. 'How can this be happening? My mother lives there.'

'It's just the early results, it will change, don't worry,' I assured her.

I'd been wrong.

Her sheer anguish at the events would lead me to believe that it was possible to love a country not for itself but for the loved ones it held.

*

We dropped the boxes on the floor in Ego's room. She'd already begun to pull items from the shelves and the wardrobes; clothes were strewn on the bed and books were arranged in boxes, and I realised just how deserted the place would be when she was gone.

'Zina, do you think I'm too nice?' Ego asked all of a sudden.

I blinked, confused by the question. 'Nooo,' I said slowly. 'Why would you ask that? Did anyone say you're too nice? You know our work culture here is different, very subservient and reliant on respect, it might take a while for them to get used to your relaxed style.'

'I think I'm too nice,' she replied glumly.

'Why?'

'All the other senior executive staff are such bullies you know, and I really didn't want to propagate the whole mean female boss stereotype and so I tried to be friendly and down to earth with everyone when I resumed; I mean I smiled till my gums hurt! Me that used to mind my business when I was in London o. And now I think they're taking me for granted. I ask for tasks to be done and mine are always done last, because no one is scared of me. The other day I held a meeting with new male hires and you wouldn't believe that they left me alone to clear the tea items. Then yesterday, a manager told me that I put on a lot of makeup for a lawyer. Of course, I told him to learn to mind his business and face his work but the fact that he had the effrontery to say such nonsense to my face! I've already given up my nice skirts and fitting dresses for trouser suits because the CEO said they were too clinging. Do I have to give up lipstick too?' She collapsed on the bed.

'You never told me all this was happening to you,' I said, stretching out on the mattress beside her.

'I didn't want you to think I was struggling. You've been

calling me "superstar" since I got back. I finally told Emeka about it and he thinks I need to put my foot down more often, stop being so polite.'

I chuckled. 'You're still a superstar to me. And I agree with Emeka: you need to put your foot down. England has softened you up. The Ego of before never let people get away with rubbish.'

She rolled off the bed and began pulling more books from the shelf. 'I don't want to be known as difficult or a witch. In the UK, I didn't care what anyone thought.'

'My dear, it's better to be a witch than to be a *mumu*. These people will take advantage of you.'

She nodded. 'You have a point. I've been back for a year and yet it still doesn't feel like I belong; I didn't belong over there and I don't belong here either.'

'Don't say that.'

'But it's true, nothing is the way I remember it, not even the food. It was too cold for me in London and it's too hot for me in Lagos. And now I'm not even Nigerian enough for work?'

'What accent do you use at the office? Maybe that's part of the problem,' I joked.

'Semi-British,' she returned and made a face.

'That sound you make when you call your friend Ceri? Is that thing a British accent?'

A book flew in my direction, I dodged it.

'Fool!'

We laughed.

The moving van came at 5pm instead of 4pm as agreed, and the driver complained of traffic on Ozumba Mbadiwe Expressway. Within an hour, Ego's room had been cleared, and the items in the storage room moved to the back of the van. We followed behind in my car.

'Your house is going to be empty now that I've moved out. You know, you're a strange one. You don't have a driver, you order all your food from caterers, no live-in help or anything, they all come and go except your gateman.'

'I enjoy being alone,' I explained.

'You lived with me.'

I shrugged.

In my early years, my mother had been a paranoid woman, she believed in witches and unknown powers, in poisoned and bewitched items, in enemies lurking, plotting to do you harm. We had no nannies, no cooks, no live-in help aside from our gateman Salau, and somehow, even though I barely shared her beliefs, I'd become just the same.

Urenna's first son turned ten that year and my mother insisted on throwing a party when my sister's husband declared he did not have money for such frivolities. Nulia forwarded the invite via WhatsApp: Ejimetochukwu, suited up at the centre, surrounded by the words, *'You're cordially invited to celebrate with the Okafors on the momentous occasion of our son turning a Glorious Ten.'*

Glorious. It was a word my mother liked. The fact that my father's surname was used on the invite was a clear shot at Urenna's husband: they would claim his wife and her children if he pushed his luck.

Nulia's message said: *'You should come, Mummy said it's going to be big this year. Come with a nice gift so they won't throw you out xx.'*

The house had begun to feel empty since Ego left. It was that thing about life where a momentary change left you unable to return to how it had been before. I stopped at a popular game store, paid for a PlayStation console and a few games – what I assumed were the perfect gifts for a ten-year-old – to be wrapped and drove to my parents' house.

The music reverberated through the compound gates, thumping from the speakers, causing the earth under our feet to quake a little. I parked my car across the street and walked to the gate with the gifts under my arm, ignoring the stunned expression on Salau's face as I passed.

Colourful inflated castles bobbed in the air, and children sprang from their confines screaming at the top of their lungs. An MC led the gatherings, urging other attendees into dance competitions and coaxing their parents into interactive games. Costumed cartoon characters ran around and danced, scaring some of the children to tears. Smoke from the back of the compound where the caterers were at work wafted through the air. It was just like it had been when we were children. My mother loved to plan parties, and regardless of circumstance, she ensured all her children had birthday parties for their tenth birthdays; except me – I'd been in boarding school then. Ifeadigo had celebrated every birthday until he left for senior secondary school, but he was their only son.

Under a canopy, my sisters were huddled together, observing the goings-on, pointing and laughing at their children's antics. Nulia was squeezed beside them, seemingly uninterested, then she sighted me from afar and she jumped to wave. I moved quickly towards them, keeping my head averted to avoid notice.

Urenna, Jachinma and Sofuchi's eyes followed my approach, their faces a blanket of disconcerted distrust. 'Hi!' I called when I was close. They didn't respond.

Nulia grabbed my arm and pulled me towards the seat she'd reserved. 'I almost thought you weren't coming. I've been so bored without you!' she effused, dragging my handbag and scattering through it. 'You'll have to *dash* me this bag, it's so fine. Which label is this?' she said, running her fingers over the leather surface.

'When you're not a thief,' I retorted and snatched my bag from between her fingers.

'Ahn-ahn. Why are you acting like you don't have finer ones? I should even visit you to raid your wardrobe. You think I don't see your pictures? We should take a picture together before you go, see we're both wearing red. Did you come with your Range?'

I laughed, not showing my discomfort. 'Nulia, are you sure you're here for a birthday party? In fact, where is the celebrant?' I asked, leaning my head to the side in search of Jimeto.

'He's inside the house,' Sofuchi answered. I turned, surprised she'd spoken to me. She averted her eyes as I studied her. I'd always thought she was the prettiest of the lot of us, with her unblemished ebony skin, but I was the fairest and so everyone said I was the prettiest. She looked pregnant, and if indeed she was, she would have been the last of my sisters to have a child; it made me wonder how much pressure she was under to fulfil this pre-eminent duty.

'Mummy is changing him into a second outfit,' Nulia adjoined. 'I don't know whether she thinks he's a girl or something. How many suits can he wear?'

'Thank you,' I said to Sofuchi and rose to go inside.

Nothing had changed: the photographs that decorated the room, the Catholic calendar plastered to the wall, the large crucifix above the television, the rosary that drooped down from above it. In a prominent corner hung a full-size portrait of the last picture we'd taken together as a family – just after my brother was born.

It didn't surprise me that there was no sign of my father on the premises; he never attended such events. He was raised to believe men provided, and he'd always done just that.

My mother emerged like a ghost from the staircase as I picked at the figurines on the étagère; my father had added new ones in my absence. 'What are you doing here?' she demanded. My nephew was by her side, peeping at me with avid interest.

I straightened my spine, forced a broad smile on my face I was sure was too bright, and stretched the wrapped presents in front of me like a shield. 'I came to wish Jimeto a happy birthday.'

I moved closer, slowly, like a zoophilist afraid to frighten their subject of interest away. When I stood in front of them, I bent to greet Jimeto. My mother snatched him behind her.

'I just wanted to wish him a happy birthday and give him his gifts,' I explained, straightening myself once more.

'Zinachukwu. I asked, what are you doing here?'

My confidence disappeared. 'I–I–heard today was Jimeto's birthday so I came.'

'Who is Jimeto to you that you think you can come in when you like to wish him anything? So after how many years, you remember you have a family? Who even told you about the party?'

I could feel the tears gathering at the back of my eyes but I was powerless to stop them. I sighed. 'What have I done that is so wrong? You told me to leave then, you said I should make something of myself and I did. You never gave me a chance but somehow I did. I might not be the biggest name in the industry but you can't say I'm a failure. Why do you hate me so much?'

My mother cackled, a sound that resembled nails against

a chalkboard, then she said, 'Success? You call the rubbish life you're living successful? You don't even go by your real name anymore, just Zina. Zina who? Go outside and look at your sisters and their families, that is success. You chose your selfish ambitions over your own family and you expect to be welcomed back like a queen. Not once have you shown any form of remorse! You've made your choice, be happy with it.'

A woman's hand grabbed my shoulder as I hurried towards the gate. I stopped to look at her. 'Ehen! I thought it was you. You're so beautiful! I really like your films. My daughter likes you too. Please can you take a picture with us?' She was already searching her phone for the camera icon, not bothering to wait for my response.

I posed for the pictures, grateful for the sunglasses I'd brought along. I pushed the wrapped gifts into her daughter's hands before I left. 'Give this to the birthday boy,' I told her. Then I rushed out the gate. I could hear Nulia's voice behind me screaming my name.

The nightmares would come, I knew – they always did after I saw my mother. Rather than await the torture, I pre-empted their arrival this time: bite, break, swallow.

A text message was on my screen when I finally opened my eyes: *'Hi Zina. It's me, Bayo.'*

26

Circumstances

We have no say in the circumstances of our birth – the very things that determine the people we become: our parents, our families, our country.

The children running around in the sandy compound of their thatched roof hut home surrounded by a thicket of bushes, shrieking their names as they play catch, pulling at the hems of each other's shirts, oblivious as to how a proportion of the trajectory of their lives' stories had been set in ink, the strength of will and force of nature it would take to turn it, the scars the efforts would leave, the country that had inherently failed them. I watched them through the window by my side, unsure of where I was exactly, uninterested in knowing.

'How long until we get to Ogbomosho?' I asked the airport taxi driver, not removing my eyes from the children. The smallest and quickest had just caught the eldest and they'd both fallen into the sand in shrill laughter, their backs covered in sand. I searched for a sign of electricity and saw a lone bulb, hanging at a corner of the ceiling of an adjoining hut. Questions scurried in my mind: did the electricity come often enough? Was that enough for them to study in the evenings? Were there any schools nearby? Such was the injustice of the lottery of birth.

'About thirty minutes, ma,' the driver said. I strained my neck to get a better glimpse of the children already disappearing into the foliage. How old were they? 'Madam, you like children? You get any?' the driver asked, smiling at me through the rearview mirror; he'd been paying attention.

I wasn't sure how to answer the first question, nor the second. If he'd asked my mother, she would have said no to the first, and for the second, she would have answered yes, only to emphasise the role I'd played in that no longer being so. No woman who loved children, who had a modicum of maternal instincts, would have done what I did.

There were gift hampers with chocolates, roses and wine waiting on my bed when I arrived at the hotel in Ogbomosho. 'We were told you'd be coming early, ma,' the steward that assisted me to my room explained. I always arrived a day ahead of everyone to enjoy a moment of solitude before the madness began – the twelve-hour days and early-morning shoots, the late nights rehearsing lines and miming scenes – but it wasn't often that I received such an affectionate welcome filming outside a major city, or with a producer who wasn't Zino.

The producers for the film had changed at the last minute, the government's latest fiscal policies were discouraging international investors despite the boom in the film industry and explosion in overseas interest.

Zino complained that many had turned their focus to low-budget movies – filmed and edited in a matter of days – that earned a quick turnover by selling to cable TV. 'Not that those are bad of course, everyone is allowed to make their money and there's a market for that, but we also need to be able to convince investors to finance big-budget projects that can move the industry forward on a larger scale. The issue is the economy and the government. Imagine investing in dollars and the naira earnings don't meet up because the exchange rate has moved against you in a matter of months, with a government that regularly interferes in the market,' he said.

This time, the producers had withdrawn after initial funds were blocked by a parastatal for supposed investigation. A local financier had eventually taken up the project but by then, filming had already been on hold for well over six months.

A card was tucked into one of the hampers and I reached for it just as my phone rang – it was Marve. It was strange; she never called. We were friends with Tare and not necessarily each other. But I'd noticed a change since our last meeting, a new willingness to trust.

Tare and Cassandra had fallen out over Cassandra liking an anonymous Instagram blog post accusing Tare's husband of an affair with another actress, an accusation Tare had asserted was contrived to dent her family's image. Cassandra insisted that the 'like' had been an accident on her part as she'd read the post, and they'd both taken to passing subliminals via Instagram stories:

'Avoid enemies cloaked as friends. And avoid marrying men old enough to be your fathers #wisdomoftheday,' was Tare's first jab.

'Exodus 20:16 – Thou shalt not bear false witness against thy neighbour #godwillfightforme. Also, my children look better than yours,' Cassandra returned.

As expected, Cassandra was absent from the get-togethers after that, and our numbers fell even further with Zahrah's absence as she travelled up north to prepare for her upcoming wedding. Marve offered to host; a neutral ground should Cassandra decide to change her mind, and then at the very last minute, Tare phoned to say she wouldn't be coming. For the first time, it was just me and Marve in the same room, forced to get to know each other.

'You have to learn to secure your options,' she told me. She had three boyfriends – an accountant, an entertainer and a businessman, even though she wasn't particularly sure of the specialty of his business.

'I don't know how you do it, I'd mix up their names and get caught,' I said.

'Mix up *ke*? You're not serious. What is your brain for? Chigbo is the accountant but his earnings are not enough to meet my needs, Pero is doing well but he's yet to blow, and Jide can afford to buy me whatever I want. One of them will eventually propose. If any of them starts acting unserious, I switch up immediately – there are many fishes in the sea. There's even one footballer that's on my case but he plays for a second division team in Ukraine. How much can he be earning there?'

It wasn't uncommon but it never failed to amaze me how easily people were willing to be duplicitous in love. I shook my head with a smile and said, 'But do you like or love any of them? You must like one more than the rest.'

She laughed, a belly-aching laughter that let me know just how funny she found my assertion. 'Love? In this economy? You're not serious. You better wake up, streets are rugged.'

I dropped the card on the hamper without reading it and picked up my phone.

Marve appeared to be in the middle of a panic attack. 'Zina, please I need your help.'

'What happened?' I asked, sitting on the bed and preparing for the worst.

'A picture I posted is on a popular blog. Oh God, what do I do?' she said.

The blogs had the power to make or mar reputations, to twist lives and tarnish relationships. We feared them, loathed their influence and paid to manipulate them to our will.

'Why did they post your picture?' I asked, relaxing now that I knew it wasn't a life-or-death issue.

'My assistant photoshopped the picture and she didn't do it well, stupid girl. The wall bent around my ass. What am I going to do? All the brands I influence for! People will say they're fake. And I just trended on Twitter the other day for tweeting something innocent.'

'You trended?' I'd never acquired the obsession with social media, the desire to grow a following like a trained pet, ready to do your bidding, the obscene power we'd accorded the opinions of others over our lives, the breathless trepidation at being 'cancelled'.

'You didn't see? I tweeted one quote I saw online o, people thought I was subbing another actress, what is her name again? *Ehen* Boma! I didn't even know she was trending for her boyfriend *wahala*. Which kind bad luck be this?'

I giggled in the face of her panic, unable to help it. 'Why are you photoshopping your ass? It's big enough as it is. And your waist is small enough.'

'Ah you know I'm influencing for this brand that sells waist trainers, buttocks cream and half-caste soap. I was just trying to encourage my followers to buy from them.'

'You don't even use any of these things. You're naturally fair and you've had plastic surgery.'

'Zina *abeg*, I called for a solution not a lecture. Can you help or not?'

I suddenly felt in need of a cigarette. 'I'll call Zino, he

knows everyone. He might be able to get it taken down, but it will most likely cost something,' I said.

Marve exhaled in relief. 'I'm ready to pay any amount. God bless you.'

The knock at my door excited me because I assumed it was the food I'd ordered – fried snail and special fried rice, the first proper meal I would have in weeks, a break from my extended diets.

Charles was resting confidently against the frame when I pulled the door open. He straightened with a cocky smile; I hadn't set eyes on him since the botched meeting at his office. 'Hello Zina. Did you get my special package?'

My face squeezed into a frown. 'What are you doing here?'

He raised a supercilious brow, then smiled. 'You had no idea, did you? That it was my company financing this project?' My stomach sank; I'd been so grateful that the project had been taken up that I'd not bothered to look into the financiers.

'Are you not going to ask me to come in at least?' he mocked when I stayed silent. He eyed my skirt. 'Is this how you travelled here? Isn't that skirt a little too short?'

I laughed at the irony, the effrontery even. 'What do you want?'

Eyes twinkling, he stretched out a hand and ran it over my hair and down the side of my face, I struggled to remain expressionless even though all I could feel was disgust. 'I don't think you need to ask that question.'

He was a man accustomed to this, to wielding his wealth and privilege as a weapon until he achieved what he wanted. I thought about how easy it would be give in, to fuck him and get it over with so I could be left alone.

I'd heard a story once, of a girl who told a persistent admirer that she'd been dedicated to a god as a child – it was why she was so beautiful – and anyone who was intimate with her against her will would die within seven days; his pursuit had ended after that. Would it be so hard to believe if I said the same?

Charles was irritated by my silence. The cavalier smile disappeared and a contemptuous sneer took its place. 'Why are you acting like this? It's not like it's your first time. I've heard the stories about you. I've even gone as far as sponsoring your film and this is how you behave?'

I slammed the door in his face.

'What happened? I hear the producers are having issues with you?' Zino asked me over video call two weeks later.

'It's nothing serious, just a minor misunderstanding,' I answered. I did not need it becoming a bigger issue than it was. Eventually Charles would accept no for an answer; he'd heard it enough in the past weeks.

'Are you sure? I've never heard anyone say you're difficult to work with. I've never found you difficult to work with either. I don't like what I'm hearing.'

I smiled at his concern. 'It's really nothing that can't be sorted, I promise.'

'You'll get tired of this act eventually. Let me know when you're ready,' Charles had said to me after I had the stewards return the baskets to his room.

Some connections were simply etched in the very lining of the cosmos. It was what I thought as I observed Ego and Emeka. I'd never told her about the times Emeka had called my phone, pretending to be interested in catching up just so he could catch an unintentional slip-up on my part about Ego, the days we'd met up for lunch and how his ears had perked up at the mention of her name, his eyes pleading with me to reveal just a little more. I'd wanted her to move on, to walk away from the murkiness of the past, but watching them as we had dinner at her apartment – the inordinate subtle caresses, the clandestine whispers, the unmistakable ardour every time their eyes connected – I realised I'd expected the impossible.

'Romance!' I texted Ego at the table.

'Can you behave? 😂' she replied and sent a warning glance in my direction.

Bayo had been calling and texting nonstop, tempting me to change my phone number. But that night, I called him.

'Hello?' he answered tentatively when the line connected, and I thought he sounded exactly the same as he had years ago, the same shy boy unsure of himself and his advances. 'Zina, are you there?'

'What do you want? You won't stop calling or texting. What do you want from me?'

'Can we meet to talk in person? I know I deserve your contempt but please give me a chance to explain.'

'Craft Gourmet. 9pm tomorrow,' I said and disconnected the call.

I found a sleeveless cocktail dress with an asymmetrical hemline at the back of my wardrobe and decided it was the best option for the evening, a dress that said the events of a decade ago hadn't, despite their best efforts, left me shattered.

I went hoping to put a stop to the nightmares that appeared to be the universe's way of telling me there were issues unresolved. He was already seated when I arrived, and I thought time had been good to him. He looked different, mature in a way that gave him presence.

'You don't wear glasses anymore,' I said.

'Contacts,' he replied with an awkward smile as he pulled out a seat for me. He still wasn't very tall.

I pulled nervously at the hem of my dress as I sat.

'What would you like to have?' he asked, placing a menu in front of me. 'I collected two when the waiter came by earlier,' he explained and I remembered he'd been like that at the start our relationship: eager to make me happy. He would buy our lunch on the way back from class and run under the rain to get a taxi so my hair wouldn't get wet.

Annoyance at the memories sprung up. I pushed the menu aside. 'Let's get this over with, what do you want? Why won't you leave me alone?'

He looked nervous again and I felt a sardonic satisfaction at watching him. 'Please don't be like that. You look beautiful,' he said.

'Be like what?' I demanded, ignoring the compliment, holding his stare and daring him to say something unflattering.

He sighed, defeated. 'Zina, I'm sorry. I'm so sorry.'

I looked away, afraid my face reflected the pain that crushed through me. 'It's been over ten years, Bayo. It's rather late for that.'

'A lot has happened since then,' he said. I rolled my eyes. 'My mother died a few weeks ago.'

The anger dissipated and I was overtaken by sadness. I'd loved his mother, her vivacious personality and zestful eagerness to assure others of her affections, and I often wondered if that was how regular families functioned, so different from mine.

My eyes closed of their own volition. 'I'm so sorry,' I said.

'Eat with me Zina, please,' he begged, placing the menu in front of me once more. 'Cancer,' he explained to me minutes later, plates of steaming pasta in front of us. 'Why do Lagos girls like pasta so much?' he'd joked when I placed my order, then asked for the same as well.

'She liked you a lot,' he said.

'I liked her too,' I heard myself murmuring.

'I told her the truth before she left; she'd been asking what happened and I finally told her.' He held my eyes. 'I told her everything: the baby, the hospital, everything. I didn't want her going without knowing. It didn't matter anymore if she was disappointed in me or not, I just wanted her to know.'

Tears converged to a well behind my eyes and I struggled to blink them away. He reached across the table and held my hands, and for a while we were both silent, caught up in the waves of the past, nostalgic for what could have been.

27

Mistakes

Life is to be lived, mistakes to be made, or at least that was what I told myself as I let Bayo into my house days after our meeting at the restaurant. He held a teddy bear in his hands and I was going to joke that he thought I had a child in the house when I thought better of it.

'Thank you,' I said instead, taking it from him and smelling the fur. My favourite perfume. He remembered.

Bayo looked around my living room like he wanted to fulfil a curiosity he'd had for a while. 'You decorate well,' he said, picking up a throw pillow and relaxing on a sofa. I perched on the arm. He was more confident today.

'Thank you,' I said, following his eyes, trying to view the curtains and paintings through them. I picked an imaginary thread from the sofa. 'Do you still practise law?'

He turned to me. 'Yes, I run my father's law firm now actually. It was really small back then, but we've been able to grow. We received an award from the Nigerian Bar Association just last year.'

'Oh wow! Congratulations,' I said. I wondered if he felt

the need to impress me, and if my desire to assure him reflected in how I said 'wow', drawing out the phonemes unnecessarily.

He gestured at me. 'And look at you, you did it. You talked so much about acting and now look at you. I passed a billboard on my way here with your face on it.'

I blushed, self-conscious.

'I watch your movies, you know,' he said.

I raised a brow. 'Really?

'Yes, really. At first, I was curious – "what does she look now? Is she any good?" – that sort of thing, then I actually enjoyed them and so I decided to see more. I have to say, they're good. I really like the fact that you pick scripts outside the usual themes, like the one about a woman's battle with her past demons and mental health, it seemed so real and personal.' He stared at me, waiting for me to say more, to admit the movie had been personal.

I waved a dismissive hand. 'Oh, well I have to give my friend Zino credit for that one. He chooses the best screenwriters and mentions my name in every casting room.'

His smile faltered at the mention of another man's name, and I didn't bother to correct his assumptions, delighting in it; I was a bundle of nerves and uncertainty and here he was acting like it was a regular day.

'I should offer you something,' I said, pushing to my feet. 'What do you drink? I won't boast but I have a decent wine collection.' I walked towards the wine bar.

His smile returned. 'Well, let's see what you have,' he said and got up to join me. We were flirting, and I wasn't sure why.

I pulled out a bottle of Château Lafite Rothschild. 'It's French,' I said with a wink.

He made a face. '*Wooh*, you drank palm wine with me at the school joint every weekend. Now you're all bougie.'

I smiled as I searched for a corkscrew. 'Please, I was just managing you then. This is my true form.'

He took the bottle and corkscrew from my hands gently and proceeded to work on the seal. 'You have only one form. You can't change.' He pulled the cork free and poured the wine into two glasses; he handed one to me.

'What?' I exclaimed in mock offence. 'Don't be so sure. It's been a long time. I have multiple forms. How do you think I play different roles?'

His stare turned intense and the room suddenly felt charged. 'I'm sure because I know you,' he said. Then he kissed me, a gentle kiss at first, uncertain – he wasn't as confident as I'd thought – then it turned deeper. We were meant to be drinking wine and catching up like old friends, but we were in my living room kissing, then we were in my bedroom, taking off each other's clothes like we were on a bunk in law school, unhinged from time: we were twenty-three again, zestful for a life we pictured together.

He stroked a hand across my belly afterwards. 'I'm so sorry Zina, I should have been there.' And I thought he sounded just as tortured as I'd been.

'You're making a mistake,' Ego said to me in my living room a week later. She was spending the weekend. 'It's lonely over there sometimes,' she said.

'Just say Emeka travelled and stop lying,' I told her.

Ego was still speaking. 'What about Halil? Does he know anything about this? It's unfair to do this to him. You're many things, Zinachukwu, but you're not a dishonest person.'

Halil had called several times for days and I'd left the

phone ringing on my nightstand, unable to face him, to think of a way out of the maze I'd created, then suddenly he was at my door, asking to know what he'd done wrong and I couldn't conjure an answer. Instead, I picked a fight, acting a part that wasn't me – surly and rude for no reason at all except my pricking conscience – and he'd left, only to return with a wrapped box and an apology, and not for the first time, I truly felt like the spawn of the devil my mother thought I was.

'Haven't you ever felt a connection that you can't explain? There are things I can talk to him about that I can't even think of mentioning to Halil. Maybe it's because of our past or because he's Nigerian and I'm not always thinking of how to explain issues in a way he'd understand or in a way that wouldn't offend his sensibilities or make him think we're strange or something,' I said.

Ego harrumphed and tore open a packet of biscuits. She stretched it in my direction. 'Diet,' I said, putting my hand up.

She hissed. 'You're always on a diet. Don't kill yourself o, this life is only one. *Aye o pe meji.*'

I laughed at her distorted Yoruba pronunciation, then I said, 'You know you're being judgemental again,' steering the conversation back to where it began. 'How's this different from what you and Emeka have?' I did not add that just like them, tragedy tied Bayo and me together.

'I get what you're trying to say, I really do, on all levels.' She held my gaze to let me know she'd heard the words unsaid. 'But Zina, I know you. You don't love him – even back then, you didn't. You liked how innocent and infatuated he was with you and everything you did. The boy couldn't believe his luck that you gave him a second glance. You barely knew each other, you still don't. I'm sure you still haven't told him about your time in Onitsha and what led you here. Or even about that married fool that is harassing you now.'

'I don't love Halil either,' I protested.

'Well fine, break up with both of them – I'll always think Halil is cute by the way – but this double life isn't for you.' She picked up the TV remote; she was done saying her piece. 'What does Zino think?' she asked, her eyes frozen on the channel scroll.

'Why would I ask Zino?'

'Well, he seems to be the one with more sense of the both of you.'

My foot connected with her side.

We'd watched several Mexican telenovela episodes in quick succession when Ego decided she was in the mood for a sermon. She flipped through the cable channels until she landed on a religious station.

'Nwakaego, stop playing around and give me the remote. I was enjoying that,' I said.

'You need a good sermon to reset your brain,' she retorted.

I'd grown up under the weight of sermons: the declarations against evil, the prayers for wayward and sinful children, the miracle services and pastors waving fingers and blowing air until members of their congregation flipped over. They were all my mother watched, her anchor in the storms of her marriage to my father. After cable TV came to Nigeria, my father paid for a decoder and the accompanying satellite dish, and soon enough, my mother gravitated towards the American evangelists, digesting their every word, discerning situations only through the tunnel of their views. My father never missed a cable payment after that, and I thought that he appreciated the distraction it gave her, the reassuring hope it ignited so she would never realise she deserved better.

Choir members led the congregation in song. Ego sang along and I wondered how she could watch anyone sing without remembering her father. Perhaps she was no longer hungry for his approval, and I felt a pang of jealousy.

'I love this hymn, it comforts me every time I hear it,' she said as the choir sang 'Amazing Grace'.

The singing ended and a young man took the stage to perform the duties of what would have been a hype man had it been a concert and not a church service: ' . . . a man of God! A man of vision! God's anointed to break every chain in your life! If you're ready to hear from heaven today I want you to raise your voiiiiccceee!' The crowd roared.

I smiled, amused by his antics. If this pastor was as good as he said, perhaps he would have a solution to my recurring nightmares. The camera panned to the seated man, his head bowed in prayer, and I felt my blood turn to ice. Ego's phone rang then. It was Emeka. 'Don't change the channel o, I'm coming back now,' she shouted as she ran out of the room without looking at the television. I was too frozen to move.

I stared at the bowed head again; I'd seen it only once but I could recognise it anywhere. I'd heard stories of him, through many others, and Ego would have too if she'd been given to gossip. He'd started his own ministry since the last time I saw him, and now he owned a private jet and was only ever clothed in designer items. He'd married his then fiancée and had two children; the stories still trailed him, but more than ever, he had the backing to squash them. Reckoning never came for evil in our world, instead it was elevated and exalted.

I watched Pastor Kamsi amble up the stage with confidence, and thought I'd never felt so much hatred for one person. How he could be allowed to exist freely and brazenly, maiming and devastating the lives of others without consequence I could never understand. Were his protectors all just like him, or were these women's lives so negligible that they could be sacrificed on the altar of ambition?

I overheard Ego telling Emeka she loved him and I realised that their conversation was about to end. My limbs loosened and sprang into action.

'This woman, why did you change the channel?' Ego whined as soon as she returned to the living room.

'I'm not in the mood for a sermon. This soap is very interesting. I've already missed some scenes and now I don't know why this guy is under surveillance,' I responded, infusing as much nonchalance as I could into my tone.

'Give me the remote,' she demanded.

'No!' I said, pushing it further into a corner behind me.

We wrestled like professionals, falling off the sofa to the floor. She was taller than me and should have made quick work of my efforts, but I had determination on my side, and when I was determined, I was undefeated.

I cut my slits with my mother in mind. Whenever the designers asked, 'How high?' I placed my finger at a point I knew my mother would consider scandalous, and as I admired the final products of their imaginations, I imagined her screaming at the photos in the magazines and on the blogs, powerless to do anything about it.

'Zina, your dress is fine o. Ahn-ahn, which designer is this?' Tare said. We were at her house preparing for the premiere of the movie I'd shot in South Africa because we'd agreed to hire out the same makeup and hair studio.

Cassandra stood to run her fingers across the mesh of the

middle and the wing of the arm. 'This is good.' It wasn't a compliment she gave out easily. 'Zina, it's like you're out to intimidate us today. Take it easy,' she said.

Cassandra and Tare had settled their differences over party invites – Tare's husband's footballer friend had organised a party Cassandra was eager to attend and Tare had gotten her the invite – and now they posted pictures together on Instagram and left saccharine comments on each other's posts to remind the bloggers they were no longer enemies.

'I still haven't done my hair and makeup, and you're talking intimidation. Just wait and see,' I boasted unabashedly. They laughed.

We could hardly hear Zahrah's voice above the noise of the blow dryer and television at the other end of the room. She waved her hand at the stylist and the noise died. The hairdresser looked disgruntled; Zahrah didn't notice. 'Zina, this is beautiful, and please don't get me wrong, but why is our fashion so aggressive? It's so in your face.'

'Hmm, Zahrah you've come again with your Americanah,' Cassandra said.

'I don't think there's anything wrong with that,' I said. 'We've never been understated people. There's no reason our fashion should become understated to appeal to certain sensibilities.'

Zahrah had already shown us her dress: a simply-cut turtleneck gown that billowed to her ankles, and Tare had asked if she intended to die of heat.

Zahrah's wedding had been a glamorous affair graced by the political juggernauts of Nigerian society. As her friends, we'd attended to plaster her with wads of cash as she danced, but we'd all noticed the sharp pivot in her style since it took place and we wondered how soon it would be before she told us she was no longer interested in acting.

I glanced at my phone as the argument continued, unsure what I was checking for. I'd invited Ego but she had no interest in appearing in pictures that might feature in newspapers.

Messages from Halil and Bayo buzzed at the same time. I never took a date to premieres because I tried to keep my relationships private but Halil had been eager to come with me, as if sensing a stutter on my part. Bayo wasn't aware there was a premiere to begin with.

My conversation with Ego had left me unsteady and anxious, and one day, as we lay in bed staring at the ceiling, wrapped in balmy silence and spent desire, I asked Bayo, 'What's my favourite colour?' It was a few months since we first met up at the restaurant.

He chuckled. 'That's a weird question.'

I sighed. 'Just answer.'

'Red?' He grinned, a triumphant grin because he'd gotten it right.

'How much do you know about me?' I asked. 'Like beyond the regular things, like my favourite colour?'

'Zina, why are you asking this all of a sudden?'

I propped myself up and said, 'My favourite colour might still be the same but I've changed as a person in many ways. Do you know that? I'm sure you've changed as well.'

His face crinkled in confusion but he said nothing.

'You come here every other day and we have sex but that's it. You've never even asked how I became an actress or what happened in between. Or when my next movie is out or even what books I read. What are we really doing? We can't keep living in the past.'

Bayo rolled out of bed and hurriedly began to pull on his clothes. I stared at him, confused. 'Where are you going?'

He sat down to wear his shoes. 'You're doing this thing you do again.'

I blinked. 'What thing do I do?'

'That thing where you act like every man is your father and you try to push them away.'

It was as though I'd been hit by a boulder, and my heart began to race. I tried to say something but the words hung in my throat; instead I watched as he stomped out of my room and seconds later, I heard the door bang downstairs. I hadn't heard from him since.

I read the texts without opening them:

Halil: 'Where are you getting ready? I want to come over to pick you up.'

Bayo: 'I think I forgot my wristwatch at your place. Please send to this address:'

I clicked my screen black.

Marve came late as usual, just as one of the hairdressers was burning curls into my wig. She dragged a sizeable box behind her.

'I know I'm late but I promise it's for a good cause. You won't believe the gist I gathered today, in fact it's so plenty I don't know where to start,' she announced, dropping her box and zipping down the front of her fashionable tracksuit. 'Remember Oma announced her engagement to her very rich *bobo* last month, that we were all congratulating her for bagging? He has been picked up by EFCC for fraud. And

Nkiruka – the tall fair one that was in that film with Bisi Somolu – fought Blessing Giri in a salon in Lekki Phase 1 for sleeping with her boyfriend, boyfriend that already has three wives o. *Omo* things are happening!'

28

Wind and truth

The wind had started in America, a turbid and sudden yet not-so-sudden wind that had taken its time to form a surge rooted in the pain of many. Then a single tweet caused it to erupt into a cyclone that rocked the world. Twitter threads were written, blog posts were put up and Facebook was flooded with harrowing recounts, heads lopped off in numbers. Women had found their voices and were no longer to be silent in the face of abuse. #MeToo.

Dera was hopeful that the same could happen in Nigeria. 'We're already seeing threads on Twitter and anonymous Facebook posts. Hopefully it can translate offline and across industries. I'm sure the stories here are even more horrific.'

She wasn't one to talk much but had brought up the topic as soon as we'd all settled in Zino's living room. There were expensive wines, cocktails, platters of canapés, charcuterie boards and trays of small chops arrayed around the plush space. Zino knew how to host a gathering.

'I'm very doubtful to be honest, but maybe I'm just pessimistic,' I said, biting into a piece of fruit. 'You need a functioning justice system that will hold people to account and we just don't have that.'

'The conversation online has been encouraging though, I must say,' Simi said, then glanced nervously at Zino as if expecting him to contradict her. She'd been that way since the evening he'd spoken to her sharply at the Cosmopolitan, jumpy, expectant of a reproval. Zino lounged on a sofa across from her, seemingly oblivious to her newfound apprehension. He said nothing.

'We have other important issues to worry about. Let's not allow ourselves to be sucked into issues in the West,' Dapo said, his voice once again reverberant. I'd come to assume that he'd been brought up in a large polygamous home and had to raise his voice to be heard. 'We started last year with scarcity of tomatoes, the economy is barely out of recession, prices are soaring, people are unemployed, insecurity is rising and now, our government is arresting and bullying reporters that criticise them. I feel like we trend a new hashtag every day for a reporter that was picked up for interrogation by the Department of State Services for simply reporting the truth. Are we going to continue living like this?'

'The whole world is forging forward and we seem to be plunging back into the ugly past days of the military regimes,' Zutere commented.

'That's what you lot get for voting in a former military dictator. It was Shakespeare that said, 'What is past is prologue', but we willingly decided to make our prologue the story again,' Zino said, finally chiming in.

Dapo huffed, exasperated. 'Zino, when are you going to forgive us for voting for this man? We were hopeful and unhappy with the previous government. We were fooled by the propaganda and people that we trusted that campaigned for him. It's been almost three years now – saying "I told you so" doesn't change anything. We're all suffering this together.'

Zino raised a nonchalant brow. 'I still told you so.'

I decided to speak. 'How come it's when women's issues come up that you people suddenly remember all the country's problems? How does women speaking up against their abusers and holding them to account affect the economy? Will these issues suddenly disappear if we don't speak up?'

'That's true,' Dera said. 'I've never heard Dapo or Zutere say we shouldn't get involved in Western issues until today, in fact we're always discussing topics outside our sphere.'

'True,' Zino chimed, a glint of mischief in his eyes.

'Oh Lord, you women have come again,' Dapo shouted, his voice even louder than usual. 'I'm saying freedom of speech is collapsing before our very eyes and you're talking about some women accusing men of abuse in the West.'

'And so?! And so?!' Dera screamed all of a sudden. A bubble within her had burst, and quiet and meek Dera had suddenly erupted into a wild woman loud enough to challenge Dapo. 'Has freedom of speech not been collapsing for years? Why is it now you want to discuss it? Are you the only person in this room?'

Zutere stared at the both of them with dilated pupils, and Simi had gone quiet again, busy picking at cheese on a board. I glanced at Zino. It was his house; he had the power to diffuse the situation.

'If you're going to fight, please just don't break my crystals. They cost quite a ton. I have to make a call,' he announced as he placed his glass on a stool and rose to his feet, making his way out of the living room. Zino gave Dera's shoulder an encouraging pat as he passed by her seat, as if to say, 'You've got this.'

Dapo remained frozen in shock. Was this the first time a woman had yelled at him?

'Let's all try to calm down,' I intervened. 'Please.' Dapo folded his arms and burrowed into his seat like a child and Dera excused herself to use the bathroom.

By the time Dera returned, Dapo had taken up a conversation with Zutere and Simi and Zino still wasn't back from his call. She poured herself a glass of white wine and found a space beside me on the sofa; I was her chosen ally.

'Hope you're calmer now,' I said, shifting to make space for her.

'I am, thank you,' she replied. 'He's so silly and misogynistic. Does he think he's the only one that can shout?'

I nodded and glanced in Dapo's direction, grateful for the size of Zino's living room in preventing them from overhearing Dera's comment and reigniting the altercation.

'He's very stuck in his ideas of masculinity. I've noticed it,' Dera continued. 'He thinks men and women are meant to speak and act only a certain way. Outdated idiot. I've heard him make shady comments about Zino's style, speech and mannerisms. He always does it when neither of you is around.' I wondered if she would have told me this if they hadn't just fallen out. Had she laughed at the jokes with Dapo then? Were they all here only for what they could gain from Zino? Was I the same as them?

Zino walked in then, holding two new bottles. 'I was going to keep them for a special day, but since we're all in a bad mood, maybe these will help lighten things up.'

Dapo jumped up to take one of the bottles from him. 'Oh wow, this costs like 5k dollz. Zino, you're the best mahn.'

*

'I want to have children,' I told Nwakaego in her apartment. She'd been back for a few years now. I could see the open ocean through the glass that bathed the room in natural light.

'With who? Me?' she joked, assuming I was joking as well.

'I'm serious,' I said, staring at her.

Her smile disappeared as her eyes widened. 'Why all of a sudden?'

I looked at the ocean again. 'I'm not sure,' I said, because I really wasn't sure. But I knew I did. 'Don't you? We're both turning thirty-seven this year and it's something I've been thinking about. I'll soon lose my chance to ever have a family. I should probably freeze my eggs soon.'

'You can always adopt.'

I nodded. 'True, but it's not something we look on favourably here, is it?' I could already see my mother passing on a message through Nulia that I take the child for deliverance from whatever demons that accompanied her.

'Yes, it isn't,' Ego acquiesced.

'You know what, maybe my mother is right, maybe this is my punishment and I'm actually just a murderer.'

'Aunty Ada said what?!'

I didn't realise I'd said it out loud. 'It's nothing, she was angry. Just leave it alone,' I rushed to explain.

I glanced at Ego. I could see her contemplating whether to indeed 'leave it alone' or take it up. She decided on the former. 'What about Bayo and Halil? Have you finally decided?'

Bayo had returned with an apology, saying I was placing too much pressure on our relationship. We'd had torrid makeup sex and the next time the conversation had come up again, the same sequence of events had taken place. The last time, I'd mentioned children in passing.

Overcome with a frightening awareness of the awfulness
of my person, I drove to Halil's house and told him the truth:
I'd been cheating with my ex-boyfriend with whom I'd had a
child, and I'd aborted said foetus. He'd stared at me in disbelief, then he'd broken into Turkish curses, then he'd dragged
me to the door and slammed it in my face. He no longer
picked up my calls. I said as much to Ego.

'Bayo's probably married or has a serious girlfriend,' she
declared. 'Also, it's unfair how you treated Halil. How did
you expect him to react? He really liked you.'

'No, Bayo is just childish and emotionally fragile. He was
the same way back then; he'll come around,' I countered. 'And
if Halil really likes me, why didn't he ever talk about starting
a family? How do I know I wasn't just a fling until he was
ready to go back to his country to settle down?'

Ego shook her head. 'Zina, I've never heard you make
excuses for someone the way you make excuses for this
fellow Bayo, and you make excuses for people you care
about a lot. At the very least, he doesn't respect your person
and emotions, disappearing and reappearing when he likes.
Come on, this is you! You're sharper than this – how can you
allow Bayo to play you?'

I smiled, a tired smile that reflected the state of my emotions. 'You've just never liked him,' I said. 'Not everyone can
be like Emeka, you know? You got lucky.'

Ego blushed and unexpected jealousy surged within me –
she was indeed lucky.

'Speaking of Emeka,' she said and abruptly bounced to her
feet. 'I have something to show you.' She scurried indoors,
and I waited, wondering what it was all about.

Ego returned with her hands clasped around an object.
'Close your eyes,' she instructed.

I rolled my eyes before I closed them. 'Nwakaego, please. We're too old for this behaviour.'

'You can open them now,' she said.

A pear-shaped diamond blinked at me from a band between her fingers. We squealed and jumped together like we'd done as girls. 'When?' I asked when we finally stopped screaming and found the sofa again.

'Two nights ago at his place.'

'Well, it only took him nearly twenty years.'

Ego slapped my arm. 'He wanted to be sure we were both ready.'

My brows shot up. 'Was that the only reason? His parents? Do they know?'

She sighed, her weariness echoing in that single puff of air. 'There's something I need to tell you. I've been talking about this with Emeka and my therapist for a while,' Ego said. My mother did not believe in therapists; they were for white and mad people alone.

'Okay,' I said, prompting her to continue.

'I'm going on leave from work in a few days,' she said meaningfully. 'I'm ready to share the truth, Zina. I know you've purposely kept this from me, but I know about Pastor Kamsi.'

I covered my face with my palms.

'I know about how well his ministry is doing and how wealthy he is. I've seen so many women share their experiences online and I feel I cannot continue to carry this baggage around with me. I didn't do this to myself; he did, and he shouldn't be allowed to continue living his life like nothing happened, possibly doing the same to many others like me. I know I'm not the only one. I don't even care if I get justice or not, the world deserves to know exactly the kind of person he is.'

I held back the tears because I knew they would only make her cry too. I nodded instead and tucked my hands between my legs. 'How do you want to go about it?'

'Social media. It's the only power I have. I'm putting it up on my Twitter, Facebook and Instagram.'

'Your Facebook is still active?' I teased. 'People are going to be so shocked when they find out NaijaUKLawGirl is you.'

She forced a small smile. 'I'm shutting down my Twitter account after that.'

My chest tightened; she loved that account.

She continued, 'I know this means his parents are most likely going to object to our getting married, but Emeka says he doesn't care, we'll get married anyway, even if we only end up going to court. He says he's going to support me in any way he can. He'll repost and corroborate my story. His fintech is doing really well and he has a good enough reputation in the startup community so he hopes that will help.'

'I'll support you too,' I murmured. 'Why aren't you asking me to?'

Ego shook her head. 'He's really popular, Zina. Many top politicians and celebrities attend his church. I don't want to jeopardise your career in any way. People don't even need to know we know each other.'

'How can you be talking about career in this type of situation? *Ehn* Ego?' I shouted. Tears slipped out the corner of my eyes before I could stop them. 'Who was the one that gave me money to go to Onitsha *ehn*? Career? Don't ever say that nonsense again.'

'I'm sorry,' she blubbered. We were both crying now and neither of us was sure how to comfort the other.

I thought about *reckoning* the following week as I typed up a note to be screengrabbed and put up on my social media accounts. Nwakaego had already made her posts the previous day, and with Emeka's backing, it had begun to make the rounds of necessary blogs and newspaper websites. Someone had figured out who Ego's father was and reached out to him for comment; he'd responded that he only had one daughter.

On social media, it had ignited a debate so fiery and caustic, it had descended into an all-out brawl – curses, screaming and abuse hurling at the audacity to speak against such a man:

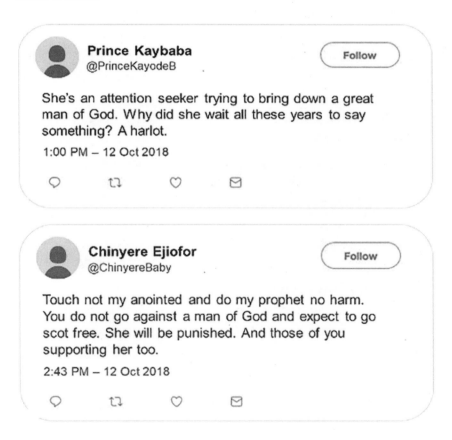

Prince Kaybaba
@PrinceKayodeB

Follow

She's an attention seeker trying to bring down a great man of God. Why did she wait all these years to say something? A harlot.

1:00 PM – 12 Oct 2018

Chinyere Ejiofor
@ChinyereBaby

Follow

Touch not my anointed and do my prophet no harm. You do not go against a man of God and expect to go scot free. She will be punished. And those of you supporting her too.

2:43 PM – 12 Oct 2018

I marvelled at the type of God they claimed to worship, if he would approve of their conduct.

But for many, it was a moment to finally share their own stories; Ego's step forward had emboldened them to do same:

Sarah Okojie
@OkojieSarah

Follow

I stand with Nwakaego Azubuike. It took me over 20 years to finally share my story with my family and they still didn't believe me. #MeToo

9:22 AM – 12 Oct 2018

Victory Osei
@VictoryOsimhen

Follow

I've never spoken about this before, but I was sexually harassed and assaulted by a colleague at work and I never spoke about it because I was scared no one would believe me #MeToo

7:42 AM – 13 Oct 2018

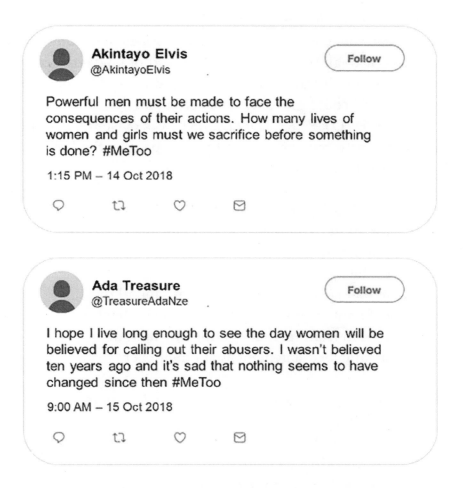

Akintayo Elvis
@AkintayoElvis

Follow

Powerful men must be made to face the consequences of their actions. How many lives of women and girls must we sacrifice before something is done? #MeToo

1:15 PM – 14 Oct 2018

Ada Treasure
@TreasureAdaNze

Follow

I hope I live long enough to see the day women will be believed for calling out their abusers. I wasn't believed ten years ago and it's sad that nothing seems to have changed since then #MeToo

9:00 AM – 15 Oct 2018

A conversation had begun, voices long suppressed demanding to be heard, for justice, for reckoning at last.

Reckoning hardly ever came for evil in our world; their sins were dismissed, washed anew as though soaked in the blood of the lamb. And I thought to myself as I clicked *'post'* that if only this time could be different, if only reckoning could consume those it needed to. Then I waited for hell to break loose.

*

A jacketed lawyer delivered the suit to my address. I'd instructed my gateman to not allow anyone – regardless of status – through but everyone was afraid of lawyers. I contemplated the ill-fitting navy suit he had on and thought to myself that I could probably do a better job.

'*NOTICE TO CEASE AND DESIST*' was plastered in bold letters beneath my address on the first page of the letter. It demanded that I:

    a.   tender a general unreserved apology in writing for all the defamatory statements made and/or published in the past within three days of receipt of the letter;

    b.   tender specific written apologies for all the defamatory statements against their client;

    c.   refrain from further making any false or defamatory statement about their client

I thanked him, then I called my lawyer, sidestepping several missed call notifications along the way.

The comments had become as ugly as I'd expected, the back and forth insulting and inflammatory, my DMs engorged with messages I didn't bother to check. Tare's handle with its blue tick was emblazoned in the thick of it, exchanging words and issuing threats and vicious curses to the trolls. There was another handle I couldn't recognise that seemed so familiar, until I realised it constructed sentences in the same manner as Marve; it was most likely her burner account. I chuckled at the irony in the bile of some of the comments – defending a supposed man of God with the very nastiness the Bible taught against. I laughed even harder, thinking of the power they ascribed their words, imagining they would land like darts, piercing and demolishing. What a waste of time, I thought – only my mother had such power.

'*Don't read any of it,*' I texted Ego to say, and Emeka replied hours later that he'd taken her devices under his care. She was fine, oblivious to it all. I drove to see her.

Emeka left us alone in the living room, the television animated in the background as the characters in the telenovela played out their roles with passion.

'*Andre, how could you?*' the female lead screamed and we laughed.

'She'll still go back to him anyways,' Ego said, then we were both silent.

'How are you?' I said finally into the loaded silence between us.

She turned to look at me for the first time since I'd arrived and I read the answer in her eyes; the memories laden with pain and something else, something that resembled peace.

'That's a tough question to answer,' she said at last.

'You don't have to answer it.'

'I want to answer it.' She paused. 'I'm feeling so many emotions at once that I'm waiting for one to finally take control. I'm scared. I know my life's not going to be the same again now everyone knows what happened. It's out there now and I keep wondering how people will react to me. Will they believe me? Will they hear my name and immediately think, "Oh, isn't that the woman that accused Kamsi?" Is that all they'll ever know me for? You know?'

I nodded encouragingly.

'I know I'll get abused, I know Kamsi is more powerful than ever.' I grabbed her hand and pulled her closer on the settee as she continued, 'I know all these things but I don't regret it. I don't regret it because for the first time in forever,

I feel free. I've carried it around for so long – the pain, the bit-
terness, wishing I'd done things differently that day, blaming
myself endlessly.'

'It was never your fault,' I cut in sharply.

Tears pooled in her eyes. 'I know that. I've always known
that, but it didn't stop me feeling that it was.' She laughed,
different from her earlier laugh in its humourlessness. 'The
brain is a funny thing, isn't it? You can know something isn't
true but it doesn't stop you feeling that way. I've borne it alone
all these years and now he can finally share the shame for
what he did to me.'

An association of pastors issued a statement two days later
to say it stood firmly by its member and that the accusations
were a demonic attempt to sully his good efforts in bringing
souls to the body of Christ.

The Actors Practitioners Guild issued a statement on the
third day: I'd failed to respond to all attempts to get in touch
with me for a 'robust' response and explanation for recent
conduct, and owing to recent complaints of insulting and
inappropriate behaviour from a recently appointed senior
member (a Mr Charles Bekinware), I was hereby suspended
indefinitely and all directors and associated organisations
barred from working with me.

On the fifth day, police vans surrounded my home. I called
Emeka. 'Are they there too? Is she okay?' I heard the strangled
fear in my own voice but I could not control it.

'Yes, they're here. I've called my lawyers and I've been
posting regular updates on social media so everyone knows
what happened if we suddenly disappear.'

'My God,' I breathed. 'These people move like the mafia.'

Nulia called me that evening, reminding me my mother

was yet to let me know just how much of a disgrace she thought I was for attacking a man of God. She was crying.

I chuckled. 'Nulia, please stop being dramatic, it's really not that bad. I'm still alive.'

'You know already?'

I paused. 'Know what?'

'Mummy didn't want anyone to tell you, but she has cancer.'

It was only then that I finally collapsed.

29

Pressure

Agwo emeghi ihe o jiri buru agwo, umuaka ejiri ya kee nku – if a snake fails to show its venom, little children will use it to tie firewood. It was what my mother said the first and only time she defied my father. He'd just returned from a business trip and she'd found something – something that looked like a sacheted balloon to my seven-year-old eye – in his bags. But that was not why she fought him. It was the scent, the perfume that permeated the four corners of the suitcase, rising from it like a burning incense; a woman's perfume that didn't belong to my mother.

I watched my mother's face contort into a mask of pain as she confronted him. 'Am I not enough for you, Uzondu? Am I not?' she asked, her voice choked with unshed tears. And I heard the wounded pride in her pain; she was Adaugo Omimi, the type they referred to as a complete package. She could have gotten any man she wanted, and there had been many – her father boasted of the offers often – but she'd chosen my father. And yet she wasn't enough?

It was a question she posed often: *'Is your family not enough for you? Is this not enough for you? Am I not enough for you?'*

Enough. Surely something had to be enough, contentment had to be established at some point. But I'd inherited my father's avarice for more.

They fought: an acerbic exchange of words followed by successive blows. My father had landed the first one and my mother had retaliated, until they tore madly at each other. Then, as if grasping the reality of what was taking place, he pushed her away and stalked out the door. By the time he returned, we were long gone to Aunty Uju's house, our boxes in their extra bedrooms. *'Agwo emeghi ihe o jiri buru agwo, umuaka ejiri ya kee nku,'* she told Aunty Uju as she narrated what had happened to her. And for the first time, I was proud of my mother.

My father searched the state for us until his hunt finally brought him to Aunty Uju's door.

'I have no idea what you're talking about,' I heard Aunty Uju tell him calmly.

My mother indicated with her finger to her lips for us to not make a sound. I did not hear what my father said next, but Aunty Uju responded with, 'And what will you do?' She was still with Uncle Gozie then and even my father knew where his money and power had their limits.

The elders settled the matter, and in public my father carried himself with bravado, mouthing a forced apology only when the elders demanded it, but behind closed doors, he knelt before my mother in contrition and pitiful plea. He shed heavy remorseful tears that he would do better; he would make sure she never had reason to leave again. And as far as I knew, he kept his end of the bargain.

The second time I was proud of my mother, my father's businesses struggled. 'We're going through a lot, these military governments really don't know how to manage the economy,' he said to her. What he meant to say was that he wasn't liquid enough to pay our school fees. He'd never let my mother work; she was too beautiful and could be taken away.

That first Monday we stayed at home, my mother went into her room and pulled an empty box from the top of her wardrobe, then she filled it with her most expensive and luxurious wrappers, and we watched with bemusement as she dragged the loaded suitcase out the door. Hours later, she returned with bundles of cash and an empty suitcase. 'Enter the car,' she told me and my sisters. In the school bursar's office, she counted the amount needed and signed all the documents and I thought I'd never seen her look more confident. But at home, she told us to go thank my father for paying our fees; she never wanted him to feel inadequate.

Memories continued to flicker through my brain like screens in a cinema. Did she ever plan to tell me? Would she rather I found out at her graveside?

I was floundering, I knew, struggling to find purchase in this new upturned world. And for the first time, I understood why my mother clung so doggedly to religion, at least she had that comfort.

I called Bayo. I wasn't even sure why, but I needed a familiar footing that assured me. He'd lost his mother recently; he would understand.

'Hello? It's Zina,' I said when he picked up, not sure if he'd deleted my number.

'Yes, I know it's you,' he grumbled, like it was an unwanted nuisance.

I forged ahead still; I was desperate. 'Are you free to talk, please?'

He sighed. 'Listen Zina, if you've called to talk about our relationship, there's no point, let's just end it properly now. In fact, that was why I picked up,' he said. 'You keep criticising and demanding, placing unnecessary pressure on me and bringing up bad memories. How could you talk about children when you killed the one we could have had? I grew up with love, I've only known love and I've realised that it's not the same for you and we can never work out. I read the news and I've seen the allegations you're levelling against that man of God and it only sealed it for me; this would never work in a million years. Imagine what my mother would say?'

For hours afterwards, I stretched out on my bed, empty bottles of wine scattered by the side; I needed them to numb me to sleep, to deter the nightmares.

I rattled the drawer of my nightstand as I pulled at it. The pills Tare had given me were still there. I poured the bottle's contents into my palm and wondered how many it would take to make sure I never woke up again. Would that make everyone happy?

I separated two pills from the others and returned the rest to their container. Then I threw them in my mouth: bite, break, swallow.

Banging. Loud incessant banging and doorbell ringing were what it took to pull me from the murky waters. At first, I assumed they were coming from inside my head, but there was no knocking under water.

I forced my eyes open. Someone was banging at my door, probably the police, having bullied their way through my gateman, Edikan. I pulled on a robe and trudged down the stairs. They could at least sit in the living room while I dressed to follow them.

The banging continued with each step I took. I would probably have to call my lawyer, I thought. And smother on enough makeup in case they'd brought the press along for dramatic effect. What casual combination of my outfits photographed really well again?

'Zinachukwu, open this door right now! I'm not leaving until you do,' I heard Zino shout from the other side. He hadn't even crossed my mind; he was meant to be out of the country on a business trip.

I turned the key and unfastened the chains and bolts. We stared at each other. He looked like he'd just found his way from the airport.

'Madam e no gree go o, e say e go make sure them arrest me too if I no open gate,' Edikan shouted from behind him, meaning the police hadn't tried to come in yet.

'I leave the country for a few days and you set everything on fire without telling me?' Zino said, his face lined with exasperation.

I turned my back to him and stumbled towards a sofa. 'The police aren't outside?'

'No. They were here?'

'They'll be back.' It was the first step of intimidation: instil fear.

Zino ran a hand over his shorn head and I thought of Halil's curly hair that he kept pushing out of his eyes. Halil that now hated me too.

'Zina, what the actual hell? What happened?' Zino said.

'Which of the happenings?' I joked, a small smile playing at the corner of my lips.

'Everything! Your social media posts about that pastor. This nonsense I'm hearing about Charles; you never told me what happened at that meeting. I knew I shouldn't have let it go. Why the police are looking for you, why you look like you've just been run over by a truck!'

I raised a hand to my forehead; I was already beginning to pay the price for all that drinking.

'For the social media posts, every single word is true. I might not have been there but I was aware of the circumstances. The police are looking for me because Kamsi has powerful sponsors ready to crush his accusers and their supporters – he's not new to this. As for Charles, he simply saw a woman he would like to fuck and hasn't let up ever since. And well I can't help how I look, can I?'

Zino's eyes narrowed. 'Why didn't you call me?'

'I didn't think it was necessary. As you can see, I'm not doing badly by myself. I don't need saving again, Zino. I haven't tried to kill myself yet.' My voice broke, I covered it up with a cough.

'You didn't think it was necessary? Have you lost your mind, Zina?!' He was yelling; Zino never yelled. Was this what I did to people? He glared at me long and hard and then his tone became gentle. 'There is something you're not saying,' he said.

The tears were coming again. I closed my eyes to keep them at bay. 'Zino, please let's talk another time.'

'Have you been drinking?'

'Does it matter?'

'Zina.' He said my name delicately, like a prayer. It was all it took.

I surrendered to the hurricane of pain that had held my heart for too long, sobbing hysterically into my palms. I heard Zino move from his seat and felt his hand begin to move soothingly across my back.

'I'm trying, I swear I'm trying,' I wailed over and again.

Later, when I finally stopped sobbing, I told him about Bayo and Halil, and then I talked about my mother. 'She might be dying and she didn't even want me to know.'

He held both my hands as he spoke. 'Listen to me, Zina. You're not going to let any of this break you. You're a diamond. You don't crack under pressure.'

I laughed. 'That's pretty corny, even for you, Zino.'

In my room, we packed a box. He did not want me staying at home alone.

'Are these prescribed?' Zino asked as I picked out the items for a shower, and I knew I'd forgotten the bottle of pills on my bed. My face gave me away; I couldn't seem to act well enough where Zino was concerned. He sighed. 'How long have you been taking these?' he asked.

'A while,' I said shortly.

'You're seeing someone as soon as things settle down, I won't let you continue like this.'

I nodded, contrite. 'You'll need to leave the room for me to get ready,' I said as I headed towards the bathroom. I turned to lower a shoulder of my robe theatrically and winked.

Zino chuckled and shook his head.

We received summons to appear at the police command headquarters as part of an investigation of 'a criminal conspiracy, falsehood, and threat to life'. Pastor Kamsi had lodged a complaint.

Echoes of support had begun to reverberate through social media. Emeka's colleagues and friends formed a ring around him, putting out messages attesting to the quality of his character. 'One thing I know about Emeka is he is honest and straightforward, judicious and hardworking. He has no reason to lie about this; he's a very solid guy. I stand with him and his fiancée. Due process must be followed and we will not allow any form of intimidation from the police or any other party,' a popular venture capitalist posted on his Facebook account. But I thought

Emeka deserved to be given the benefit of doubt even if he wasn't a 'solid guy'.

The police released a statement denying involvement in any form of intimidation tactics and the vans disappeared from around Emeka's house; Edikan called to inform me that they'd left my house as well.

Tare put up a video on her Instagram page cursing the board of the actors' guild. 'Foolish old men, you should be ashamed of yourselves! Suspending an actress for standing with a victim of rape. How exactly has she shamed the profession? Who is Charles? Let him come and tell us exactly what Zina has done.' Marve and Cassandra congregated in her comments cheering her on and issuing their own share of insults. The guild announced they were suspending the three of them for disreputable behaviour. It was then other actors and actresses poured out in protest.

'We are with you, Zina. Don't even worry about it,' Tare messaged me to say. *'I'm a South-South woman, they can never intimidate me. They should go and ask about my ancestors, they fought the British with their last blood, these people don't know who they're joking with.'*

The guild issued a statement not long after rescinding all suspensions, including mine.

'Good people will always rise when the time comes,' Zino said. 'This country has good people. Sometimes we forget that because we're so overwhelmed by the bad.'

Zino brought on Dr Ojeme, SAN, OFR, a well-known, seasoned lawyer to take on the case. 'A senior advocate of Nigeria? You want to finish all my money?' I protested.

'He offered to do it pro bono actually, and even if he didn't, you think I would have allowed you to pay for that?'

Dr Ojeme wore his glasses on the bridge of his nose,

bringing to mind a character from a comic skit that broad-
casted on the government-owned television station in the late
'80s. 'You all have to be prepared, mentally and emotionally.
This is a process that will take time; our judicial system isn't
exactly the quickest,' he said. We were gathered in his office to
discuss the next steps. He stared pointedly at Ego; she would
be the one to bear the brunt of it.

She was already under pressure at work. 'They want me
to retract the statement. They say that it's placing an unnecessary spotlight on the company and their work. I've taken
an indefinite leave of absence,' she'd told me just days before.

Emeka placed a hand over hers as Ego nodded solemnly.
'I understand.'

Dr Ojeme continued, 'Unfortunately, at this moment, the
statute of limitations for rape in Nigeria is only two months
so we cannot file another criminal case against him. The perfect time would have been when it happened. I understand
that the case was botched, but the fact that you filed back
then provides a good basis for our case. There are no time
limitations on a civil case and a police investigation. We also
have a DNA sample. There aren't many forensic labs in the
country, so we would most likely have to cover the costs for
that. I have to say, your mother was a very wise woman for
taking you to a hospital first.'

Eriife's caller ID took over my screen the morning we were to
head to the police station. Zino was dressed in a suit despite
my insistence against it. 'You weren't summoned, it's just the
three of us,' I'd told him.

I considered not picking up; we had nothing to talk about,
except she'd somehow found the time to read about the case in
the midst of the frenzy of political gatherings and machinations.

Campaigns for national elections were already in over-drive even though they were several months away; I was still yet to wrap my head around the fact that almost four years had passed since the last election. Before the blow up with Dera at Zino's place, Dapo had talked about the likely can-didates to emerge from the major political parties and Simi had questioned the integrity of voting for only candidates from major political parties. 'It's the same in America, they only vote for the two parties and talk about how things are the same.'

'It's about practicality over morality,' Dapo responded. 'Which of these other guys can actually win without the backing of the grassroot infrastructure these major parties have built over the years? Does the average man in my village know any of these other guys? It's about a choice between the lesser of two evils. I can't be wasting my vote on someone that can't win please.'

'But everyone is saying this candidate is a thief,' Simi said.

Dapo rolled his eyes. 'Aren't they all?'

I accepted Eriife's call, and we went through the perfunc-tory greetings.

'I'm calling to discuss this with you because I understand how sensitive this is, but you've always been very realistic,' she said. 'Nwakaego needs to be convinced to drop the case against this pastor. He possesses a significant level of influ-ence amongst the young people in the country. With elections coming up, many campaigners have planned visits to his church and are dependent on his endorsement and support. This case is making things difficult for them, especially now that social media is divided over this issue.'

'Is this really why you called me?'

'Listen, I'm only doing this because I care deeply about the both of you. I do not want you to be casualties in this; they're willing to go to any length to squash this.'

'Ready?' Zino asked me, peeping his head into the room.

I tucked my phone in my handbag without ending the call and left Eriife to speak to herself.

30

Outcomes

Churches and hospitals. Two sets of places I avoided for the unpleasant memories they managed to stir, memories I would rather forget. That Christmas, I drove down the main Lekki expressway until I sighted an illuminated metal cross on the arched rooftop of a cathedral, coloured stained-glass windows danced in the setting sun like rainbow rays. I pulled into the crowded car park and turned off the ignition. Men, women and children milled into the two-story edifice in time-honoured Christmas colours: red, green, blue, gold. I rubbed a sweaty palm across the ruffled skirt of my red dress and buckled my gold sandals; at least I'd gotten the dress code right.

'We hold the best Christmas cantatas every year. Every top celebrity attends, even those that don't go to church on a regular day,' Tare had boasted. 'You should come; you would enjoy it. You need your spirit uplifted after the year you've had.'

'I don't enjoy such things,' I'd said. Yet here I was in a crowded car park, a brand-new Bible peeping out of my bag. I'd tried to get Zino to come as well.

'What are you talking about? I'm at the airport.' He was spending Christmas with his mother in Germany, their first holiday together in over two decades, brought about by the most unlikely circumstances.

The court ruling had come first, expedited by the intensity of public interest. 'The Nigerian legal system isn't built to protect victims of sexual violence, unfortunately,' Dr Ojeme explained after a High Court in Abuja threw out Nwakaego's case and ordered that she pay a significant sum for wasting the court's time prior to completion of a police investigation.

The disparagers had returned to my comments to jubilate. God had done it. He'd disgraced the wicked and lying serpents that had tried to pull down a man of God. I'd stopped answering calls from unknown numbers at that point, bored of the constant threats and attempts at intimidation.

'But there's DNA evidence and precedence,' Emeka protested, looking ready to drag the lawyer by his collar. Several other women had come forward to anonymously share their experiences at the hand of Pastor Kamsi. I tried not to be offended by their cowardice, to understand why they'd chosen to shield themselves from the venom of the religious public, but their chosen shield was my friend, and it was difficult not to bear a grudge.

'There's still hope,' Dr Ojeme said, adjusting his glasses and ruffling through the papers on his desk. 'The police are completing their investigation; afterwards, they will forward their findings to the Ministry of Justice for prosecution. We just have to be watchful and ensure that the powers that be don't scupper the case.'

In front of Ego, I was confident and reassuring. 'We will see this to the end. Kamsi will be held accountable. Dr Ojeme is very experienced, I'm sure of it,' I said to her, gripping her hands tight and willing her to not lose hope.

'We were always prepared for a long-haul battle,' Ego replied with a peace that confounded, then she smiled. 'I know you don't believe me, Zina, but I'm very aware of the reality of this country. I'm tougher than you think.'

In the privacy of my home, I shattered glass, a single swipe of my hand sending the variegated bottles of perfumes and oils on my dresser flying to the floor, clogging the air with an asphyxiating blend of lavender, musk and spices.

I called Zino crying. In Sunday school, our teachers had taught a scripture: *'Be sure of this: The wicked will not go unpunished.'* My mother had recited it often during her vigils, screaming the words as she prayed against her enemies. Then why did they seemingly prosper? Why were they venerated, even in death, enduring monuments erected in their honour?

That evening, Zino put out a statement via his social media accounts. He used them only for work; I'd doubted he even knew the passwords. In his statement, he denounced the efforts to scuttle the case, but that was not what caused conversation. It was the name he signed at the end, a name I'd never identified with him. A name with a powerful surname.

There was a Christmas play. A boy in a curly wig played Joseph, and I wondered from my seat in the back pew since when Joseph had had blond hair, or if it was the only wig the frazzled children's church teacher that stood by the side of the stage coordinating their activities could find in the market. A fair-skinned girl with naturally loose curly hair that didn't need a wig played Mary, and I thought she looked familiar from a distance. Cassandra ran forward then with a photographer and her phone to take pictures. The girl appeared embarrassed as she tried to focus on her role. She was to turn ten in a few months; I knew because Cassandra would not stop talking about the grand plans she had for the party. I did the maths in my head, trying to calculate how old the baby would have been. Would I have been a parent like Cassandra, ever present and over the top? Or more measured like Tare, who complained about attending children's parties, 'They're always screaming!'

I didn't regret the decision; I never had. Though for years, I thought it made me devoid of good. But the child and its murky waters hadn't visited in many weeks; Zino said it was because I was finally confronting my repressed demons. I went to see a gynaecologist about the possibility of having a child sometime in the future and she'd run the tests and returned with a verdict: yes, it was possible, but the likelihood dwindled with each moment that passed.

The children joined hands in a line when the three wise men arrived, directed by a star that dropped from the ceiling. They sang traditional tuneful Christmas carols and the choir and congregation joined in, reading from the hymnals arranged on the pews. Cassandra was still knelt at the front, taking pictures, a glittering Christmas hat tied on her head.

The priest shared a brief sermon afterwards. He hadn't intended to, or so he said. But it had been a difficult year for many, with the floundering economy and collapse of many businesses, and he felt it necessary to instil hope in the doubting. 'The hymnist Horatio Spafford suffered many losses when he wrote "It is Well". He had lost his businesses, his children had died at sea, with only his wife saved, yet like Job, he remained faithful. And so, I'd like the choir to offer a rendition of this hymn to remind us all that it is well.' Robed men and women rose to their feet and their seraphic voices soon filled the auditorium.

When peace like a river attendeth my way
When sorrows like sea billows roll
Whatever my lot, Thou hast taught me to say
It is well, it is well with my soul

I hunched over the pew and shed uncontrollable tears.

My mother was raised to never misbehave in front of visitors, and it was why I took Zino with me to the hospital to see her. Ego had travelled to America to visit her mother; I hadn't told either of them about her illness. My mother spoke to Aunty Uju often enough to tell her herself if she wanted to.

It was the day of her surgery and my father was seated in the hospital hallway, his head bowed over like a man who was about to lose his most valued possession. He lifted his head in the barest acknowledgement when I called him – *Daddy* – then returned his stare to his hands. In them a rosary was tightly clutched and his lips moved with sullen desperation.

At first, my mother had refused treatment, and the single lump discovered in her breast during a routine checkup had remained unchecked. She couldn't be sick; she'd always been in perfect health, and by some miracle her body would return to its normal perfect self. But months later, the doctors warned that the tumour had spread to the second breast and she would need to undergo a double mastectomy. It was then we'd discovered the true reason for my mother's denial.

'She said Daddy will leave her for a younger woman if she has no breasts, that it's what makes her a woman,' Nulia explained to me. The doctors offered implants but she turned them down. No, she will not carry 'plastics' in her body.

Faced with the stark reality of death, she eventually

accepted treatment, but only after my father swore he wouldn't marry another woman even if she died. Aunty Chinelo's husband had married another woman several years after her passing and my mother never forgave him. If there was one thing Adaugo Okafor née Omimi knew how to do, it was hold a grudge.

Nulia called again, 'The doctor said it's a routine surgery, afterwards they will start chemotherapy. But nothing is ever guaranteed, there have been a few cases of women not waking up from routine surgeries.'

I decided then that I was going to see my mother, even if she cursed me on her deathbed.

My sisters and their husbands were present in the ward, and I tried to recall their husbands' names as I greeted them. The men looked varying degrees of preoccupied and troubled as they glanced up to acknowledge my greeting and nod at Zino. My sisters turned their heads with unconcealed disdain. Except Nulia. 'Good afternoon, sir,' she greeted Zino, bobbing her head. And I burst into a shrill inappropriate laughter that made the others glare at me.

'What?' Nulia asked, her eyes squinched in innocent confusion. 'He's older than you, meaning he's older than me.'

'Not *that* old,' Zino drolled, sending me a side-eye.

I made the introductions.

'She asked us to wait outside, that we're making her sad,' Nulia whispered to us. Yes, that sounded like my mother. 'I didn't tell her you were coming; the doctor said they should start in an hour.'

I knocked before I turned the doorknob then observed as my mother's eyes lit up with unremitting hostility and dimmed as she saw Zino walk through the door behind me. She adjusted her hospital gown. I knew her well.

'Good morning, Mummy,' I said. I hadn't called her that in a long while.

Zino greeted her respectfully, adding 'ma' at the end, a salutation I'd never heard him make use of. 'Good morning, young man! Hope you're well. What's your name?' she responded with overt enthusiasm.

Zino responded and my mother hung on his surname. 'Ah, that sounds very familiar. I might know your family!' Eventually, he excused himself so we could talk but made sure to emphasise that he was waiting just outside the door, a signal to my mother that her words would be heard by a visitor.

We stared at each other in strained and prolonged silence, then my mother said, 'Why are you looking like that? I'm not dying. I already chased your father out of here for almost crying, you better not behave like him.'

I laughed, realising for the first time just how alike we were; I would never let anyone cry, even at my deathbed. Somewhere along the line, my mother joined me, cautiously at first, then the years melted away and we were both sharing a laugh at something only we understood.

'It's the same way he cried at my father's funeral,' my mother said, still chuckling. 'My brothers' and sisters' spouses were comforting them; I was the only one comforting my husband. Who does that?' We howled with laughter.

'Who is that? Is he your fiancé?' my mother asked later, gesturing with her head towards the door.

I smiled. Of course, she would think that. 'No, he's my friend.'

She tilted her head to the side. 'Well, it's a start,' she said. 'That his surname, I think I know his family, their village is not too far from ours. They're very popular and rich. Grab your copy now!' She winked. We laughed.

Then she told me she'd seen a movie of mine.

'It was showing in the shopping mall I went to buy household items at. It was very good. I asked Nulia to buy DVDs of the old ones for me. You're doing well.' She said this like she'd surprised herself by her own admission.

They were words I'd never expected – or dared to hope – to hear from my mother. I took in her expression, her eyes glazed with childlike uncertainty, her lips upturned in a wobbly smile, the way in which she'd mouthed the words. I committed them all to memory, wanting to always recall, even in my dying moment, the time in a blazing moment of shared laughter, my mother had thought good of me.

'Power retained by oppression is illegitimate,' Zino said.

'It's still power,' I replied. 'Power is power.'

After several months of propaganda and a tendentious rewriting of the last few years in lieu of a dignified campaign, elections were finally underway. Tribal tensions had been stoked to a frenzy and it was clear despite the tireless declarations of 'One Nigeria' that we were anything but one.

'These guys are united in robbing the country of its future but they stoke these tensions and draw the lines to deceive us into their agenda,' Zino said. It was the first time I'd ever known him to implement a sit-at-home policy during an election, but he'd declared that he wouldn't participate in such a farce.

The people had declared they would kick out an incompetent government and the machinery had clicked into gear. Scattered ballot boxes, disappearing electoral officers, fractured heads, broken spirits. Just another election.

'The origin always determines the outcome,' Zino said. 'The police force hasn't progressed beyond the colonial construct of intimidation it was intended to be, its masters have only changed.'

The results were evident before they were announced. The ruling party was declared victor. At Eagle Square, they gathered for a charade of a swearing-in ceremony, garbed in party colours, waving party flags and brandishing sunglasses and hand signals. Eriife flashed briefly across the screen, seated in the VIP box, chatting animatedly with a senator's wife.

Zino and I were to leave for Onitsha for work but decided to hold off until tensions cooled.

And Nwakaego got married.

We were a party of less than ten: me, Zino, Nkechi and her husband, and the besotted couple. The police had concluded their investigation and forwarded their findings to the Ministry of Justice, and nearly one year since Ego had made her first post about Pastor Kamsi, justice was yet to be served.

She'd resigned from her job at the multinational and we'd held several directionless conversations about what she could do next. Then one day she said, 'Let's start a production company.'

I sent her a sardonic side-eye. 'I'm the one that cracks the jokes.'

'I'm serious,' she averred.

'How?'

'You're passionate about film and we both have a decent amount of money saved. You'll handle all the technical aspects I have no idea about and I'll run the legal and the day to day of everything else. We can actually do this.'

The proposition seemed nebulous and farfetched at first, but steadily, the idea began to take a form of its own. Name ideas popped up of their own volition, flashes of the pictures we could produce glinted in my mind, stories of the reality of the country we lived in, outside the borderlines of the Lekki Ikoyi Bridge.

None of these things appeared to weigh on Ego's mind as she exchanged rings with Emeka at the Ikoyi courthouse, or as they sliced through a cake in the garlanded hotel garden a few hours later.

'Must be nice,' I murmured to Zino with a sigh, moments after watching Emeka and Ego take to the floor for their first dance, Luther Vandross' 'Here and Now' serenading them. We chuckled together.

'How did the gyno visit go?' he asked, popping a samosa in his mouth.

'Okay, I guess. I have frozen my eggs now. I just have to find an unfortunate man willing to father a child with me.'

He seemed to contemplate something on the table. 'Why not me?' he said casually, the way one would say, 'Do you want rice or fufu?'

I leaned over to pick a stick of meat from his plate. 'Zino, *abeg*, be serious.'

He looked up. 'I'm serious,' he said. I was silent, unsure of what to say next as he forged ahead. 'Look at it this way, you're almost forty, and I'm almost fifty. We've known each other for almost twenty years and get along really fine.'

'You're bossy,' I mouthed.

He pretended not to notice. 'We both want children and can afford to take care of them, and we're friends. That's a lot more than many children can say about their parents. If IVF doesn't work, we can adopt together. And you come around often enough that we might as well live with each other.'

I pushed the piece of meat into my mouth and chewed on it slowly, just to keep my brain moving.

Zino was still speaking. 'You know I was reading this article about how much emphasis we place on romantic relationships and how we tend to overlook how much more important friends are. Many people are changing that with their living arrangements.'

I laughed, incredulous at what he was suggesting. 'Zino, this is Nigeria. You're the one always reminding me of that.'

'It's the twenty-first century.'

Our first night in Onitsha, I booked a taxi to the River Niger Bridge. It wasn't the same taxi man that had driven me all those years ago, and I wished it were, just so I could thank him for playing Ebenezer Obey for me that night, creating a fleeting moment of happiness in what I'd decided was my last hour.

I walked along the bridge and clung to the railings. I'd been called *mami water* all my life even though I'd never learned how to swim. It was almost comical how I'd forgotten my fear of heights that night.

A man passed by, then he paused. 'Madam, is everything okay?' he asked, like he expected me to jump.

I smiled. 'Yes, I'm fine,' I assured him before turning to stare into the depths of the murky waters.

My grandfather, my father's father, a man I never met, had perished in this same river during the civil war. He'd fought in the rebel army for a vision of the country he believed in. Then my grandmother had written to say that three of their five children had succumbed to the hunger blowing through like a dirgeful wind during the blockade. My grandfather had gone to the bridge and never returned.

I wondered what he would think of the country as it was now, of the way we seemed to meander in circles,

tussling with the very same issues that had led to a fruit-
less war, of my attempt to join him, of the man that had
stopped me, of my unspoken plans to still join him someday. Just not yet.

3

ERIIFE

Power does not corrupt. Fear corrupts ... perhaps the fear of a loss of power.

JOHN STEINBECK

31

Differences

The difference between us was that I'd long accepted the reality of the existence we occupied. Ego lived in a quixotic universe, where right was right and wrong was meant to be punished, where patriotism was rewarded and systems served the people. Zina bordered more on the edge of things, cynical and practical, yet behind all that cynicism was an almost delusional hope that lingered, daring the universe but trusting it to prevail. But me? I was firmly rooted in the reality of who, what and where we were. Perhaps it was because I was a trained doctor; they do say that after a few years in a hospital ward, you lose your heart.

You see death, watch it claim and claim until you know its name and recognise its abiding presence. The child that calls out to his mum as the jagged lines of the monitor smooths straight, the woman with the prolapsed womb that always wanted children of her own, the man that holds on to the edges of your scrubs pleading for a miraculous feat – his wife's return. Under the illumination of torchlights, you perform your surgeries and pray that the power returns just in time so a patient can make it through the night.

In the early days, you shed feeble tears as you wonder if your only purpose is to be a futile escort to the other side. Then one day, your supervisor pulls you aside and demands of you, his stethoscope coiled around his neck like a pet snake: *'Do you want to be a doctor or not?'*

That was me, and I'd seen it all. I'd also chosen to marry into politics, a game where there were no permanent enemies or lasting friends. And I'd witnessed the extent humans were willing to go to accomplish what they desired, the fickleness of people and the meaninglessness of our very existence. But perhaps what kept me most entrenched and awake to all that surrounded us was my mother – a woman who'd lived her life for others, taken away at the very precipice of success. With her passing, I'd realised that we were little more than animals; you either looked out for yourself or died at the very mercy of others. At your funeral, they would cry remorseful tears and roll in the dirt around your grave, but eventually they would move on and your sacrifice would have been all for naught.

I scrolled through the latest national headlines on my iPad in the executive lounge of the Murtala Muhammed International Airport, nothing out of the ordinary: the state of the economy and rising unemployment numbers, advice for the soon to be inaugurated second-term government, the usual entertainment news. Then a caption from a popular internet blog caught my eye: 'KAMSI ACCUSER TO MARRY FIANCÉ.' I clicked on it to be sure.

Nwakaego Azubuike, the estranged daughter of promi-nent businessman and socialite Chief Chigozie Azubuike, who a little over a year ago accused popular mega pastor Kamsi Aguta of raping her in 2004, is set to tie the knot with her fiancé very soon, we can exclusively confirm. Details are being kept hush hush, but should we find out more, trust us to let you know.

Ego was getting married. To Emeka.

Soye extended his neck in my direction, and I felt the *aso oke* of his *fila* brush my *gele* as he read over my shoulder, the uneasiness with which he monitored my every activity never failed to irk, like a single move on my part would bring the house of cards he'd carefully constructed crumbling down. 'She's getting married?' he murmured.

'It would seem so,' I replied shortly.

'You're no longer in touch? Good. Hope no one outside that company knows about your friendship? You know the newspapers would carry it immediately if they got wind of it.'

'Soye, how many times are you going to ask me the same question?' I asked, letting my irritation show but keeping my volume low. To any observer, we were having a normal conversation. 'I didn't tell anyone else, and who else do I have to tell?'

He adjusted the collar of the kaftan underneath his *agbada*. 'Good, good,' he murmured, appeased.

A stewardess moved towards us then. 'Sir, the plane is ready,' she said courteously.

'Oh wonderful!' Soye exclaimed theatrically, then to the larger room, he said, 'Gentlemen, I believe we're ready to leave now.'

The men bounced to their feet and arranged the wings of their *agbadas* over their shoulders in unison, and I thought that they looked like members of a drummers' troupe. I was the only woman in their midst; the others had sent their wives and children ahead on first-class flights, but Soye knew better than to treat me that way.

In the plush interior of the private jet, the men shared jokes and a bottle of champagne. 'This is really a moment of celebration,' Soye said, and the other men laughed. There always seemed to be a lot of laughing in their midst, servile and fawning laughter; what exactly was persistently funny, I wasn't sure.

'Ah Madam Adebowale, you won't join us?' Yunusa asked, raising his flute in my direction.

'I'm not feeling too well,' I lied before Soye could speak on my behalf; his lips had already moved.

'Hope madam isn't pregnant? This one Soye takes her everywhere with him like his handbag,' Onomavwe said, and the others laughed again – no one dared not laugh at his crude jokes. I forced a smile. Just a few years ago, Onomavwe, a former governor, had been serving time in a jail cell in the UK on myriad money-laundering charges, but he'd patiently served his time, buoyant in the assurance of his eventual return to his stowed-away loot and kingly influence. 'It was all politics. They sold me out to the Brits because a lowly Niger Deltan like me wanted to become a vice president against their preferred candidate and they were angry,' he always said when he spoke of those years. He saw no use in contesting for electoral offices now, not when he could control events just the same from behind the scenes. A true godfather.

Soye answered this time. 'We're happy with our daughter, sir.' He didn't add that I couldn't have children.

Onomavwe tutted. 'I have six and my father had twenty!' He laughed again, and the others laughed with him.

An air hostess waltzed in then to inform us that the flight would take off soon.

Onomavwe nodded, suddenly seeming agitated, and turned to the man seated next to him. 'We need a spiritual man to lead us in prayer. You know there have been crashes in recent times. The nation cannot afford to lose men like us. Yunusa, you can lead us in an Islamic prayer for balance when he's done.' I could have laughed then. A man like Onomavwe was scared to die?

Kamsi bowed his head and stretched forward a hand; a diamond-studded Rolex watch glimmered on his wrist. 'Let's all close our eyes in prayer. Father in heaven,' he started. The men all followed his lead while he led the cabin in prayer. I stared, wide-eyed, unable to hide my disgust.

'What a powerful prayer. God is with us!' Onomavwe declared afterwards. The men chuckled and nodded their heads. Yunusa raised his palms to take his turn. The plane moved then.

'I've not forgotten about that file at the Ministry of Justice,' Onomavwe said to Kamsi when we were in the air. Soye glanced at me nervously. I turned away to look out the cabin window at the disappearing cluster beneath us.

Onomavwe was still speaking. 'My men are working hard but that woman has some strong people behind her. They've assured me that they will make the file disappear regardless. Power pass power.' He guffawed. The others joined in; I thought Soye sounded choked.

I returned my mind to the story I'd read in the terminal. Nwakaego was getting married and she hadn't bothered to invite me, not that I was particularly deserving of an invite considering who I currently shared a plane cabin with, but at the very least, I'd thought she would have sent a text, even if it said I couldn't come. Perhaps it was Zina's influence; she'd always been far more unsparing than Ego, except where it concerned those she cared about, and I'd long ceased to be on that list.

'*Your mother would consider you a disgrace,*' Zina had written to me the day I'd called to talk her into convincing Ego to withdraw the case. *A disgrace.* So easy for her to say. An actress whose face alone guaranteed attention. She had no idea what it was to live as women like me who had no blinding beauty to guarantee they escaped rigorous scrutiny. Unlike her, I'd had to work to not be ignored, to be listened to, to have meaning.

But had Zina influenced Aunty Uju too? Following my mother's death, when Aunty Ada had been too devastated to even try, Aunty Uju had been the one to attach herself to me like an epiphyte, refusing to let go even while her own life quickly fell apart. She'd been present at my wedding and called at every turn to remind me she was there should I ever need her. The year before, she'd called the morning of Prince Harry and Meghan Markle's wedding. It was 3am on the east coast of America where she lived. 'I'm just calling to remind you that Harry, *nwa* Diana is getting married today, make sure you don't miss it.' She'd done the same for his brother's wedding, but this time was different. He was marrying a black woman. 'Our sister,' Aunty Uju said. They'd loved Diana, all three of them, but especially my mother. She kept newspaper clippings of her dresses to show to her tailor to replicate and included her in our evening prayers. 'We know what it's like not to be liked by our in-laws,' she said. The year my mother passed, Diana had gone not many months later, and for some reason, I'd been grateful that she hadn't been alive to witness the devastating sadness of the event.

Ninety-seven was meant to be a good year. My mother was in love again, not with my father – that was more or less a given – but with the life growing inside of her. I was to turn fifteen, an age where boys were a befuddling fascination and life was an expanse of assignments, teenage fashion and the Spice Girls. But because my mother had been eager for me to establish the sort of sororal bond she enjoyed with her friends with those friends' daughters, I'd started schooling earlier than others and was in my final year of secondary school.

'Have you decided on what you're going to study now?' my mother asked when second term resumed that year. We were in the living room, me in my green school skirt and jacket, and she in her trouser suit, her belly protruding, ready to leave for work. The time to register for all the school leavers exams that determined most of the rest of our lives was drawing closer and I still felt unprepared for such a consequential decision.

I shrugged. 'No, not yet.' I knew I enjoyed biology, chemistry and mathematics and did well in all, but that was as far as my decision-making abilities stretched. My mother – unlike me as she'd been in so many ways – had studied business administration at the university and worked her way up the ladder of a manufacturing company. Early on, she'd spotted the differences in our persons and guided me towards the sciences.

She nodded thoughtfully and picked up her handbag, indicating it was time to go. She was going to make Vice President; I'd heard my father say so. 'Maybe I should speak with your school guidance counsellor so we can think of ways we can help you decide what's best for you, maybe we can find some professionals to give your class talk, I could come as well,' she said with a smile. I'd taken it for granted then, her unstinting love and infinite patience, the brightness of her smile and ebullience of her laughter.

It was that very laughter my father claimed to have fallen in love with when they'd met on the first day of campus opening. In the large hall to welcome new students, he'd been seated beside a girl whose laughter was a little too loud, and he'd told himself he wanted to hear that laugh for as long as he lived. He was a Nupe boy from a small village along the middle belt of the country – a place designated under the old Northern Region – lucky to be selected for a scholarship to study chemical engineering, and she was an Igbo girl who'd been brought up in the modern ways of the city of Lagos, an almost improbable match if there was one, but he'd made a go for it anyway. 'The most she would have said was no,' he always said smugly years afterwards, even though his actions remained that of a man who couldn't believe his luck.

Their parents formed a stumbling block. He was a Northerner, she was Igbo, they'd lived through the civil war. But my parents remained resolute until their dissenters had had no choice but to let the wedding hold.

Eriife – *evidence of love* – was the name they chose when I was born, a name outside of both their tribes that many would consider unusual, a representation of their love. The oil sector was booming then and my father's job at an oil company, together with my mother's, guaranteed a stable life for them. My brother came afterwards, and for a while, we were a relatively normal family. If their tribal differences created any problems, they were not very evident, or perhaps my parents were so enamoured of each other that those differences meant little more than momentary interruptions to them. Then at the close of '94, my grandfather – my father's father – passed away and my grandmother moved in with us because my mother did not want her lonely and neglected in the village; a good deed that spun the sequence of occurrences that would result in her eventual demise.

The plane taxied along the runway as we landed in Abuja. Several others just like it lined the tarmac. An event such as this came once in four years. Onomavwe rubbed his hands together in intemperate relief. 'We thank God, that was a smooth flight!' The others murmured their agreement. Kamsi said a brief prayer of thanks.

'The party this time will be different,' Yunusa commented when it was time to alight the aircraft.

'You mean the inauguration party? In what way?' Onomavwe asked, running a hand across his rotund belly.

Soye was running a thumb along the vessels that lined my knuckles, a silent imploring gesture. I removed my hand from under his.

Soye chuckled. 'I think what he means is that last time we weren't even sure about a transfer of power.' The men laughed again.

We had been the underdogs the last time around, the antithesis of the ruling party, working against a state machinery that had yet to be defeated since the country's return to democracy in '99.

'I don't think it's possible,' Soye told me after party members had informed him of their plans to unseat the government in the coming elections. He was the man connected to the streets, the one who could make some of it happen. Winning a state seat was easy; it was time to take it national.

'Anything is possible,' I told him then, because that was the role I played in our relationship.

The months that followed were a testament to the fact that the powers that be had chosen their candidate and the man in power was not to be the one. Alliances were formed across the Niger, each wielding its own agenda for a future shot at power, tribal differences were put aside, new languages were spoken and traditional garments exchanged. The people were hungry for a change and the time was right.

In drafting manifestos, foreign consultants were employed – to differentiate us from the incumbent – and new media were deployed in dispersing the message. Despite his brief moment of crippling unbelief, Soye was desperate to prove he was ready to play a bigger role in the party and take on a mantle of leadership. He knew the locale of the Southwest like the back of his hand – after all, he'd spent enough years hiding in them as he'd dodged the wrath of the military dictatorships. When the time came, it was easy to mobilise the young who looked up to him as a contemporary hero. Then he took his campaign online, forming narratives and countering propaganda with that of their own.

Then Soye told me, 'You know how to speak with people in a way that they'll listen.' Before then, I'd played more of a behind the scenes role, visible yet unseen – now he was ready for me to step out from behind the curtains.

On the night the results were officially declared on the national television station, the air crisp with exhilaration, we celebrated with others, patting ourselves on the back for a job well done, raising crystalline glasses in toast. The numbers had come together and we'd accomplished the unimaginable.

That night, Soye made love to me for the first time in months, fevered and frenzied, high on the adrenaline of history-making, just like the days on campus when he'd taken to his first ballot in almost a decade in '99, as if desperate, yearning to pour his ambitions into something or someone.

32

Circle

Soye sat at the head of the dining table, an open laptop in front of him as he picked at a breakfast plate.

'Moses!' he screamed for the chief steward as I approached the table. 'Bring more orange juice, madam will soon be down; the jar is almost empty.'

'Good morning,' I murmured as I took a seat.

'*Iyawo mi,* good morning,' Soye said. He placed a hand over mine on the table and leaned in to peck me on the cheek. I pulled away.

'*Ahn-ahn.* You're still upset? Don't be like that,' Soye said. He pushed the laptop in front of me. 'Come and see, our pictures are everywhere, all the blogs and newspapers. Even our pictures with the vice president and senators' families.'

We'd only just returned from Abuja the night before. Camera flashes, synchronised and blinding, had greeted us as we alighted the limousine that transported us to Eagle Square and trailed our every step as we were escorted along the red carpet to our seats. It was only to be expected that our pictures would appear on the usual sites and in the pages, but for Soye, the fact that we'd been thought important enough to post in the dailies, to name – Chief and Mrs Adetosoye Adebowale – denoted an elevation of status: we were no longer to be ignored.

He put a hand on my thigh, and slowly moved it in soothing circles, like one petting a wild animal. 'Senator Majekodunmi was telling me how impressed everyone was with our galvanising. I'm being seriously considered for a national legislative seat come next elections, and this is just the beginning. This state legislative seat is just a stepping stone. From there I can move to the Senate, even the Presidency. Who knows? Anything is possible.' He was using my words on purpose.

'That's nice,' I said as I placed a teabag in a mug, before covering it in hot water.

Soye flicked a finger under my chin. 'Stop being like this now. I know you didn't want to travel with Kamsi, but it was Onomavwe who brought him along, you know he's very scared of flying and I couldn't say no. There are things you put aside for the sake of politics, you should know this. We've been in this long enough.'

'There should be a limit somewhere,' I said. 'We've given everything, must we sell our souls too? I've known Nwakaego all my life and now she won't even speak to me; imagine she found out I flew with him.'

He caressed a hand across my cheek and returned his attention to his plate. 'Smile, you look finer when you smile. You know everyone kept mentioning how beautiful you looked yesterday, like they were just finally noticing. I told them no be today, my wife has always been beautiful.'

I wasn't always beautiful; beside my mother I'd looked like a derelict urchin, and it wasn't because she was fair skinned.

Aunty Ada was dark and everyone considered her beautiful. But there was a phosphorescence about her, an unalloyed and irreplicable cheer that attracted and retained attention. My father talked often about how others on campus had tried to lure my mother away from him because they'd wanted some of her light. And when she'd passed, it was as though a candle had been snuffed out from within and we were left to meander life's maze in impermeable darkness.

In '98, I'd volunteered to escape her memory, the crushing weight of its omnipresence. It was my first year of university and all I could think about was how much I wanted her to be there; the times we'd talked about it: me studying at the University of Lagos just as she'd done with her friends, her visiting too often and me eventually complaining about it, everyone asking, 'Is that really your mum? You look nothing alike'.

A flyer stuck on the hostel notice board drew my attention to a student union meeting at the back of Omotola Multipurpose Hall. The first year of medical studies at the Akoka campus wasn't cumbersome back then; we still had time for club meetings and make-up.

A man who did not look like a student was speaking when I snuck in over an hour late and crammed myself into the nearest seat at the back. Student politics, he was saying, served as a good training ground for future political involvement. The head of state's death had only just been announced and people were already speaking about democracy.

He was tall, a lanky sort of height I thought more appropriate to basketball than politics, but from the manner in which he spoke, it was clear he'd chosen his path. The audience listened, enraptured by a voice I found too eager, too determined to convince. When he was done, they erupted in applause and the student that took over to ask for questions bowed over his hand as he shook it. The questions filled in what I'd missed – a biography of a faithful martyr to the cause of democracy, a man who'd dared to question a dictator, who'd campaigned for Abiola and led protests when the results of the June 1993 elections were scuttled.

A union secretary diligently penned down names of volunteers and I moved forward to be included amongst them. Being busy meant no time to think, and no time to think meant no time to feel.

I waited till the crowd around the man dispersed and the hall had finally emptied, leaving just him and the student-appointed officials. He pulled on a grey jacket and moved towards the exit; I moved to block his path. I observed as he once more put on the persona of a politician.

He stretched a hand and I took it. 'They haven't started releasing political prisoners yet. How come you aren't in prison?' I said.

He looked dumbfounded. I was accustomed to that – intimidating people into silence. In secondary school, the boys had avoided me; I was the girl with a tongue she wielded like a weapon. I knew too much, said too much, always had an answer. And I wasn't even pretty enough to be worth the trouble.

He smiled, a slow smile that said he found my boldness endearing. 'Well, I somehow managed to escape,' he said finally.

I returned his smile, then tutted. 'Too bad. You'd have had more stories to tell us.'

'What's your name?' he asked.

'Eriife.'

'I'm Adetosoye, but everyone calls me Soye.' Later, he

would tell me how his names bore 'Ade' because he was a distant relative of a crown, a poor distant relative. He was twenty-four, I was sixteen. Ego said it was inappropriate and I told her to mind her business. We would not take it to the next level until I was eighteen. He was solace in a time I needed it most. Then, in my penultimate year of medical school, I discovered I was pregnant. Fear that I would end up like my mother clamped around my heart.

'Let's get married,' Soye said.

I turned him down; I'd promised my mother I would finish university before I married. 'But you've spent almost nine years in school for a seven-year course because of strikes. How long are we going to wait? I'm already in my thirties,' he said. I told him I wasn't the one who'd asked him to date a younger woman.

One night, I woke up to a bed drenched in blood; I'd lost the baby. And in that moment, I felt more relief than pain. I graduated from university the following year and a few months later, we got married in the chapel my mother had attended, sunlight streaming from the windows like a halo.

A year passed, then two, then three, and Soye fretted about our not having children. I agreed to visit the O&G ward for a checkup just to stop his diatribes. I had fibroids that prevented a fertilised egg attaching itself to the lining of my womb and I needed to undergo surgery. A few days before my scheduled surgery, Soye returned home with a little girl with skin like polished wood, a girl whose sharp features were all too familiar.

He wanted me to know the truth if something went wrong. It had happened once, one time when he'd grown wary of waiting for me. He hadn't known how to tell me but he hadn't wanted me to find out on the other side.

'Adelola said to tell you she's coming home in July for the summer holiday,' Soye said now, downing the glass of orange juice that Moses had just refilled.

I looked up from my plate. 'July? Don't universities in America go on holiday in May/June?'

'She's going on a trip with some friends around Europe. She said she knew you wouldn't like it so she called me instead.'

'She called you because she knows you always say yes,' I said.

Guilt was what made him so pliable, he was eaten up by irremissible guilt for how he'd left her in his mother's care, for his failure to acknowledge; her mother had been too young to bear such a burden of who she really was.

Adelola's entrance into our lives motivated me to have children, if anything, to assuage my pride. I began treatments in earnest and reduced my hours at the clinic. Then the doctor recommended I remove my womb.

Radio Democratic Nigeria was Soye's claim to fame. A radio station broadcast in hiding as the military dictatorship clamped down on dissent following the annulment of the '93 elections. Soye had led marches demanding a return to democracy, and the government had come after them with a vengeance. Many fled the country, others not so fortunate were abducted, tortured and jailed. On the run and at the height of oppression, Soye and several others launched a guerrilla radio station. The government intensified its search, and several of them were taken in the most unlikely of circumstances, many never to see the light of day again. But they'd given their lives for a noble cause, to see their country free, democratic.

It was this goodwill that allowed Soye to permeate the

political space, ascending from a lowly local government chairman to a state legislative member. Before Radio Democratic Nigeria, Soye had considered himself a disciple of Awolowo – a democratic hero – espousing his politics, consuming his books, reciting his speeches verbatim, blind to his flaws. By '91, he'd participated in his first protest as a secondary school student, against another military dictator and was detained at the local army barracks until his mother came to plead on his behalf that he was only a boy who had no knowledge of left from right.

In the early days of our relationship, Soye spoke of the state of the country often – what it could be and the role he intended to play within it. My mother had lived most of her life under the instability of military dictatorships. She'd witnessed Nigerian independence, the coup that came only six years later and the civil war it led to, the rotations of military governments afterwards, the assassinations and brief whiffs of democracy. And I thought that my meeting Soye was a sign; it would be only right that I played a part in creating a country she'd longed for but had never gotten to see.

For the '99 elections, we went door to door, convincing reluctant voters, galvanising support for party candidates and hiring buses to transport people to polling units. On Democracy Day, we set up a canopy on campus and shared packs of jollof rice even though our candidate had lost the presidential elections. Soye appeared in a white *agbada* and green cap, and every time the hired cameraman passed, he said excitedly, 'Let's take a picture, let's take a picture'. For him, it hadn't mattered that we'd lost – Nigeria had won.

Otunba Bankole's Prado Jeep was parked in our compound when I returned from the clinic weeks later; as one of Soye's benefactors, he visited often. Technically, I didn't need to go into the clinic much. Soye had seen to that when he'd built a private clinic and staffed it, but going in reminded me of the reasons I'd chosen to become a doctor, and gave me a purpose outside being Soye's handbag, as Onomavwe had put it.

Otunba Bankole was chewing on a fried chicken thigh when I walked in, his lips glazed with oil; in front of him was a wide serving stool crowded with plates of chicken, a bottle of red wine and a wine glass. His skin was a splotchy shade of yellow with green veins that protruded, like he'd tried to use bleaching creams but only had access to the cheap ones. But Otunba was anything but cheap. It was whispered that he'd made his money at the start of the internet boom via *wire wire* or credit card fraud and still ran a small unit of boys in America who remitted money regularly to him to be laundered. Like many big men, he dispensed a decent proportion of his wealth on two items: women and politics.

I knelt to greet him. He tapped my back with the side of his wide monogrammed fan. 'Stand up, stand up. Thank you, my daughter,' then to Soye, he said, 'She's so well behaved, I'm always surprised that she's not Yoruba. It's our women that understand respect like this, even her name belongs to us.'

'Thank you, sir,' Soye responded, beaming like a proud father.

I took a seat. 'Is that enough? Should I get you anything else?'

'No, no. I'm fine. It's good you're back. I was just asking your husband to help me with advice for a small problem I have. But now that you're here, I think you'd give me better advice. You're a smart woman.'

'Ah, of course. Any way I can help you, Otunba,' I said.

'Thank you my dear. It's my second and third wives. The

second, Bosede, is really jealous of my girlfriends. I've tried
and tried to talk to her but she won't listen, in fact, she wants
to call her people to negotiate a separation. If I didn't keep girlfriends after marrying my first wife, would she have become
my second? You women can be so unreasonable sometimes.
We men are born polygamists, forget all this white people
nonsense. A man keeping other women doesn't make him a
bad person.' He shook his head, sincerely wounded.

'And your third wife, Otunba?' I asked.

'Ireti? That one is a completely different story. She doesn't
even act like I exist, whether I come or go isn't her problem,
as long as her account is topped up every month, she is fine.
I would have suspected her of having a boyfriend but she's
always with women. In fact, I think she might be a lesbian.
Your husband here said I should hire a private investigator
to trail her.' I sent Soye an astonished look. 'But I think that
might be a little too much. My dear, what do you think?'

Soye blinked quickly at me from his end of the room. I
looked away and pretended to think before I told Otunba
what I knew he hoped to hear. 'Otunba, you know we women
are emotional, they should know you're an elderly man, they
shouldn't be troubling you like this.' Otunba nodded appre-
ciatively. 'I think hiring a private investigator to trail your
Aunty Ireti might be too much but you can try speaking to
her to find out if she's unhappy about something, maybe she
feels you've been giving too much attention to your other
wives and she's jealous; women express jealousy in different
ways. Aunty Bosede is also jealous and is expressing hers
more vocally. Try to appease her by opening a new shop
for her or paying for a trip to Dubai. Women like things
like these.'

Otunba's face brightened, making it appear waxy, as a

smile stretched from one side to the other. He turned to Soye. 'You should count yourself lucky; you married a very wise woman. Do you know that?'

Soye bowed his head slightly. 'Ah, yes, sir. I'm very aware.'

I excused myself from their midst a few minutes later, citing tiredness. As always, it was in my absence that the conversation about the real reasons behind Otunba's visit started. I passed by the corridor adjoining the living room to catch snatches of their conversation. Soye was speaking. 'How much is that?' I peeped in. They were writing on plain paper like secondary school boys doing their homework.

'Two hundred million.'

'Good,' Soye said. 'We can include another two hundred thousand naira contract under the state agric ministry. I'll call the commissioner first thing tomorrow morning. The budgets will still come to our committee for approval anyway, we'll make sure you're not left out.'

'So that's five projects now?' Otunba asked.

'Yes,' Soye said, drawing a double line under a sum.

'Soye, you've done well.'

'Otunba, it's the little I can do for financing our campaigns.'

Otunba relaxed deeper into the settee. 'It's because you're an honest boy, you think so. You sponsor some of these non-sense boys and they forget you once they get into power and start misbehaving. They give all the contracts to their family and friends and forget those who helped them thinking four years is forever. But you? You're loyal.'

Soye laughed, that same fawning laughter. 'Thank you, Otunba.'

There was a time Soye would have denounced behaviour such as this. In fact, it had been one of the improprieties he'd held up against the military regimes, Fela's 'Army

Arrangement' his anthem as he berated them: 'Thieving bastards!' But that was before he'd understood how campaigns worked, the requirement to *settle* people, the ease with which they could be bought – a bag of rice, oil, fees for the children's next terms.

And I'd long accepted that in criticising others, we overinflated our own perceived righteousness. We claimed to loathe power, but in truth, we worshipped it, eager for our own opportunity for a whiff of its might. In the meantime, we told lies, beautiful lies to appease the conscience we claimed to possess.

Otunba swished wine about his wine glass, exhibiting the placid contentment characteristic of the Nigerian wealthy.

'Otunba, what about Agude that you sponsored for governorship? I heard he won. How is that going?' Soye asked, to fill in the silence, I felt.

Otunba hissed. 'That fool? He was humble and grovelling when he was still looking for a ticket. Within how many weeks, he's already arresting people that criticised him instead of focusing on important things. I don't want my name associated with such nonsense. If anybody asks you, I don't know him.'

33

Spoils of war

My great-great grandfather – my father's father's father's father – fought in the First World War, recruited by the colonial masters to fight on behalf of their government and king. He'd witnessed the amalgamation of the Northern and Southern protectorates – for budget deficit reasons – to become Nigeria. He'd been a storyteller, and so he told his son, who'd told his own son, until it got to my father.

His son would serve in the Second World War, and his grandson – my grandfather – would keep the uniforms hung as a reminder of our history in the library of his corrugated sheet-roofed house.

My grandfather was a learned man and my first introduction to politics. In his library, where the bookcases brimmed with aged, scuffed spines and the breeze from the window made the uniforms sway like reluctant flags, he told me the stories his father had told him, and passed on his informed views on the politics of the country. I was the only grandchild interested in his stories, the only one willing to sit quietly in a locally crafted chair for hours as he narrated events and postulations I didn't always understand, nodding anyway because I was aware it made him happy.

Unlike my parents, he hadn't been brought up under the fist of military coup rotations, and unlike me, he hadn't been subjected to a revised history while the perpetrators still dwelt in our midst; his mind was unfettered in a way ours weren't, in a manner we didn't even know we were handicapped. He'd been a witness to the nation at different phases: reluctant colonial union, hopeful democratic nation, plaything for a selected ruling class.

When the civil war broke out in '67, he declined to take up the uniform like his fathers before him – he would not fight for a cause he didn't believe in. 'The coup should never have happened in the first place; it became a justification for future atrocities,' my grandfather always espoused, his thick-lensed round glasses making his eyes appear smaller than they were, like narrow slits in a wall. Other times, he was more agitated: 'Ironsi made a mistake tearing up the regional governance agreement. A big mistake! This country is not meant to be centrally governed, we are a nation of over three hundred tribes and five hundred languages forced together into cohabitation by the imperialists. Those who won the civil war have taken up the country as spoils of war while the people continue to suffer.'

Perhaps it was because he was from the middle belt and a minority tribe and so he viewed his surroundings without the arrogance the major tribes possessed, refusing to admit the wrongs of the past, the ills others had been subjected to; one side in particular denying it had committed a colonial-assisted genocide.

On some days, my grandfather found humour in our predicament. And when he did, he joked about how some of the others now knew how it felt to be a minority within their own land – to be subsumed within a larger mass, forgotten in the time of major policies, to have legitimate grievances dismissed as statistical noise, to only become relevant political pawns when the numbers were needed.

My father thought his father was a mad man, consumed by too much knowledge and the stories of his fathers; I thought him tormented by a country that never came to fruition.

Soye was seated in front of the large television screen in the living room downstairs. It was July and the rains had returned in torrents, turning roads impassable and causing gridlock traffic. Nzube, Soye's longtime friend, had come to visit, and they were watching the national news and making boisterous comments.

I'd first met Nzube as a university student. He'd studied journalism, eager to partake in holding the government to account, and had gone on to work for one of the nation's largest newspapers after graduation, gaining acclaim as one of the government's loudest critics, reporting without fear or favour, leading several labour marches and protests against government maltreatment. Now, he sat on a state government cabinet, a state government that reportedly owed its workers nineteen months' worth of salaries.

Newly released unemployment numbers flashed across the screen, closely followed by a secretly recorded video of a state governor brazenly demanding bribes from his visitors and going on to tuck bundles of dollar notes in his *agbada* when they obliged. A panel had been assembled by the news network to analyse the events, and already the individuals gathered looked unsure of where to start.

The anchor, a balding man in an oversized suit, introduced

the participants, then said, 'Let's begin with the unemployment numbers and brain drain in the nation. The Federal
Minister of Information and Culture has denounced these
numbers as inaccurate, even though they've been released
by the National Bureau of Statistics. The Federal Minister
of Labour has commented. Let's take a quick look then
discuss.'

The Minister of Labour appeared on the screen, a dimin-
utive, bearded man. 'The issue with our young people is that
they want white collar jobs, they want to work in offices with
air conditioners. This is why they are running to Canada
and America. Well, we have many more to replace them so
let them continue running. There are farms in the villages,
left to lie fallow; let those that don't have jobs return to the
farms and feed the nation.' Soye and Nzube nodded vigorously together.

Discussion began immediately. Dr Chukwu, the first
person to speak, was incensed. 'The problem with this government is that fact has become the enemy, propaganda is
now truth. Instead of speaking of solutions, they deny the
truth of their failed policies. How can the Minister of Labour,
a trained medical doctor, speak such nonsense? It's because
there are no consequences for actions here. We have a governor boldly collecting dollars as bribes and yet to resign. Until
actions start to lead to consequences, nothing will change.'

Mrs Fagbemi, a lawyer, spoke next. 'Just last week, we were
here to discuss the unprecedented rise in internet fraud. If
a country where a significant percentage of its population
consists of young people fails to provide jobs, we shouldn't
be surprised when they turn to crime or seek opportunities
outside. The Minister of Labour is a doctor – if he'd been told
to return to the village to farm, would he be where he is now?

Would he say the same for his children? These people send their children abroad and leave ours to rot within the system.'

The pro-government person on the panel, Mr Okhai, was given the floor. Also a lawyer, he'd been recently awarded the Senior Advocate of Nigeria (SAN) title, more for his sycophantic antics than his legal resume.

Soye and Nzube started their commentary then. 'Government this, government that. Is the government meant to do everything for the people?' Nzube said, then sipped on his bellini.

'My brother, are you minding these young people? They don't want to work, they think we got here by accident,' Soye said. 'They forget that we had to work very hard, it wasn't easy at all.' Power, it would seem, had a way of manipulating memories.

Nzube nodded in agreement. 'It's the internet age, they see all these American celebrities wearing diamonds and riding Rolls-Royces and think they can wake up tomorrow and get that without working. Now you see them doing all these funny jobs like YouTube channels.'

'That's for the ones that aren't addicts or doing fraud business.'

'Thieves, and they want to take over from us? *Tahh.*'

They turned back to the television. The panel had moved on to discussing the governor and his *agbada* crammed with dollar notes.

'Are we going to keep blaming the colonialists or past governments for this country's problems? When are our leaders going to take responsibility for the state of the country?' Dr Chukwu was saying in response to something the government's spokesperson Mr Okhai had said.

Mr Okhai attempted to interrupt and the anchor said,

'Gentlemen, let's endeavour to give room for everyone to air their opinions.'

'This anchor is biased against the government,' Nzube complained. 'How many minutes has this doctor fellow been speaking for? Was Okhai allowed to speak for this long?'

'Most of these journalists are very dishonest and biased,' Soye grunted.

'Rubbish,' Nzube said. 'It reminds me of that fellow that wrote an article criticising your road project in the slums. Hope you dealt with him like you said you would? I haven't heard anything from him recently; he must be sleeping behind a cell.'

Soye stiffened, as if suddenly taking note of my – until that moment – taciturn presence. He sent a furtive glance in my direction and Nzube's eyes flashed with acknowledgement.

Pasting a smile that was too bright to be real across his face, Nzube said, 'Madam, you've been very quiet. What do you think about what they're saying?'

I mirrored his smile. 'Nzube, do you want me to tell you what I really think or what you think I should think?'

His smile wavered. 'Of course, I want to know what you think, Madam Eriife.'

I nodded, slowly, methodically. 'Okay, would you allow your university-educated children to work as labourers on a farm?'

'Why did you talk to Nzube like that?' Soye demanded later after Nzube departed in a far less cheery mood than when he arrived. Before he left, he told Soye he was headed to Abuja in the coming days. 'What's happening in Abuja?' Soye asked.

'A major market caught fire last week and the governor wants me to submit pictures of the damage to the presidency,' Nzube responded. 'We have to let them know what's going on; maybe the state government can be assisted with a loan to help rebuild the market.' Nzube sent me a meaningful glance, then he added, 'Before they say we're not doing anything.'

'How did I talk to Nzube?' I asked calmly, unperturbed by the annoyance I read in Soye's gaze.

'Eri, why would you ask him such a question, simply because he said we need more youth farmers? Don't we need more farmers?'

'Listen, I've supported every move you've made. I even pretend not to notice the things you don't want me to know. But the least you can do is not lie to yourselves about the state of this country. We both know I detest pretence and cowardice. If you're going to do something, you might as well do it with your chest.'

That evening, Adelola called to inform me she was returning home the following week – her father had sent her the money for a first-class ticket.

'So, you've finally remembered me *ehn*?' I told her.

'Ahn-ahn, Mummy, it's not like that.' I'd never met her mother; I wasn't sure she had either. And so she called me 'Mummy' and I responded like I was indeed her mother.

The day Soye had brought Adelola home, after my return from the hospital, we'd stared at each other with uncertainty, neither of us seemingly sure how to play the roles we'd been cast in. Day by day, we learnt, helping the other, each new experience exposing my incompetence. I missed my mother most in those moments.

I found Soye holed up in his study, as he'd been since Nzube's departure, refusing even Moses' offer of dinner. I sat in one of the leather armchairs facing his desk. He pretended to not notice, keeping his head burrowed in shuffling pages.

Mildly amused, I said, 'So you're not going to talk to me again because I asked your friend a simple question *okwa ya?*' I spoke Igbo – my mother's language – only when I needed to tease Soye.

Soye sighed and looked up from his papers. 'You need to start a major pet project and spend less time at the clinic,' he said.

I stared at him, taken aback. 'Why? What is wrong with going to the clinic? I've already reduced my hours enough as is.'

He pulled off the reading glasses he'd recently taken to donning – a reminder that we were ageing. 'If I'm going to move up, I need to show that my wife is committed to service. You have to have a big project that can be pointed to as a success.'

'I have to totally give up working at the clinic for that? Isn't being a doctor commendable enough? I'm literally saving lives!'

From Soye's perplexed expression, I could tell he'd expected me to give in easily. 'Eriife, we both committed to making sacrifices when we started on this journey. Why the sudden change in behaviour?'

I pushed out of my seat and said, 'Maybe it's because I'm no longer the naive girl you married, Soye. I didn't realise you expected me to lay down my life as a stairwell to your ambitions.'

My father called me the next day. I watched his number on my screen for several seconds before it shrunk to a missed call bubble. I missed his calls more often since his remarriage five years ago.

His new wife looked nothing like my mother. Perhaps if she had, it would have been easier to forgive, to understand his decision to finally move on. But to see him with a woman who was so unlike her, a woman from his tribe, approved by his mother, made the sore of my mother's passing fester even more. I'd been conspicuously absent on their wedding day and my siblings had called until my phone's battery ran out. My brother, who was a year younger, had sent a text that said: *'You're so childish. Grow up!'*

'Never allow a woman to disrespect you,' was what my grandmother – my father's mother – used to say. As children, my brother had annoyed me by breaking an expensive porcelain doll my mother had bought me. He'd shattered it into hued pieces that decorated my bedroom floor. I'd charged at him, spurred by fury boiling like lava, and landed a slap across his face.

He let out a loud wail and my grandmother rushed out of her bedroom to examine the finger-shaped welts rising on his skin. Then she went into her room again; when she returned, she held a long thin stick. She handed it to my brother and said, 'Beat her. Beat her now! Never allow a girl or woman to disrespect you.'

My screams alerted my father and he stepped out of his study; my mother had gone to the market that morning. He'd collected the stick from my brother and pulled him aside, then he'd asked his mother 'why?' in a tone that sounded more like a plea than a reprimand. He was soft-spoken and gentle, a man not given to conflict and who never seemed to comprehend how others could muster the strength for it.

It was the same way he reacted on the days she taunted and harassed my mother about having only one son, pushed her to try for more children even though the doctor had warned of the consequences. What if something were to happen to my brother? What would our family do then?

Hypertensive cardiomegaly. I'd overheard my mother and Aunty Uju discussing it, arguing about it. My mother was trying for another child and Aunty Uju kept crying that she was sick. My father talked of moving countries but my mother was reluctant to leave my grandmother alone, reluctant to see my father lose the ground he'd gained at his workplace, to become a second-class citizen. It was how she was – selfless, always thinking of others.

My father's text came in: *'I called to check on you. I miss you. I'm sorry.'*

34

Juggernaut

Chandeliers dangled from the ceiling like upturned lit wedding cakes, casting the hotel ballroom in an iridescent glow. Voices hummed, barely taking note of the keynote speaker, a seasoned expert on girl child issues in the country. In the past, I'd avoided such gatherings, but with Soye's insistence that I play the role of a political spouse more, I'd decided to attend.

'WOMEN IN POLITICS: *How We Can Play A Bigger Role,*' the banners mounted on the stage and outside the hall announced, but as I'd expected, it had turned into a social gathering of political wives eager to make the next connection.

At my table were four other women, one of whom was Chief Mrs Abisola Aluko, a woman considered by many to be a political juggernaut, the power behind her husband. A descendant of a moneyed royal bloodline and married to old Brazilian settler Lagos money, her father had served a minister during the First Republic, her father-in-law was the largest shareholder in one of the country's largest oil companies, her late mother a former *iyal'oja* of Lagos, and her husband a sitting senator.

Famously religious, she only ever appeared in public in glittering scarves tied in a turban, and was a deaconess in her church, attending vigil services and chairing women's groups. In the past, we'd crossed paths at social gatherings but had never been formally introduced.

'You're Soye's wife, right?' she asked me now, raising a perfectly arched brow. She was clothed in gold – it was around her neck, wrists and swinging from her ears – a fine carat gold that looked specially handcrafted.

'Yes, ma,' I said, surprised she knew who I was. I extended a hand, suddenly feeling nervous; her gaze gave an impression of omniscience, like she could read the thoughts I was yet to have. 'I'm Eriife Adebowale.'

She eyed my hand. 'No need for that, my dear, we all know each other here one way or the other. You just don't attend enough of our meetings. Or am I wrong, Enitan?'

The woman beside her, a local government chairman's wife, leaned in. 'Yes of course, I know Mrs Adebowale and she knows me. We all know each other. How's the clinic doing?'

'Very fine, we thank God,' I said and nodded in Enitan's direction.

'It's good to see you take an interest in our activities outside election season, my dear,' Mrs Aluko said. 'From what I hear, you're a better politician than your husband.'

I chewed on a corner of my lip and tried to smile. 'Thank you, ma, I won't say I'm a better politician but I try my best.'

'No need to be modest, and I'm not asking, I'm telling. You would do well to be more active. We need more level-headed people in our midst.'

Hassana, the woman to my right, shoved her iPad on the

table and pointed at the bright screen. She adjusted the hijab draped around her hair and shoulders. 'Have you all seen this?' she asked. Her husband, a Northerner, was a member of the House of Representatives.

On the screen was a picture of a sitting senator knelt before Onomavwe, his hands clasped in a pleading gesture. 'Are they not agemates? What rubbish,' Hassana said.

'It's not about age, my dear,' Mrs Aluko said, 'it's about power.' She sounded like she knew what it meant to wield that magnitude of power.

'Senator Anaborhi must have offended him,' Enitan observed. 'You know he's planning to run for governor of the state come next elections, he cannot afford to be in Onomavwe's bad books.'

'An ex-convict?' Hassana said.

'No need to be so self-righteous, we all have our own dirty laundry, including your *husband*,' Mrs Aluko replied. And I thought she must be good friends with Onomavwe.

Hassana bristled and pulled her iPad from the table. Mrs Aluko didn't bat an eyelid in her direction; she was accustomed to this – putting others in their place.

Saratu, the woman seated opposite me, joined the conversation. Her birth name was Sarah, a Christian from Uromi, Edo state, but together with her husband, they'd both taken to adopting the Arabic versions of their names and dressed only in jalabiyas and kaftans to blend with the Northern sect in power. She wore a hijab, and whenever she was greeted, she responded with '*as-salamu alaykum*'. Political Islam, Soye called it. Beliefs easily traded like wares, attires transformed, tongues twisted, on the altar of power.

'Did you hear that Hauwa Bintu lost her seat in the Senate?' Saratu said.

'It's all over the news; it's rather hard to miss it,' Mrs Aluko drolled. She sounded bored and I wondered what it took to ignite her interest – she'd seen everything.

'She was the only female senator from the North, you know. That means the women in the senate are less than ten, out of one hundred and nine? That's poor,' Enitan said.

'I'm not sure if that's a good or bad thing,' Hassana commented. 'Wasn't she accused of corruption? That's why she lost her seat; she lost it to a young vibrant man from her village.'

'Haven't most of them been accused of corruption?' I said, surprising myself. I hadn't intended to make a comment.

Hassana stared at me like I'd grown a second head. 'What do you mean?'

I dusted imaginary lint from my skirt. 'Let's be honest. Many House of Assembly members have been accused of corruption, many of whom we know. If we're going by that, why haven't they lost their seats? Why is she being held to a different standard than the rest of them? Does being a woman automatically make her an angel? Women can be corrupt too; we're human beings.'

'Hmm,' Hassana murmured and adjusted her scarf. Saratu looked uncomfortable and I was certain I'd performed a misstep.

Mrs Aluko chuckled. 'Well, you have a point,' she said, suddenly interested in the conversation. 'Speaking of the young man that replaced her, from what I've heard, he's not very experienced or qualified. Many of these young politicians have not proven to be any different or better than their older counterparts. I even think quite a few of them are worse. They're just noisemakers. I'm quite tired of the whole thing being one big boys' club.'

Saratu leaned forward and dropped her tone to a whisper. 'Do you plan to run for a seat next time around, ma?'

Mrs Aluko laughed, sounding genuinely amused by the mere thought. 'Of course not, dear. I prefer to remain where I am, thank you very much.' The woman behind the power, not the power itself.

And I thought, what if I wanted the power itself?

My phone vibrated as Soye's text delivered: *'How is it going? Did you meet Mrs Aluko?'* And it occurred to me that he'd orchestrated our being seated together.

'Yes. I think she likes me,' I replied.

'She doesn't like people easily. Keep up the good work,' he sent, a heart emoji attached at the end, and I thought he must have picked up the use of emojis from Adelola.

I excused myself from the table. In the bathroom, orange lights gleaming against porcelain sinks and modern fittings, I washed my hands until they turned ghostly; the handwash smelled like cough syrup. Then I pulled out my phone and called Ego. I listened to the ringback tone, hopeful that at some point her voice would replace the sound and felt a stab of pain as it disconnected. I tried two more times; the same happened, just like the several times before. She would not forgive me and I did not deserve to be forgiven. I opened the message app and wrote: *'Congratulations on your marriage. Wishing you and Emeka all the best. Love, Eri.'*

In secondary school, our skirts had been identical – all three of us – sharp pleated skirts that rose just above our knees and made us feel grown and speak of the future with sprightly enthusiasm. It was a time when Zina crafted scripts and invented personas, pitching project after project to imaginary directors whose places we took, shaking her hand in congratulations, and Ego took part in every debate club activity to prepare, she told us, for the courtroom. Zina and I would stand at the back of the room and clap the loudest when she spoke until others threatened to kick us out. Life had been different then – simpler. It had never occurred to me that a time would come when we would not be on speaking terms. I stared at the picture that now occupied my home screen – one of us in pleated green and white, taken on the last day of secondary school. 'Three of you stand together, let me take a picture,' my mother had said, holding up her Polaroid. And we'd thrown our arms around each other and screamed, 'Cheese!' And now, I'd been smoothly carved out. I swallowed the tears constricting my throat and walked out of the bathroom, distracting myself with the sound of my clicking heels.

'I hear you're thinking of starting a pet project. Do you already have something in mind?' Mrs Aluko said when I returned, confirming my suspicions that Soye had contrived our meeting.

'Yes, ma,' I murmured, not trusting the sound of my voice. 'I have a few projects I'm looking at.'

'Good. I'm happy you intend to participate more.' She pulled out a card and scribbled an address on it. 'Come see me sometime this week. I know just the people to connect you with,' she said, handing me the card. 'You know I told Soye the other day that he's too eager. All that *gra gra* is good at the early stages, but as you go higher, you need a level of calm. I told him to look at his wife.'

Mrs Aluko's offices were located within the mini-estate situated in Banana Island that housed her family home. The unabashed opulence brought Ego's father to mind, and his alabaster winged angel that occupied the central spot in his monument to himself; even that paled in comparison to the grandeur of Mrs Aluko's home.

A security detail escorted me to the waiting area. Thirty minutes later, a skinny-legged secretary led me into a space that looked more like a penthouse than an office.

Mrs Aluko relaxed on a sofa in leggings and a robe dress, a tray with packs of juice and crystal tumblers arranged in front of her. 'Sit down, my dear, we don't have much time, there's so much to do,' she said.

The internet had said she was fifty-five but the smoothness of her skin leaned more towards the late thirties, closer to my age. 'Money is good,' my mother used to say. She was right.

'So tell me, what do you have in mind? It would do good to focus on your areas of strength,' she said when I was seated, adjusting cat-eye framed glasses on the bridge of her nose. The realisation hit me then that this was the life Soye desired: to reside in a mini-estate such as this, in the most expensive parts of the country guarded by sophisticated security details, to run its politics from a windowed penthouse office, to be untouchable. I tried to imagine myself in a dress robe, seated in an office like this.

I pulled out the dossier I'd prepared from my handbag and arranged the pages on the centre table. 'A foundation supporting maternal health and family planning,' I announced, feeling proud of myself. I'd only chosen my profession following my mother's death, ticking through the form we'd planned to fill out together with tear-blurred vision, Zina and Ego huddled beside me with their own forms, leaning in to ask if I was alright. I could not think of a better extension of my mother's legacy. I was desperate for her to be proud of the woman I was, and haunted by the feeling that she would have despised me.

'I've been reading up on the situation in the country and it's quite dire,' I said.

'Everything in the country is dire, my dear,' Mrs Aluko murmured as she shuffled through the pages I'd laid out.

'Our maternal mortality rate is one of the highest in the world,' I said.

'I'm glad you've done your research, dear, and as I can see here that there are several local and international organisations already working to tackle the issue.'

'Yes, I'm hoping to partner with some to identify the areas I can provide support.'

Mrs Aluko pulled the glasses from her eyes and pushed them into her hair. 'You're not planning to run this yourself, are you, my dear?'

My mind blurred. 'Well, yes.'

She grinned like a Cheshire cat, and I thought it was the most authentic smile I'd ever seen her wear. 'Who do you think you are, Jesus Christ?' She laughed. 'That's what money is for. You hire the experts, they run it, you check in every now and again and show up when it's time to take pictures. Don't get me wrong, I think this is brilliant and I appreciate your enthusiasm but running a private clinic in Lagos isn't the same as any of this.' She pulled out her phone. 'Let's see, I have some top contacts within the NGO space that can provide assistance.'

The weeks that followed were spent holding meetings, setting up office and signing documents. Adelola returned in the midst of the foray, alight with the nonchalance of youth, a life lacking strain. 'You're always busy, let's go to the beach. Let's go for a party. There's a new movie out.'

'Go and disturb your father, some of us are busy,' I told her. Soon, she stopped asking and arranged meet-ups with her friends, teenagers whose parents owned speedboats, yachts and beach houses; teenagers who, like her, had never known what it was to live in the real Nigeria.

The skies in Ilorin were foggy, heavy with forthcoming rainfall, and when we landed, I could hear the murmur of thankful prayers coming from the economy cabin.

'A bit of a turbulent flight *aye*?' the foreigner seated beside me commented.

'Yes, very turbulent,' I said, wondering what business had brought him to the ancient city.

The consultants had recommended travel to properly conduct a landscape assessment, to see for ourselves the issues we planned to tackle head on. 'We can handle it,' the lead consultant said when I volunteered to go to Ilorin; it was clear she had never had a client volunteer to participate in field work before. In the end, we'd settled on another consultant meeting up with me in Ilorin.

Grass, rangy and unattended, grew up the sides of buildings in the ministry complex. Goats wandered unbounded, stopping every now and then to chew on some of the grass.

'I said take me to the State Ministry of Health,' I told the driver, believing he'd misheard my instructions.

'Na the ministry be this,' he said and pointed at the fading paint letters on a wall. I reached for the door handle. 'Dem never come by this time.' It was eight in the morning.

The state consultant who was to assist me was yet to arrive as well. I called her.

'Ah, ma, you should have told me before going, nobody resumes this early.'

By 9.30am, they milled in, bearing black leather bags and paper files. The state consultant had arrived fifteen minutes earlier. Before we left Lagos, we'd held a virtual brief with the entire team on how the process worked. We were to submit letters at certain offices and wait for a response, in the meantime, we would reach out to contacts directly in charge of the issues and begin conversations.

'The commissioner has not resumed but you can drop your letter,' the civil servant at the desk informed us. In front of her was a large tray of melon seeds she was carefully dehusking.

'What time does he resume?' I asked.

She dropped the seed between her fingers in the tray and sat up. 'He hasn't resumed office. None of the commissioners have resumed.'

'It's September,' I said, disbelieving. Swearing in ceremonies had been held in May.

Her eyes asked me the question she was too polite to utter: *Are you new here?* She shrugged. The consultant hurried forward and began to make conversation, asking questions about who we could speak with.

'Is this normal? Why is she peeling *egusi* in the office?' I asked the consultant when we had exited the building.

'This is good. You need to go to some states where they have full-blown kiosks,' she said.

Eventually, we were pointed to a director's office, who received our letter lamenting the underfunding of his department. On the ceiling above him, rotated a fan I'd last seen at the end of the '90s.

In my hotel room, I called Mrs Aluko, unsure of the next step to take.

'You didn't tell me you were going this week, my dear. A

state assembly man's wife should not be running around like this,' she reprimanded. 'Anyways, since you're already there, I'll call the governor's wife to see if she's in town. You know she lives in the UK and only visits from time to time.'

35

Noble cause

Oh God of creation, direct our noble cause
Guide our leaders right
Help our youth the truth to know

To open and close the meeting, we bowed our heads as we mumbled the national prayer that served as the second stanza of the national anthem.

Political infighting within the party had erupted in the past weeks and emergency meetings were called from above to ensure calm.

The party had become the government and the government the party; two indissoluble elements such that we did not know where one began and the other ended. Power blocs had formed to take advantage and soon enough, the blocs had risen up against each other. This wasn't the selfless service Soye had promised at the start of our journey.

'It's not even six months since the swearing-in and they're already fighting over who will take over in 2023. Unserious people,' Nzube said to Soye whilst the meeting was ongoing.

'My brother, by the time we get to 2023, they will have finished sharing everything. Be alert, don't be caught sleeping on a bicycle,' Soye responded, rubbing his palms together as if in preparation for a fight.

They agreed to congregate at our house when the meeting was over.

'Madam Adebowale is such a wonderful host,' Nzube said – to my surprise – and their friends concurred. Soye beamed like he had been paid the compliment.

'Hope we're not imposing, madam?' Yunusa asked, leaning towards me from the other side of Soye. His constant deference and effort to acknowledge my existence had endeared him to me over time, and amongst Soye's friends, I considered him the most refined of the lot. Soye insisted Yunusa was infatuated with me, an incorrigible puppy love.

'You're the type of woman he would have married if he hadn't gone ahead with the political marriage his father arranged,' he blustered. And I could tell he wasn't yet sure whether to be offended or flattered by Yunusa's attention to his wife.

'He's just being polite. You know it's possible for a man to be polite,' I said.

In our larger living room, they agreed that tech was the new oil money. 'These young boys are making so much so quickly. Just the other day, my friend's nephew raised two million dollars for his fintech startup. Another young man sold his company for just over a hundred million dollars. Dollars o,' Akamnachi was saying. He was from a major political family in the Southeast.

'We have the local talent,' Yunusa said, picking from the plate of small chops in front of him. 'I was speaking to someone in the space and there are so many talented young men building the future of tech here, many foreign companies are even poaching them.'

'How can we get in and take advantage?' Nzube asked.

Soye laughed and said, *'Ahn-ahn* Nzube, government money is not enough for you?'

'My brother, does one ever have enough money?' Nzube returned. They all chuckled.

'If you ask me, the government should stay out of it. They've been doing well without our interference,' Yunusa said. 'We can only flourish as a nation when the government starts sticking to the issues of governance and nothing else, the market will take care of itself.'

'See Yunusa oppressing us with his Cambridge economics degree o,' Akamnachi said, and they all laughed.

'But what is wrong with the government trying to control things? Or trying to benefit from the success of companies?' Danladi, a party member who happened to be visiting Lagos from Zamfara, asked. Soye always called him a *money miss road*, the type that had stumbled on wealth via government contracts and didn't know how to comport himself.

'The recent policies coming from the top aren't helping the sector,' Yunusa said. 'If anything, they are making life difficult for the companies and discouraging investors. It's why we're ranked so low on the ease-of-doing-business scale.'

I thought of Ego and the several conversations we'd had about how the restrictive central bank policies were affecting Emeka's startup enterprise. 'We cannot keep innovating around incompetence,' she would say. Then I'd nodded in agreement with her.

'We should not use all these foreign scales to rate our

performance; they're biased against us,' Akamnachi said, sipping from his whisky tumbler.

Yunusa relaxed in his seat and wiped at his lips with a napkin. 'They might be biased against us, but we can still say the truth. We've carried our rent-seeking behaviour to the tech sector – this isn't oil.'

'Don't be a hypocrite, Yunusa. We've all pocketed something at some point in time or the other,' Nzube said.

'Speak for yourself,' Yunusa murmured, and the air crackled with challenge.

'And if you haven't, it's because not all us are from old Northern money,' Nzube retorted.

Danladi bit into a meat pie, the crust scattered on his lips like stardust. 'Yunusa's problem is that he's read too much. He thinks this is England,' he said.

'Our problem as a country is that we engage in low quality theft,' Yunusa said. 'We have people who have only ever been in politics running important sectors. Even if we want to steal, we should at least not do so at our own detriment. Allow businesses to flourish and tax them to their teeth.'

Nzube looked down at his empty plate and raised a hand towards the direction of the dining area where I was pretending to be engrossed in coordinating the stewards in arranging food trays and setting the table for their lunch. 'Madam, any more puff-puff?' Nzube asked.

Yunusa tapped him lightly on the shoulder. 'Nzube, is that how to speak to the madam of the house? You think you're in a *mamaput*?' Then to me he said, with an alluring smile, 'Madam, please don't mind Nzube, our friend is a village man.'

Soye held my gaze as if to say: *I told you so.*

*

We'd concluded our landscape assessment and set up temporary offices in selected states of the country to provide support.

'Start small then expand into other areas and gain more partners. But I'll advise you to limit your expectations,' Mrs Aluko said.

I handed over management of the clinic to a medical director and poured my hours into coordination efforts. Then one day, a staff member from up north called. One of our officials had been picked up by the Hisbah police for running a kiosk selling alcohol from his home, and his sister for indecent dressing. Before this, we'd faced pushback from some of our political associates. 'Madam it is against the will of God to regulate the number of children.' An official in another state had blatantly informed us not to expect significant support from the governor as he was a 'staunch Catholic'.

Mrs Aluko had laughed the next time we'd spoken. 'They need the population numbers to rig the elections their way.'

In the middle belt, we were facing a different sort of crisis: insecurity. There had been several clashes between herdsmen and the local farmers who didn't want their farms decimated by the herdsmen's grazing animals. I thought of my grandfather and what he would say of the government once again ignoring the cries of the minority, of our people. His farmlands had been sold off not long after his death. But for years, I'd harboured thoughts about buying them back, of returning to the corrugated roofed room with the handcrafted hardback chair and reliving those moments with him. And now even that seemed impossible. 'Nigeria giveth and Nigeria taketh away,' he'd loved to say.

When Soye returned that evening, his kaftan wrinkled

in several places by activity, his only interest was food. 'I've been in meetings all day!' he said as he wolfed down the meal prepared by Moses.

I pushed an empty glass tumbler in front of him and filled it with water, listening to him vent about the day he'd had. He eyed me with open suspicion. '*Oya* talk,' he said.

'I don't understand,' I replied, feigning innocence.

'You're watching me eat like you kept gold in my mouth. You want something. You think I don't know you this woman?'

I chuckled and rolled my eyes. 'Soye *abeg*.'

He held my hand and rubbed a thumb across my knuckles. '*Iyawo mi*. I'm happy you're pursuing this project the way you are. Thank you for doing it for me, I know you didn't want to give up the clinic,' he said. Maybe that was the problem – I'd always been willing to do anything for him. At some point in our relationship, his wants had become mine, his ambitions my ambitions. We were bound by more than name – Love? Obsession? Time? – and sometimes I thought that if someone were to cut him, I would bleed instead.

'One of our officers and his wife have been arrested,' I said.

His brows creased with worry. 'Why? What did they do?'

'Alcohol and indecent dressing.'

He sighed. 'I'll try to make some calls.'

'How is this allowed to happen?' I fumed. 'We can't be living in the same country and existing under different laws? It's ridiculous. Alcohol is illegal in certain parts but VAT from alcohol sales is collated and shared nationally. What even is indecent dressing in a secular democracy? Where is the bottom? You should bring it up on the floor of the assembly!'

Soye started. 'Are you trying to destroy my career? I've

already said I'll make some calls so your people get released. What more do you want?'

'And what about those that don't have connections?'

'See, I think you're overestimating the level of influence I have. I'm just a state legislative member. Eri, I've had a long day, please I'm tired.'

I got up and left him at the table. In our room, I paced, agitated. I picked up my phone and thought of who to call to vent the emotions boiling within me, someone who would understand without taking Soye's side or returning it back to him. And at that moment, I realised I had no friends. My life had become subsumed within his; his friends were my friends and my friends were wives of his friends. The only friends I had, I'd lost.

He massaged my shoulders later that night as I sat in front my dressing table, his fingers kneading their way in and out above my clavicle.

'Soye, please leave me alone,' I muttered, feeling small and feeble. I would give in, I knew. I always gave in.

'Are you sure about him?' Aunty Uju had asked with barely concealed concern on the morning of our wedding. And I thought then, as I did now that she must have seen something in him that I couldn't. But it was too late to turn back – I had no one else.

Soye dropped a gold-backed scroll in front of me. 'Look what was delivered to my office today,' he said.

'What's this?' I asked, as I unfurled the object.

'Senator Balarabe's son is getting married to an emir's daughter and we're invited.'

I read the golden words on the scroll and handed it back without a word.

'Eri, why are you being like this? Do you realise how huge this is? Not everyone can get an invite like this. It means we're making all the right moves. Even the president will be in attendance; we can make all the right connections.'

'This is all you care about, so I'm happy for you,' I said and turned around to look at him. 'When did you become this person? I'm not expecting you to transform the system, I'm not even expecting you to be incorruptible. But do you even care about doing the bare minimum? You weren't like this when we met.'

He frowned. 'See, the issue is you're too involved in this project. I expected you to do as much as you could and leave the rest in the hands of the experts. All this is unnecessary.'

Kano was coated in dust like a carapace. I itched to peel it back just to see what the city looked like underneath.

'It's the harmattan. You know it's almost the year end,' Soye explained, grinning out the cabin window like a child on a school trip as we landed at the airport. Private jets scattered like toy aircraft across the tarmac. Soye continued to chat animatedly. 'I've counted more than forty jets, and there are still many more on the other end. Were there this many jets for the inauguration ceremony?'

'Definitely more. Is a wedding more important than the swearing in of a sitting president?' Nzube responded.

'I hear all the five-star hotels in town are fully booked; we were lucky to get the rooms we did,' Soye said.

A week of festivities had been ongoing before our arrival – glitzy polo matches, a bride-price-exchange ceremony, an ornamental-henna night, amongst others. Newspapers and blogs flooded with pictures of each festivity, underlined by dolorous complaints from residents and rogue imams about such an exuberant display of wealth in the midst of endemic poverty. Before the festivities, official pre-wedding photos of the couple had been released – a wide-nosed young man whose eyes held the cameras in a commanding glare and a wispy thin girl who looked to be about Adelola's age; I found it strange that they did not smile at each other in any of the photos.

The wedding fatiha had been held early in the day at the palace mosque and a giant elaborate marquee had been erected within the palace walls to house the weekend festivities. Heavy security presence dotted the landscape: police, military and paramilitary officers in bulletproof vests, wielding automatic rifles. And I thought of the article lamenting the tremendous disparities. One woman had told the paper: 'When our children are being killed, these security personnel are nowhere to be found but suddenly we're seeing machine guns and weapons just because their children are getting married. God will punish them!'

'So you mean to tell me if someone were to blow up this place that would be the end of most of this country's ruling class?' Mrs Aluko joked and a chill of dread ran down my spine at the thought. Would Ego and Zina mourn my passing? Would Adelola have a hard time recalling my face? The first time I'd struggled to remember my mother's face, I'd scattered through my belongings in deranged craze, until I'd found the picture of her I'd hidden away at the bottom of a drawer, her broad smile lighting up the frame. Then I'd traced a finger over the lines of her face, willing my mind to commit every single one to memory, to never forget.

Mrs Aluko chuckled, enjoying her own grim humour. 'Don't look so startled, dear; I have no plans to blow up this place. I have too many friends here.'

Both aisles of the political spectrum had converged for what many had branded the wedding of the year. Here, there was no need to play-act enmity; hugs were shared, handshakes exchanged, conversations loud and boisterous. Soye moved within the crowd like a whirling breeze, table to table, making new friends and lasting impressions. I'd grown tired of the performance when he'd pulled me towards Onomavwe's table where Kamsi – whose sight still revolted me – was seated and returned to our assigned seats instead.

Enitan glared at the white roses and potted bare-branch trees crusted with crystals and LED lights that served as our table's centrepiece, then she turned her head to look around at the painted white manzanita tree branches and lampstands that bordered the aisle, the crystal garlands, candles, flakes and petals that covered the cavernous hall, all reportedly flown in for the occasion. 'What theme is this meant to be?'

'Winter wonderland,' I guessed.

'In Nigeria? Do we have snow in Kano?' Enitan said.

'No, but we have money in Nigeria and money can buy snow,' Mrs Aluko said and picked up her wine glass.

The bride emerged to applause an hour into the reception in a sculpted couture dress, sheer nude material covering her shoulders. The groom escorted her down the aisle towards elevated palatial thrones. At the other side, I spotted Soye shaking hands with a man who'd referred to him as a buffoon during the last elections.

'How old is she? She can't be that old,' Enitan said. A server in a waistcoat approached our table to take our order, interrupting conversation.

'Probably nineteen or twenty, maybe twenty-one? Not very old,' I said when he was gone.

'She's nineteen,' Mrs Aluko said with certainty.

'No wonder she doesn't look very happy,' Enitan said. 'They should have allowed her to enjoy her youth a little more before marrying her off.'

'Maybe she just doesn't smile much,' Mrs Aluko drolled.

'They don't look like they love each other,' I observed.

Mrs Aluko huffed. 'Only the poor can afford to marry for love, my dear; we have more important things to worry about, like power and money. Even the middle-class marry to improve their options. At the end of the day, we're all trying to escape poverty.'

The conversation shifted towards my work when Mrs Aluko asked how the project was going. I told her of the arrest. As promised, Soye had secured their release but Yusuf's wife had been instructed to return to the headquarters for Islamiyya sessions for six months.

'Why didn't you inform me?' Mrs Aluko asked.

'I felt it was something Soye could handle. I didn't want to bother you,' I said.

'You should have called me; it's never a bother,' she said with finality.

My eyes caught Yunusa's across the room. He smiled and winked like we shared a joke. I laughed.

'What's so funny? Share the joke,' Mrs Aluko said.

Enitan was still thinking about what I'd shared. 'But isn't the bride also a Muslim?'

'Enitan, are you going to spend the evening asking questions?' Mrs Aluko retorted, with a hint of exasperation she did not often show. 'Rules are for the poor.'

Adelola called me the next day to say she'd seen my pictures on social media; she'd returned to school at the beginning of the new semester. 'You looked so pretty,

Mummy!' Conversation had erupted online on the bride's dress and the hypocrisy of the Hisbah police. Days later, it released a statement saying it was against religious tenets to criticise a leader publicly.

36

Sachet economics

Death came in the midst of chaos in early December that year.

'Have you heard the news?' Soye asked me. 'Rabiu Harouna is dead,' he said when I shook my head.

We turned on the television and scrolled quickly to a local news station. *'BREAKING: FORMER GOVERNOR RABIU HAROUNA DEAD AT 85'* was emblazoned on the screen as the leading story. A reporter was saying he'd passed away in a hospital in London and they would have more details later. The news ticker at the bottom of the screen crawled by in brilliant yellow, the only byline that would matter for a while – *'Breaking News: Elder statesman Rabiu Harouna passes. Nation in mourning.'*

'What sort of year is this? From one problem to another,' Soye said. And I thought the human memory was as fickle as humans themselves. Just months before, we'd celebrated a victorious election cycle, and it had only been weeks since the senator's son's wedding, but a succession of unfavourable events was all it took to turn Soye's perception of the year around.

An unlikely TV documentary broadcast in two parts in October and November had resurrected Kamsi's case – 'Sex for Grades'. Female journalists had gone undercover in academic institutions in Ghana and Nigeria to obtain proof of sexual harassment and assault endemic in the system. The ensuing online debate had caused a wide-reaching stir as calls for reckoning for the lecturers caught on camera came:

'This has been going on for decades and nothing has been done about it. Women are not protected in our society,' one person commented on a news site.

'Nothing will change. Nothing ever changes,' another said.

Then a single tweet that lit the embers:

A Distinguished Field Marshal
@General_Chinwe· **Follow**

Whatever happened to Pastor Kamsi's case? So many people spoke up in support of the victims, including a popular actress and nothing has been done. We were told there's DNA evidence. But what has happened? If that case could disappear, what hope is there for the rest of us?

10:35 AM · 20 Nov 2019 · Twitter for iPhone

The Police Command issued a statement saying it had concluded its investigations and the onus lay on the Ministry of Justice to act based on the investigative report, effectively laying the blame at the ministry's feet. Forced to defend its delay in addressing the case, the Ministry of Justice released a statement that said prosecution would have to wait for the conclusion of internal due process.

Onomavwe called, unhappy. How could Soye have allowed the online discourse to escalate to such perilous levels? What had happened to the influencer farm that had won them the elections? Soye lamented about social media after that: how it had become a dangerous tool of expression and slander. I told him he'd loved social media when it had helped to get rid of the then incumbent president.

Then a US associate of Otunba Bankole was taken into custody by the FBI, facing criminal charges for conspiracy to launder money obtained from business email compromise fraud and other related scams. Within weeks, Otunba Bankole and a high-ranking member of the police force – a recent recipient of a national award – were labelled as persons of interest and declared wanted. Pictures surfaced online of Soye in Otunba's company, and he was branded a fellow criminal. Soye read out one of the news site comments to me, his voice trembling: 'A member of a state legislature! We're truly a country run by criminals.'

The following morning, Soye issued a statement disassociating himself from all criminal activity, but the conversation had been started.

Otunba Bankole called Soye, screeching through the speaker phone at the highest decibel. 'Adetesoye, what is the meaning of that nonsense statement? Are you calling me a criminal?! Ehn? Shey o ya werey ni? Have you gone mad? Iwo? After all I've done for you? Ah! O ma gba gbe? You've already forgotten? Is this how you treat your friends?'

An emergency meeting was held at the top in Abuja to decipher a solution. Threats and warnings had been issued; Otunba and the high-ranking police officer were determined to not go down alone.

Soye returned from Abuja admonished and subdued, like

a dog left out in the pouring rain; this wasn't the triumphant end to the year he'd hoped to have.

'You're still young. This will pass. Our people forget easily,' I told him because I couldn't bear to see him so dejected.

Rabiu Harouna's death would only serve to prove me right. On the panels discussing his death, he was referred to as a national hero, a man who had lived a life of service to his country.

There were no mentions of his past as a commanding officer of the Nigerian army division that had perpetuated the Asaba massacre, his role on the dubious petroleum trust under the leadership of a late dictator, nor the several corruption scandals that trailed his time as a governor. Before his demise, he'd sat on an economic council that had overseen the country's plunge into a recession.

The voices online were raised in contest:

E. O.
@NedCruz_Utd · Follow

Who and who are mourning? The nation is not in any mourning. In fact he lived too long. Good riddance!

10:15 AM · 5 Dec 2019 · Twitter for iPhone

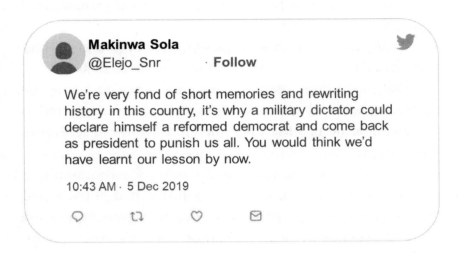

Makinwa Sola
@Elejo_Snr   · Follow

We're very fond of short memories and rewriting history in this country, it's why a military dictator could declare himself a reformed democrat and come back as president to punish us all. You would think we'd have learnt our lesson by now.

10:43 AM · 5 Dec 2019

Soye wasn't taking any chances this time, and influencers were unleashed to turn the conversation around:

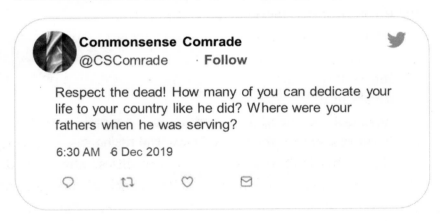

Commonsense Comrade
@CSComrade   · Follow

Respect the dead! How many of you can dedicate your life to your country like he did? Where were your fathers when he was serving?

6:30 AM 6 Dec 2019

'I met Senator Rabiu Harouna a few times,' a guest on a news network informed the viewers. He tapped a handkerchief on the skin underneath his eyes. 'We would discuss policies and books we read over tea. A very refined and dignified fellow. He will be greatly missed.'

*

A glossy magazine cover was the right way to announce success.

'That's how you let everyone know you've arrived,' Mrs Aluko said.

The foundation's work had been recognised on a random international end of year list and Mrs Aluko thought it was just what was needed to boost my profile in the political arena. A few calls in her penthouse office and the editor of a newspaper magazine made space on the cover of its end-of-year issue. 'I want her to look like a future president's wife,' she told the editor. 'The piece must be tastefully done; no second-rate nonsense. Hope you understand?'

When the call was over, she grinned with self-satisfaction and pressed a little knob on the side of her table. A steward in white appeared and she asked him to bring her a bottle of Pol Roger and two flutes. 'We need to celebrate.'

'What are we celebrating?' I asked, sincerely puzzled.

'The magazine cover, of course.'

'But we haven't accomplished much yet. Isn't it a bit early to talk about it?'

She shook her head as if saddened by my naivety. 'You really don't seem to understand how the higher-level works, my dear. This isn't local government politics,' she scoffed. 'Anyways, it's why you have me. You think all the people you see on these covers have actually accomplished much? It's all about presentation! You need to blow your horn; sell your story so others can believe it. Otunba who is wanted by the FBI was just on a magazine cover lauding his business exploits and you think you shouldn't talk about this? How else do you plan to attract attention to yourself and build your profile?'

The steward returned minutes later with a laden tray and

she told him to return the bottle for an older vintage. 'Are you trying to make me look cheap?'

As we sat sipping from our flutes, the floor-to-ceiling windows creating an illusion of being suspended in the sky, Mrs Aluko said, 'You're doing a good job, my dear. But I need you to talk to your husband. He needs to calm down, all this *gra gra* will lead nowhere. What was that statement he put out about Otunba?'

The morning of the shoot, the team offloaded their equipment in our garage and the shoot coordinator threw instructions around like he owned our home: 'Put it there. Yes, over there. No no, not there. Over there! Watch what you're doing!'

The interviewer, a woman dressed in an abstract jumpsuit that was intended to be fashionable but ended up appearing as though the tailor had gotten her measurements wrong, spoke in an accent that had been American at some point but was now stolidly somewhere in between. 'I'm Klara, ma. It's so lovely to meet you. The work you're doing is absolutely phenomenal,' she said, shaking my hand enthusiastically, and I wondered how often she'd spoken those words to an interviewee.

In our living room, Klara opened her binders to explain the concept they had in mind, 'Somewhere between chic and boss lady,' and shared a copy of the interview questions. 'Let me know if there's anything you're uncomfortable with and we'll take it out. I've already shared them with Mrs Aluko but she says you should have a say as well.'

Soye walked in as we sorted through concept photos, dressed in a collared polo shirt and shorts that stopped above his knee. He'd recently taken to playing golf because a friend had mentioned it was the best way to socialise with the upper class. 'What's going on?' he asked, looking around at the magazine staff and equipment with open curiosity.

I excused myself to speak with him. 'Today's the shoot I told you about,' I said.

'Oh, oh, I totally forgot about that.' He looked over my head to speak with Klara. 'Are you the interviewer?'

'Yes sir,' she said, rising to her feet. 'Good morning, sir.'

Soye stepped around me to speak with her. 'Good morning! It's good you're here, I had some ideas in mind,' he said as he plopped down to occupy the seat I'd only just vacated. 'We can do a couple shoot, then you can ask her some questions. Afterwards, we can do a brief column on the role she's played in supporting me in my career and my plans for the future and the country.'

Klara looked between me and Soye, confusion written in the lines of her face. She stuttered as she spoke. 'W–well the shoot is meant to be about just Mrs Adebowale and her foundation's work on maternal health care.'

'Yes? And? You're saying there's no space to discuss my work afterwards? It's not like much has been done with the foundation anyways.' He wouldn't know; he left the files I handed him unread.

'Sorry sir, but Mrs Aluko gave clear instructions about what we should do, and we can't change that,' Klara insisted.

Soye brooded when the team left. The shoot had concluded on a high note and the interviewer commented that it was one of the best ones she'd done.

'So is this how it's going to be now?' he said.

'How is what going to be?' I asked as I wiped the makeup from my face.

'You're just going to focus on yourself? The whole purpose

of you starting this project was to boost my profile and you wouldn't even let me participate in your interview.'

I laughed, incredulous. 'Soye, you're interviewed every other day. You can't be serious!'

Hassana was campaigning for votes for a Big Brother house-mate in our WhatsApp group chat when Mrs Aluko sent the galley proofs. I'd been added to the Women in Politics group after I'd attended the meeting at the hotel and like most groups, it often pivoted from its main purpose.

> **Hassana:** Please you people should vote so she doesn't
>   get evicted
> **Enitan:** With all the problems affecting this country? This
>   is a serious group Hassana
> **Hassana:** At least your votes count here

Then Mrs Aluko sent the pictures with the caption: *'Let's all congratulate our very own Mrs Adebowale on her award and magazine cover spread.'* And all other conversation was abandoned to do as Mrs Aluko said.

Hours later, Saratu returned with other news: *'This is so sad,'* she wrote as she shared a blog post. The caption read: *'Actress Zina's Mother Down With Cancer.'*

I was fifteen, losing my mother again, watching her body lowered as the pastor mouthed the burial service in the Book of Common Prayer, but Aunty Ada had taken my mother's place, and Zina, Ego and I were rolling in the dirt by the graveside.

My vision stuttered as I struggled to read the article – she'd been undergoing treatment for a year. A year and I'd had no idea. I swiped through my phone frantically, searching for the social media apps I almost never used except to keep tabs on my friends. But Ego had stopped using Twitter since she'd outed Kamsi.

Zina's Instagram was the same as ever – premieres, events, promotion for her movies, an announcement of a new production company with Ego; she wasn't one to show weakness.

'What do you want to do now?' Zina had asked me when I returned from the hospital after the surgery to take out my womb. I hadn't told her about it, but somehow she'd found her way to my home when I needed her the most.

'What?' I said, unable to comprehend what she was asking.

'What do you want to do now?' she repeated, her eyes clear. It was how Zina moved through life – propelling forward through action, refusing to be stopped. 'Do you want to stay with him?'

Ego, Zina, Aunty Uju. What was it about Soye they'd all seen that I was blind to? 'We're married.'

She shrugged. 'And?'

'I thought you liked him?'

'I liked him more than Ego did, which isn't saying a lot, but I thought he made you happy,' she said.

'And you don't think he does anymore?'

'I don't think you even remember what that feels like. You're too busy making *him* happy.'

Adelola returned from America for the Christmas holidays the week the magazine cover was released. Digital versions were broadcast across blogs and social media and I received further requests for interviews. 'Don't respond to them yet. You have to appear scarce and unavailable,' Mrs Aluko advised, and so I scrolled through their fawning emails instead, wondering when they would discover the fraud I was.

On the coffee table in our main living room, a stack of glossy proofs was arranged and Adelola took a copy along every time she went out, only to return without it. 'My friends keep asking for copies. Everyone says you look so fine. And I'm like "yes, that's my mum!"' she said.

Soon the stack had reduced to a small pile of copies that Soye largely ignored. 'It's nice,' he finally said one afternoon, skimming through. 'They could have done better with some of the pictures. I'll arrange a better interview for you.'

They'd included a brief mention of my parents and my 'multicultural' background, and my father messaged to say congratulations: *'I'm proud of you, your mother would be too.'* I cried for my mother because I didn't want her proud of me from a metaphysical other side; I wanted her there in my living room, leafing through the glistening pages and laughing at the pictures, always laughing. 'You never take anything seriously,' Aunty Ada used to complain.

One day, Adelola asked to come with me to the salon. 'I need new braids for Christmas,' she said. And I agreed because I knew it was just an excuse to go out with me.

As a child, she'd emulated my mannerisms, wanting to be like her mummy. In school, she'd told everyone she was going to be a doctor and that we looked just alike. I'd felt guilt for taking the place of a mother she'd never known. Even though she was now old enough to understand the truth of our circumstance, neither of us would acknowledge it.

Aunty Hannah – my father's distant relative – owned a salon in Bariga, and because she did, I never went elsewhere to get my hair done. Growing up, she would ask my mother to allow me to spend the weekends in her salon because she never married or had children of her own. 'I don't want any man collecting my money,' she always averred.

In the confined container of her salon, large peeling posters of hairstyles on the wall, the air thick with hair spray and jerry-curl chemicals, I'd learnt the ways of hair and adults, and listened to the stories my mother had been too protective to tell me. And even though I'd offered several times to help her get a better place in Lagos Island, Aunty Hannah refused to move from her salon on the mainland. Soye said it was good I still went there – it was a good way to feel the pulse of the people.

A film was playing on the television in the corner when we arrived. Aunty Hannah was pulling at attachment and giving instructions to a younger girl.

'Aunty Hannah, I'm here,' I said as I pulled back the sliding glass door, and she shouted, throwing her arms wide open, '*Ay!* My daughter is here o.'

Later, I was seated under a dryer and two girls surrounded Adelola, their arms moving deftly as they wove through waist-length braids. A woman in faded clothes was mixing *akamu* in a bowl to give to her little daughter. 'Check that cupboard there for milk,' my aunty said, and the woman got up to tear out a sachet from the line, murmuring thanks.

'This country is so hard,' Aunty Hannah said when the woman was gone. She was sewing a weave into a woman's hair. 'People cannot afford basic things. The other day I went to the market and when I saw the price of things, I screamed. How is the regular man expected to survive?'

'My sister,' said the woman whose weave she was sewing. 'And our wicked politicians are just living their lives and travelling up and down like nothing is happening. God will punish them and their generations.'

Adelola sent a panicked glance my way.

'Businesses are closing every day,' another woman said. She was under a dryer as well and was almost screaming to hear herself. 'My friend's husband just lost his job because the factory closed and moved their operations to Ghana. Businesses that are not closing are trying to adapt. Almost everything is in sachets these days so people can afford to buy. The other day I saw Baileys in a sachet. Baileys!'

'You must know how to practise sachet economics to survive in this country,' a woman who'd only just arrived said, her scarf still tied on her head.

'Which one is Baileys again?' Aunty Hannah asked. 'You know I didn't go to school like you people.'

'It's an alcoholic drink, aunty,' I explained.

'Oh! People still have money to drink? Anyways, na only woman and drink dey to comfort people,' Aunty Hannah said.

'Why don't you move abroad and set up a salon there?' the woman in front of her said. 'If you hear how much these black Americans are charging for braids that we make here for how much *ehn*? No wonder they're always carrying their hair for three months.'

The woman with the scarf pulled it off and ran her fingers through the shrub of hair underneath. 'Everyone is moving abroad these days. My colleague and her husband just sold off all their furniture because they got Canadian permanent residence. If it's not Canada, it's Europe. America is not the in thing like before, it's too hard to move there. Me too, let me start planning my *japa*, can't be dulling myself.'

'Do you know how much it is to apply for Canadian PR? Even to run away, you need money,' the woman under the dryer shouted.

'I'm too old to move,' Aunty Hannah said. 'If all of us move, how many of us will remain in this country?'

Before we left, I pushed a thickened envelope into Aunty Hannah's apron, ignoring her protests. 'Buy more dryers – the place is looking fine,' I said.

She smiled, a motherly smile that exposed the new lines around her eyes, and patted my cheek. 'Call your father, I know he has offended you but call him.'

I nodded, not saying anything, not committing.

'And tell that your husband to come and see me. When it's time to campaign for votes, he'll be everywhere like a tsetse fly.'

In the car, Adelola leaned towards me and asked, her eyes clouded with a new sadness of awareness, 'Is Nigeria that hard?'

37

Consequences

'New Year! New Decade! New Things!' Kamsi proclaimed from the altar of his new auditorium, an altar fashioned from pure flamed marble. 'God is about to transform your life beyond your wildest dreams,' he shouted into the microphone and the packed auditorium surged to its feet screaming 'Amen!'

Soye was amongst them, raising his arms to the high ceiling, the wings of his *agbada* falling to his shoulders in loose folds.

Outside the new building, protesters formed a gathering of their own, raising placards and screaming epithets that could be overheard when the din of voices and musical instruments died down; a line of young male ushers had formed a protective border to keep them from rushing in to disrupt the service.

Kamsi had taken to trotting his wife about as a heraldic shield. In the past, she'd been a silent appendage, taking to the stage once in a while and never appearing in flyers. Now she was plastered on billboards across the city – her name, then his, followed by other popular pastors whose names were meant to whitewash his. I thought it a compromise in exchange for her silence. Occasionally, he brought in prominent American evangelists and splashed pictures of them in chauffeured Rolls-Royces across the internet.

Onomavwe decided Kamsi needed more conspicuous and prominent support from the political class, and as he wasn't always in Lagos, he instructed Soye to take up the duty.

'I'm not going. You can do it alone,' I told him.

Soye's face fell. 'Why are you being like this? This isn't the oath we took o. It's for better or worse,' he pleaded.

'This was not the "worse" I had in mind when we exchanged our vows,' I retorted. 'Are you not tired of being that man's lackey? At what age? You can go alone,' I said.

'If I go alone people will start asking questions. We go everywhere together. Next thing you know, divorce rumours will start surfacing and people will start digging around for what is not there.'

I spotted the jib crane camera moving towards where we were seated and stretched my fan wider, pulling it closer to cover my face. Zina was right; my mother would have been ashamed of me.

Midway through the service, Soye was invited to the altar to share a few words of exaltation. In his introduction, Kamsi quoted a special scripture: 'When the righteous rule, the people rejoice.'

Aunty Ada wasn't expecting me; her bemused expression said as much, but it also said she'd heard about everything else. I studied her face as I stood outside the door to her home – she was still beautiful; it was impossible to take that away from her. But a gauntness had crept into the structure of her cheekbones and the flatness of the scarf on her head told me she'd lost her lustrous thick hair.

Like Zina, Aunty Ada was unpredictable, and I waited with hitched breath as she decided what to do with me. On the way, I'd bought baskets of oranges and apples because my mother always took fruit along when she visited the sick.

'Come in,' Aunty Ada said finally and pushed the door open wider.

I walked the familiar path through the narrow corridor to their living room, remembering all the times I'd come there with my mother as a girl.

'Sit down,' Aunty Ada said, waving towards the settee.

I extended the bags in my hands. 'These are for you, aunty.'

She eyed the packages in my hands, then took them. 'Thank you,' she murmured. Aunty Ada was never rude to visitors. 'Do you want anything to drink?' she asked, moving towards the kitchen. 'There's juice and cold water but I can ask someone to buy Coke for you.'

'Water is fine, aunty,' I said, balancing my weight on the edge of a settee.

Aunty Ada returned minutes later with a bottle of cold water – the surface radiating a chilly steam – and a tumbler. She placed them on a wooden stool and took a seat at the other end of the room.

'To what do I owe this honour?' she asked. Her tone was intentionally sardonic, her eyebrows arched with scepticism. In no way did it sound like she considered it an honour and I wondered if I'd made a mistake in visiting.

'I heard about your health and wanted to check on you,' I said.

She hissed, dismissive. 'These blogs that never mind their business, always invading people's privacy and the law protects them in the name of freedom of speech. I wonder how they found out I'm Zinachukwu's mother in the first place. Uju has already called me from America to cry and cry. She says she's booking a flight to come down next week. Ego came the other day with her husband and gift baskets. My own children visit me almost every day. How am I supposed to get better when everyone is acting like I'm dying *ehn*? Even if I'm dying, it's not like I don't have people waiting for me on the other side.'

I cleared my throat to rid myself of the sudden thickness that gathered there. 'We don't think you're dying, aunty,' I said. 'We're just concerned.'

'You should all be more concerned for yourselves.' She tapped her chest emphatically with both hands. 'Well, as you can see, my breasts are gone. But I'm alive and well. I can't die easily.'

'How's the treatment going?'

She sighed. 'I should be done with chemotherapy in a few weeks. We started late because of my stubbornness.' She chuckled to herself. 'I didn't want to lose my breasts. But look at me now. Hopefully my hair will eventually grow back.'

'I'm sorry, aunty.'

'No need to be sorry; it's not your fault.' Aunty Ada shifted so she could relax her back against the sofa. She folded her arms across her planed chest, and for several seconds, she stared at me, not saying anything. It felt like being observed under a microscope.

'Your mother is the only reason I opened my door for you today,' she said eventually. 'If not ...' She let the *'if not'* hang like a shadowed threat. 'Does Zinachukwu know you're here?' she asked.

'No,' I said.

She laughed, a loud hearty laugh. 'Is this how you plan to live the rest of your life?'

I wasn't sure how to respond to that or what exactly she meant, and so I remained silent.

Aunty Ada rubbed a hand across her chest, like she was still getting used to the loss of her breasts. 'Akwaugo,' she called suddenly, startling me. Only my mother had ever referred to me by that name. 'That is the Igbo name your mother gave you, right?'

I stared at my hands ashamedly. 'Yes.'

'Do you know the meaning?'

I shook my head no.

'It means "Precious daughter",' she said. 'Over time I've tried not to meddle in your affairs because I know how painful it was to lose your mother. In fact, most times I don't want to remember she's gone. But I'll tell you something I wish our mothers had told us, something I'm sure your mother would tell you if she were here with us. Akwaugo, you need to stop living your life solely for others, even those you love very much.'

An unlikely pandemic pulled all plans to a standstill. Soye was to travel to a remote part of the US to receive an honorary doctorate award from a remote college. He'd grown pensive since the magazine cover release, and I understood that a marked tilt had occurred in our relationship. The cover line had said: 'Dr Eriife Adebowale: The Political Wife Quietly Changing Lives.' And several people had approached me to say they'd been unaware I was a medical doctor, in a way that suggested that had they known, it would have affected their interactions with me.

Otunba Bankole, who'd resumed his relationship with

Soye after much pleading, now addressed me as, 'My Very Own Doctor,' even though he'd been aware of my training and the clinic. But I'd begun to notice the discomfort in Soye's countenance whenever we were introduced as Mr Adetosoye and Dr Eriife Adebowale. An unexpected light had cast me out of his shadow, and he was unhappy about it.

At first, no one took it seriously, this strange novel virus that had forced a nation like China into lockdown. Theories flew around as to its origin and Soye forwarded conspiracy theories over WhatsApp until I threatened to block him.

As always, the elite class continued its regular activity. A party was thrown in London to celebrate a birthday and several flew out to attend. Soye only happened to miss the party because his interview at the American embassy was scheduled for that week and he lamented endlessly about the missed opportunity. Then everyone started to fall ill.

Further information continued to be released about the virus and within weeks, the world had gone into lockdown, including Nigeria. Just before the airspaces closed for an interminably long period of time, Adelola returned to continue her classes online from home. 'It's too lonely over there,' she said. I realised I'd never asked her about her friends in the US: if she had any and, if she did, what sort of people they were.

'It's good you no longer run the clinic. Imagine the kind of danger we would all have been in with you going there every day,' Soye said, settling into life at home as the number of cases in the city surged and isolation centres were flooded with the sick.

A lone skeletal figure lay in the middle of a dirty street. Flies gathered, feasting on the remains of a carcass. Children hovered from a distance, unsure of whether to approach. A news reporter announced that the person had starved to death as the ongoing lockdown put a stop to business.

'When bread is no longer available, the people will eventually revolt,' Yunusa was telling Soye. They were in the living room, seated at the separate extreme ends and sharing wine and stories. 'Happened with the French in the 1700s, happened during the Arab Spring. We must try to avoid it here.'

At first, many had celebrated the virus as retributive karma against the ruling class in the country. The global borders had shut and they were trapped like the rest of the populace, forced to reckon with their own refusal to equip local healthcare facilities. Now they would die just like the average man: surrounded by underpaid and overworked physicians in buildings that had long seen better days.

But then the virus had spread beyond the exalted social stratosphere and lockdown began to affect businesses and household incomes. The people now feared hunger more than they feared the virus, a nigh alarming situation. The country had gone into lockdown because other countries had gone into lockdown, not because it had a plan.

'Our people are not given to revolts,' Soye told Yunusa. After Yunusa had called him that afternoon about his intention to visit, Soye had said the man missed seeing my face – 'No more events to meet you at – he's carried his toasting to my house.' But they were seated like friends, eating snacks and drinking wine. 'They're docile to a fault,' Soye continued. 'If you push them to a wall, they would rather break through the wall than fight back. The military broke something fundamental in us. Whatever it was, they squashed it under their heels.'

'Don't be so sure, Soye,' Yunusa said. 'Look at the rest of the world – protests everywhere. This is unprecedented; people are frustrated.'

Hong Kong had opened the year with protests, a spillover of demonstrations from the preceding year, women had taken to streets in March across the globe, demanding for their rights. But it was George Floyd's death that lit a match that would cause a global eruption and discussion of race. Soye and I had watched the gruesome video in muted silence, tears obstructing my vision as he called for his mother. 'What is happening over there is terrible,' Soye espoused.

'Have you been to a police cell in this country?' I retorted.

Doctors went on strike not too long after Yunusa's visit, to protest their working conditions in the country even as other countries openly made calls for medical professionals looking to migrate to greener pastures. A Middle Eastern country set up office at a hotel to recruit, and queues stretched across their lawns. News stations broadcast videos of medical practitioners on the lines arranging copies of their credentials in brown envelopes and school bags as they waited. Mysterious armed government men materialised the following day, shooting bullets in the air, dispersing the crowd and driving recruitment underground.

Adelola referred to me as *'old school'*. Lockdown had brought us closer; we watched movies together to fill the idle hours, and in the quiet of evening we listened to music and chatted about boys.

'Was he always this serious?' she asked me of her father once.

Adelola danced one afternoon during lockdown, a strange movement of arms and feet that appeared far too strenuous to be enjoyable, and I stopped at her door, stared for a moment and asked, 'What are you doing?'

'It's this new trend on TikTok,' she responded, sounding out of breath. 'Don't come too close or you'll get into my video.'

I blinked. 'What's TikTok?' I knew about Facebook, and Nwakaego had introduced me to Twitter and Instagram. Soye only ever seemed to complain about the content on there: the extremities of opinions and their hatred for people like him, and invariably, me, and so I'd taken to using them only to spy on my friends. But this was new to me.

Adelola guffawed, a sound I didn't hear from her often, then said, 'You're really old school', a phrase we'd used against my mother whenever she played Kool and the Gang and called it 'better music' than our '90s RnB.

'I'm not old school. How old do you think I am?' I protested. Had so much time passed that such a statement could apply to me? I pulled my phone from the pocket of my house gown and handed it to her. 'Help me download it. Let me see what's happening. Update the other ones too.'

The barrage of nonstop information that existed in this new cyberspace was staggering and overwhelming, yet a fleeting happiness bubbled within me as I scrolled, tickled with anticipation of the next post, and I understood why Adelola was addicted.

I wondered why a young man would have 'Kaduna Nzeogwu' as his Twitter name given its history, and what it meant to be 'dragged'. Soye peeped in my direction often, questioning the cause of my constant laughter.

It was on Twitter that I first read the news of the collapse of Kamsi's investment initiative. He invested regularly in his members' businesses, doling out inordinate sums to their ventures and interests in exchange for profit and fealty. But at the start of the year, he'd floated his own investment vehicle, a venture whose activities were cloaked in dim shadowiness.

Onomavwe shelled out over a hundred million naira to show support, an encouragement to his associates to follow suit. Soye opted out, claiming to be temporarily illiquid, but at home, he told me he would not put even the change lying around the house in such nonsense.

'My money! My money!' Onomavwe screamed over the phone when the venture collapsed, sounding more like a character in a Nollywood picture than a real person. 'This fellow has stolen my money!'

Kamsi's arrest was televised in a manner that left me viewing the whole scenario as a theatrical performance.

The police commandant in charge of the case gave an interview as Kamsi was led away. 'Criminals will always face the consequences of their actions in this country no matter who they are,' he said.

On Twitter, Zina posted a vague tweet about criminals and comeuppance. Ego's Twitter remained silent.

38

Uprising

If anyone had asked me what would light the match that would set it all ablaze, leaving me engorged in the embers, I never would have thought it would be an internet video of a young man rolling out of a moving vehicle.

October 1st 2020. Independence Day. Sixty years since our country's independence from British colonial rule. The pandemic had moderated plans for an all-out celebratory festival to be replaced by a watered-down parade at the Eagle Square. Hoisted flags fluttered from salient poles; sirens rang on the streets of the capital as preparations were underway. At seven in the morning, the president was plastered on our screens. *'Sixty years of nationhood provides an opportunity to ask ourselves questions on the extent to which we have sustained the aspirations of our founding fathers. Where did we do the right things? Are we on course? If not, where did we stray, and how can we remedy and retrace our steps?'*

'*Iyawo mi*, hope you didn't forget our invites,' Soye told me in our hotel suite. He was seated in front of the television, his neck stretched out like he couldn't afford to miss a word.

'Yes, they're with me,' I said. Mrs Aluko had made sure we were included on the reduced guest list for the celebratory parade.

Later, from our vaunted seats in the stadium, the atmosphere effete with perfume and jubilee, attired in matching green and white outfits: *God bless Nigeria.*

On social media, the tone was radically different: *'Sixty years of independence and twenty-nine of those spent under military regimes. What really has changed since then? Journalists are still arrested for criticising the government, freedom of speech is curtailed and we're fed daily propaganda to prop up a failing government. Military authoritarianism garbed in democracy,'* a man wrote on Facebook and others congregated in his comments to applaud him.

October 3rd. A video emerged on social media of a young man being pushed out of a vehicle and shot by armed members of a special police unit. It wasn't the first time this unit had been accused of abusing its power. In '99, as medical students, we'd studied cadavers on gurneys in our classrooms, rumoured to be from hospital morgues where the police had abandoned the bodies of their victims, unidentified and lost to their loved ones. We'd scoffed at these tales as works of fiction, until one afternoon, in the middle of an anatomy class, the lecturer had lifted the cloth from the body we were to study and a classmate had run out screaming and crying. The face had been that of his longtime friend, two bullet holes decorated the right side of his chest.

Demonstrations against the Special Anti-Robbery Squad (SARS) had taken place before; there was nothing particularly new there. Each time, the government put out a perfunctory message, claiming a reorganisation, dissolution or ban on the unit's activities, and each time, they continued their reign of terror uninhibited: picking up young men for owning nice phones and laptops, accusing them of trumped-up criminal activity, disappearing fathers for walking at night and resting gun barrels on sternums for the crime of disagreement.

But in October of that year, there was a shift, a caving in the minds of the people that would turn it all on its head. For days, social media raged. I read in horror as people shared tales of their experiences:

Enahoro Frances
@Enahoro_F   · Follow

My brother ran a barbing salon in '98. One day they raided his shop for cutting hair for some young men they accused of being armed robbers. We've not heard from or found him since. We act like he never existed because that is the only way for my mother to stay sane.

9:12 AM 5 Oct 2020   · Twitter for iPhone

Juliana Okai
@JOkai   · Follow

My father went out to deliver my sister's wedding invite to a friend by 6 p.m. on November 2nd, 2005, I can never forget. We've not seen or heard from him since they arrested him for loitering.

11:15 AM · 5 Oct 2020   · Twitter for iPhone

A young man in a photograph, his eyes light with future promise, was found in the custody of SARS in Awkuzu, Anambra state – a chapter of the unit particularly notorious for its blood-stained record – after being missing for months, one of the lucky few to be found alive, although he did not last long as a gunshot wound had been left to fester and breed infection.

But it was the story of Chijioke Iloanya, arrested at twenty in 2012 at a child dedication ceremony that would haunt me. His family selling off their property to pay for his release, the commandant having drained them of funds, allegedly looking them in the eye and saying he'd been killed, and nothing could be done about it. His father forced to swim in a river of dead bodies off the cliff behind the prison walls in search of his son's body, if only to give him a decent burial.

People rallied: enough was enough. The first protests were just a small number, gathered at the government office. Celebrities lent their voices, announcing they would be physically present at protest grounds, and the numbers surged. Then someone volunteered to cook for the protesters, spearheaded by a group of women that would become the Feminist Coalition and people offered to donate. The donations poured in from across the globe as the hashtag #EndSARS trended worldwide, far exceeding what was required, setting in motion a string of events that would create one of the largest protests in Nigerian history.

'Nothing will happen. Not today, not tomorrow,' Soye said to me dismissively as news came from the capital that a dissolution of the unit had been ordered. We were watching the events unfold. A television crew was at the Lekki toll gate that had been blocked for days, interviewing protesters.

A stunning light-skinned woman stepped forward to

speak, then proceeded to lambast the government. Soye turned to me. 'Isn't that your friend?' he demanded in an accusatory tone, like I was somehow responsible for Zina's actions. He did not notice a girl behind her who looked very much like him.

The protests were decentralised and peaceful, purposely so, to avoid avenues for disruption by government agents. In Anambra state, protesters marched for miles in the rain to the Awkuzu station, singing songs of protests.

Mounted speakers reiterated songs of protest across the country, from the resistant tunes of Fela to the insulting lyrics of 'FEM', the latter played when a governor attempted to address a gathering of protesters. It was what I'd always imagined a revolution would look like. Fists raised, fingers flipped in the direction of those in power. Like my grandfather, a good number were too young to remember the days of the military, and like him, they were unfettered, alight with a courage to act.

'They're very brave,' I told Soye. He eyed me with palpable irritation, saying nothing. From a bank account I kept hidden from him, I made a sizeable donation. Because I recognised the hope in their eyes: it was the same light that once burned in Soye's.

The police retaliated, descending on protesters with batons and violence. Bullet pallets were fired, water cannons launched, many dragged on the ground to waiting police vans, yet they remained undeterred.

Donations were utilised to hire ambulances and private security, a network of lawyers volunteered to provide bail representation for arrested protesters, a call centre took emergency requests and responded with prompt efficiency across several parts of the country. For many in the crowd, it was the first time they would witness the machinations of a working system and it spurred in them further hope for a different future.

'Who is their leader?!' a voice I didn't recognise was demanding over the phone from Soye.

'They're insisting there is no leader, sir,' Soye responded, subdued. There was no one to compromise; no one to pay off to make it all go away.

'There's an uprising under your nose and you've done nothing to control the narrative online? Are you a serious person?' the voice screamed. I imagined this person's veins standing out on their neck, their eyes red from unrestful sleep.

The blaze of protests had spread like an irrepressible forest fire, progressing beyond the rogue police unit to demands for better governance and a decent country. After over a week of impassioned demonstrations, those at the centre of power were ready to take notice as international voices joined the deluge. As the momentum ricocheted towards parts of the Northern axis of the country, government agents spread word amongst religious leaders and offline populace that the protests were against their religion, and I understood that the widespread low-education levels were purposeful, not a glitch in a system, but parts of a well-intentioned system to retain power and control.

Then to cut off funding, the Central Bank declared protest donations illegal and labelled their organisers terrorists. Bank accounts were blocked, donation links disabled. Protesters switched to digital currency.

'Some of our usual influencers are refusing to take the job sir. They're saying that anyone identified as a government mouthpiece would be ostracised,' Soye explained.

'Who is paying these people? Who is trying to bring this government down?'

It amazed me how certain they were that someone – a hidden hand – was behind the protests, that the people could not demand better of their own accord.

I'd always avoided policing Adelola's activities because I never wanted to be labelled an evil stepmother. But this time, I had no choice because I feared for her safety. I waited until Soye was asleep; it wasn't often he went to bed early, and that night felt like a gifted opportunity. I knocked on her door before I pushed my way in. She was on her phone, typing furiously away. And I questioned if her online friends were aware of her father's identity, that he was one of the people they campaigned against. She sat up.

'When did you start going to protests?' I asked, not wasting any time.

She appeared stunned. 'How did you know?' she asked.

'I saw you on the news.'

'What?'

'You were standing behind Zina during her TV interview at the Lekki toll gate. You're lucky your father didn't notice you. Do you know that?'

'But I'm doing the right thing. Didn't he participate in protests himself back in the day?' she returned, defiant.

'That was then. It's dangerous; you could get arrested or injured. What would you tell your father?'

Adelola rolled her eyes; she would never do that to her father. 'What could be more dangerous than a military government? Courage is dangerous. At least I'm doing something, not being a coward like you.'

I bristled at the insult. 'What is that supposed to mean?'

'You think you're better than him because you sit beside him and give fancy retorts to the nonsense he says and run your NGO. But how are you any better? You follow him everywhere, do everything he tells you to, and never speak up publicly for anything important. You heard your aunty talking about how hard the country is the other day and you couldn't contribute to the conversation because you know you're part of the problem. Coward!'

In the Women in Politics WhatsApp group chat, conversation had gone unusually quiet, with an occasional quip from Hassana about her shows. I decided to initiate the discourse. Adelola had referred to me as a coward and I was determined to reject the label.

'*What does everyone think about what is currently happening in the country?*' I wrote, then thought to myself as I sent it that even that was a cowardly way to begin.

Hassana: '*Absolute nonsense, these young people are determined to tear the country apart. They are sponsored by terrorists.*' She seemed to always be beside her phone.

Saratu: '*We need to start working towards moderating social media to prevent such nonsense from happening again.*'

Me: '*You don't think they're fighting for a legitimate cause? Some of these stories are heartbreaking.*'

Mrs Aluko: '*Madam Adebowale, you're getting soft.*'

'*Mothers are coming out to protest. We should lend our voices too and join them,*' I typed in the message bar, then deleted. It was a waste of time. Adelola was right, I was a coward.

Enitan: '*How can we cause confusion in their midst to scatter this? Riff raffs and insurgents.*'

Underneath their derisive sneers and blustering, I sensed a fear about what would become of them in a country where they no longer yielded power, where every citizen was treated as equal.

That evening, Soye came home screaming at the top of his voice. He'd watched the news at the office and spotted a familiar face in the crowd.

October 20th.

It had been about two weeks since the protests started. Soye was in a much better mood than he'd been a couple of days before. Adelola had promised to stop going to protests; some influencers had stealthily begun sowing seeds of discord amongst online protesters and an emergency meeting the night before had yielded some results and a continuation was to be held that morning.

'Since it will all be ending soon,' Soye boasted, 'maybe I should approach one of their gatherings and try to talk to them. You know, build my rep amongst the youth.'

12.00pm. The state government suddenly announced a curfew for 4pm in a state known for its traffic-clogged roads.

Soye called, 'Make sure Adelola doesn't go out!' I had no way of telling him she'd already left – to see her friend, she'd said, but I knew better.

I phoned her, putting on my best impression of a strict mother. 'Make sure you start coming home now!' By 2pm, she stalked through the front door, refusing to glance at me.

2.40pm. A video was going viral on the protest hashtags. A politician had attempted to speak at a gathering of protesters at Abule Egba. Annoyed at their refusal to listen to him – they stoned him instead with sachets of water – he'd pulled out a shotgun as he drove away and shot in the air, hitting two innocent bystanders. A journalist had caught the latter end of the event on camera. Efforts were underway to identify the Prado Jeep. I watched the video, the scenes clear and yet unclear, as my heart beat with sudden terror, remembering Soye's words from that morning.

3.00pm. Interest in the video was overtaken when pictures surfaced of technicians taking down CCTV cameras at the Lekki toll gate. People tweeted, pleading with protesters to leave the toll they had blocked for a better part of two weeks, keeping watch at night in tents, safeguarding what they saw as a path to a future for their country.

Adepeju Orawuola
@PejuOrawuola · Follow

Go home! Go home! They're taking down cameras. You can only protest if you're alive.

3:17 PM 20 Oct 2020 · Twitter for iPhone

I checked on Adelola, and although she wouldn't speak to me, I felt relief at seeing her curled in bed.

4.00pm. Protesters were sat on the floor, waving flags and singing the national anthem. *'We're prepared to die,'* one posted along with a self-facing picture of the crowd behind him. Someone dug up a vague statute in the law concerning the national flag:

#ENDSARS Amarachi
@AmarachiO   · Follow

They cannot kill us if we protest peacefully and wave
the flag, it's against the law.

4:30 PM 20 Oct 2020   · Twitter for iPhone

6.29pm. Army vehicles were spotted leaving Bonny
Camp, an army camp minutes away from Lekki toll gate.
Someone tweeted:

Daniel #ENDSARS
@DanielPE   · Follow

They're coming

6:30 PM 20 Oct 2020   · Twitter for iPhone

6.40pm. Toll gate floodlights and advertisement billboards
were turned off, leaving only foreboding darkness. Mobile
networks antennas in the area were switched off.

Esther Ganiyu #ENDSARS
@EstherGaniyu   · Follow

My network stopped working, I live near the toll gate. I
had to switch to WiFI

6:41 PM 20 Oct 2020   · Twitter for iPhone

'*Go home,*' people pleaded. But the protesters stayed, waving
and singing.

6.45pm. Another tweet:

Esther Ganiyu #ENDSARS
@EstherGaniyu   · Follow

I can hear gunshots, I live near the toll gate

6:45 PM 20 Oct 2020   · Twitter for iPhone

Soon after, a video of men in military uniform at the back of
three Toyota Hilux vans arriving at the toll gate was posted.
Almost immediately, a rain of bullets began into the crowd of
protesters. My fingers shook as they held my phone.

7.00pm.

DJ Switch a female DJ who only a few weeks before had spearheaded a party in the Big Brother house, a party I'd watched because of Hassana. I sat in our living room transfixed, my fingers moving between applications as I searched to find her page.

'*Let them shoot. Let them shoot,*' someone was saying in the dark. Protesters carried on singing even as the sound of bullets like firecrackers continued unabated, their voices cracking under the weight of their tears and fears: '*Arise O Compatriots.*'

'*They're taking the bodies,*' someone said, raising the alarm. A man was bleeding profusely on the floor, others gathered around him, struggling to keep him alive. The DJ was calling for an ambulance and turned the camera to show her audience, that now included CNN, the fire started by the army to keep protesters from accessing help. A bullet was pulled from the bleeding man's leg, his wound wrapped in a bloodstained flag. People were still singing the anthem.

9.30pm. Soye stumbled into our living room, sweating profusely. I was in the same spot I'd occupied since the shooting began, unable to move, incapable of any rational action. I turned to stare at him; his eyes were dilated, the collar of his kaftan open like he'd been running.

I raised the phone in my hand, slowly, almost mechanically; a picture of a bleeding protester was plastered on the screen. I tasted salt at the corner of my lips and realised I was crying. 'Soye, did you know about this?' I demanded, my voice a tremulous whisper. 'Did you?!'

Something in my eyes alarmed him. He raised his hands in a calming gesture. 'Eri, please calm down. I swear I didn't know this was what they were going to do. The agreement was to take drastic measures.'

'You're killing people's children now? *Ehn* Adetosoye?!'

He looked around me. 'Where's Adelola?'

'Soye, answer me!'

'Where's my daughter?!'

'She's in her room,' I answered.

He moved around me and raced up the staircase in the direction of Adelola's room. A few seconds later, he was out and clinging to the banister with desperation. 'She's not there,' he announced, the words like a death knell.

39

Time

I was crying. I couldn't stop crying. Zina's phone kept ringing.

'Please, please pick up,' I begged the invisible Zina on the other end.

On the very last ring, Zina answered, her voice frail like she'd been crying. 'This isn't a good time, Eriife. But in case you're calling because you saw me at the toll, I'm fine, I left early.'

The spectral hand around my rib cage loosened just a little. 'Zina, my daughter,' I choked out. 'Please, I need your help.'

Zina was many things – erratic, audacious, impetuous – but she wasn't cruel. 'What happened to your daughter?'

'She was at the toll,' I sobbed. 'I can't find her anywhere.'

'I can't hear you well,' Zina said, her end of the line crackling. The network was still unstable around the island.

'My daughter, she was at the toll.'

Zina was immediately alert. 'Have you tried her phone number?'

I tried to steady my voice. 'Yes, it's not going through. Her phone is switched off.'

'Do you have a recent picture? Send it to me and meet me at the Lekki Phase 1 gate,' Zina said. I could already hear the jangle of her keys.

Soye had already left with his security detail. Before he'd left, we'd searched the house – the extra bedrooms, the other living rooms, the guest house – screaming Adelola's name. We tried her phone number as we moved through the rooms, then the gateman informed us she'd left through the back gate sometime after 4pm.

'How didn't you notice? What kind of mother are you?' Soye screamed in my face before he stormed out, clutching his phone to his ear as he made desperate phone calls to his contacts.

Fifteen minutes after our call, Zina was already parked at the gate. Gunshots were still ringing, the source uncertain as the soldiers had already left; eyewitnesses would later say the police had returned to finish what the army started. Someone had set the toll gate on fire and the flames blazed upwards, like a beacon.

I sent the driver back, not wanting to put him at risk, and got into Zina's car. A scarf was tied around the cornrows on her head – she hadn't bothered with a wig – and her blouse looked like it had been pulled on in a hurry.

'Ego will meet us on the way,' she informed me as soon as I was seated and set the car into motion.

On the way, she told me several injured protesters had been taken to hospitals that had volunteered free care for the wounded. I no longer ran the clinic, but I called the management to suggest they do same.

'It's not safe to go towards the toll; the soldiers have carried most of the bodies away,' Zina said. 'We should check hospitals first, if we don't find her.' At the mention of the possibility,

I burst into another bout of tears. 'We can check the shanty towns around. Some people ran in that direction when the shooting started.'

We drove slowly, paying attention to every movement around us, checking the few faces we saw, hoping to see Adelola amongst them, and stopping to pick up injured people or those who just needed help getting away from the scene. Was this what it felt like to live in a war zone?

The first hospital was overladen with the injured, fully in a state of mayhem. The hallways, beds and corridors crowded with bleeding heads, arms and legs. Physicians and nurses ran around attending to the most critical first, like the man who had received two bullet shots at the side of his chest. We searched the wards, bed to bed, and showed the frazzled nurses pictures, asking if they'd seen a patient that looked like her. Ego arrived as we left the first hospital; we hadn't found Adelola.

She looked between our disappointed faces. 'Any luck?' she asked.

Zina shook her head slowly. I covered my face with my hands and wept. I felt their arms engulf me.

It was the same at the next hospital and the next and the next, until we'd searched five hospitals. As daybreak approached, the darkness already beginning to lift, Zina suggested we try one more hospital before heading towards the shanty town.

We found her there, unconscious with a head trauma and attached to a ventilator. A kind someone had brought her in after she'd fallen in the stampede that had followed the beginning of the shooting. She wasn't yet stable, but the doctors were hopeful she would survive.

Outside the hospital walls, anarchy was unleashed, security

agents conveniently absent from every corner as complexes were looted, homes robbed, people harassed and shops burned, many losing lifetime investments. The message: they were willing to let the city burn to bring the people to heel. A 24-hour curfew was announced, closely followed by an announcement of a three-day curfew.

The governor gave a speech, a poor-spirited and cowardly speech. I fumed as I watched on the large TV screen from Adelola's bedside. *'For clarity, it is imperative to explain that no sitting governor controls the rules of engagement of the army … while we pray for swift recovery for the injured, we are comforted that no fatalities were recorded as widely circulated on the social media,'* he said.

A coordinated campaign of misinformation had already begun, first with the army denying any involvement in the attack on protesters, then systemic circulation of falsified images and videos to make it appear as though there were no casualties. By the third day, I'd begun questioning my own sanity. Were it not for Ego and Zina assuring me that they'd also joined the livestream and witnessed the massacre, and Adelola's unconscious state, I might have believed that it had all been a figment of my imagination.

The president was more forthright. 'Did this man just basically say the international community should mind its business?' Zina asked, disbelieving from the other side of the room.

'It sounded more like "if you protest again, I'll have you killed. We're doing our best,"' Ego said. She sounded resigned, and I wished she hadn't returned to the country – another mishap I was to blame for.

'People are yet to bury their dead and this is the insensitive nonsense we have to listen to?' Zina said. She sent me an apologetic glance. I didn't mind the conversation, it kept me from thinking; not thinking was the best thing I could do.

They had not left my side since I'd called Zina in desperation. When one left to shower and return with food, the other stayed behind to keep me company. The first morning I was alone with Ego, I finally had the opportunity to apologise like I'd been meaning to.

'I knew you were sorry. I just didn't want to hear it,' she said to me with an understanding smile.

But I needed to explain. 'It's not an excuse but I knew how powerful the people behind Kamsi were. I told myself I was trying to protect you, but I was being a coward and protecting Soye's position.'

She put a hand over mine. 'Let's talk about it later.'

Soye had Adelola moved to the ICU of our private hospital with foreign doctors and nurses. While we waited for her to wake up, he stayed away, checking on his business interests. At the end of each day, he called me, demanding, 'Is she awake yet?' We didn't speak otherwise.

The media were wary of letting the government propaganda define the narrative around the events of the movement and took to the streets to gather evidence as to what really happened at the Lekki toll gate.

What took place after the military left? Who set the toll on fire? Why were gunshots still heard until the early hours of the following day? Had the curfew allowed the authorities time to cover up? It was all shrouded in unspeakable darkness. The government threatened sanctions even as interviews and eyewitness accounts were broadcast.

'There is no scratch of blood anywhere there,' the state governor asserted in an interview with CNN, but bodies had floated up the lagoon and behind people's homes. Residents of the shanty town claimed there had been more, many who would retain that unresolved status of 'missing'. Months later, the state government would announce plans to clear out the slum.

In the shadow of the aftermath of the massacre, messages poured in from within the region and across the Atlantic, many in condemnation of the state-inflicted violence on its citizens, but some called for 'calm and dialogue between parties', and it made me wonder how we were meant to negotiate with the barrel of a gun.

'Some of these statements are just so strange. I'd have preferred it if they didn't say anything,' Zina said, folding her arms across her chest in disgust.

'They can't be more forceful; they don't want new immigrants,' Ego said. 'As long as the country is "stable" with a functioning government, most of the international community is okay, regardless of the price to the citizens. Besides, there are too many pro-government NGOs lobbying on behalf of our leaders and improving the general perception of the situation here. It's the same for many countries across the world.'

Zina huffed. 'Anyways, it's not like their meddling in other countries has even yielded many positive results.'

We were quiet for a few minutes, staring at the floor to avoid looking at the beeping machines, then Ego said, 'I understand the international community, but why aren't the African Union and ECOWAS being sterner in their response?'

Zina hissed, 'You want people to condemn what they themselves are guilty of? Take a look at the continent, my dear.'

That night, the monitor flatlined and Adelola was gone.

'We're not sure what went wrong but it could have been

complications from a clot or bleed,' the doctor tried to explain in between my screams as my friends struggled to pick me up from the floor.

'... *earth to earth, ashes to ashes, dust to dust.*' It was the same pastor who'd officiated my mother's funeral, the resonance of his voice diminished by age and time's passing. Tears slipped down from underneath the sunglasses that covered my eyes.

Where had it gone wrong? At what point had I turned down the path and ignored all the warning signs? Was it the day I'd precociously blocked the path of a man I barely knew, in awe of his person, in need of a distraction from my mother's death, and introduced myself? Or had it started before that, the moment I'd desired some form of attention my father had been too overwhelmed by grief to give?

'*Thy will be done, on Earth as it is in heaven.*'

I could still see Adelola, as she'd been before the protests, so young, filled with so much life. Unburdened and carefree. How could this be anyone's will? *Mummy*, she'd called me and yet I'd let this happen.

Soye gripped my shoulder, pleading and comforting at the same time, and I shrugged his hand away. There was little to be said now. We both knew it was over; our marriage could never recover from this.

He'd tried to explain his side of the events of that day. Yes, he'd attended meetings, but at no point had it been made clear what sort of actions would be taken. I couldn't bring myself to believe him because I had lost a sense of who he was, of how far he was willing to go to achieve his ambitions. Until the moment the politician in the video had been identified, I'd found myself believing it was Soye, believing that he was capable of pulling out a gun and shooting out of his car because protesters had refused to listen to him. The young man with a flaming torch for the nation was gone and I had no idea who I was married to.

My father approached me when the service was over. His black suit hung from his frame, and I was astounded by just how much he'd aged since I saw him last; I was once again close to losing a parent. He placed a hand on my shoulder, unsure whether to reach out for a hug, afraid I would reject his comfort. His eyes said he recalled the similar service we'd attended over two decades before, just as I did.

'Time heals all wounds,' someone had said to us when my mother died, but if anything, we were proof that wounds festered, only to be replaced by more torturous ones.

40

New life

I hadn't been to see her in a while, but it was her birthday so I took a broom and flowers along. Zina and Ego were to meet me there, delayed by a business meeting ahead of their first production. Their production company had already started to take off, the future path of their lives becoming clearer by the day while mine had turned hazy with fog. What was I to do next?

In the traffic, a hawker approached, plastering a state gossip magazine with coloured pages against my window. I turned to glance at the cover, only to recognise myself at the top right corner. It had been three months since I appeared in public with Soye and suspicions had already begun to rise. *'Separation Rumours Plague House Rep,'* the headline screamed.

He wouldn't stop begging. He'd called my father, my brother, even my youngest sister who lived in the UK. When he'd exhausted my limited nuclear family, he'd extended his pleas to Aunty Ada and Aunty Uju and their children. But I'd remained resolute. Mrs Aluko had been a sort of last resort on his part.

'We political wives are made of different stuff my dear,' she said to me over the phone. 'We know what we see daily and the things we have to put up with to keep it together, but this is our God-appointed role. They can't do anything without us. You can't just up and leave because of a mere scandal that – if we're being frank about it – he wasn't directly involved in. If so, why hasn't the governor's wife left? Or the president's wife? You're made of far better stuff than that. There's so much more to gain than to lose. Do you know the things I've seen in all my years? Adetosoye needs someone like you beside him to keep his head straight; you're his backbone. It's why I liked you even before we met; you're tough and brutally honest. And I might deride him every now and then, but at least he's different from the others in that he's loyal to you. Give it a thought, my dear. We still have so much to work on together.'

I was still yet to call a lawyer, yet to find a place to live while I shared Zina's large duplex, yet to figure out what to do with the NGO. I was even unsure if I could still run the clinic while Soye sat on the board and shared ownership. Our lives had been intertwined for so long that it seemed impossible to extricate myself in any way.

'How did your mother do it?' I'd asked Ego one day as we sat in Zina's back garden splitting groundnut pods open and sipping orange juice, amid a bloom of colour and the mingled perfume of gardenia, jasmine and crinum.

'Do what?' she asked, pouring a pod's contents in her mouth.

'Leave a man like your father,' I told her. 'I know it's not the same but . . .'

'Well for one, there was no internet back then, and hence no useless blogs,' Zina retorted.

We laughed. Zina never missed an opportunity to take a dig at internet blogs; they were a thorn in her side.

Ego paused to give it some thought, then she said, 'I don't know.' She shrugged. 'That's just the truth. I don't know how she was able to do it.'

Aunty Uju wanted me to come over to America, to write the medical exams and start over to avoid any vindictiveness on Soye's part. I wanted to say Soye wasn't like that; he wouldn't act like Chief Azubuike, unleashing every tool of power at his disposal. But how was I to vouch for a man I didn't know? A man entrenched in a game that chipped slowly away at your conscience and person?

Panels had been established across the country to investigate what had taken place and prosecute offending officers, but like most people, I was wary. There had been panels before, their reports still lying on the shelves of some government ministry collecting dust, the offenders running rampant. We were a collectively traumatised country pretending to move on.

I laid the flowers at the bottom of the headstone and stared at the words, still unable to believe they were true.

CHINELO NDAGI NÉE NWAEZE
LOVING MOTHER AND DAUGHTER
1957–1997

I tried to think of what she would say if she were with me, what she would advise I do. I was in need of my mother and she was still gone.

Zina and Ego came with wine, almost two hours later than agreed. 'I'm so sorry,' Ego apologised. 'My uncle Ikechukwu went for his friend's father's burial and insulted the elders and now his friend is angry because he's been asked to pay a fine before they can bury his father.'

I laughed; I needed it. 'It's fine.'

'I brought wine; I thought you'd need it. I won't be having any though,' Zina said, shoving it in my direction.

'Since when don't you take wine? I know Ego doesn't drink, but you?'

She shrugged. 'It's temporary.'

Ego turned a curious eye in her direction. 'Zina, are you trying to tell us something?'

Zina looked shy; I couldn't remember the last time I'd seen Zina look shy. 'Maybe?' she offered.

Ego was screaming, Zina was tearful, I was laughing; we were all sharing a hug, asking if it was a boy or girl and trading possible names. It was another thing I was still learning since my mother's death: even in the darkest moments, the universe still managed to breathe new life.

Acknowledgements

A first book is a blessing but a second book is a gift. This has been a gift. I want to start out by thanking the readers and fans of my first work, *Tomorrow I Become A Woman*; the book clubs, the messages, the social media posts and memes. Your praise and support have helped uplift and encourage me to embark on this second venture. I put my heart into this and I hope you feel it as you turn the pages.

I would like to my wonderful agent Cathryn Summerhayes for the constant support and encouragement, and for reading early drafts of this that were far from perfect.

Kaiya Shang, for being not just an editor, but a friend. Your faith in me is humbling, and I cannot express just how much it means. Your ideas and suggestions (sometimes unintended) helped make this book what it is now, and you never let me forget just how much you love it. Thank you.

Sophie Missing, for your kindness and patience throughout this process. We didn't start out working on this together but we've gotten along so well that most times I forget that. I'd been told good things about you and it's been a joy to learn that they were all true, if not understated. Your edits were incisive and helped transform this from a very wordy draft into the book is it now. Thank you for being so supportive.

A special thanks to Ella Fox-Martens and everyone at Scribner/Simon & Schuster UK for your efforts on this and for all the lovely messages letting me know just how much you've enjoyed reading this; they mean so much.

Many thanks to my Iowa Writer's Workshop lecturers and classmates who took the time to read through the lengthy manuscript and provide insightful suggestions and advice: Abby Geni, Margot Livesey, CJ, Zkara,

As always, my deepest gratitude goes to my family and friends. To my mother, Dr. Sarah Odafen, for your encouragement and patience with me every time I got into one of my moods during this process. Writing can be so emotionally taxing and I know there were times I wasn't the best to be around. Thank you for seeing me how I don't see myself. I'm not sure there's anyone that has as much faith in me as you do. I love you so much.

My father, Mr. Ehimhanre Odafen for not always agreeing with my decisions but for loving me regardless. I love you always.

Salome, Oseiga, Ireneosen, Sona, and Gideon Odafen. My siblings that continue to inspire and push me. I love you.

Gabriella Njiokwuemeni, my trusted manuscript reader and love. You're the best friend a person could ask for. We've always joked in the last decade plus of our friendship that if we don't have partners, at the very least, we have each other. It remains true my dear.

Diligence Inubuaye Omimi, my smallie. Thank you for being a listening ear and my gist partner, and for telling me how much you hate literary fiction but I should send my manuscript over anyway. We get each other so much and it's exactly why we're bad for each other.

Ayo Arikawe, my dear dear friend. We fight all the time but have somehow remained friends, and it's mostly because of you but hey, that's what friends are for. Two books in from that very first conversation when I ranted about writing about my frustrations. I still owe you royalties. Haha.

Tobi, Sharee, Nneka. My Kdrama girlies. Thank you for being some of my loudest cheerleaders. I truly value the friendship we've formed and appreciate the sisters we've become.

Samantha Dion, Christina Montilla, Michaeljulius Idani, Yinka Oduwole, Olamide Adelugba. For your long calls and support.

My grandparents, Late Pa Joseph Taiwo and Ma Romula Elizabeth Moses, for your prayers and old copies of Shakespeare. My uncle and aunty Rev and Rev. Mrs. Taiwo for getting copies of my first novel and telling me to keep writing because you loved reading it so much. Thank you so much.

To everyone that I've been unable to mention that has contributed in one way or the other to this work and/or the person I am today, I express my deepest gratitude.

It is only right that I close this out by once again thanking my God who has been a source of unwavering assurance that all things do indeed work together for good. I've not always understood life's events, but I'm learning to trust as you've been with me through it all.